JUSTIN W. M. ROBERTS

# THE POLICE WOMAN

Copyright © 2016 Justin W. M. Roberts.

All rights reserved. No part of this book may be reproduced, stored, or transmitted by any means—whether auditory, graphic, mechanical, or electronic—without written permission of both publisher and author, except in the case of brief excerpts used in critical articles and reviews. Unauthorized reproduction of any part of this work is illegal and is punishable by law.

ISBN: 978-1-4834-5983-7 (sc)
ISBN: 978-1-4834-5984-4 (hc)
ISBN: 978-1-4834-5985-1 (e)

Library of Congress Control Number: 2016917042

Because of the dynamic nature of the Internet, any web addresses or links contained in this book may have changed since publication and may no longer be valid. The views expressed in this work are solely those of the author and do not necessarily reflect the views of the publisher, and the publisher hereby disclaims any responsibility for them.

Book cover designed by Deranged Doctor Design
Book formatting by Istvan Szabo, Ifj.

To protect police officers and special forces operatives from around the world, almost all combat tactics and police/military procedures depicted in this book are <u>INTENTIONALLY DISGUISED</u>.

> 'We are the pilgrims, Master, we shall go,
> Always a little further; it may be,
> Beyond that last blue mountain barred with snow,
> Across that angry or that glimmering sea.'
>
> - James Elroy Flecker, *Hassan: The Story of Hassan of Baghdad and How He Came to Make the Golden Journey to Samarkand*

# CONTENTS

Glossary .................................................................................................. i
Prologue ................................................................................................ 1
Chapter 1: Deployment ....................................................................... 3
Chapter 2: International Criminal Police Organization–Interpol ............... 9
Chapter 3: Five Paragraph Order ...................................................... 18
Chapter 4: Reconnaissance By Fire .................................................. 49
Chapter 5: Close Quarters Battle ...................................................... 67
Chapter 6: The 22nd Regiment, Special Air Service ................................. 108
Chapter 7: The Fan Dance ................................................................ 138
Chapter 8: The Killing House ........................................................... 147
Chapter 9: KGM ................................................................................ 185
Chapter 10: Close Target Reconnaissance .................................... 198
Chapter 11: Fish & Chips ................................................................. 215
Chapter 12: Snatch Operation ........................................................ 254
Chapter 13: Hostage Rescue ........................................................... 288
Chapter 14: Last Post ...................................................................... 310
Chapter 15: Tiger Kidnap ................................................................ 349
Chapter 16: Satuan Bravo – 90 ....................................................... 375
Chapter 17: Detasemen Khusus – 88 ............................................. 394
Epilogue ........................................................................................... 422
About the Author ............................................................................ 424

# GLOSSARY

**ENGLISH**

| | | |
|---|---|---|
| 2 i/c | : | Second-in-Command |
| 3 i/c | : | Third-in-Command |
| AAC | : | Army Air Corps |
| AAR | : | After-Action Report |
| ABS | : | Advanced Bomb Suit |
| Adquals | : | Additional Qualifications |
| AFO | : | Authorized Firearms Officer |
| AGC | : | Adjutant General's Corps |
| AWOL | : | Absent Without Leave |
| Bone | : | Stupid (English slang) |
| Casevac | : | Casualty Evacuation |
| CCTV | : | Closed-Circuit Television |
| CGC | : | Conspicuous Gallantry Cross |
| CO | : | Commanding Officer |
| CQB | : | Close Quarters Battle |
| CT | : | Counterterrorist |
| CTR | : | Close Target Reconnaissance |
| DA | : | Direct-Action |
| The Det | : | See SRR |
| DMP | : | Drug Manufacturing Plant |
| DS | : | Directing Staff |
| DSF | : | Director Special Forces |
| DSO | : | Distinguished Service Order |
| EOD | : | Explosive Ordnance Disposal |

| | | |
|---|---|---|
| ERV | : | Emergency Rendezvous |
| ETA | : | Estimated Time of Arrival |
| FAP | : | Final Assault Position |
| FIBUA | : | Fighting In Built-Up Areas |
| FISH & CHIPS | : | Fighting In Someone's House & Creating Havoc In People's Streets |
| FMJ | : | Full Metal Jacket |
| FOB | : | Forward Operating Base |
| Foxtrot | : | On foot |
| Frag | : | Fragmentation grenade |
| FRIES | : | Fast Rope Insertion/Extraction System |
| FRV | : | Final Rendezvous |
| Garda | : | See *An Garda Síochána* |
| Garda ERU | : | Garda Emergency Response Unit |
| Garda NDU | : | Garda National Drug Unit |
| Garda NSU | : | Garda National Surveillance Unit |
| GC | : | George Cross |
| GCB | : | Knight Grand Cross of the Most Honourable Order of the Bath |
| Gimpy | : | See GPMG |
| GM | : | George Medal |
| GMP | : | Greater Manchester Police |
| GMT | : | Greenwich Mean Time |
| GPMG | : | General Purpose Machine Gun |
| GPNVG | : | Ground Panoramic Night Vision Goggles |
| GPS | : | Global Positioning System |
| Green slime(s) | : | Member(s) of the Intelligence Corps (British Army slang) |
| Head shed | : | Boss/commander of a special forces unit (British Army slang) |

| | | |
|---|---|---|
| HQ | : | Headquarters |
| HVT | : | High Value Target |
| ICPO | : | International Criminal Police Organization, see Interpol |
| IED | : | Improvised Explosive Device |
| INP | : | Indonesian National Police |
| INT | : | Intelligence |
| Interpol | : | International Police |
| IRA | : | Irish Republican Army |
| IRT | : | Incident Response Team |
| ISTAR | : | Intelligence, Surveillance, Target Acquisition, and Reconnaissance |
| IWB | : | Inside Waistband |
| JHP | : | Jacketed Hollow Point |
| JSFAW | : | Joint Special Forces Aviation Wing |
| KCB | : | Knight Commander of the Most Honourable Order of the Bath |
| KGM | : | King's Gallantry Medal |
| Kremlin | : | RHQ, SAS Barracks |
| LOE | : | Limit of Exploitation |
| Longs | : | Assault rifle (British Army slang) |
| LUP | : | Lying-Up Point |
| MACP | : | Military Aid to the Civil Power |
| MC | : | Military Cross |
| MCDO | : | Mine-warfare and Clearance Diving Officer |
| MDMA | : | Ecstasy |
| The Met | : | Metropolitan Police Service |
| MI5 | : | Security Service |
| MI6 | : | Secret Intelligence Service |

| | | |
|---|---|---|
| Mike(s) | : | Minute(s) |
| MO | : | Modus Operandi |
| MoD | : | Ministry of Defence |
| MOE | : | Method of Entry |
| MPGS | : | Military Provost Guard Service |
| MTP | : | Multi-Terrain Pattern |
| Mufti | : | Civilian clothes (British Army slang) |
| NAPS | : | Nerve Agent Pre-Treatment Set |
| NCA | : | National Crime Agency |
| NCB | : | National Central Bureau |
| NRO | : | National Reconnaissance Office |
| OC | : | Officer Commanding |
| OP | : | Observation Post |
| P Company | : | Pegasus Company |
| The Paras | : | Parachute Regiment |
| PATA | : | Pontrilas Army Training Area |
| Pinkie | : | Nickname for the Land Rover 110 |
| Pissed | : | Drunk/intoxicated (English slang) |
| Player(s) | : | Terrorist(s) |
| PSNI | : | Police Service of Northern Ireland |
| PTSD | : | Post-Traumatic Stress Disorder |
| R&R | : | Rest & Recuperation |
| R2I | : | Resistance to Interrogation |
| RAF | : | Royal Air Force |
| Recce | : | Reconnaissance |
| The Regiment | : | See SAS |
| RGR | : | Royal Gurkha Rifles |
| RHQ | : | Regimental Headquarters |

| | | |
|---|---|---|
| RIB | : | Rigid Inflatable Boat |
| RSM | : | Regimental Sergeant Major |
| RTB | : | Return to Base |
| RTU | : | Return to Unit |
| Rupert | : | Officer (British Army slang) |
| RV | : | Rendezvous |
| SAS | : | Special Air Service |
| SBS | : | Special Boat Service |
| Scaley(s) | : | Member(s) of the Royal Corps of Signals (British Army slang) |
| Scoff | : | Food (British Army slang) |
| SDR | : | Surveillance Detection Route |
| SFSG | : | Special Forces Support Group |
| Shorts | : | Pistols (British Army slang) |
| SHQ | : | Squadron Headquarters |
| Sitrep | : | Situation Report |
| Slime | : | See green slime |
| Slot | : | Kill (British Army slang) |
| SOAS | : | School of Oriental and African Studies, University of London |
| SOP | : | Standard Operating Procedure |
| SRR | : | Special Reconnaissance Regiment |
| SSE | : | Sensitive Site Exploitation |
| SSM | : | Squadron Sergeant Major |
| Switched-on | : | Smart/intelligent (English slang) |
| Tango | : | Enemy/Terrorist |
| TAOR | : | Tactical Area of Responsibility |
| UAV | : | Unmanned Aerial Vehicle (drone) |

| | | |
|---|---|---|
| UK | : | United Kingdom of Great Britain and Northern Ireland |
| UKSF | : | United Kingdom Special Forces |
| US | : | United States of America |
| UXO | : | Unexploded Ordnance |
| VC | : | Victoria Cross |
| VCP | : | Vehicle Check Point |
| VP | : | Voice Procedure |
| VRN | : | Vehicle Registration Number |
| Weean | : | Child (South-Ulster slang) |
| X-Ray | : | Terrorist |
| Yankee | : | Hostage |

## GAEILGE

| | | |
|---|---|---|
| BMC | : | An Bonn Míleata Calmachta (The Military Medal for Gallantry) |
| BSD | : | An Bonn Seirbhíse Dearscna (The Distinguished Service Medal) |
| Cigire | : | Rank in the Garda equivalent to Inspector in the UK |
| Éirinn go Brách | : | Ireland Forever |
| An Garda Síochána | : | Police Force of the Republic of Ireland (The Guardians of the Peace) |
| Leifteanant-Cheannasaí | : | Rank in the Irish Navy equivalent to Lieutenant-Commander |
| Leifteanant-Choirnéal | : | Rank in the Irish Army equivalent to Lieutenant-Colonel |
| Maor-Sáirsint Cathláin | : | Rank in the Irish Army equivalent to Battalion Sergeant Major |
| Mo ghile mear | : | My gallant darling |

| | | |
|---|---|---|
| Sáirsint | : | Rank in the Garda equivalent to Sergeant in the UK |
| Sáirsint Complachta | : | Rank in the Irish Army equivalent to Staff Sergeant |
| Sciathán Fiannóglach an Airm | : | Army Ranger Wing |
| Slán go foil | : | Goodbye |

## BAHASA INDONESIA

| | | |
|---|---|---|
| AD | : | Angkatan Darat (Army) |
| AKP | : | Ajun Komisaris Polisi (equivalent to Inspector) |
| AL | : | Angkatan Laut (Navy) |
| AU | : | Angkatan Udara (Air Force) |
| Bibi | : | Affectionate name used for Indonesian housekeepers |
| Brimob | : | Brigade Mobile (Paramilitary Unit of the INP) |
| Denjaka | : | Detasemen Jala Mangkara (Counterterrorist Unit of the Indonesian Navy) |
| Densus-88 | : | Detasemen Khusus – 88 (Antiterrorist Unit of the INP) |
| Dik | : | How older siblings address younger brother/sisters |
| Ditreskrim | : | Direktorat Reserse Kriminal (Criminal Investigations Directorate) |
| Gegana | : | Counterterrorist Unit of the INP |
| Kak | : | How younger siblings address older brother/sisters |
| Kapolri | : | Kepala Kepolisian Republik Indonesia (Indonesian Chief of Police) |

| | | |
|---|---|---|
| Kapolsek | : | Kepala Polisi Sektor (Head of Police Precinct) |
| KOOPSUS | : | Komando Operasi Khusus (Special Operations Command) |
| Paskhas | : | Korps Pasukan Khas (Special Forces of the Indonesian Air Force) |
| POLDA Metro Jaya | : | Kepolisian Daerah Metropolitan Jakarta Raya (Police Force for the Greater Jakarta Area) |
| Satuan Bravo-90 | : | Counterterrorist Unit of the Indonesian Air Force |
| Sersan | : | Rank in the TNI equivalent to Sergeant |
| TNI | : | Tentara Nasional Indonesia (Indonesian Armed Forces) |
| WIB | : | Waktu Indonesia Barat (Indonesia Western Standard Time) |

# PROLOGUE

00:55 GMT
Tuesday April 14, 2026
Spitalfields Chemical Warehouse
Spitalfields and Banglatown, London, England

The warehouse is in a deserted industrial complex in the East End of London. This night, all the heaters are turned off and the cold inside the warehouse is unbearable. In the office part of the building, there's a large steel table with a naked English woman lying on top, handcuffed to the table legs. Her wrists and ankles are scraped, bruised, and swollen from friction with the restraints. Her eyes are closed and her breathing ragged. A large, hot spotlight is pointed at her. The lamp should have warmed her body, but she's still shivering from cold. A video camera is above her, recording her predicament.

The woman is quite attractive, with blue eyes and shoulder-length blonde hair. She's in her thirties with a firm, well-conditioned body. Unfortunately, a deep slash cuts through her abdomen, from beneath her sternum to just below her navel, which has caused most of her entrails to spill out. A man is beside the table, holding a small, bloody knife.

"Karen," says the man in an Irish accent. "Karen, wake up!" His left hand caresses her hair.

Karen struggles to open her eyes because of the dazzling spotlight.

"Karen," says the man again.

Karen finally opens her eyes. She looks frightened and in pain.

"Please… stop…" she begs.

The man only smiles.

"Niall… please… I've… told you… everythin'…" begs Karen again, her Manchester accent quivering.

"I know, my dear."

"Why… keep… hurtin'… me?" she pleads, starting to cry.

Niall wipes her tears with his left hand and shakes his head. "Why, Karen, I'm just doing this for fun."

Karen cries even louder.

"Ye will die today, Karen," says Niall, "in a few hours from now."

He makes a small cut on Karen's innards with his knife. Karen can feel the knife slicing her intestines and she screams in agony! All she can do is scream and writhe around, causing more injury to her wrists and ankles.

Her screams of pain last more than three hours. They finally stop, just before dawn.

# CHAPTER 1
# DEPLOYMENT

05:08 WIB (GMT+7)
Friday May 2, 2026
Taman Impian Jaya Ancol
Pademangan, North Jakarta, Jakarta

A few weeks later, on the other side of the world, Sarah is doing her morning run, accompanied by a large German Shepherd. A brunette with fierce blue eyes and light-tan complexion, she's clearly of Eurasian descent. She's tall and athletic with broad shoulders and a slim waist. Her body is toned and pleasingly muscular. She's stunningly beautiful, even with sweat dripping from her morning run.

Sarah's running toward her house in Jaya Ancol Seafront, a luxurious complex near the Taman Impian Jaya Ancol resort in North Jakarta, Indonesia. When she enters the main gate of the housing complex, both on-duty security guards come out of the guardhouse, stand to attention, and give her a crisp salute.

"*Selamat pagi, Komandan!*" they say. *Good morning, Commander!*

Sarah nods and smiles at them, her usual response. About a year ago, she volunteered to be the chief of security of the housing complex. All the security guards under her command speak fluent English, a requirement for the job as so many foreigners live in this complex. Visitors from the UK are always surprised when they talk to the security guards because their English accent sounds quite posh. They learned that from their commander.

About half a mile from her house, Sarah starts to sprint. As usual, her dog races past her. A few moments later, a black Toyota Fortuner honks its horn and also passes by. Sarah smiles in recognition and kicks her pace up a notch. Arriving home, the Fortuner has already parked in front of the house and its driver playing and talking in German to the German Shepherd.

The driver is a young man with Eurasian features. With his blue eyes and two-day stubble on his face, he's what some would call rakishly handsome. He's tall, athletic, and has a swimmer's physique.

"*Hai, Kak,*" greets Sarah to her older brother.

"*Hai juga, Dik,*" says Tony.

"You're early," Sarah points out. "My flight doesn't leave until nine."

"Yeah, well, I have a good reason to eat Bibi's fried rice for breakfast then," says Tony, grinning.

"Hmm... Lydia's fried rice not tasty enough for you?"

"Bibi's tastes better."

"I'm telling Lydia you said that."

"Don't you dare!" says Tony, punching his sister's shoulder.

Brother and sister laugh as they go inside the house, followed by the family dog. Bibi, their housekeeper, has cooked them an Indonesian version of a full English breakfast. After taking a quick shower, Sarah joins Tony.

Tony looks at her eating. "You don't usually eat this much for breakfast, *Dik.*"

"You think you're the only one who likes Bibi's fried rice?"

Tony laughs. "Lydia is jealous of you, you know."

"How is that?"

"You eat so much but you still have a six-pack."

It's Sarah's turn to laugh. "Tell her to return to the gym, *Kak.*"

"She'll probably start again after Jonathan stops breast-feeding."

"How is Jonathan?" asks Sarah, thinking about her adorable baby nephew. "What can he do now?"

"He rolls around a lot. He keeps trying to stand up, but ends up falling arse over teakettle."

Sarah laughs.

"By the way, has Interpol told you yet about what sort of job you'll be doing in England?" asks Tony.

"Not yet. They told me to go to Manchester and meet the boss. He'll be the one giving me the full briefing. They only told me to be ready for a six-month assignment. I've no idea what I'll be doing there."

"Any plans to visit Poole?" asks Tony.

"Maybe during the weekends."

"How about Credenhill?"

"I'm not military," says Sarah, surprised at the stupid question. "Why on earth would I go there?"

"Just asking," answers Tony, trying to look innocent.

Sarah frowns. She thinks her brother has been hiding something ever since he returned from Credenhill a couple of years ago. She's gearing up to ask him about it when they hear someone coming down the stairs. Their twelve-year-old sister, Cindy, is in her uniform, ready to go to school. Her features are a photocopy of her older sister's, but her skin is distinctly more Asian. All three siblings get their extremely good looks from their European mother.

"*Hai, Kak,*" greets Cindy to her older brother, kissing him on the cheek.

"*Hai juga,*" says Tony. "Join us for breakfast, *Dik.*"

"*Oke deh,*" says Cindy, sitting next to her sister.

Cindy is the quietest of the three, but has countless friends. Only a few seconds after she sits down, her smartphone's bleeping away, indicating the arrival of emails, tweets, Facebook notifications, and texts from around the world. She ignores them all. They're not allowed to play with their smartphones at the dinner table.

If she *were* allowed to look at her Facebook account, she'd only see pictures of herself and her friends. Cindy loves her brother and sister, but she isn't allowed to share pictures of them. This is because her siblings' jobs prohibit them from having their photos taken and featured on social media. Her older sister has a Facebook account, but the family know that it's only used as cover for her secretive day job. Sarah hasn't updated it for a while, not since she was transferred to an even more secretive role.

"Remember to bring some souvenirs from England, *Kak,*" reminds the young girl.

"What do you want me to bring?" asks Sarah.

"How about a good-looking English boyfriend?" suggests Cindy, a big grin on her super-cute face.

Sarah laughs. "Why not ask me to bring home Prince George instead?"

"Yeah! That's even better!" exclaims Cindy excitedly.

"I think *you* will get married before your older sister, *Dik,*" comments Tony.

"Why?"

"Sarah doesn't respect anyone who can't take her down in unarmed combat, you know."

Cindy laughs. "Is that why all her ex-boyfriends need cosmetic surgery?"

They all laugh, taking the mickey out of each other all through breakfast, until Cindy leaves for school and Sarah goes to the airport.

17:15 WIB (GMT+7)
Friday May 2, 2026
Terminal 3, Soekarno-Hatta International Airport
Kota Tangerang, Tangerang, Banten

At the same airport that afternoon, an Irishman is picked up by Santoso, his chauffeur. Besides being his chauffeur, Santoso is also the chief of security and butler for his house in the Pondok Indah area, an elite district in South Jakarta. They greet each other in Bahasa Indonesia, the official language of the Republic of Indonesia.

"How are you, Santoso?" says the Irishman.

"Fine, *pak* Patrick," answers Santoso with a friendly smile.

Patrick has asked him many times not to use the word *pak*, which means mister, but always in vain. "How's the family?"

"They're well, *pak*."

"Good to hear."

"Do you want to go home first or go straight to the factory, *pak* Patrick?" asks Santoso.

"Let's head home first. Could you please take me to the factory later this evening?" orders Patrick.

"No problem, *pak* Patrick," answers Santoso.

Santoso drives the car to his employer's house in Pondok Indah. His house is much larger and more luxurious than his house in North West England, and more than big enough to accommodate over fifty of his organization's men, who are mostly Irish. They need almost three hours to reach Patrick's house because of the heavy traffic, which is typical for Friday afternoons in Jakarta. Patrick is in a sour mood when he finally arrives home.

"I see ye've had a pleasant journey, Paddy," says Richard, sarcastically.

"Fuck off!" snaps Patrick, giving him a nasty look. "Any grub here before we go?"

Richard accompanies him to the dinner table, already loaded with Indonesian food. Quite unlike Patrick's house in England, his house in Jakarta has twelve housekeepers, mostly members of Santoso's extended family. They're tasked with doing all of the cooking, washing, and cleaning.

It's no wonder Patrick and his men prefer to stay in Indonesia instead of the UK or Ireland. Despite having left the European Union, the UK is still an economic superpower and everything is cheap in Indonesia, including sex. The Brits here can live like kings, meaning they can have daily sex parties with Indonesian women who look like actresses or supermodels.

"Where's the package Frag sent ye?" asks Patrick.

"I sent most of the longs and all of the shorts to the factory as soon as they arrived. I'll give ye the honour of distributing them to the fellas," answers Richard.

"How's production?" asks Patrick, taking some food from the table.

"Still not enough to produce for the Australian market, let alone the Indonesian market," answers Richard. "I'm even having problems fulfilling the quota for Ireland. The problem is in the supply chain, not in production."

Patrick nods. "I'll send Frank here again so he can also sort out the supply chain cock-up for Swan's Mill. Any problems with the local authorities?"

"None that needs Niall's help," says Richard, "but I think we're ready to proceed with Phase Three."

"Did ye get the info from Lukas yet?"

"Last night," answers Richard.

"How?"

"Easy... I got him really pissed," says Richard, smirking.

"Can't ye do Phase Three yerself?"

"If I could then we wouldn't need Niall, would we?"

"In that case, I'll text Niall and have him fly over. Frank will then come here to continue with Phase Four. Ye should gather intel based on the info from Lukas before Frank arrives," orders Patrick.

"Aye," says Richard.

Patrick finishes his dinner then opens a small bottle of Bir Bintang, their favourite Indonesian beer. They are then driven by Santoso to their factory in Bogor, which just happens to be the largest ecstasy factory in the world.

# CHAPTER 2
# INTERNATIONAL CRIMINAL POLICE ORGANIZATION–INTERPOL

08:58 GMT
Monday May 4, 2026
Interpol Manchester
Central Park, Manchester, England

Sarah arrives on schedule at the office of Interpol Manchester. Its office, in northeast Manchester, is in the same building as the Greater Manchester Police headquarters. She has just been invited into her new commander's office and immediately introduces herself.

"Good morning, Mr. Broussard. I'm AKP Sarah Michelle Dharmawan from the Indonesian National Police. Reporting for duty, sir!"

Sarah salutes and stands to attention in the manner of the Indonesian National Police (INP). Her rank is AKP, or Ajun Komisaris Polisi, which is somewhat equivalent to Inspector in the UK.

Christopher Broussard glances at the beautiful, confident young woman in front of him. Sarah speaks in perfect English. Like most Brits, Broussard is sensitive regarding one's accent and he's a bit taken aback by this young Indonesian policewoman speaking with a West Country accent with a touch of Spanish. She doesn't sound at all the way he'd imagined of an Indonesian woman. She's wearing a simple, grey business suit with a white shirt and black shoes. She has dressed to blend in and even her Samsonite briefcase is simple, although it looks heavy.

"Good morning, Sarah," says Broussard, standing up. "Stand easy, please."

Sarah stands at ease in the INP manner and shakes hands with the head of Interpol Manchester.

"Let me be the first to welcome you to England, Sarah," says Broussard warmly.

"Thank you, sir."

"Oh, just call me Chief like the others around here."

"Sure, Chief."

"I would also like to thank you for coming here and thank the INP for sending you."

"You're welcome, Chief, glad we're able to 'elp."

"Please sit down. Would you like anything to drink? Some coffee, perhaps?"

"That would be lovely, Chief, thank you," says Sarah.

Broussard calls his secretary to order a couple of cups of coffee.

"And how was your flight?" asks Broussard, opening some files on his tablet.

"'Orrible, Chief," replies Sarah, smiling, "but at least I managed to survive the British Airways grub."

Broussard laughs. He has also had bad experiences tasting the food of British Airways. Broussard's secretary comes in with their coffee, which they sip before getting down to business.

"So, Sarah, your personnel file was sent by e-mail from NCB Indonesia last week, but I've only managed to skim through it. Maybe you can kick things off by telling me about yourself? Could you please start with your family?" says Broussard. He's still friendly, but there's no mistaking this for anything other than a direct order.

"Well, my dad is a retired general in the Indonesian Marines and Mum owns a successful cosmetics company in Indonesia. I 'ave one older brother in the Indonesian Air Force and a little sister in secondary school."

"Pardon me for mentioning this, but you don't look or sound like any of the other Indonesians I know."

Sarah laughs. "Well, Dad is Indonesian, but Mum is 'alf English and Spanish. They met when Dad was stationed at Poole on a secondment with the SBS. About six years after I was born, Dad was sent to Poole again for six years so the 'ole family moved there. My little sister was born in England just before we 'ad to return to Indonesia. My brother and I went to Bournemouth Collegiate School at Poole. So, basically, English is my first language."

"That explains your accent then," says Broussard, smiling.

People from West Country usually don't pronounce the letter 'h', which is known as aitch-dropping. Broussard usually associates the West

Country accent with farmers... or pirates. But he has to admit that it sounds nice coming from the stunningly beautiful Indonesian policewoman in front of him, even if it's ever so slightly unnatural.

"Why did your father stay so long in Poole on his second tour?" continues Broussard.

"Dad went to 'Amworthy Barracks almost every day, but 'e never did told us about what 'e 'ad done back then," explains Sarah. "While 'e was in England, 'e also took the time to study for a master's degree in War Studies from the University of Kent in Canterbury."

Broussard smiles again. It's really quite a thing, her voice in full flow. "How about your career in the INP?"

"Well, after I graduated from the Police Academy, I decided to join Brimob, and then was almost immediately inducted into Gegana," says Sarah.

"Brimob?"

"It's a paramilitary unit of the INP, like The Met's SCO19 that 'andles extraordinary crimes."

"And Gegana?"

"It's a step up from Brimob, but with a greater emphasis on EOD and counterterrorism."

Broussard continues without looking at his tablet. "And then after that, you were hand-selected to join Densus-88?"

Sarah tries hard not to react, but she eventually blushes. "I'm sorry, Chief, but I'm not allowed to talk about that."

"No, no, don't apologize. I shouldn't have asked that question," says Broussard, smiling. "And I assure you that I will be the only one here who knows that particular bit of information. I happen to know this because I got to know your Police Brigadier General Prasetyo when I was assigned as a liaison officer to NCB Indonesia quite a few years ago. Don't worry, I told the other team members that you were from the Traffic Management Centre before they transferred you to Interpol."

So her Interpol commander knows Police Brigadier General Prasetyo, the commander of Detasemen Khusus-88 (Densus-88), which is Indonesia's leading antiterrorist unit. Sarah is relieved, because all members of Densus–88 are obliged to conceal their membership.

Sarah continues. "About a week ago, I received orders to transfer to the

Interpol National Central Bureau for Indonesia and they then told me to immediately sort myself for Interpol Manchester."

"Right, so here you are. Do you know why you've been sent here?"

"I 'aven't the foggiest, Chief," answers Sarah.

Broussard nods, unsurprised. "My team and I will give you a full briefing in a few minutes, but let me ask you a question. You joined Brimob, then Gegana, and then, well, you know where. Why?"

"Well, I never wanted to be just a regular policewoman in the INP. The INP initially wanted me in Public Relations for some reason, but I preferred a much more active role in combatting crime. My dad was once the commanding officer of Denjaka, which is a counterterrorist unit of the Indonesian Marines, and my brother is now a detachment commander of a counterterrorist unit in the Indonesian Air Force. My brother would probably take the mickey out of me for the rest of my life if I 'adn't qualified for… you know… that unit you mentioned."

"I'm sure your parents are very proud of you two."

"Actually, Mum complains that no one in the family wants to take over 'er business when she retires. Even my little sister wants to join the navy."

Broussard laughs and continues studying the file in front of him. "It says here that other than Indonesian and English, you are highly proficient in Spanish, French, Dutch, and German?"

"Mum can speak those languages and she taught all of us, including Dad. She made all of us practice every day. We even 'ave a schedule. For example, on Mondays I'm only allowed to speak French, my brother is only allowed to speak German, my little sister Spanish, my dad Dutch, and Mum Ba'asa Indonesia. The next day we switch languages and so on. We were only allowed to speak English when Mum wasn't around."

"What do you usually use all those languages for?" asks Broussard.

"Oh, I usually pray in Spanish, speak French to my boyfriend, curse in Dutch, and talk German to my German Shepherd," answers Sarah.

Broussard laughs out loud, but Sarah wasn't joking. Their family dog, whose name is Jürgen, was taught German commands by her family and it's the only language he understands. Broussard's file isn't up-to-date. Sarah can also speak fluent Arabic, but she decides her new commander doesn't need to know that unless it becomes relevant to her job in England.

"We could certainly use your language skills here, but what we really need is your experience in investigation and intelligence gathering. Not so much your combat skills," says Broussard. "I hope you're not too disappointed."

"I think I've 'ad enough action in the INP to last a lifetime, Chief," says Sarah, smiling.

Broussard laughs again. "Right then, let's meet the team, shall we?"

He stands and leads Sarah to the meeting room near his office. Inside are five people who all seem to be from the UK. All of them are in their late thirties, except a young woman who looks in her late twenties. Barring her new commander, who's wearing a business suit, the rest of the team are dressed in business casual, which makes Sarah feel like she's wearing the wrong costume to the party.

"Good morning, everyone. I would like you all to meet our newest team member, Inspector Sarah Dharmawan from the Indonesian National Police," says Broussard.

Everyone comes forward and shakes hands with Sarah.

"DCI Matthew Gallagher, Police Service of Northern Ireland. Please call me Matt."

"Detective Chief Inspector Arthur Grimes, Metropolitan Police Service."

"James Hicks, Security Service."

"Sáirsint Elizabeth O'Connell, An Garda Síochána. Ye can call me Liz."

"I'm Paul Elliot from the National Crime Agency. *Hoo yee gannin', pet?*" asks Paul, the final member of the team, at high speed.

Although Sarah has heard the Geordie accent before, it takes her a second to understand him. "I'm all right, Paul. Thank you for asking."

"Wow! Can ye really understand him?" asks Liz with her thick Irish brogue.

"I took a shot in the dark," says Sarah, joking. "Actually, I don't understand any of you."

Everyone laughs, including Broussard, who's laughing the loudest. It seems Sarah's new commander also has trouble sometimes understanding his team members.

"Where's Michael?" asks Broussard to his team.

Liz answers. "He just got back from Belfast and will be in shortly. He said he needed to download and print some files first."

"Right then. Can everyone please take their seats?" says Broussard.

Everyone sits down and Liz directs Sarah to a chair opposite Broussard. On Sarah's left sit Arthur, Paul, and James, and on her right, Matt and Elizabeth. The chair beside Liz is empty and so is the one beside Sarah. She also notices that James, Matt, and Elizabeth are Irish. Just after everyone has settled themselves, the door opens and another person walks in carrying some files.

"Michael, I would like you to meet Inspector Sarah Dharmawan from the Indonesian National Police," says Broussard.

Sarah stands and shakes hands with Michael, whose hand feels as rough as sandpaper and whose face is full of scars. He seems to be in the same age group as Sarah and Liz.

"Major Michael Adrian, British Army," says Michael, blinking as if he's seen Sarah before.

Sarah gets the feeling Michael recognizes her, but that's impossible unless he reads Indonesian fashion or fitness magazines. Sarah's intrigued to have a representative from the military in this team, but no representatives from the GMP, the Greater Manchester Police. Michael has a King's English accent with a touch of Irish, unlike Broussard and Arthur, who have an Estuary English accent, commonly used by people from South East London.

Michael gives the files he brought to James. "I've e-mailed you the file and here's some info on Rory Hanrahan, courtesy of the Intelligence Corps."

James, the MI5 man, opens the files and studies them quickly. "I owe ye a big, fat, juicy steak, mate. I'd like to follow up on this immediately, Chief," he says, standing up.

Broussard nods and James leaves the room. Michael then sits beside Liz.

"How was your weekend in Belfast, Michael?" asks Broussard, preparing his tablet.

"Fine," answers Michael curtly.

"What did you do there?"

Michael thinks for a moment before answering his commander. "I met an old girlfriend."

"Ah… so you've been dating your old girlfriend, then?"

"Indeed, Chief," answers Michael with a cheeky grin.

"Did you bring her with you to Manchester?"

"The thought crossed my mind, Chief... but then her husband probably would've objected."

Paul chokes on his coffee while the others try hard to stifle their laughs. They fail miserably and Broussard is not amused. It takes a while for the room to settle down.

"Let's not wait for James to return. Since we have a new member, I would like to start from the beginning," says Broussard, glowering at Michael.

Broussard connects his tablet to the TV behind him via Bluetooth and it shows a map of Ireland. A formal briefing usually starts with the Preliminaries, and continues with Situation, Mission, Execution, Command, and Support. This is called the Five Paragraph Order. The briefing contains everything from the most general matters to the most specific. After the briefing, even the dumbest person in the room should have understood the goal of the assignment and what role they would play.

'And the dumbest person in the room is *me*,' thinks Sarah. 'First day of work and there's so much information to absorb from such a dry, formal briefing.'

"Let's start with the Preliminaries," says Broussard. "As you can see on the screen, this is the map of Ireland..."

Broussard starts with the geography of Ireland, its demographics, its history, and then on a part of Irish history called The Troubles. "The Troubles was caused by the disputed status of Northern Ireland within the United Kingdom and a sense of discrimination against the Nationalist minority by the dominant Unionist majority. As early as 1969, armed campaigns began by paramilitary groups to end British rule in Northern Ireland and to create a new 'All-Ireland', 'Thirty-Two County' Irish Republic. These paramilitary groups were responsible for countless bombings and lost lives in both Britain and Ireland. The ranks of these groups were filled with 'professionals', who didn't have daily jobs or careers and had dedicated their lives to the cause in which they believed. To fund their activities, these groups relied largely on the drug trade, from cocaine, heroin and cannabis, to ecstasy."

Sarah is familiar with some of the details Broussard's reciting, but is grateful to him for bringing her up-to-date. James enters the room and sits down in his previous place.

Broussard continues. "The Good Friday Agreement in 1998 was a major step in the peace process. One aim of The Agreement was that all paramilitary groups in Northern Ireland would cease their activities and disarm. In response, the UK government announced military cuts which included the Royal Irish Regiment, in which three of its five battalions were disbanded in 2007. I will explain the significance of this later."

"It was not until June 2009 that all paramilitary groups officially decommissioned their arsenals. However, they still retained a considerable amount of weaponry beyond what was needed for self-defence. This left us with a new issue; their so called 'professionals' had employment problems and chose to continue their drug operations. Not for the cause, this time, but for personal wealth. This group of criminals has evolved into one of the world's most organized and sophisticated crime syndicates. Their experience in smuggling weapons is now focused on smuggling narcotics. Their original members were mostly from Ireland, either from Northern Ireland or from the Republic of Ireland, but now their members are from all over the UK… and much more dangerous."

Broussard pauses for effect and Sarah looks up from her tablet. Her new commander, she realizes, is a natural storyteller.

"More dangerous because, since the year 2020, almost all of their core members are ex-soldiers of the British Army."

The others in the room nod. They know this all already, but it still carries impact every time it's said.

"Following the 2010 General Election, the new government instituted a new defence review called Army 2020, which was to reduce the size of the British Army from approximately 102,000 members to nearer 82,000 members by the year 2020. As part of this objective, the infantry was reduced in size from thirty-six regular battalions to just thirty-one."

"As a result, the army-restructuring policy caused employment concerns for the UK. Most of the ex-army personnel found employment in law enforcement and some others chose to join private security companies. After most of them were disbanded in 2007, scores of ex-members of the Royal Irish Regiment joined the French Foreign Legion. There is such a significant number of ex-Royal Irish Regiment members in the 2nd Foreign Infantry Regiment that they started calling themselves the 2nd Royal Irish Regiment of the French Foreign Legion."

Sarah's teammates smirk when they hear that. Broussard waits until the room settles before continuing his briefing.

"Most of the rest found work in one role or another, but a minority became criminals. A recent independent study of the prison population in the UK showed that almost twelve percent are ex-servicemen from all branches of the armed forces. After serving their sentence, some of them eventually found their way into this organization. The irony is that most of the senior members of this organization are ex-members of the Royal Irish Regiment, who gave operational support to the RUC and then later to the PSNI in the war against the paramilitaries. Now it seems that they have allied themselves with the ex-paramilitaries in forming this drug syndicate."

"This group have called themselves The Irish Drug Cartel. Ever since their formation, they have been using tactics from the South American drug cartels. They bribe, intimidate, torture, threaten, maim, and assassinate anyone who gets in their way. Especially law enforcement personnel and local politicians. They have a habit of not just torturing and killing their target, but also the target's family members as well, and hundreds of these drug-related deaths have been attributed to The Cartel.

"These past three years, The Cartel has concentrated their efforts in the production and distribution of MDMA, better known as ecstasy. The street name in the UK is 'Mandy' and it is mostly free of adulterants. MDMA can induce euphoria, a sense of intimacy with others, diminished anxiety, and mild psychedelia, and it's a highly popular drug because it's not addictive. MDMA is a Class A drug and is illegal to have, give away, or sell. Possession can fetch one up to seven years in prison, and supplying to someone else, including your friends, can mean a life sentence as well as an unlimited fine. We believe they have drug manufacturing plants, or DMPs, within the UK, the Republic of Ireland, and abroad."

Broussard stresses the word 'abroad' and once again, all eyes turn to Sarah. "We have only recently acquired intel that, most unexpectedly, the largest drug factory of The Cartel is not in the UK nor Republic of Ireland... but in Indonesia.

"This is why you are here, Sarah. Paul and James will give you a more detailed briefing regarding this new intel after the meeting. This concludes the Preliminaries and now James will continue with the Situation."

Sarah nods. Now she understands who and what she's up against and why she's needed on this team.

# CHAPTER 3
# FIVE PARAGRAPH ORDER

10:19 GMT
Monday May 4, 2026
Interpol Manchester
Central Park, Manchester, England

James presents his part of the formal briefing. "Like the Chief said, the leadership and senior members of the Irish Drug Cartel are mainly ex-British Army and most of them hail from the Royal Irish Regiment, three battalions of which were disbanded in 2007. We believe The Cartel has up to 250 core members and almost all of them are ex-army, laid off in 2020. Here's the Situation, starting with what we have on the top echelon of their organization."

"The leader is Patrick 'Paddy' Dunbar. He was the Regimental Sergeant Major of the Royal Irish Regiment before he took the redundancy package in 2007. His entire career was built upon Operation Banner, supporting first the RUC and then later, the PSNI, in asserting the authority of the government in Northern Ireland. His experience as an RSM has undoubtedly served him well as a leader of a crime syndicate."

Unlike Broussard, James's presentation style is dry and dull. Sarah knows that this information will be extremely important for their mission, but she finds herself struggling to concentrate.

"The second-in-command, or 2 i/c, is Steve Dunbar, the younger brother of Paddy Dunbar. He followed his brother into the Royal Irish Regiment and made Regimental Quartermaster Sergeant before he took the package. We think he's in charge of the finance and administration side of The Cartel," says James, presenting photos of Steve, who looks like a thinner, bespectacled version of his brother.

Sarah thinks Steve looks more like a bookkeeper than one of the leaders of a major crime syndicate.

"Don't be fooled by his appearance," reminds James. "He may look like a milksop, but he's extremely skilled in unarmed combat and a world-class marksman with a pistol."

Sarah feels sheepish for underestimating Steve Dunbar. She should know better than that.

"The 3 i/c is Rory Hanrahan. Rory came from the Intelligence Corps and thanks to Michael, the Ministry of Defence has finally sent us his file. It turns out he's had multiple aliases since his retirement, including Timothy Murphy, Finn Langley, and John Kearney. We think he's in charge of intelligence gathering and counterintelligence in the organization," says James, presenting some photos of Rory. In most of the pictures, he's photographed with Paddy or Steve. One picture shows him talking to a tall, fit, red-headed woman, her back turned towards the camera.

"Another senior member is Carraig 'Frag' O'Lenihan. We think he's the oldest in the top echelon and probably the only one without a military background. Prior to the Good Friday Agreement, he was the head of the Provisional Wing of the IRA. We think he's in charge of the production and distribution of MDMA for Great Britain and the procurement and smuggling of all weapons, from automatic weapons and pistols to explosives. His friends call him 'Frag' because he carries an old fragmentation grenade with him at all times. He's been heard saying many times that he doesn't want to be taken alive and would rather blow himself up and everyone else with him if we ever caught up to him. Please take his words seriously!"

Sarah types that information into her tablet. She must treat Carraig O'Lenihan as a potential suicide bomber and this isn't the first time Sarah has had to deal with people like Carraig.

"The next is Richard Callaghan..." James continues with the names and background information on all known Cartel members. "Frank Llywelyn... Seamus Fitzgerald... Declan Mulcahy... Brian Turner..."

Sarah's head starts to swirl from all the information.

"We think there are more than ten people in the top echelon of this organization, but we don't have names or photos for them all," continues James, completely oblivious to the fact that his teammates are losing concentration. "We still don't know who's in charge of production and distribution of MDMA in Ireland, for example. However, there are a couple of names that I want ye to pay special attention to. The first is Niall Iollan Schroeder."

Sarah notices that almost every member of her team suddenly tenses up on hearing that name.

"While he was with the Royal Irish Regiment, he was court-martialed for torturing and mutilating a female civilian after the Battle of Musa Qala in Afghanistan. His psychological profile, taken before his court-martial, states that he's a textbook psychopath with an absolute disregard for human life. Niall somehow managed to escape the Military Corrective Training Centre in Colchester, Essex before his sentence was carried out. Like the Chief said, the Irish Drug Cartel is employing tactics from the South American drug cartels and Niall is their chief executioner. He's in charge of the torture and murder of police, politicians, and civilians who get in their way," says James, holding back some emotion.

Sarah observes that her teammates are showing signs of distress and all of them are avoiding looking at the screen, except for Michael, who remains expressionless.

"The second person is Donald Mullins, affectionately called Tiny by his close friends. He's called Tiny because he's well over two metres tall and weighs almost eighteen stone of pure muscle. He's the only senior member we know of from the Republic of Ireland and he used to be in the Sciathán Fiannóglach an Airm, or the Army Ranger Wing, which is the counterterrorist unit of the Irish Defence Force. He used to box for his unit until he was sacked for 'accidentally' killing his opponent in the ring during practice. We think he's in charge of the security and paramiltary side of the organization."

Sarah sees that Tiny is absolutely huge. Tiny was a boxer and no matter how tough someone is, if they're hit by a man as big as him, they're out for the count.

"Tiny is the most dangerous of the lot, so please be careful if ye manage to locate him. A couple of Rangers from the Army Ranger Wing once tried to take him down by themselves when they accidentally ran into him outside a pub in Dublin, but ended up getting themselves killed. Tiny defeated both and broke their necks. He is rarely seen in public and if ye do see him, under any circumstances, ye will *not*, I repeat, ye will *not* try to apprehend him by yerselves. Ye should *always*, I repeat, *always* call and wait for backup to arrive. Trust me on this, it is better to have him escape than to have any of ye try to take him out by yerselves."

James stares hard at each member of the briefing until he's sure they've taken him seriously.

"We have reports that there are female members in the top echelons, but those reports are unconfirmed. The UK Police and the Garda have managed to apprehend many of the dealers, but none of The Cartel core members. Those dealers who were apprehended do not talk about their suppliers because they all know the consequences of talking, which usually ends with the most violent death someone like Niall Schroeder can bestow upon ye."

"This concludes what we have on the opposition. To face them, the Home Office has requested ICPO-Interpol Headquarters at Lyon, France to form an Interpol Incident Response Team, or Interpol IRT, led by Christopher Broussard from Interpol. Since The Cartel has become a matter of national security, MI5 has become involved and I will be the liaison between this team and MI5. Paul will liaise between this team and the NCA, and Liz, Matt, and Arthur will be the liaison between this team and their respective constabularies. The Cartel has been such a disruption to civil order and represents such a clear and present danger to our society that two months ago, His Majesty's Government declared War on Narcoterrorism and initiated the MACP. This means that His Majesty's Armed Forces, *not* the police force, will be the ones involved in handling The Cartel once we've located them and a 'shoot-to-kill' policy is applied to the core members of The Cartel. This is why Michael is here, as the liaison between this team and the Ministry of Defence. As for ye, Sarah, as stated before, we have acquired new intel that their largest factory is in Indonesia. We would like ye to be the liaison between us and the INP."

Sarah nods. MACP stands for Military Aid to the Civil Power, which means the provision of armed military assistance in its maintenance of law, order, and public safety using specialist capabilities or equipment in situations beyond the capability of the Civil Power. One of the instances in UK history where MACP was activated was during the Iranian Embassy Siege at Princes Gate, South Kensington, London, in 1980. The hostage rescue operation, called Operation Nimrod, was successfully executed by B

Squadron, 22$^{nd}$ Regiment, Special Air Service (SAS) and this was the first time most people became aware of that special forces unit.

The War on Narcoterrorism, Sarah knows, has raged around the world, but so far only the UK has involved their armed forces to combat it. Other governments still place narcoterrorism under the jurisdiction of law enforcement, not military. In the US, their armed forces are even *prohibited* from being involved because of the Posse Comitatus Act, which prohibits the US Armed Forces from being involved in enforcing the law. Similar laws to the Posse Comitatus Act are applied in almost all democratic countries.

'I guess I'm all the way here just to be a liaison officer,' thinks Sarah, feeling a bit let down. Her job in England turns out to be not challenging after all.

Sarah will realize a few minutes later that she couldn't be more wrong.

At this point, Broussard takes over the briefing. "Thank you, James. We have quite a monumental Mission on our hands, which is to assist the Ministry of Defence of the United Kingdom of Great Britain and Northern Ireland in locating all members of the Irish Drug Cartel and their headquarters, drug manufacturing plants, and distribution centres. I repeat, our mission is to assist the Ministry of Defence of the United Kingdom of Great Britain and Northern Ireland in locating all members of the Irish Drug Cartel and their headquarters, drug manufacturing plants, and distribution centres."

Sarah makes note of the mission in her tablet and highlights it. Next comes 'Execution', where Paul will outline the strategy designed to accomplish the 'Mission'.

Paul explains in his hard-to-understand Geordie accent that Liz, Matt, and Arthur will concentrate on investigating the downstream, which is the distribution side of MDMA. Paul, James, and Michael will investigate the upstream, which is the production side. They will also search for the location of their headquarters, drug factories, and distribution centres. Once these are located, Michael will liaise with the MoD for the raid. If any of The Cartel members are seen or located, the military will be the ones handling them because regular armed police would not be able to handle Cartel members, who are military-trained and armed with automatic weapons. Paul then asks Sarah to concentrate on locating their largest factory which, based on the latest intel, turns out to be in Indonesia. Sarah is advised to coordinate with Michael, who has experience in locating and decommissioning drug factories.

Paul's presentation finally ends and Sarah breathes a sigh of relief. The heaviest part of this formal briefing is finally over.

Broussard takes over again. "Thank you, Paul. Our chain of command will be as follows: I will be in command of this Interpol Incident Response Team, with James Hicks as 2 i/c and Paul Elliot as 3 i/c."

Broussard then displays everyone's contact number and e-mail address. Sarah adds her contact details to the list. The team is not allowed to save the names and contact numbers in their smartphones to avoid The Cartel taking one phone and tracking the other team members' smartphones with a sophisticated phone-tracking application. Team members may send each other encrypted text messages, but only on the condition they erase them immediately. They are also prohibited from giving their contact numbers to other people outside the Interpol team, especially constables from the GMP.

The final part of the briefing is 'Support', which is about the supporting units and the logistics needed to accomplish the 'Mission'. Broussard explains that basically all territorial police and military units can be deployed to support the team, as long as he can convince the Home Office that such support is really needed. Theoretically, with the activation of MACP, Michael can have MoD deploy the whole 3$^{rd}$ Mechanized Infantry Division from the British Army if it's really needed by the team. Broussard hopes that Sarah can also convince the INP to deploy all assets necessary to locate and decommission The Cartel's factory in Indonesia.

"Due to the high-risk nature of this assignment, all of you are authorized and required to carry firearms at all times," says Broussard. He gives Sarah some official-looking letters and a couple of ID cards, one which identifies her as an Interpol officer and the other which identifies her as an AFO or Authorized Firearms Officer. "After this meeting, the first thing you should do is to proceed to the GMP's armoury, show your AFO card and give them these papers. In return, they will give you a sidearm, a backup sidearm, and magazines for both weapons. I'm sure you are familiar with the Glock 17, which is GMP's standard issue sidearm, but you might want to take some non-lethal weapons as well, like pepper sprays, telescoping batons, or Tasers."

Sarah wants to say something, but then closes her mouth. Her commander takes notice.

"Do you have anything to add, Sarah?" he asks.

Sarah is still hesitant, but she then takes a chance. "I 'ope this is all right, but I've brought some kit with me from Indonesia."

She places an empty HK P2000 pistol on the table, two magazines loaded with bullets, a small Smith & Wesson HRT3 knife inside its holster, handcuffs, and an ASP telescoping baton. All of the team members look at her kit with wide eyes except for Michael, whose eyes are focused solely on her handcuffs.

"How on earth did ye smuggle these into England?" asks James.

"*Hoo* did *yee* get them through airline security?" asks Paul.

"How did you get them past GMP security?" asks Broussard.

Everyone looks shocked except for Michael, who only smiles at Sarah. She smiles back at him. Sarah already has an idea which regiment Michael comes from. With Sarah's weapons still on the table, the other team members are keeping a wary eye on them. Even at this high level, UK police officers rarely handle firearms. Watching somebody waltz through security with them has put almost everyone on edge.

"Well, I feel naked without a weapon so I decided to bring them to England. I 'ope you don't mind," says Sarah.

The eyes of all the men in the room instantly become unfocused when Sarah says 'I feel naked', but soon return to normal. Liz notices and rolls her eyes.

"I'm sure glad you're on *our* side, Sarah," says Broussard, finally able to smile again. "Before you receive further briefing from James and Paul, do you have any questions?"

"I 'ave some basic questions," says Sarah. "First, why are we based in Manchester? Isn't there an Interpol Dublin?"

"Ye might have heard on the news a couple of months ago that there was a huge explosion at the International Liaison Building of the An Garda Síochána Headquarters," says Liz, the anger apparent in her voice. "The bastards killed almost all of the Interpol agents that handled this case and maimed the rest."

"The results of the forensic analysis say that they used PE4 for that one," says James. "Michael is looking into how they managed to procure it."

"We had to start from practically square-one because almost all of the agents assigned to this case are dead and much of their investigation along with them," says Broussard, sadly.

The news *had* reached Indonesia and Sarah remembers feeling saddened by the event because of the dozens of people killed in the explosion. Sarah suddenly realizes that this assignment is much more dangerous than she'd previously thought. "Second, I'm just wondering why there aren't any representatives from the GMP in this team?"

Everyone is silent and Sarah wonders what she's said wrong. She also notices Liz's eyes getting moist.

"Arthur will brief you on that," says Broussard softly, staring at the empty chair next to Sarah while the other team members just look down.

Sarah wonders about their reactions, but decides now is not the time to pursue it. Although she still has plenty to ask, she nods to Broussard to signal that she's done.

"Jolly good then. Let's get back to work everyone," orders Broussard, dismissing them.

Sarah starts to stand.

"Sarah, may I have a few words before you meet with James and Paul?"

"Sure, Arthur."

They stay in their chairs while the others leave the room. Sarah takes her weapons and straps them on again. Only AFOs, like the people in this room, may carry concealed weapons in the UK. Arthur waits until the room is clear before he begins.

"We used to have a representative from the GMP Criminal Investigation Department. Her name was Karen Wilson. She got a little too close to The Cartel members and they snatched her. She was killed last month, leaving behind a husband," says Arthur, sadness in his voice.

"Oh, Arthur," says Sarah. "I'm sorry."

"It's the way she was killed that is most distressing. Niall Schroeder tortured her for several hours before she finally died," says Arthur in his soft Estuary English accent.

"And 'ow do you know Niall did it?"

Arthur shifted in his chair before answering. "He left a copy of the video at the crime scene. The arrogant bastard even called The Met to tell us where to find her body." He began connecting his tablet to the screen in the briefing room by Bluetooth. "Now, I know you don't want to see this, but it will give you some insight into our opposition, especially Niall Schroeder."

The screen shows a naked woman in her thirties, spread-eagled on top of a steel table with her arms and legs handcuffed to the table legs. She's crying.

"Please, Niall, don't do this," begs Karen.

"But I want to, Karen," says Niall Schroeder, who suddenly appears on screen carrying a small knife.

Sarah automatically notes that the small knife Niall carries is a Gerber Guardian, similar to her Smith & Wesson HRT3. The only significant difference is in the tip; where Sarah's knife has a spear tip, Niall's Gerber Guardian has a tanto tip, stronger at the end and less likely to break. Niall traces Karen's body with his knife, starting from her neck, down to her breasts, and then her stomach, which makes Karen cry in fear.

He then inserts his knife into Karen's navel and applies some pressure. Karen seems to know what's going to happen to her so she clenches her abdominal muscles, as if trying to prevent the blade from entering her body. More pressure is applied and the blade slowly goes into her. Karen's whole body now tenses from the pain. Watching the scene, Sarah feels herself wince.

Karen flinches hard when the tip of the blade touches her intestines, but then Niall stops pushing the knife in. Karen clenches her mouth, determined not to scream.

"Scream," orders Niall.

Karen shakes her head and keeps clenching her jaws together. The small knife is barely halfway in and hasn't perforated her bowels yet, but she's clearly in pain. Niall starts wiggling the knife, moving it inside her like a toy. Karen can feel the knife moving inside her and she's in agony.

"Scream!" orders Niall, the frustration evident in his voice.

Karen tries hard not to scream and Niall keeps wiggling the knife around. Eventually, she can't take it anymore and finally screams out loud! As soon as he hears her scream, Niall starts slashing downward, disembowelling her. He takes out his knife and smiles like a child at Christmas when he sees the peristaltic movement of Karen's intestines.

Sarah is shocked, but becomes even more shocked when she sees what happens next. Niall starts caressing Karen's innards like they're something beautiful. Sarah feels sick and covers her mouth with both hands. She steals a glance at Arthur and sees that he's looking down, avoiding the screen. Her eyes return to the screen when Karen's screams grow even louder. Niall is now slicing open her upper abdomen. Now there's a deep slash from just beneath her sternum to down below her navel, which causes most of her entrails to spill out. Once again, he starts fondling her squirming intestines. He even starts kissing them, which makes Sarah so nauseous she almost throws up! Niall stops what he's doing when Karen stops screaming. She has fainted.

The Bluetooth is suddenly disconnected by Arthur and the screen goes blank. Sarah keeps her hands over her mouth until the last wave of nausea passes. She's successful in holding her emotions, but her eyes are glassy. She notices that Arthur's eyes are glassy too, although he must have seen this video many times before.

"You don't want to see the ending or even need to," says Arthur. "But just so you know, Niall started slashing her intestines with his knife. It took a few more hours before she finally died from hypovolemic shock."

Sarah still can't say anything yet. She can only stare at the blank screen, the images from a moment before still vivid in her mind. They're both silent for a few moments.

"What can you deduce from that video, Sarah?"

"*Dios mío!*" exclaims Sarah, her voice shaking. "I don't think Niall is 'uman. Even animals don't do that."

Arthur only nods in agreement. Sarah sees that Arthur looks quite a bit older than a few minutes ago. She can't even imagine how it must feel to see someone she knows be the subject of torture like that.

Arthur continues his briefing. "Niall is turned on by the screams of his victims. The more they scream, the more excited he becomes and the more damage he inflicts."

"Do 'is male victims receive the same treatment?"

"No, he only disembowels his female victims. For the men, he likes to beat them to death, first with a pair of brass knuckles for a few hours, then finished off with a wooden board with nails hammered through."

Sarah thinks hard for a moment. "Why did I need to see this video, Arthur?"

Arthur takes a long breath. "Before I joined The Met, I was an officer in MI6. Before every deployment to the Mid-East, my superiors always ensured I carried an L-pill. I always laughed at their insistence. After seeing that video, though, the thought has crossed my mind that I would rather take one than be subject to torture like that."

Arthur opens a ring box to reveal a diamond ring. "Only an expert would notice that this is really not a diamond. Should the need arise, all you have to do is bite into the 'diamond' and swallow the potassium cyanide inside. Death will come to you within minutes, instead of hours at the hands of someone like Niall Schroeder."

Sarah observes the 'diamond' for a few seconds and imagines that it contains the Ángel de la Muerte, ready to collect her soul. Arthur's ring is as deadly as her HK P2000 pistol.

"No, thank you," she says without taking her eyes off the ring.

Arthur sighs as if he'd already known what Sarah's answer would be. "Are you sure?"

"I don't believe in suicide for *any* reason, Arthur," says Sarah firmly.

"You might regret it when Niall is in the process of disembowelling you."

"Even so," says Sarah, "I'll just 'ave to endure it and wait for reinforcement to arrive."

Arthur shakes his head. "Whom the Gods would destroy, they first make proud," he quotes.

Sarah recognizes the mangled Euripides quote and smiles. "I don't think that's the way it goes, Arthur."

Arthur shrugs and takes back his ring box. "I like that version better."

"Did any of the other team members take the ring?"

"No, Sarah, and neither did I. Come on," says Arthur. "I'll take you to James and Paul."

They exit the meeting room and head to their office area. They bump into James and Paul on their way there.

"We have a lead that Paul and I want to follow through immediately," says James. "Maybe ye can meet with Michael first? We can meet tomorrow morning."

"Sure, James," answers Sarah.

Arthur escorts Sarah to her desk, which is in the same area with James, Paul, and Michael. At Michael's desk, Liz and Matt are swarming over Michael's shoulder, who hurriedly shuts off his tablet when he sees Sarah coming towards them.

"James 'as asked me to meet with you first, Michael. Do you 'ave time right now?" asks Sarah, giving her teammates a quizzical look when she sees them start to blush.

"It's almost lunch time, so how about we all grab some scoff?" suggests Michael.

They all agree and go together to the GMP cafeteria.

18:55 WIB (GMT+7)
Monday May 4, 2026
Markas Besar Kepolisian Negara Republik Indonesia (INP HQ)
Kebayoran Baru, South Jakarta, Jakarta

At the same time, more than 7,000 miles away, the commander of Densus-88, Police Brigadier General Prasetyo has just finished meeting with the Chief of the INP when he receives a call from his colleague.

"Good afternoon, Chief," answers Prasetyo warmly.

"And *selamat malam* to you, General," greets Broussard. "*Apa kabar*, my good friend?"

"Very well, Chris, thanks for asking," replies Prasetyo. "I presume you have met the officer I sent you?"

"I have indeed and I would like to thank you very much for sending her. She should be a great asset to my team," says Broussard.

"Yes, of course. She's one of the best officers in the INP and that's why she was working for me in the first place, Chief," says Prasetyo, dryly.

Broussard hears a trace of bitterness in his friend's voice. "Well, I'm glad you could spare her for Interpol, General."

"What kind of job will she be doing, if I may ask? How dangerous will it be?"

"My team is taking on the Irish Drug Cartel and we have received intel that their largest ecstasy factory is in Indonesia. She will be the liaison between my team and the INP."

"The Cartel has set up a factory in Indonesia?" asks Prasetyo, incredulously.

"Indeed, Pras," confirms Broussard.

Prasetyo falls silent for a few seconds. He has heard about The Cartel's exploits and becomes worried that they are in Indonesia. He then makes a decision. "I heard about the bombing at Interpol Dublin, Chris, and we will give you our full support. She's under your command until you accomplish your mission."

"That's good to hear and I thank you very much for your support on this."

"Please keep her safe, Chris. Do keep in mind that she's a rising star in the INP and we would prefer to have her back in one piece," says Prasetyo, dry once again.

"Indeed, Pras," replies Broussard, smiling. His colleague from Indonesia seems to have picked up a touch of British humour.

"And don't keep her in Interpol for good. I will need her back one day."

"Of course. Thanks again for sending her."

"Cheers, Chief."

"And cheers to you, General."


12:03 GMT
Monday May 4, 2026
Interpol Manchester
Central Park, Manchester, England


"So, Sarah, how *did* ye manage to smuggle those weapons into England?" asks Liz.

Before Sarah can answer, Michael gives them an explanation. "Her briefcase, although it says Samsonite, was actually produced by Heckler & Koch."

Arthur, Matt, and Liz nod knowingly. Sarah smiles at Michael. His explanation confirms Sarah's suspicions about him as only certain people could identify her briefcase, which was produced by Heckler & Koch firearms manufacturers. The briefcase can disguise its contents from X-Ray machines and can smuggle anything anywhere, including weapons, ammunition, and even explosives. The briefcase is not sold to the public, for obvious reasons, and can only be procured by specialized units in the police and military.

"Did ye accept Arthur's ring, Sarah?" asks Matt, smirking.

"Of course not," answers Sarah, laughing. "I don't know 'im that well and the situation was less than romantic."

"Indeed, Arthur. If you'd offered her the ring during a nice, candle-lit dinner, she probably would have accepted it," says Michael dryly.

Everyone laughs and Sarah gets the feeling this isn't the first time Arthur's ring has been laughed at. Brits enjoy dark humour, revolving around sarcasm, irony, taking the piss out of each other, and making fun of one's self. Jokes are often delivered with a straight face, which leaves most foreigners more than confused. The funniest British film Sarah ever saw is a favourite of her mum's, called 'Monty Python: Life of Brian'. Sarah, her siblings, and her mum laugh from start to end whenever they watch it. Her Indonesian father, despite speaking fluent English, doesn't get the jokes… and thinks his whole family is completely mental.

Almost half an hour later, Matt, Liz, and Arthur receive a text message from Broussard, who has asked them to meet him in his office. They've already finished their lunch so they head off, leaving Sarah and Michael alone.

"Which regiment are you from?" asks Sarah.

"I'm from the Parachute Regiment."

Sarah keeps a straight face, but she's thinking 'bullshit!'

Michael continues. "What about you? What were you before you were assigned to Interpol?"

"I was a traffic constable," answers Sarah without changing her expression.

'Bollocks!' thinks Michael, also with a straight face. He then continues. "And how did you acquire your charming West Country accent?"

"I spent six years in Poole when my dad was seconded to the SBS," answers Sarah, watching Michael's face closely for a reaction.

As Sarah expected, Michael's eyes flicker at the mention of one of UK's special forces units. She allows a knowing smile to creep onto her face. "Now why don't you stop bullshitting me and tell me which regiment you're really from?"

"Only if you bin your West Country bullshit and start using your real accent," says Michael, seriously.

Sarah's stunned and her smile fades away. She falls silent for a few seconds, observing Michael's masculine features. His face is ordinary-looking, but full of scars. He has brown longish hair and a two-day stubble like her brother. Sarah knows that someone from the Parachute Regiment would never be anything but clean-shaven.

"What makes you think this isn't my real accent?" asks Sarah.

"Your West Country accent is just an affectation to gain acceptance from the Chief and your older teammates. You don't need to do that," suggests Michael.

"And what do you think is my *real* accent?"

"RP," answers Michael, giving her a piercing stare.

Sarah and her brother were taught Received Pronunciation when they studied at Bournemouth Collegiate School. She decided to use her West Country accent because she didn't want to be considered old-fashioned by her teammates. Now it turns out that Michael could tell she was faking. Sarah is actually relieved that she doesn't have to pretend anymore.

"Right then, I'll drop the West Country accent," says Sarah in her real accent - King's English with a touch of Spanish. "So... which regiment are you really from?"

"I'm from the 22$^{nd}$ Regiment, but only the Chief knows that. I told the others that I'm from the 2$^{nd}$ Battalion of the Parachute Regiment, which is my former unit."

Like Sarah, Michael has to keep secret his membership in a special forces unit. The 22$^{nd}$ Regiment, Special Air Service (SAS) is considered the finest and most experienced special forces unit in the world, and Sarah is begrudgingly impressed with Michael.

"Which squadron?" asks Sarah.

"Actually, I'm the OC of B Squadron."

"Why are you here instead of running your squadron?"

"My squadron can run on autopilot," says Michael. "I have good men under my command and they really don't need me there every day. I'm only required to check on them a couple of times a week."

"An Indonesian special forces unit went to Credenhill to train with your regiment a few years ago. Do you remember any of the members?"

"Indeed. A nice gentleman named Anthony Dharmawan and his whole unit trained with us a couple of years ago. I noticed you share the same surname. Is he your brother?"

"You knew the moment we met that I'm his sister, Michael, so you can cut the bullshit," says Sarah, a bit sharply but with a smile.

"How is Captain Dharmawan these days?" asks Michael, starting to blush. Actually, she's right. Michael recognized her the moment he met her because he has Sarah's picture... and that picture is posted on his office door in Credenhill.

"He's now a Major and the commander of Detachment 902. He got married soon after he returned from England and has a five-month-old son now," answers Sarah.

"That's marvelous!" says Michael. "How about you? What unit were you really from before Interpol?"

"I was a team leader in the Strike Force of Densus-88. Like you, only the Chief knows this so I'd prefer you keep it quiet."

Michael nods and looks impressed. Although Densus-88 is police instead of military, it's quite well-known in the special forces community. "Right, so let's get a few things squared away between us. First of all, are you single?"

Sarah is taken aback by the question and becomes embarrassed because she didn't expect Michael to be so direct. "Indeed."

"Splendid! This means we are the only ones who are single in this team. Are you currently seeing anyone?"

"No," answers Sarah, becoming even more embarrassed. "How about you? Do you have a girlfriend?"

"A girlfriend? No..." answers Michael.

Sarah smiles. At least she can hang out with Michael during her deployment in England.

"... I have lots," he continues with sparkling eyes and a cheeky grin.

Sarah's smile disappears.

"I was just yanking your chain, of course," Michael laughs. "No, I don't have a girlfriend."

Sarah's annoyed, but then laughs with him. "What do you carry?"

"Sig Sauer P226. Why do you ask?"

"Well, I can see why you don't have a girlfriend. Your sidearm's better looking than you," quips Sarah.

Michael laughs out loud. Sarah is not that interested in Michael. Although he's tall and athletic, which Sarah likes very much, Michael's face is too manly for her taste and the scars on his face make him look too masculine. Sarah prefers sweet-looking men with tall, athletic bodies. Tony always made fun of her for having the same tastes in men as their little sister, Cindy. Too bad Michael doesn't fit their tastes.

Although... Michael isn't good looking, but Sarah has to admit that there's a strong aura and certain mystique about him that attracts her. But Sarah presumes that this is only because she knows he's an SAS officer and this intrigues her.

"Is your sidearm standard issue for Densus-88?" asks Michael.

"No, the standard issue is the Glock 17. My dad bought me the P2000 for conceal carry."

"I've noticed you only carry two mags with a ten-round capacity," comments Michael.

"Why? How many mags do you carry?"

"I carry six and a P228 with four mags for backup," answers Michael.

"That's a lot of firepower, Michael," comments Sarah. "Are you planning to take on a whole regiment or do you plan to miss a lot?"

Michael laughs out loud, but then gives her an explanation. "If members of The Cartel try to slot or snatch us, they'll probably ambush us with a minimum of three men, like when they snatched Karen outside of a hotel in London. I urge you to bring more mags and a backup sidearm."

"Well, I don't plan on missing any of my targets then," says Sarah, giving him a wink and a smile.

Sarah is implicitly telling him that she's an expert shot with a pistol, which makes Michael laugh again. He continues. "And what's the knife for?"

"You don't carry a knife?"

"I wouldn't know what to do with it," Michael shrugs.

"What do you use to keep your fork company when you eat?" quips Sarah, poking fun at him once again. 'Wait a minute... why am I being so aggressive with him?' she thinks suddenly.

Sarah is surprised at herself, but Michael laughs at her joke. "The British Army has never issued an official knife for the infantry except bayonets and the khukuri knives for the Gurkhas. Even in the SAS, we were never taught how to slot an enemy with a knife. In unarmed combat training, the only time knives are involved is when they teach us how to defend ourselves against someone wielding them."

After finishing their lunch, they walk slowly back to the office.

"So why did you decide to join the police force?" asks Michael.

# THE POLICEWOMAN

Sarah goes silent for a few seconds. She always gets emotional whenever she remembers why she decided to join the police force. "A close friend of mine during secondary school was given a free sample of heroin and got addicted. She OD'd about six months later. I hate drugs and everything that goes with them, ever since then."

"I'm sorry to hear that."

"How about you? How did you end up in the army?" asks Sarah.

"Actually, it's a family tradition. My father's a retired general from the Irish Guards and so are my grandfather and great-grandfather. My little brother is carrying on the tradition. He's just graduated from Sandhurst and is now a Second-Leftenant in the Irish Guards. As for me, I've always wanted to join the SAS and the best way to do so is through The Paras. I then joined the SAS after I received my Captaincy and passed their rigorous Selection."

Michael and Sarah finally arrive in the Interpol area, but James and Paul are nowhere to be seen. They sit at their respective cubicle and it turns out that Michael's desk is right next to Sarah's.

"Right then, so how about we get back to work?" invites Sarah.

"What do you know about the production of MDMA?"

"Not much... I have experience investigating the downstream part, but I don't know much about the upstream side of the business," answers Sarah.

When she first joined Densus, Sarah was asked by her commander to be active as a model, which resulted in her being on the cover of various fashion magazines in Indonesia. After her body grew more toned and muscular, Sarah became known as a fitness model and was frequently featured in health and fitness magazines. Her Facebook account contains her modelling portfolio, but has no indications whatsoever that she's a policewoman. Not many people know that and even her secondary school friends think that she's just a model. In the world of intelligence, Sarah's cover is called a legend. So far, no one seems to have uncovered her legend.

Sarah's early career in Densus-88 was in the Intelligence Sub-detachment. Her main job was to monitor the circulation of narcotics in socialite circles and in the entertainment industry of Jakarta. Her side career as a model enabled her to easily infiltrate the socialite circles and thus gain access to Jakarta's night life for the rich and famous. Sarah sometimes found it hard to believe that she was being paid by the INP to party almost every weekend with other undercover policewomen of Densus.

Last year, Sarah was transferred to the Special Actions Sub-detachment and has several times led Strike Forces in raiding terrorist hideouts and drug manufacturing plants. Her side career as a model was put on hold, although there were still plenty of offers from her modelling agency. Sarah was really enjoying her work in Special Actions so she was quite disappointed when she was suddenly transferred to Interpol.

Michael starts his briefing. "Well, first of all, the chemical compound safrole is a precursor for the clandestine manufacture of MDMA…"

For a few hours, Sarah listens attentively as Michael briefs her on the production of MDMA. Michael is excellent at explaining things clearly, but even so there's a lot for Sarah to take in on her first day of work.

19:34 WIB (GMT+7)
Monday May 4, 2026
Jagorawi Toll Road
Citeureup, Bogor, West Java

After a two-day inspection at his drug factory in Bogor, Patrick has to return to the UK. He's taken to the airport by Santoso, accompanied by Lukas, a local partner. Lukas is Richard's deputy, and controls the local workers and the supply chain of MDMA. The location for their factory is ideal and easily defended. Unfortunately, it only has one access point for entering or exiting the compound. This makes Patrick's men from the UK uneasy.

"When will you start building the tunnel?" asks Patrick in his fluent Bahasa Indonesia.

"The problem is with the contractors. Small contractors don't have the capability. I'm still looking for a contractor who can not only make the tunnel, but can also keep their workers' mouths shut," explains Lukas.

Patrick nods. This means that Frank Llywelyn has to stay a while in Indonesia to design, build, and supervise the development of their escape tunnel. Frank, who used to be in the Corps of Royal Engineers, had developed and built the tunnel for their factory in the Republic of Ireland.

"How are the locals?" asks Patrick. "Any problems with them?"

Lukas shakes his head. "As long as they get paid on time, I don't think there'll be any problems. They would like for this collaboration to last."

"Any complaints from them?"

"Their only complaint is that the factory is extremely hot and humid because we have no air conditioning in the factory area, but I've explained to them that we have to avoid using electricity and use our generators only to power the production machinery. Once production is stable and no one dares to bother us, then we can start thinking about luxury. There were a couple of men who wanted two-day holidays each week, but I already told them it's impossible because of the high production demands."

Patrick nods again. Lukas was the first person he recruited in Indonesia and he's reliable. Some two years ago, Lukas ran his own ecstasy manufacturing plant, which was bought by Patrick for a reasonable price. But then Patrick gave Lukas capital to develop the plant. Not for the Indonesian market, but to export their products to Ireland. Ecstasy that was once sold by Lukas in the Indonesian rupiah is now sold in pound sterling and euro, which has quadrupled Lukas's profits.

During his inspection, Patrick sees that the locals are content and hard-working, the opposite to his men in the UK, who tend to be lazy, fussy, and demanding. Fortunately, the locals don't know that they receive far lower wages than their UK counterparts, despite doing the same work, and they're happy with the money Lukas pays them each week. They were practically ecstatic with Patrick when he gave them each an old Ruger Speed Six revolver with ammunition and holsters. Most of these men had never held, much less fired, a pistol before, but they'll be taught by Richard and his UK associates.

Unlike the locals, all the men from the UK received Glock 17 pistols and M4 Carbines, weapons that are stored in an armoury behind the factory. The carbines and pistols were smuggled into Indonesia by Frag O'Lenihan before Patrick arrived in Jakarta. Also unlike the factories in England and Ireland, almost all of the UK men stationed in Indonesia came from the infantry, so they are adept using assault rifles and well-trained in combat tactics.

"If there are any problems, could you please inform me about them?" orders Patrick.

"*Siap, Komandan!*" answers Lukas, which in the Indonesian military means the same as 'yes, sir'.

Patrick returns Lukas's smile before entering the terminal. Lukas has no idea he only has weeks to live.

16:03 GMT
Monday May 4, 2026
Interpol Manchester
Central Park, Manchester, England

They go to the cafeteria for afternoon tea.

"Where are you staying?" asks Michael.

"Stay Deansgate Apartments. How about you?"

"3Towers, only a couple of miles from here," answers Michael. "How do you plan to get to work?"

"I took the Metrolink this morning, but I'm thinking about run-commuting."

"What do you usually do in your free time back home?"

"Other than working out at the local gym, I volunteered to be the chief of security of my housing complex. I command sixty-three security guards there."

"And what do you plan on doing in your free time here in England?"

"I haven't planned anything yet. There's a Lifestyle Fitness near the flat and I'll probably visit Poole during the weekends," answers Sarah.

"There's a complete gym here at GMP HQ. Why not just work out here?"

"I like Lifestyle Fitness because it's a women's only gym."

"Oh," says Michael.

"Why do you ask?" asks Sarah with a knowing smile.

"I presume you're highly trained in counter-surveillance drills?"

"I-I-Indeed I am," stammers Sarah, thrown by the change in direction.

"I just want to remind you to remember your tradecraft. Always employ counter-surveillance measures, never be conspicuous, know your environment, always choose a different route to and from the office, and be on alert if anyone is following you. This includes during weekends."

"Oh," says Sarah, still somewhat taken aback. She had thought that

Michael was going to ask her to work out with him so she's a little embarrassed.

"Since this is your first day, it's highly unlikely the opposition knows about you. During your first month here, I suggest you recce various alternative routes, choke points, and ideal ambush or snatch sites that may be used by the opposition against you. I suggest you do the recce during the weekends also."

Sarah can only nod.

"Since you live in Deansgate, there are a number of alternative routes you can take to get to the office. Please get in the habit of *not* taking the same route every day. This includes taking different routes in the mornings and evenings. Everyone in this team is doing the same thing," continues Michael.

Sarah nods again.

"If you think you're being followed, you should immediately execute counter-surveillance drills to confirm it. If someone is *really* following you, please *do not* confront them. Try to lose them and if you can't, call any one of us and we'll send in reinforcements. All right?"

"I'll do that," answers Sarah.

"Don't underestimate the opposition, Sarah. Karen got careless and that's how she got snatched," says Michael, a hint of sadness in his voice.

Michael seems dead serious and Sarah nods again. After their afternoon tea, Michael continues his briefing until late into the night. After work, she takes the Metrolink to her flat in Deansgate.

'This assignment is turning out to be a lot more dangerous than I previously thought,' thinks Sarah, reflecting on her first day in England.

She's also disappointed that Michael didn't invite her for dinner after work.

06:35 GMT
Tuesday May 5, 2026
Stay Deansgate Apartments
Deansgate, Manchester, England

The next day, Sarah wakes up and does her routine exercises. After warming up, she lies on the floor and crunches 1,000 times. She's done this every morning since secondary school. After she's done, she changes into running gear and puts on a running backpack. Her gun is holstered into an IWB (inside waistband) holster and her knife is strapped to her ankle beneath her socks. Looking at her, no one could ever guess she's armed and deadly.

Sarah takes the stairs down from the fourth floor. Her parents always insisted she use the stairs, no matter how tall the building. On Michael's suggestion, she keeps an eye out for places where the opposition could ambush her. Fortunately, it would be difficult for them to set up an ambush because there are so many different routes available to her. She only needs to be extra careful when entering or exiting her building and GMP HQ.

While running down Oldham Rd towards a street called The Gateway, which takes her straight to GMP HQ, Sarah recognizes Michael from behind walking leisurely to the office. He has earphones in his ears, both hands are playing with his smartphone, and he appears indifferent to his surroundings, walking as if on vacation.

'How can you walk like that when yesterday you gave me a bloody lecture on counter-surveillance?' thinks Sarah, irritated at him.

When Sarah is a few steps behind Michael, she reaches out towards him. She wants to tweak his ear as she passes by to teach him a lesson. But Sarah is surprised when Michael suddenly shifts his body and Sarah's fingers miss his ear by inches! It turns out Michael has excellent situation awareness, always fully aware of his surroundings.

When she turns left towards The Gateway, Sarah steals a glance towards Michael. He's grinning from ear-to-ear and the satisfied gleam in his eyes makes Sarah embarrassed.

"*Verdomme!*" curses Sarah in Dutch when she feels her face turning red.

Sarah hotfoots the last 200 metres to GMP HQ. She's gleaming with sweat so she takes a shower at the gym. By 08:52, she's changed into business casual attire and enters the Interpol area. Her teammates are already at their desks except Michael, who's nowhere to be seen. Maybe he's outside, still grinning to himself.

"Good morning, everyone," greets Sarah cheerfully.

"Good morning, Sarah," return her teammates. They notice that she has dropped her phony West Country accent and sounds several degrees posher.

"Where's Michael?" Sarah asks James.

"Right behind you," answers Michael from behind her.

Sarah quickly turns around and sees Michael entering the Interpol area. Sure enough, there's still a huge grin on his face and a half-eaten doughnut in his hand. Sarah quickly turns back to James before Michael can see her blush again.

"Can we meet now, James? Paul?" invites Sarah hurriedly.

"Sure," answers James, standing up, followed by Paul.

They enter one of the meeting rooms.

"How was yer first day yesterday?" asks James with a friendly smile.

"Quite insightful," answers Sarah, returning his smile. "So, which branch of MI5 are you?"

"I'm from the T Branch. We handle terrorism," answers James.

"Oh, I thought you were from D Branch? Organized crime?"

James nods. "There was debate among the senior management of MI5 whether narcoterrorism in general, and the Irish Drug Cartel in particular, is considered organized crime or terrorism. They decided on the latter… for now. This is why T Branch is involved and we have Paul here from the NCA, who's an expert in organized crime."

"Oh, okay. How about you, Paul? Where do you come from?" asks Sarah, observing Paul's face. He's quite silly-looking, but his eyes show high intelligence.

"I'm from The Toon," answers Paul.

Sarah wants to laugh on hearing Paul's answer, but she's able to control herself. Geordies like to call their hometown, Newcastle upon Tyne, The Toon. The Toon is also the nickname for their football club.

"Are you a fan of The Toon FC?" asks Sarah, smiling.

Paul laughs. "No, I support Chelsea."

"So, how did you manage to find out that The Cartel has a drug factory in Indonesia?" asks Sarah, back to work.

"When we were conducting our investigation in London, Karen overheard a couple of Cartel members - Seamus Fitzgerald and Declan Mulcahy - at a pub, saying that the next cargo from Indonesia was due to arrive within a week. They also said they had to start the journey to Ireland within the next couple of days to help unload the cargo. Karen immediately called Liz about the new information," says James.

"What's interesting is that she says 'help unload the cargo', meaning that the goods are most likely being transported by ship rather than by air," says Paul.

"That was the last time we heard from Karen… she didn't return to her hotel room that night," says James. His face remains expressionless, but Sarah can feel the sorrow behind his mask.

Sarah nods. She already knows the rest of the story.

James continues. "We don't know anything else besides what Karen told us. We don't know exactly when the factory started producing for them or how many shipments they've made so far. However, a couple of weeks after Karen's message, the price of MDMA in Ireland dropped like a rock, while the price in Great Britain remained stable. This means that the supply of MDMA in Ireland outweighed demand. This was *not* the first time this has happened so we are assuming that that was *not* their first shipment from overseas. This price fluctuation has happened every other month for the past two years."

"Are they producing MDMA just for the Ireland market or for the Indonesian market as well?" asks Sarah.

"That's an excellent question and we don't have an answer to that… yet. That's yer job to find out, Sarah."

"Well, I'm new at being a liaison officer, so maybe you two can help me on what I should do for now?"

"What kind of constable were ye before ye were assigned to Interpol?" asks James.

"I was a traffic constable," answers Sarah without changing her expression.

James and Paul give her disbelieving looks, but they don't pursue it.

James continues. "First, NCB Manchester will issue Red Notices for NCB Indonesia, so the INP can arrest Cartel members if they ever show up at your airports or ports. In the meantime, you can check the prices of MDMA in Indonesia. Have there been any fluctuations these past few years? If the price drops, we can assume they're supplying for the Indonesian market also. Ye can also check the price by region. The lower the price, the closer ye are to their distribution centres or drug factories."

Sarah nods and adds that information to her tablet. Paul then briefs her on how they distribute the MDMA in the UK and Ireland. What's interesting is that the price of MDMA is lowest at a chain of night clubs called Gwilliam's, scattered throughout the UK and Ireland. The results of police raids failed to provide any link between the owner of Gwilliam's and their employees to the dealers who use that venue to distribute their goods. All of the detectives handling this case suspect that the owner of Gwilliam's, Gwilliam O'Donnel, is a Cartel member. He could even be a senior member, but till this day they've not been able to prove his involvement with The Cartel. Dealers caught in his night club absolutely refuse to divulge any information on how they got their hands on their drugs. They'd all prefer a longer prison sentence than a horrible death at the hands of The Cartel.

For The Cartel to achieve smooth operations in Indonesia, Paul suspects The Cartel must be cooperating with at least one local syndicate. In The Cartel's birth in the UK, they forcibly acquired other syndicates one by one until they eventually monopolized the narcotics industry, from upstream to downstream. They would probably do the same in Indonesia. Sarah should also be on the lookout for drug-related murders in Indonesia. If any MDMA players have been tortured to death, it can probably be attributed to Niall.

Once The Cartel has a strong operation running, they will then start narcoterrorism in Indonesia. Narcoterrorism is the attempt to influence the policies of the government or society through violence and intimidation, and to hinder the enforcement of anti-drug laws by the systematic threat or use of such violence. This means that The Cartel will kidnap, torture, and assassinate police officers and government officials to ensure the continuity of their operation, just like the drug cartels of South America.

Sarah is not entirely confident she'll find anything as she has thin leads. What's worse is that she can't conduct her own investigation and must rely on other officers in Interpol NCB Indonesia and the INP to follow up on it. But James and Paul seem to understand her predicament, because that is the job of a liaison officer in Interpol. They too must rely on other police officers to do *their* job and they know it takes time indeed.

Sarah spends the rest of the morning at her desk, writing a report to the Secretariat of Interpol NCB Indonesia and coordinating with them by phone and e-mail. Her teammates seem to be as busy as she is, except for Michael, who again is nowhere to be seen.

Without her realizing it, Sarah's spending a lot of time looking out for him.

16:21 WIB (GMT+7)
Tuesday May 5, 2026
Terminal 3, Soekarno-Hatta International Airport
Kota Tangerang, Tangerang, Banten

At the Soekarno-Hatta International Airport that afternoon, Santoso picks up another man.

"How are you, Santoso?" greets Niall pleasantly in fluent Bahasa Indonesia.

"Fine, *pak* Niall," replies Santoso.

"How's the family?"

"They're well, *pak*," replies Santoso.

"Good to hear," says Niall.

Santoso always gets the same greeting whenever he picks up his boss's associates at the airport. It might sound like small talk, but it's actually intelligence tradecraft. If Santoso senses any trouble at the airport, he's required to answer that 'his wife is sick' on the second question. If this happened, his passenger would give Santoso his luggage and pretend to need to go to the restroom and Santoso would drive away to wait near the Central Park Mall in West Jakarta. The passenger would then have to conduct counter-surveillance measures and find some other means of getting to the mall, where he'd be picked up by Santoso. Santoso knows how to do this because he once worked in intelligence in the Indonesian army, before he was dishonourably discharged for 'accidentally' killing a civilian. So far, Santoso's wife has always been 'healthy'.

"When will you return to Ireland, *pak* Niall?" asks Santoso.

"Sunday, early morning, on the twenty-fourth. Could you please take me to the airport on that day?"

"Of course, *pak* Niall."

"Also, could you please lend me your car? I'll need it every night in Jakarta," orders Niall once again while he takes the disguise off his face.

"*Baik, pak* Niall," answers Santoso.

They talk about other things on the drive to Pondok Indah.

11:36 GMT
Tuesday May 5, 2026
Interpol Manchester
Central Park, Manchester, England

Towards lunch time, Sarah receives a text from Michael's smartphone number, asking everyone for a meeting. As per SOP, Sarah immediately deletes the text. Everyone can attend except the commander.

Michael starts his presentation once everyone is present. "Right, the MoD has conducted an audit of all armouries, which are under the supervision of the Royal Logistics Corps. A major finding is that there are eighty kilograms of PE4 unaccounted for from an army training area in Pontrilas, Herefordshire."

"Isn't that a training area for the UK Special Forces?" asks James.

"How would I know?" retorts Michael with a straight face.

James only shrugs, also with a straight face.

Michael continues. "Anyhow, officers from the Special Investigation Branch of the Royal Military Police are currently investigating that army base. With any luck, they'll send the results of their investigation to us sometime next month."

"How much PE4 is needed to bring down the International Liaison Building?" asks Liz.

"Well… ehm… I wouldn't know about that either. The Paras are basically airborne light infantry and we don't handle explosives. I'll try to find out, though," says Michael.

Michael looks uneasy as he notes Liz's question in his tablet while his teammates smirk at his reaction. Sarah has a satisfied smile on seeing that Michael's uncomfortable with Liz's question.

Arthur suddenly looks at Sarah. "What do you think, Sarah? How much PE4 is needed to bring down the International Liaison Building?"

Sarah's smile disappears. "I was just a traffic constable before they sent me to Interpol… so I wouldn't know about it either," she shrugs.

"Bullshit! Ye're Densus-88 or at least Gegana," says Matt, smiling at her.

Sarah struggles to remain expressionless. "How did you get that idea?"

"We studied yer Facebook yesterday and it doesn't mention anything about ye being a traffic constable. A real traffic constable would've had no problems mentioning *that* in their modelling portfolio. Ye should always update yer legend before ye go on to another assignment, ye know," suggests Matt with a wide grin.

Sarah can't believe her teammates have already studied her Facebook account! Her face starts to turn red, especially since there are several sexy modelling photos in her account. Sarah's lost for words, which makes her teammates laugh. She sees that Michael is laughing the hardest and it annoys her even more, as she suspects that it was Michael who showed them her Facebook in the first place. However, Michael's fun doesn't last long.

"Michael, the UK Special Forces Group should conduct their own investigation. As part of The Paras, maybe yee could help them?" suggests Paul, smirking.

"Only the 1$^{st}$ Battalion of the Paras are part of the UKSF Group, Paul. I'm from the 2$^{nd}$ Battalion, remember? I'll contact one of the ruperts in the 1$^{st}$ Battalion to see if he can help," says Michael. He makes another note in his tablet and looks uncomfortable again.

"Maybe you should get in touch with your DSF so you can coordinate with him on the investigation?" suggests Arthur.

"I don't know what you *mean* by DSF, Arthur. I'm from the Parachute Regiment!" says Michael, getting exasperated.

"Bullshit!" Matt snorts. "Ye're SAS."

"You must have mistaken me for someone else, Matt," says Michael.

"Oh, I'm sure Michael's *not* from the SAS, Matt…" says Liz seriously.

"Thank you, Liz," cuts in Michael, looking relieved.

"… because he doesn't fit their profile," continues Liz. "The fellas from the SAS are supposed to be really tough."

Michael's jaw drops.

James immediately responds. "Actually, I think Michael fits their profile perfectly. The SAS fellas aren't really that tough anymore," he says, trying hard to keep a straight face.

Michael's jaw drops even further and his teammates finally laugh. Sarah's delighted that it's Michael's turn to be slagged off by her teammates.

Matt continues. "That's right. Didn't the SAS get bested by the Royal Gurkha Rifles on some endurance race about a year ago?"

Everyone nods and laughs even louder, recalling an article from last year's Daily Mail. The article said that during an endurance race held by the British Army in the mountains of Wales, the entire UK Special Forces were outrun by the infantrymen from Nepal. The UKSF were so embarrassed that they daren't race against the Gurkhas anymore.

"Yeah, right," Michael snorts. "Why don't *you* try running up and down the bloody Brecon Beacons for twenty-four kilometres in under four hours carrying a bloody fifty-pound bergen on your back!"

"So… you're either SAS or a Gurkha then," says Arthur. "You're quite a bit taller than any Gurkha I know so you must be SAS."

Michael finally raises his hands in surrender and the others can only roll in laughter at his reaction. Paul then invites them all for lunch at the cafeteria. All through lunch, they continue to take the piss out of Michael for his lousy acting. Like Sarah, they'd all suspected he was from the SAS since day one. Sarah's glad her Interpol team is so easy to get along with.

Throughout the rest of the month, Sarah concentrates on coordinating with other liaison officers at Interpol NCB Indonesia. The rest of the time she spends studying the intelligence data, especially the opposition's names and faces. Sarah's job is boring, especially compared to her job in Densus. Sarah also feels quite lonely, as no one has asked her to hang out and she seldom sees her teammates, who often work in the field.

All of this will change in the upcoming month.

22:09 WIB (GMT+7)
Saturday May 23, 2026
Roxy Indigo Spa
Taman Sari, West Jakarta, Jakarta

Every Saturday, the Indonesian factory workers all go together to have fun in the city. These petty criminals have never had so much money before and they go mental every weekend.

Lukas is forty-four years old. He's single and intends to stay that way. His face and body are not attractive so he prefers to pay for sex. While his men like splurging at seedy bordellos and bars in Jakarta's red-light district, Lukas prefers to visit the type of lavish spa that offers more than just massages, called *spa plus-plus* in Indonesia.

Tonight, he picks a new, pretty therapist with a slim figure, calling herself Donna. After the 'therapy' session, Lukas is so satisfied with Donna's 'service' that he immediately asks her to continue in his home. They ride in Lukas's Jaguar to his house in the Kebayoran Baru area, another elite district in South Jakarta. Every weekend, from Friday night till Monday morning, Lukas gives the housekeepers the weekend off so that he can be free to have his sex parties. The housekeepers will return on Monday morning to clean up. Lukas and Donna don't realize that someone is waiting for them inside Lukas's house.

Monday morning comes and there's uproar at one of the luxurious houses of Kebayoran Baru. The owner has been found, beaten to death with a wooden board full of nails and a naked woman beside him, disembowelled with her intestines slashed to bits. The police are baffled. No valuables were stolen and they can find absolutely no forensic evidence. They don't know that the perpetrator left Indonesia just hours after completing his 'job'.

Phase Three of The Cartel's plan has been concluded and Phase Four is about to begin.

# CHAPTER 4
# RECONNAISSANCE BY FIRE

06:51 GMT
Sunday May 31, 2026
Stay Deansgate Apartments
Deansgate, Manchester, England

Without realizing it, Sarah has spent a month in England. This morning she wakes up and does her daily exercises. She'd originally planned to visit Poole every weekend but instead she's promised Michael she'll spend her first month conducting recces of her routes to and from GMP HQ.

After running around Manchester throughout the day, Sarah decides to try out The Castlefield Spa at the Y Club for her routine skin care. The skin care has made Sarah's skin glow, which makes her look even more exotic than normal. She looks incredibly sexy in her tank-top, gym shorts, and running shoes.

On exiting the spa and passing through the gym, Sarah sees it full of people working out. She rolls her eyes when several men clock her and make their way towards her. Fortunately, her smartphone rings. It's Michael number.

"Yes, Michael?"

"Are you busy tonight?" asks Michael without preamble.

"Not really. Why?"

"I was wondering if we could have dinner together."

"Are you asking me out on a date?" asks Sarah, smiling to herself.

"Actually, it's a working dinner. I have an idea that I want to discuss with you regarding our mission."

"Oh," says Sarah, disappointed.

"So, are you available?" asks Michael.

"Sure, where are you now?"

"Right behind you."

Sarah immediately turns around and sees Michael walking a few metres behind her, his signature cheeky grin on his face. She can't help smiling seeing his silly grin. This is the first time Sarah's seen Michael in casual clothes. Michael's wearing a T-shirt with the word 'Bulmers' emblazoned across the chest, jeans, running shoes, and a backpack on his back. He looks like he's just finished taking a shower after a workout. He has muscular arms, covered in scars, and a broad chest and shoulders. Too bad he's starting to sport a pot-belly. Too bad.

Sarah turns off her smartphone, waits for Michael, and then puts her arm through his while they exit the gym. The men following her look disappointed and scatter. She lets go of Michael's arm as soon as they've exited the gym. Michael knows she only used him as camouflage to avoid being swarmed by the gym-rats buzzing around her, but he doesn't mind. In fact, he'd felt a jolt of electricity and his heart rate had increased when she'd grabbed him. Sarah actually felt the same way, but neither one shows it. They walk towards the Sapporo Teppanyaki Restaurant near the Y Club. It's almost empty as it's not dinner time yet. After reading the menu, they both agree on the Emperor Set, a set meal for two, and large glasses of an Australian Riesling. They watch the chef prepare their food in front of them. The sounds of the chef's cooking can mask their talk.

"I thought you worked out at the GMP gym?" asks Sarah.

Michael only shakes his head and smiles.

"Why not?" asks Sarah.

"Well, compared to the Y Club, it's not really a nice place to meet girls, is it?"

Sarah rolls her eyes.

"So how was your recce?" he asks.

"The routes I can take to and from my apartment are almost infinite. All I have to do is change my route and vary my working hours and it'll be difficult for the opposition to snatch or ambush me, unless they have unlimited resources, which is highly unlikely."

"That's excellent, Sarah!" says Michael.

Sarah only smiles at him.

"Do you have a specialty in Densus?" he asks next.

"My experience is mostly in intelligence and EOD, but I was a team leader in the Strike Force before they sent me to Interpol."

"How good are you in unarmed combat?"

Sarah thinks for a moment before answering him. Besides her training at Brimob, Gegana, and Densus, her dad had also drilled her and her siblings in intensive hand-to-hand combat since they were young. She doesn't want Michael to think she's overconfident.

"I'm sure I could give a member of the SAS a hard time," answers Sarah, giving him a smile and a wink.

Michael's pleased with Sarah's answer. "Now let me ask you a question. How much do you know about the Battle of Waterloo?"

Sarah again takes a moment before answering him. Sarah and Tony like to discuss military strategy with their dad, as he's considered an expert in that field. Truth be told, Sarah and her family probably know more about the Battle of Waterloo than most Brits.

"I've read about it…" she answers carefully.

"Now, disregarding the outcome of the actual battle, who would you rather be? Field Marshall Sir Arthur Wellesley, who was the ultimate master of defensive warfare? Or Emperor Napoleon Bonaparte, the ultimate master of offence?"

"I'd rather be Sir Arthur Wellesley," answers Sarah without any hesitation.

"Why?" asks Michael, giving her another smile.

"Defensive warfare means we can choose the battleground and force the enemy to come to us, minimizing our losses even against a superior force. I'd rather *not* go on the offensive unless I have, at the very least, a three-to-one advantage to ensure a decisive victory."

"What if you're on the offensive, but you don't have superior numbers?" asks Michael.

"Besides having good intelligence, a good strategy, and good officers under my command, I would need to have speed, surprise, and violence of action to overwhelm the enemy."

"Wow! That's very good!" says Michael.

Sarah smiles happily at being praised by an officer from the finest special forces unit in the world.

"Anyhow, here's my idea…" he continues.

Sarah listens attentively as he tells her his idea, which is to provoke The Cartel into coming out of their hideout. Michael's idea sounds audacious and will need meticulous planning, but she likes it very much. At least they can be more proactive instead of just acting as liaison officers and waiting for other people to do their job.

"Well? What do you think?" asks Michael.

Sarah considers her answer before replying. "Actually, your idea reminds me of the Battle of Agincourt more than Waterloo."

Michael becomes speechless. It takes him a moment to answer. "You're absolutely right, of course."

Sarah *is* right. Michael's idea is more similar to the Battle of Agincourt. But Michael hadn't expected the Indonesian policewoman to know about Agincourt, which was why he'd compared it less accurately to the more famous Battle of Waterloo.

"Any other comments?" he asks.

"How come you don't seem particularly concerned about being snatched by them?"

"Well, they'd more likely slot me on the spot than snatch me if they knew I was from the SAS. It would be utterly daft for The Cartel to snatch and torture to death an SAS trooper, let alone a squadron OC. I'd hate to think about the consequences for them if they really did that," he explained.

"What would happen to them if they did?" asks Sarah.

"Nothing," answers Michael, winking. "However, their mates would probably have a hard time finding them because they would have somehow vanished without a trace."

Sarah smiles. She had heard rumours about how the SAS prefer to make disappear those who cross them. A perfect murder is a murder with no dead body. Without a dead body, the police don't have a case for murder.

They discussed Michael's idea until late at night. Overall, Sarah enjoyed her dinner with Michael.

18:12 (GMT+7)
Monday June 1, 2026
Murphy's Irish Pub & Restaurant
Mampang Prapatan, South Jakarta, Jakarta

Frank Llywelyn is picked up at the airport by Santoso. He's needed to execute Phase Four of their plan, which is to dominate the supply chain of ecstasy. He has also been asked to design and supervise the development of an escape tunnel at the rear of the factory.

Frank has an appointment with someone this afternoon at one of Jakarta's Irish pubs. All the tables are full of foreigners, even though it's not yet dinner time. Frank waits for his guest, who finally turns up almost fifteen minutes late. He stands to shake hands with the man, who appears to have brought four bodyguards with him. The five men keep their jackets on. Frank doesn't need to frisk them to know these men are armed.

"Thank you for seeing me, Nafiri," greets Frank in fluent Bahasa Indonesia.

Nafiri only nods.

"Would you like to order some food?" offers Frank. "The Celtic Chicken here is excellent."

"Get to the point! Why do you want to see me?" asks Nafiri, sharply.

Frank only smiles at being treated like that. Nafiri has positioned himself as someone *needed* by The Cartel and not the other way around. Nafiri is the largest importer of raw materials for ecstasy in Southeast Asia and he doesn't like being summoned like this, even though The Cartel is his biggest customer.

"We need more raw materials than before, not just for our factory in Indonesia, but also for Ireland. We also need them to be delivered according to our agreed schedule. There've been a number of times where they're delivered late and this has disrupted production," says Frank.

"How can you expect prompt delivery with that kind of price? Do you want to do business with me or extort me?" asks Nafiri, looking mean.

"Of course we want to do business with you, Nafiri," says Frank, patiently. "We just want assurance that you can and will fulfil all our needs."

"What if I just say no?"

"That's your call, but my boss wouldn't like that," says Frank.

Nafiri gives a loud laugh. "So what if your boss doesn't like it?"

"If you won't cooperate with us, we'll be forced to take over your business," says Frank calmly.

Nafiri stands up angrily. "Who do you think you are?"

His four bodyguards start to open their jackets to reveal their pistols. The other people in the pub look at them quizzically.

"You only have two options, Nafiri. One, you can *voluntarily* hand over your business to us…" says Frank.

"Yeah, right!" shouts Nafiri angrily.

"Or two, we can *force* you to hand over your business," says Frank.

Nafiri starts to reach for his gun under his jacket, followed by his bodyguards. The five men don't get the chance to unholster their guns before all the other patrons pull out assault rifles from under their tables. They immediately overpower the four bodyguards and start to beat them with the butts of their rifles. Nafiri is shocked that all the other patrons are Frank's accomplices, but there's not much he can do about it. Once they're finished beating the four bodyguards into bloody pulps, the rifles are pointed towards Nafiri. The M4 Carbines look so frightening that Nafiri can only freeze in fear, while a couple of the men frisk him and take away his weapon.

"Decision time, Nafiri," says Frank.

Nafiri keeps silent. He's not about to let go of something that took him fifteen years to build. Frank takes out a folder that Richard had given him. Inside are photographs of Nafiri's wife and his four kids in various activities.

"You don't want anything bad to happen to your family, do you?" asks Frank.

Nafiri starts to turn pale, but he is still defiant. "You Brits wouldn't dare hurt women and children."

"Maybe you don't know this, but one of our colleagues is a psychopath. An absolute, bona-fide psychopath. He doesn't care who his victim is, whether it's a man, woman, or child," says Frank. "In fact, he enjoys hurting women and children."

Frank turns on a video on his tablet and puts it in front of Nafiri. Lukas is seen strapped to a chair, in front of a pretty girl strapped on top of a table. Nafiri knows Lukas well because he's one of his customers and it's Lukas who always orders raw materials from him. Lukas had withheld information regarding Nafiri, just so he could have some leverage with Patrick. Lukas became more and more demanding until Patrick finally decided that Lukas was more of a liability than an asset. Richard succeeded in getting Lukas to reveal the name and contact number of their supplier and then Lukas was no longer needed by The Cartel.

Nafiri sees the pretty girl scream in pain when Niall stabs his knife into her navel and eviscerates her. The next scenes are even more terrifying, especially when Niall starts to finish off Lukas with a wooden board embedded with nails. Niall roars with delight when he hits Lukas, who is still alive, as bits of his face start flying off from the blows. Nafiri is forced to watch until he can't take it anymore and begs Frank to stop playing the horrifying video.

Over the next few hours, Frank 'coordinates' with Nafiri the details of handing over his business to the Irish Drug Cartel. The biggest supplier of raw materials for ecstasy will now fully supply The Cartel's drug factory in Indonesia and Ireland.

If no one stops them, the Irish Drug Cartel will become the largest crime syndicate in the world.

09:03 GMT
Tuesday June 2, 2026
Interpol Manchester
Central Park, Manchester, England

The downstream investigation by Arthur, Matt, and Liz shows that the MDMA is sold at its lowest prices in three places; in North West England, in County Donegal in the Republic of Ireland, and in County Derry in Northern Ireland. This tells the team where The Cartel's factories most likely are.

Broussard, Paul, and Arthur will concentrate on investigating North West England, while James, Matt, and Liz, who are Irish, will focus on County Donegal and County Derry. Sarah has to stay in Manchester to work on finding the factory in Indonesia and Michael still has to liaise with the MoD on the missing PE4s. The others will deploy once they've presented their plans, including all the necessary budgets, to Broussard, who asks them to present to him within the next three days.

They all object to the timetable, but Broussard disregards their objections. "Three days. That's all you have."

Sarah is baffled by her teammates, but Michael only smirks at their behaviour.

"The team seem pessimistic about the work assigned to them," she comments after the meeting.

"No, they're just full of shite as always," says Michael.

"How is that?"

"What do you usually say when your boss gives you a challenging job?"

"I say 'Yes, sir!' as always," answers Sarah with a raised eyebrow.

Michael shakes his head. "The secret to becoming a legend in the workplace is to always remind your boss how impossibly challenging your job is. Once you accomplish the impossible task, your boss will appreciate you more because you achieved 'the impossible'. This way, your boss won't take you for granted anymore. So even though our friends said that they can't finish their work in three days, I wouldn't be surprised if they submit tomorrow."

"I'll keep that in mind," says Sarah, trying not to smile.

After lunch that day, Michael invites everyone back into the meeting room. Once everyone is present, Michael passionately presents his idea.

"Rather than splitting the team and having them investigate different areas, we can all go together on this. All this time, we've been passive in our search for The Cartel members and it's high time we do something more proactive. Although we haven't proven it yet, we know that The Cartel distributes their goods to the dealers by way of Gwilliam's. Frankly, we might never prove that. It's better if we take the initiative so I propose a more active method to provoke the members of The Cartel into showing themselves.

"In military terms, this is called reconnaissance by fire. In essence, the plan is simple. I go inside Gwilliam's, identify the dealers, and then 'ask' for members of The Cartel to meet me. Before that, we should blanket the area with the police and even military. If any members of The Cartel take the bait, all I have to do is lure them into our ambush positions. It will be just like the opening of the Battle of Agincourt…"

Michael tries to present his idea with gusto, but his enthusiasm makes him look silly. Nevertheless, his plan is solid. Basically, he's suggesting provoking The Cartel in all the Gwilliam's clubs in Great Britain and Ireland. Using a map displayed on the briefing screens, Michael presents all the locations of Gwilliam's clubs and also places where they can conduct an ambush. Michael then presents a detailed plan using the Five Paragraph Order, right down to the budget needed for this to work.

"So… that's my idea," says Michael proudly. "What do you think?"

Everyone is silent. Sarah and her teammates are trying hard not to laugh after seeing Michael's presentation. Broussard, on the other hand, has gone red in the face.

"Michael, are you on the piss?" asks Broussard, angrily.

"Of course not," says Michael. "What's wrong with my idea?"

"Surely you can't be serious about this?" asks Broussard, giving him an incredulous look.

"I'm serious… and don't call me 'Shirley'!" quotes Michael, pretending to pout.

It's a line from the old movie "Airplane!" and the team finally laugh out loud. Broussard still looks angry, but Sarah can see that James and Paul are interested in Michael's idea.

"This sort of thing is *not* the mission of the Interpol IRT! Our mission specifically states that the military is involved only when we have found Cartel members, drug factories, or distribution centres. They are not involved in locating them. That's *our* job," explains Broussard, trying to be patient.

"I'm still in this team, am I not?" asks Michael.

"Indeed. But that doesn't mean you can intimidate people, beat them up, and break their bones. Not to mention breaking half a dozen civil laws in the process!"

"The drug dealers, or even The Cartel, can just sue me for that, Chief," says Michael, grinning broadly. His teammates smile and Michael becomes even more confident he can bring Broussard round to his way of thinking.

"And there's no way you can go inside Gwilliam's alone, either," says Broussard, starting to get impatient.

"Sarah will be my immediate backup," says Michael.

"Sarah was from the Traffic Management Centre before she was transferred to Interpol. How the devil could you choose her as your backup?" asks Broussard, frowning.

"I don't think anyone here believes that, Chief," says Michael, smirking.

The others laugh while Broussard glowers at Michael, but he only grins at his boss.

"Sarah is here as a liaison officer to locate The Cartel's factory in

Indonesia, not to conduct offensive operations against them," says Broussard firmly.

James seems to want to say something, but then shuts his mouth. Broussard notices this.

"Do you have anything to add?" he asks, turning his glower on James.

"Ye could've asked for anyone from the INP for a liaison officer, but I found out ye specifically asked them to send someone from Densus-88," says James. "Ye have a couple of highly-trained individuals in this team, Chief, so I suggest we make use of them to our advantage, rather than merely employing them to liaise."

James is right and Broussard starts to calm down. He thinks hard for a few seconds before continuing. "Sarah, what do you think of Michael's plan?"

"It's audacious, but I like it," answers Sarah. "The Cartel members are in constant seclusion so I don't think we'll be able to flush them out without provoking them. As in any defensive warfare strategy, if they *do* come out and try to attack us, it would be on *our* terms rather than theirs. I think we need to be more unconventional in our tactics against them and this is one way we could do it."

Her teammates nod in agreement except their commander, who still looks hesitant. He has already lost one team member on this mission and Michael's plan carries high risks.

"What do you think, Paul?" asks Broussard finally.

Paul shrugs. "The opposition won't expect it. It's such a bone plan, but brilliant enough that it might work."

"Why not just say it's brilliant?" asks Michael, frowning.

"Whatever," says Paul, smirking.

"Arthur? Matt? Liz?" asks Broussard.

"All these months and we've yet to succeed in apprehending core members of The Cartel. I think we have to try something different," says Arthur.

"There are still a lot of risks involved, but I agree with Arthur," says Matt.

"Concur," says Liz.

Broussard again thinks hard for a moment. He has promised Police Brigadier General Prasetyo he'll keep their best police officer out of danger.

But James is right; it would be a waste of talent to have people of Michael and Sarah's calibre on his team without utilizing them to their full potential. Broussard knows that he might regret this decision, but he and his team have been unable to show any results these past few months and the Home Office and his superiors at Interpol are starting to breathe down his neck.

"All right then, we'll do it your way. However, we will only do it in three cities. Letterkenny, Derry, then Liverpool, in that order. If we don't get any reaction from them in those cities, then we will *never* get any reaction from them. Let's also leave the military out of this operation for now, except for Michael. Matt, Liz, and Arthur can deploy immediately to coordinate with the local CT units. Michael, I want you to brief the non-Irish members for deployment to Ireland," orders Broussard. "Could you please have your material ready to present to us first thing tomorrow morning so we can all depart at noon?"

"I still have to coordinate with the Royal Military Police today regarding their investigation in one of our army bases," says Michael, stealing a glance at Sarah. "You're asking a lot, Chief, but don't worry. I'll get it done."

Sarah stifles a laugh when she sees Broussard roll his eyes. It looks like he already knows his team's bad working habits.

18:22 GMT
Tuesday June 2, 2026
Letterkenny Court Hotel
Letterkenny, County Donegal, Republic of Ireland

They all check-in at the Letterkenny Court Hotel at An Phríomhshráid (Main Street). Michael immediately conducts a CTR, or Close Target Reconnaissance, of the local Gwilliam's. After Michael is finished with his recce, it's then Sarah and Liz's turn. They walk leisurely to the club and although Sarah has spent a month with her team, she seldom chats with anyone bar Michael.

"So, who are you married to, Liz?" asks Sarah.

"My husband is a Scotsman, actually, and a Captain in the British Army."

"Really? Which regiment?" asks Sarah.

"He's in the Special Investigation Branch of the Royal Military Police. We met during one of the joint investigations we often conduct together," says Liz. "What about ye?"

"I'm still single," answers Sarah.

"How are things with Michael?"

"What about things with Michael?" asks Sarah, smiling.

"Well, I can see that ye're attracted to him," comments Liz, giving her a knowing smile.

Sarah only laughs and ignores her question. They both finally reach and enter Gwilliam's, which is almost empty, and they order two sparkling waters. They continue talking, discreetly conducting their recce.

"It's all right and it's nothing to be ashamed about. Look at me, I used to date someone on my team and ended up marrying him," says Liz. "Michael is very much attracted to ye too, ye know."

"Really? What do you think of him?" asks Sarah.

"In a nutshell, he's one of those 'adorable arsehole' types," says Liz dryly.

Sarah laughs. "What sort of a person is that?"

"Well, he's charming and funny. He's really fun to be with, but there are times ye just want to throttle the cheeky bastard instead."

Sarah laughs louder. She knows exactly what kind of person Michael is because he's like her brother. When Tony was courting Lydia, who is a former Miss Indonesia, he sometimes made her feel so exasperated that she felt like throwing both hands around his neck and choking the life out of him. However, Tony's personality intrigued Lydia so much that she finally picked him to be her partner, even though there were hundreds of other men trying to win her heart.

"He's one of those 'bad boy' types, isn't he?" asks Sarah.

Liz thinks for a moment before answering her. "No, I don't really think so. A few months ago, he told me he was looking for a committed relationship. He wants to find the right girl, settle down, get married, have kids, et cetera, et cetera."

"Oh," says Sarah, a bit disappointed.

Sarah's too engrossed with her work and has no intention of getting married. She hasn't found a man yet to win her heart, anyway. Although

## THE POLICEWOMAN

Sarah is interested in and enjoys hanging out with Michael, she still hasn't really connected with him yet. Looking at his style and behaviour so far, she can't entirely believe that he's a squadron commander in the SAS. For now, she just considers him her friend and co-worker.

After an hour observing the interior of Gwilliam's, they walk back to the hotel. The Interpol team, along with the commander of the Garda ERU, a man named Clive who immediately looked smitten on being introduced to Sarah, then meet at the Lemon Tree Restaurant, not far from the hotel. Liz has reserved the whole restaurant for them and the small but luxurious place can only accommodate their team. They eat and compare notes from their recce.

Gwilliam's has a dance floor half the size of a football field in the middle of the venue. The dance area is surrounded by lounge seats with long bars on the four walls. Clive tells them that dealers usually offer MDMA to people seated at the lounge seats.

Michael's plan is simple. Michael, supported by Sarah nearby, will identify the dealers. Michael will then intimidate and provoke them so The Cartel will start looking for him. Michael hopes The Cartel will try to snatch or kill him, just like they did with Karen. However, the Garda Emergency Response Unit (Garda ERU), the counterterrorist unit of An Garda Síochána, will prevent this from happening when they apprehend or kill Cartel members who show up. One weakness of Michael's plan is that he might be recognized as someone hunting The Cartel. However, The Cartel couldn't possibly identify Michael because of his status as a member of the SAS, which means his identity is classified as Top Secret.

Clive ends his briefing. "By 22:00, all Garda ERU personnel will be ready at their assigned positions. We'll be close to ye, but probably not close enough if they attempt to kill ye on the spot."

"Right. That's why Sarah will be nearby as my immediate backup inside the night club. She'll only be a few metres away from me," explains Michael.

"Sarah's yer immediate backup?" asks Clive, looking doubtful.

"She's from Densus-88, Clive," explains Michael.

"Oh, okay," says Clive, nodding. "But will she be yer *only* backup?"

"Indeed," answers Michael. "Why?"

Clive gives Sarah a wide grin. "She's not exactly inconspicuous, ye know. How can she be effective as yer backup when she'll always be surrounded by fellas offering to buy her a Guinness or two?"

The others also start staring at Sarah, making her feel awkward and sheepish. Clive has pointed out a major flaw in Michael's plan. If Sarah goes to the night club alone, she'll most definitely be swarmed and this will prevent her backing up Michael effectively. Michael winces as he hadn't calculated for that, but then Clive offers a solution.

"So, Sarah, how about if I join ye as Michael's backup?" suggests Clive. "Ye can go inside as my date, ye know."

Michael hastily adds. "The Cartel knows who you are, Clive, so they would probably slot *you* instead of me. You're right about Sarah being surrounded, though, so she should be *my* date instead. That way, we can support each other."

Everyone laughs as it's crystal clear Michael would be jealous if Sarah goes out with someone else. Only Broussard doesn't laugh along.

"That puts both you *and* Sarah at risk of being identified by The Cartel. I don't mind if you risk your own arse on this bone plan of yours, but I won't risk Sarah's," says Broussard.

"Sarah's what, Chief?" asks Michael with his cheeky grin.

"Sarah's ar… I mean, Sarah's life," says Broussard, with a voice that suddenly sounds curt.

The team laughs, but Broussard does not. Sarah sees how serious he is and how close he is to getting angry.

"We're already committed to doing this, Chief. I don't mind providing close protection for Michael," says Sarah.

"But The Cartel will most likely identify you!" protests Broussard.

"That's highly unlikely unless they know I'm from Densus and they have someone there in their payroll."

Broussard thinks for a moment before commenting. "You're taking a lot of risks here."

"I can take care of myself, Chief," says Sarah.

"That's exactly what Karen said!" says Broussard, emotionally.

Everyone goes quiet and looks away at the mention of their deceased teammate, except Michael, Sarah, and Clive, who give sharp looks at Broussard. They're all silent for a few seconds.

"Karen didn't have backup at that time, Chief," says Michael softly, but giving his commander a hard look.

# THE POLICEWOMAN

It's Broussard's turn to stay silent. He wants to abort this plan, but he doesn't have a better idea. They are committed to the operation, especially since they have already deployed the Garda ERU.

Broussard sighs. "Fine. The plan is a go, but let's take it one step at a time."

Everyone is relieved, but they then tense up when they realize that two of their members are about to enter one of The Cartel's strongholds. Broussard asks for the bill, but it turns out Liz has already taken care of it.

"What's the occasion?" asks Arthur.

"This afternoon I got an e-mail from Garda HQ. I've been promoted to Cigire," says Liz, proudly.

"That's bloody marvellous, Liz! Congratulations!" says Broussard. He shakes her hand, followed by the others, who are also happy for her.

It's a happy ending to a tense meeting.

22:02 GMT
Tuesday June 2, 2026
Main Street
Letterkenny, County Donegal, Republic of Ireland

Michael and Sarah walk leisurely towards Gwilliam's. Both Sarah and Michael have a radio receiver and transmitter implanted inside their ear. Michael's call sign is Mike, Sarah is Sierra, Broussard is Zero, and Clive is One.

"Thanks for backing me up back there," says Michael.

"Well, I'd rather pretend to be *your* date rather than Clive's," says Sarah, making Michael laugh out loud. Clive is even more unattractive than Michael.

They keep on walking and enjoying Letterkenny's main street, which is quite hot this evening. Despite the heat, Sarah's wearing a long-sleeved shirt so her toned arms and shoulders won't attract too much attention. Michael, on the other hand, prominently displays his muscular arms and broad chest and shoulders in a Polo shirt. When they pass other girls, lots of them smile at Michael and he always smiles back. Sarah feels something strange whenever Michael does this. Never in her life has she felt something like this and it confuses her.

Sarah suddenly remembers the first time she talked to Michael. There was something about him that intrigued her, even though he wasn't good-looking and his face was full of scars. At that time, Sarah thought that Michael was interesting as an officer of the SAS. However, it turns out that other girls who don't know him also find him attractive. Sarah still doesn't understand why she, and apparently other girls also, are so drawn to Michael.

Unconsciously, Sarah grabs for Michael's arm. Just as it had been at the Y Club, both Sarah and Michael feel a jolt of electricity when they touch. Just as it had been then too, neither one shows it. Girls who pass them no longer smile at Michael, but instead flash Sarah unfriendly looks. For some reason, this makes Sarah satisfied.

In front of them walk a pair of sexy girls. One is wearing a crop top and low-rise jeans. There's a pinstripe tattoo on the small of her back and Michael keeps staring at it. That is, he's either looking at the tattoo or at the girl's firm, rounded arse. Michael keeps looking at the girl's lower backside, which makes Sarah's strange feeling rise again.

"Enjoying the view, Michael?" asks Sarah.

"N-N-Not really," stammers Michael. "I don't fancy girls with tattoos."

Sarah starts to pout, as she knows that it's not exactly the tattoos that grabbed Michael's attention. "Why? It looks sexy to me."

"Well, if you're already hot and sexy, you don't need tattoos to show off," answers Michael. "It's like putting bumper stickers on a sports car. I mean, you didn't put bumper stickers on your Huracán, right?"

"No," answers Sarah. "But wait! How did you know I have a Lamborghini?"

"Tony once told me your mum bought you a car to go to work after you graduated from the police academy," answers Michael, trying not to laugh.

Sarah's proud of her supercar, but embarrassed that Michael knows she couldn't afford a car on her own. She wants to pinch Michael's arm for embarrassing her but unfortunately, they've arrived at Gwilliam's. The music is deafening as they enter the club. There are still several empty tables so they immediately take a seat and order Guinness.

"Zero, this is Mike and we're in position," reports Michael.

"Zero roger," answers Broussard through the receivers inside their ears.

Michael and Sarah observe the people dancing while looking out for dealers. They don't have to look hard, as one soon comes up to them. He's tall and huge, built like a boxer.

"Want some Mandy?" asks the dealer.

"Sure, how much?" asks Michael.

"Twelve quid a pop."

"Bullshit! It costs less than ten quid."

"Okay, I'll sell it to ye for eleven quid then."

"Tell your supplier to meet me here!"

"Fuck off!" curses the dealer, giving Michael a mean look.

Michael suddenly stands up while punching him in the solar plexus. The dealer folds in pain and Michael slams his face hard into the table. The dealer's nose is smashed and blood starts spouting everywhere. He takes out something from his pocket, but Michael seizes it and slams his face again into the table. One of his teeth was left on the table top, now splashed with blood. Michael hands Sarah what he'd taken from the dealer, which turns out to be a cheap switchblade.

"Tell your supplier to meet me here, right this second!" orders Michael.

The dealer looks absolutely terrified.

"Now fuck off!" snaps Michael.

The dealer staggers away with his nose and mouth pouring blood. A number of people saw the whole thing and they keep looking at Michael and Sarah, who ignore them and go back to drinking their Guinness. Michael looks at Sarah and she just looks back at him, smiling.

Sarah's not remotely bothered by Michael's actions, as she often treats the criminals she catches the same way. Her friends at the Direktorat Reserse Kriminal (Criminal Investigations Directorate) are even more ruthless as they would happily shoot the legs of suspects who were 'escaping arrest'. It's almost impossible to shoot a running man in the leg and most Indonesian policemen are shitty pistol shooters so those suspects were allegedly 'shot in the leg' while in custody. This is a violation of the law and human rights but Sarah thinks those criminals deserve it, especially dealers who sell their drugs to minors and get them addicted. If her conscience starts bothering her, Sarah only has to remember her close friend who OD'd. Michael is right. If the dealers object to his treatment, they can just sue him.

Michael and Sarah wait to see whether The Cartel will react. Although they act cool and seem nonchalant, they are on high alert and are aware of their surroundings. They drink their Guinness with their left hands and keep their right hands hidden from view. After more than three hours without a reaction from The Cartel, Michael and Sarah finally exit the nightclub. They execute counter-surveillance measures, backed up by plain-clothed members of the Garda ERU. After walking around Letterkenny for an hour, it's determined that no one is following them so they return to the hotel.

The Interpol team has just initiated their first offensive against the Irish Drug Cartel.

# CHAPTER 5
# CLOSE QUARTERS BATTLE

17:51 GMT
Wednesday June 3, 2026
City Hotel – Derry
Derry City, County Derry, Northern Ireland

The following day, the Interpol team check in at the City Hotel in Derry City, on the borders of Northern Ireland and the Republic of Ireland. In Derry City, there are two Gwilliam's clubs, one in the middle of the city on Shipquay Street and one in front of the River Foyle on Bay Road. Just like in Letterkenny, they conduct recces of the surrounds. Michael takes the Gwilliam's on Bay Road and Sarah covers Shipquay. This time, Sarah's with Matt.

"Why did you decide to join PSNI, Matt?" asks Sarah. This is the first time she's worked closely with Matt and she takes the opportunity to observe him. With his healthy beard, he looks like a young Captain Haddock from the Tintin comics. Only a hell of a lot better looking.

"I've always wanted to be a copper," answers Matt. "It must've been those TV shows I watched as a weean."

"What was it like during The Troubles?"

"I didn't experience any violence, but my parents did. Especially as they've always supported the Unionists, even though they're Catholics. That didn't win them many friends. See, you had the Unionists, who were mostly Protestant, who wanted to stay with Great Britain. And you had the Nationalists, who were mostly Catholic, who wanted a united Ireland. The Nationalists, who are a strong minority, still want a united Ireland, but now it's all done through talking. In those days, it was shooting people or blowing them up. On both sides, mind. There used to be discrimination against us Irish Catholics, but that's mostly been disappearing since the Good Friday Agreement."

"I'm Catholic myself. There used to be discrimination against Irish Catholics?" asks Sarah, frowning.

"Oh, aye! A couple of decades ago if I had joined the RUC, the Protestants, who are mostly Unionists, would've given me a hard time. Catholics don't usually fare well in government service unless they're Unionists, and even then, they still face being discriminated against by the Protestants. Nowadays, discrimination - whether we're Catholic or Protestant, Nationalist or Unionist - is all illegal. So now, for people in government service, Catholics like me and Michael won't get discriminated against whether we're Nationalists or Unionists," says Matt, smiling when he sees Sarah's eyes suddenly light up on finding out that Michael is also Catholic.

"What's crime like in Northern Ireland compared to the rest of the UK?"

"Northern Ireland is unique because of The Troubles. It's the only place in the UK where many people carry guns. The fact that Northern Ireland has the highest unemployment rate doesn't help either. This is why the PSNI is the only constabulary that issues guns to every single officer," says Matt.

"What do you carry?"

"Glock 17 and a Glock 19 for backup. I suggest ye carry more mags for yer pistol, Sarah."

Sarah only smiles at Matt. Of all the firefights she's encountered, she has never once emptied her magazine, even though it only ever contains eight rounds.

The layout of Gwilliam's in Shipquay is the same as in Letterkenny, so they decide not to spend much time there. They then meet at one of the hotel meeting rooms with Rudy, the commander of PSNI's Special Operations Branch.

Unlike their previous operation, this time Michael and Sarah will visit both places in one night. Rudy complains that the Gwilliam's on Bay Road is in a deserted area near Derry's industrial complex; there are no buildings on the flanks nor behind the club. The Bay Road is in front of Gwilliam's and across it is the River Foyle. This will make things complicated for Rudy and his unit providing cover for Michael and Sarah. They can't get too close else they'll be seen and the mission compromised. Instead, they'll have to deploy some way back. This means that if Michael and Sarah need back up, it'll take close to two minutes for his unit to reach them.

"You have snipers, right?" asks Michael.

"I can deploy them, but they'll be at least 600 metres away. I'd rather *not* order them to shoot while ye are involved in a scuffle. Ye should call for backup once ye're engaged because ye'll be on yer own until reinforcement arrives. They will not deploy unless ye call for them," explains Rudy in his thick South-Ulster accent.

"If I may suggest, you could deploy your snipers as observers. You can shoot them if any of them draw their firearms," suggests Michael.

Rudy glances at Broussard, who looks unhappy with the idea, but then nods in agreement. The location of Gwilliam's Shipquay is bang in the middle of the bustling city. The main problem with this site lies with the back door, which opens into a narrow, deserted alley. Rudy and his unit also can't give cover to Michael and Sarah in this area. Broussard looks worried about this, as there'll be too much drama if too many of the opposition attack them.

"Michael," warns Broussard, "if you bugger this up and get hurt, I'll come down there and finish you off myself. Am I being clear?"

"Clear, Chief," answers Michael. He reminds Broussard again about the Battle of Agincourt, in which the opposition's number did not pose a problem.


20:13 GMT
Wednesday June 3, 2026
Gwilliam's Quay
Derry City, County Derry, Northern Ireland

Gwilliam calls Patrick, who is currently visiting their factory in Ireland. "Ye should know that two fellas caused a scene at my place in Letterkenny."

"What kind of scene?" asks Patrick.

"A fella broke one of my dealers' nose and chipped his front tooth. I've already sent the stills from the CCTV cameras to my contact at the Garda, but he can't identify them. He also said that the Garda ERU had deployed that day, but he doesn't know for what operation. Any suggestions?" asks Gwilliam.

"What did the fella want?"

"He said he wanted to speak to us."

Patrick thinks for a moment before answering. "I think the Garda are desperate and they're just trying to provoke us. Send their pictures to all yer bouncers and let them in so the boys can have fun with them if they ever show up again. And send me their pictures as well."

"Aye," answers Gwilliam.

Gwilliam sends the pictures by e-mail to Patrick, who then forwards them to his contacts at all the UK territorial police forces. As an afterthought, Patrick also forwards the pictures to his contact in the British Army.

Unexpectedly, Patrick's contact in the British Army replies to his e-mail only a couple of minutes later. What's written in the response makes Patrick's jaw drop! He immediately sends a text to all senior members who are in Ireland to meet with him at the Gwilliam's Bay at once.


23:13 GMT
Wednesday June 3, 2026
Gwilliam's Shipquay
Derry City, County Derry, Northern Ireland


At first, Michael and Sarah think that the two huge bouncers are going to refuse them entrance, but this turns out to be not the case and they enter without much trouble. However, the bouncers give them piercing stares on their way in, which both Michael and Sarah notice. The night club is not as full as the one at Letterkenny so they easily find a lounge chair. As before, they order a Guinness and discreetly observe their surroundings. They're quickly offered ecstasy by one of the club's dealers and they reject it. They watch the dealer go back to his table, occupied by other dealers. There are three dealers at the table, including the one they just met.

Michael and Sarah don't waste time. They stand up and Michael goes to the dealers' table while Sarah watches his back from near a pillar. A man in an unbuttoned shirt sees her and starts to come over. Sarah flashes him a 'fuck off!' look. He's taken aback by Sarah's deadly look and immediately returns to his seat, tail between his legs.

"Tell your suppliers to meet me at Gwilliam's Bay at one o'clock tonight," orders Michael.

The dealers only stare at him.

"Who the fuck are ye?" asks the dealer who'd offered them ecstasy.

"Fuck off and just do what I say!" orders Michael.

"Ye fuck off!" says the one nearest him.

Michael pours his Guinness on the man's head, which makes him stand up fast. It turns out he's much taller and bigger than Michael, and thoroughly pissed off.

"Tell your suppliers I'll be at Gwilliam's Bay at one o'clock tonight," says Michael, calmly.

Michael then walks towards the back door. He knows they won't dare make a scene inside Gwilliam's, but Sarah still must keep watch, just in case. In front of him, Michael sees Sarah wipe her eyebrow, which is a signal that confirms he's not being followed. A few seconds after Michael passes Sarah, she can hear his voice from the receiver in her ear.

"Sierra, this is Mike in position."

"Copy," says Sarah.

Sarah then goes toward the exit with Michael covering her. They both leave the club. Michael turns left and Sarah goes right, flanking the door.

"Zero, this is Mike and we're in position," reports Michael.

"Zero roger," answers Broussard, sounding tense. Final responsibility for this mission lies with him, but rests now on Michael and Sarah, who are on their own.

"How long do you think until they finally decide to come out?" asks Michael with his signature cheeky grin.

"Probably no more than fifteen seconds," answers Sarah, smiling while arming her telescoping baton.

Both of them look like they're gearing up for a few laughs rather than getting ready to beat other men into bloody pulps. Less than fifteen seconds later, three men suddenly burst out of the door. Michael and Sarah wait as they're sure more will follow. Sure enough, two more men burst out. Michael and Sarah immediately slam their batons repeatedly into the two newcomers, who turn out to be the bouncers from the entrance. Both bouncers drop like flies and the first three men finally realize they're being ambushed. Two of them attack Sarah and the other attacks Michael.

Because the alley is so narrow, it makes no difference whether two people or twenty people attack Sarah, as only two people can walk shoulder-to-shoulder in the confined space. Just like in the Battle of Agincourt, where 6,000 English soldiers beat 36,000 French, the French were unable to deploy their forces simultaneously.

One of the men attacking Sarah equips himself with a telescoping baton and the other pulls out a knife. The first tries to hit Sarah's head with his baton, but Sarah can easily deflect it with her own. Surprising them both, Sarah goes forward, swinging her baton towards the elbow of the man wielding the knife. Sarah's swing is on target, making him drop his knife and hold his elbow, his eyes crossed in pain. Without stopping, Sarah swings her baton back towards the first dealer and hits him right in the ear. He falls hard, but isn't knocked out yet. Still not stopping, Sarah returns her baton to the kneecap of the other man, who also falls to the ground. Sarah then clubs him on top of his head, which knocks him out with blood gushing out of his head. Sarah can now concentrate on the other dealer, who has already risen and is about to attack her again. Before Sarah can hit him once more, Michael hits his head from behind him and knocks him out.

Michael and Sarah have expertly implemented the basic principles of Close Quarters Battle (CQB), which are 'speed, surprise, and violence of action'. Once the battle starts, the next principle is 'hit hard, hit fast, and hit often', as popularized by Admiral William F. Halsey of the US Navy during World War II. The hard, fast, repeated blows from the two special forces operatives have knocked out five of the opposition in under ten seconds. Only Hollywood bullshit would depict special forces operatives fighting hand-to-hand combat for longer than ten seconds. If they can't floor their opposition in less than that, then it's time for them to bugger off.

Only one of their opponents is still conscious and he's moaning in pain from his shattered bones. Michael grabs his hair to look at him. It turns out he's one of the bouncers from the entrance.

"Tell The Cartel to meet me at Gwilliam's Bay at one o'clock tonight. Got that?" asks Michael.

The bouncer can only nod, wincing from the pain. Michael and Sarah leave the men lying where they've fallen.

"Zero, this is Mike and we're in the clear," reports Michael, once they're away from the alley.

"Zero roger," answers Broussard, sounding relieved.

"Hey! That last chap you knocked out was mine!" protests Sarah.

"Well, it looked like you needed help," says Michael, grinning.

"Says who?"

They tease and argue with each other, fun back and forth, during the walk away from the field of battle. After the engagement, both feel more emotionally attached to each other than before.

00:36 GMT
Thursday June 4, 2026
Gwilliam's Bay
Derry City, County Derry, Northern Ireland

All senior members of The Cartel are present at the Gwilliam's Bay. Besides Patrick, there's Steve Dunbar, Gwilliam O'Donnel, Rory Hanrahan, Carraig 'Frag' O'Lenihan, Donald "Tiny" Mullins, and Niall Schroeder. The head of The Cartel's factory at Swan's Mill, which is only thirty minutes from Derry, couldn't attend because there are still problems at the factory. But everyone else is present. The third floor of Gwilliam's Bay is one of the hideouts of The Cartel's elite. Gwilliam must ensure Gwilliam's Bay is free of drugs so PSNI never have reason to raid it. This is why Gwilliam's Bay has up to ten bouncers at any one time, including the head bouncer, who used to be a professional MMA fighter and trainer.

Patrick starts his briefing. "These two are trying to provoke us. They caused a scene at the Gwilliam's in Letterkenny yesterday and at Gwilliam's Shipquay here in Derry a few minutes ago. They have sent a total of four of our dealers and two of Gwilliam's bouncers to the hospital. The fella said he wants us to meet him here at Gwilliam's Bay at one o'clock."

"Ye should've picked another place for this meeting!" says Donald 'Tiny' Mullins sharply. "Why the fuck did ye pick this place?"

"We only found out about this a few minutes ago, so fuck off!" says Steve firmly.

Tiny shuts up and Patrick continues his briefing. "Our contact in the British Army has somehow managed to identify them. The fella is Major Michael Adrian, OC of B Squadron, SAS and the girl is Sarah Dharmawan, a policewoman from the Indonesian National Police."

Everyone is surprised by two things. First, that an SAS squadron commander and an Indonesian policewoman are cooperating to find them. And second, how on earth did their British Army contact identify *both* so fast? They're still debating the implications of the news when Gwilliam receives a call from his manager.

00:56 GMT
Thursday June 4, 2026
Gwilliam's Bay
Derry City, County Derry, Northern Ireland

After executing counter-surveillance measures, Michael and Sarah split up. They plan on meeting inside the Gwilliam's Bay at 01:00 because there's a chance the bouncers will recognize them if they go in together. Michael arrives early, so he goes to the bar to order a Guinness. There's a huge mirror behind the bar facing him so he can see when Sarah arrives. A gorgeous brunette is sitting alone at the bar. She looks stunning and really sexy wearing a black strapless dress. Michael gives her a friendly smile as he sits next to her.

"Not interested!" snaps the pretty girl.

Michael is taken aback as he hasn't even opened his mouth yet.

"Yeah, right... neither am I," Michael snorts, "... and I just got out of jail."

It's her turn to be taken aback and she looks as if she's trying not to laugh. "Just got out of jail, eh? So what are ye? A bank robber or something?"

"Bank robber? Good heavens, no," says Michael in an exaggeratedly posh accent. "I'm a serial killer."

The girl finally laughs. "And they just let ye out?"

"Of course not," answers Michael. "I escaped."

She laughs harder. "Wearing a bespoke suit from Savile Row?"

"I nicked it before coming here," says Michael, signalling the barman to give her a drink.

"And how will ye pay for this drink?" she asks. The man beside her isn't good-looking, but he has a powerful aura that piques her interest.

"Actually, I was about to ask you for a loan," says Michael dryly.

The pretty girl laughs out loud and gives Michael a playful pinch on his waist as he pays for the drinks. Michael is pleased, but then notices from the mirror that Sarah is already sitting at the table behind them.

"Pardon me," says Michael, giving the girl another friendly smile. He takes his drink to go sit with Sarah.

'Oh, fuck,' thinks Michael when he sees Sarah's expression.

"Enjoying yourself, Michael?" asks Sarah, in a voice as cold as the Guinness in Michael's hand.

"I was indeed… thank you for asking," answers Michael. He arranges his face into an innocent expression, though he's actually terrified of the look Sarah's giving him right now.

"Were you trying to pick her up?" asks Sarah sharply.

"Why would I want to do that?" asks Michael, still innocently. "I already have you *pretending* to be my date."

Sarah's face hardens. These past couple of days, she has come to feel more emotionally attached to him than before and she's suddenly identified the strange feeling she'd experienced when Michael had returned the smiles of all those girls. Sarah is fully aware that this is *not* a real date, but the jealousy is almost overwhelming her.

A waiter comes over. "Would ye like to order a drink, madam?"

"Guinness," answers Sarah curtly.

"Very good, madam. Anything else for ye, sir?"

"Indeed. How about a new date?" asks Michael, still with a face like butter wouldn't melt in his mouth. "This one has come over all sulky."

The waiter then notices Sarah's pouty lips and almost laughs out loud. "I'm afraid ye're on yer own on this, sir."

"I thought so. Thanks anyhow," says Michael, giving the waiter a friendly smile.

The waiter gives Michael a small bow and leaves, still trying hard not to laugh. Sarah's a bit calmer, but she's still annoyed with Michael.

"What were you two talking about?" she asks, still with ice in her voice.

"Oh, the usual. The life of a rupert in The Paras... a few war stories... all the medals I've received," says Michael dryly. "I was about to show off my battle scars when you showed up..."

Sarah laughs out loud and Michael can finally breathe a sigh of relief. They talk about other things and focus on taking in their surroundings.

01:01 GMT
Thursday June 4, 2026
Gwilliam's Bay
Derry City, County Derry, Northern Ireland

"They're already fucking here!" shouts Gwilliam, hanging up his phone.

They all go to the CCTV screens. Niall's eyes go wide when he sees Sarah, who looks especially gorgeous wearing a long-sleeved black shirt and dark blue jeans.

"Let's snatch them!" he says excitedly.

"Not now and not here," says Gwilliam firmly.

Patrick thinks for a moment. They can't take care of these two while they're inside the building. However, neither can their actions be tolerated. "I'll have our contact send more info on them. In the meantime, there are only two of them so here's what we're going to do..."

He lays out his plan.

"They defeated five of our fellas in a narrow alley... now let's see how they handle ten of our bouncers in the open," says Patrick, smiling sadistically.

03:09 GMT
Thursday June 4, 2026
Bay Road
Derry City, County Derry, Northern Ireland

After spending a couple of hours inside with no sign of The Cartel, Michael and Sarah exit the building. They already suspected The Cartel would leave them alone inside Gwilliam's Bay. Outside, however, they become alert. Michael and Sarah leave the road to walk on the river bank. It's quite romantic and for a second, Sarah imagines she's dating Michael. Without thinking, Sarah puts her arm through his. Both feel sparks as muscle touches muscle, but they remain on high alert.

Michael's smartphone suddenly goes off and he frowns when he sees the name on the screen. He takes the call and Sarah can only hear one side of the conversation.

"Yes?"

"..."

"No, but why are you calling me at this hour?"

"..."

"No… I'm still in… ehm… Manchester."

"..."

"The squadron will be 'On The Team' starting July, remember?"

"..."

"Probably in August after the Fan Dance. Why?"

"..."

"No, not yet."

"..."

"What for?"

"..."

"Fine."

"..."

"Right, see you at PATA," says Michael, hanging up his phone.

Sarah notices Michael's expression. "Is there something wrong?"

"No," answers Michael, still with an irritated look on his face.

"Who was it?"

"Just an ex-girlfriend."

Without being able to control it, red-hot jealousy again rages inside Sarah. "Do they always check up on you like that?" she asks sharply, giving him a hard look.

"Just this one. We broke up a couple of years ago, but she's been calling me around the clock these past few months."

"Why?"

Michael shrugs. "Haven't the foggiest… she probably still finds me irresistible, I guess."

This time Sarah doesn't react to Michael's joke. She keeps silent and pouts.

"Anyhow, you've been great these past few days," says Michael.

Sarah knows that Michael is trying to change the subject so she keeps silent.

"You're excellent at hand-to-hand combat and you handle yourself very well," praises Michael again.

Sarah ignores him although she's actually flattered.

"You could be my backup anytime," says Michael.

Sarah still ignores him.

Michael finally snorts. "Well then… if you're going to sulk like that all night then maybe I *should've* picked up that lovely girl at the bar…"

Sarah suddenly grabs Michael's arm, lifts him up on her shoulders, and slams him unceremoniously to the ground. She expects complaints but Michael laughs out loud instead, making her feel more annoyed.

"What did you do that for?" asks Michael, still laughing.

"That's for winding me up, you git!" snaps Sarah, red-faced.

Michael laughs louder, making Sarah even more annoyed with him. He can sense that Sarah's jealous and this makes him happy, as he's had a crush on her for two years, since long before they met a few months ago. Sarah tries hard to maintain her expression, but finally joins in laughing at how silly this has become.

"Help me up…" says Michael with gleaming eyes and his cheeky grin, thrusting his hand towards her.

Sarah starts to give him her hand… but then withdraws it at the last second.

"Do you really think I'm *that* stupid?" she snaps, pouting again.

Michael laughs even harder. Sarah has guessed correctly that he was going to pull her down to the ground as well. Still laughing, Michael tries to get up by himself when Rudy's voice is suddenly heard through their receiver inside their ear.

"This is One. Cut that fucking shite out! Ye have ten players coming at ye from two directions! I repeat, ye have ten players coming at ye from two directions!" says Rudy, observing them from across the river.

"Roger that," says Michael.

"Copy," says Sarah.

They make like they're still joking around to prevent the opposition from becoming suspicious. While bantering, they glance about and spot six men walking fast towards them from behind and four from Bay Road to their right. They keep acting like nothing's happening, joking around as if they're unaware they're about to be ambushed from two flanks.

"All players are armed with batons!" says Rudy, tensely. "Those behind ye are closing fast... ten metres!"

"We'll counterattack the ones behind us," says Michael. "Ready?"

"Let's do it," answers Sarah.

"Standby... Standby..." says Michael.

"Five metres!" shouts Rudy.

"Go!" orders Michael.

The only way to counter an ambush is to counterattack as violently as possible. They turn around, arm their telescoping batons, and attack the six men behind them, screaming at the top of their lungs. Four men are immediately knocked out in the flurry of swirling sticks and the remaining two panic and run away.

Now they only have to concentrate on the four men coming from the direction of Bay Road. One aims a baton at Sarah's head, but Sarah can easily evade it. The man then gets a mouthful of Sarah's baton, which sends most of his front teeth flying and his body crashing bloodily to the ground. Sarah's about to face the other man when she suddenly sees something coming towards her midsection.

An extremely powerful blow from a steel baton lands on her stomach!

03:17 GMT
Thursday June 4, 2026
River Foyle
Derry City, County Derry, Northern Ireland

Everyone across the River Foyle saw what just happened.

"Oh, fuck!" shouts Rudy. He shouts an order to one of his sniper teams. "Five-Oscar, standby to fire on my command!"

"Roger that," answers the sniper, extremely tense as he struggles to keep his crosshairs on the attacker, his finger on the trigger.

Broussard is on edge because he knows it's almost impossible for a sniper to hit a moving target from 600 metres, especially when friendlies are in the immediate area. One stray shot and Sarah could get hit!

03:17 GMT
Thursday June 4, 2026
River Foyle
Derry City, County Derry, Northern Ireland

Sarah barely had time to clench her abdominal muscles before the steel baton hit her stomach. To everyone's surprise, the baton bounces off Sarah's stomach and flies out from her attacker's hands. The attacker looks momentarily surprised before his MMA training kicks in and he then throws his body towards Sarah, who's still reeling from the powerful blow to her stomach. The hard slam to her body knocks her baton out of her hand and they both enter the river bank with Sarah underneath him. Sarah gasps when her body hits the freezing waters of the River Foyle. The river bank is knee-deep and her opponent starts strangling Sarah with both hands and submerging her head, trying to drown her.

03:18 GMT
Thursday June 4, 2026
Gwilliam's Bay
Derry City, County Derry, Northern Ireland

"Now she's dead," says Patrick with a satisfied smirk, watching what's happening through his binoculars.
  Everyone else smirks with him except Niall, who's frowning because he wanted to torture the Indonesian policewoman instead of just killing her. They carry on watching the fight between Sarah and their head bouncer, who's just about to drown her.

03:18 GMT
Thursday June 4, 2026
River Foyle
Derry City, County Derry, Northern Ireland

After the initial shock, Sarah's training kicks in. She gives her opponent a hard kick to his groin and he suddenly lets go of her neck. She immediately follows up with another kick to his chest. Her opponent staggers back and Sarah easily gets up. To her opponent's surprise, Sarah throws herself onto him, pushing them both towards the middle of the river.

The two wrestle underneath the cold, dark waters of the River Foyle. Every time her opponent tries to swim up to breathe, Sarah pulls him back under. Sarah can feel her opponent starting to panic! Beneath the pitch-black, terrifying waters, Sarah calmly manoeuvres into a position behind her attacker and places him in a choke hold, which knocks him out within seconds.

Once he's out for the count, Sarah swims up to catch her breath. After a few seconds sucking in gulps of needed air, she tows her unconscious opponent towards the river bank. She doesn't want him to drown, but she does take the opportunity to give him a hard stomp on his arm with her boot. A sickening crack is heard, which is both his ulna and radius bones breaking and jolting out of his arm. Sarah looks toward Michael, who's just standing there, watching her with a wide smile. His two opponents are on the ground, bleeding and with broken bones all over their bodies.

"All right, Sarah?"

"I'm all right," says Sarah, still panting.

"Who taught you how to fight in the water like that?" asks Michael, very much impressed with her.

"My dad. He was once the CO of Denjaka."

"That's the equivalent to the SBS, right?"

"Indeed. How about you?" asks Sarah. "What do they teach you in the SAS?"

"They taught us a mixture of MMA and street fighting," explains Michael. The SAS call it jap-slapping, but Michael is afraid Sarah would be offended if he said that.

Sarah picks up and secures her telescoping baton while Michael checks the men around them. Both Michael and Sarah are disappointed that not even one of the floored men is a core member of The Cartel.

"Zero, this is Mike and we're in the clear," reports Michael through his transmitter.

"We can see that, you dickhead!" shouts Broussard, barely in control of himself. "You two get your fucking arses back to the hotel for the fucking debrief! Zero out!"

Michael and Sarah are stunned and their eardrums ring. They've never heard Broussard this angry before.

"Well… it seems that our gallant chief is bloody pleased with what we have accomplished," comments Michael dryly.

Sarah laughs. Michael takes off his suit and wraps it around Sarah's shoulders. Strange as it may seem, this event has made the relationship between them even closer.

03:23 GMT
Thursday June 4, 2026
Gwilliam's Bay
Derry City, County Derry, Northern Ireland

"Jesus fucking Christ!" says Gwilliam, his mouth open in awe.

They can see the fight clearly through their binoculars. The senior members of The Cartel can't help but be impressed by Michael and Sarah's skill in unarmed combat.

"What is she… a fucking Navy SEAL?" asks Carraig incredulously to Rory, whose jaw is still open though the fight is over.

Patrick can only shake his head in amazement. He didn't expect them to get away with nary even a scratch. He makes a mental note to have the two bouncers who ran away taught a lesson. Steve is the least impressed because he knows they fought ten men with more brawn than brains. If Patrick had deployed their core members, who are mostly ex-army, the results would've surely been different. However, Steve is impressed with the policewoman. He also thought that she was finished when her head was dunked into the water by their head bouncer. But she easily managed to escape and ended up enticing an ex-MMA fighter to a fight in even deeper waters. Only Navy SEALs and Swimmer Canoeists of the SBS are comfortable fighting in the water like that. Steve imagines how challenging and arousing it would be to fight the beautiful policewoman. Preferably while she's naked.

"Let me out and I'll take them down," says Tiny to Patrick.

Niall snorts loudly. "They'll probably take *ye* down, Tiny."

Tiny's offended. He looks like he's gearing up to punch Niall in the face, but withdraws when he sees Steve flashing him a stern look.

"Negative," says Patrick. "They're just trying to provoke us so we'll let them have this round. After a month or so, ye can lead the team to slot them. In the meantime, let's try to gather more intel on them."

"Slot them? Why not snatch them and let me have fun with them?" asks Niall, disappointed.

Carraig shakes his head. "The fella's SAS. They're professionals and they'll understand if we kill him in a firefight, but not if we intentionally snatch and torture him to death. Let's not give those SAS fellas any more incentives to hunt us down."

"How about if we snatch the girl and give her to Niall instead of just slotting her?" suggests Rory. "That way we can also send a message to the INP not to mess with us."

Niall looks excited at the idea.

"Ye can snatch her if possible," says Patrick to Tiny, "but I don't want ye to take any unnecessary risks. If she looks like too much trouble, just shoot her fucking head off."

"I can ensure a snatch if we bring longs," says Tiny.

"Negative. Just bring the shorts. The longs are for defensive purposes only. Go and draft me a plan, but I suggest ye take at least twenty of our core members for the hit. Take the fellas from Swan's Mill instead of Liverpool," orders Patrick.

The Irish Drug Cartel has two drug factories in England, one in the Republic of Ireland, and the largest of them all in Indonesia. The factory at Swan's Mill is still having problems so they currently don't need that many people there. It usually only takes three core members to conduct a snatch, but this time they'll have to deploy more men after seeing how those two fought.

04:01 GMT
Thursday June 3, 2026
City Hotel – Derry
Derry, County Derry, Northern Ireland

Once they enter the meeting room they'd rented at the hotel, Broussard chews on Michael. "What the fuck do you think you were doing? You were supposed to call for backup once you were in contact, you arsehole!"

"We were always in control and we were never in the shite, Chief," answers Michael.

"They could've brought guns!"

"That's why we have snipers."

"And I thought I told you to take them down, not cripple them!"

"Like I said, Chief, they're free to sue us," says Michael with his cheeky grin. The others, out of sight of Broussard, wryly smile.

Sarah can't believe Broussard's face could go even redder.

"And you!" he shouts towards Sarah. "That chap was already unconscious! You didn't have to break his fucking arm, you know!"

"I… ehm… stepped on his arm by accident, Chief," says Sarah, trying to give her commander an innocent look.

Her teammates start giggling and Broussard really blows his top. "This is not a fucking joke! I'm not taking any more risks and aborting this fucking operation! Liverpool is cancelled!"

"But Chief, I've already coordinated with the North West CT Unit for tomorrow," says Arthur.

"Call it off! Liz and Matt will stay in Ireland to handle any fallout from this bone operation and the rest of us will head back to Manchester at noon!" orders Broussard, still fuming as he leaves the meeting room.

After Broussard slams the door behind him, shaking the pictures on the walls, Rudy asks Sarah. "Are ye all right?"

"Of course, Rudy," answers Sarah. "Why do you ask?"

"During the scuffle I saw ye get hit by a baton," says Rudy, frowning.

"She got hit by a baton?" asks Michael, giving Sarah a concerned look.

"Aye, she got hit in the stomach. I almost gave an order to one of my snipers to shoot the fella when she went underwater," says Rudy.

"I guess my abs could take it then," says Sarah, giving them a wink and a smile.

Every eye in the room looks towards Sarah's stomach and they all try to imagine how hard her abdominal muscles must be to take a powerful blow from a steel baton like that.

15:10 GMT
Thursday June 4, 2026
Gwilliam's Bay
Derry City, County Derry, Northern Ireland

That afternoon, while Tiny and the other senior members plan for the snatch/assassination bid, their British Army contact sends them Michael's data, including his date of birth, his address in Belfast, his family, his career in the British Army, the address of his flat in Hereford, and even the vehicle registration number of Michael's Range Rover and his smartphone number. Their contact told them that Michael is currently seconded to Interpol and has rented a flat at the 3Towers Apartment while in Manchester.

Regarding Sarah, their contact says she has an older brother named Anthony Dharmawan, who's one of the detachment commanders from Satuan Bravo-90, the CT unit of the Indonesian Air Force. His whole unit was once trained by Michael and B Squadron at Credenhill around two years ago. Sarah has a little sister, but their contact doesn't know her name. Their contact only knows that Sarah is a policewoman from the INP and lives in Jakarta, Indonesia but doesn't know what unit she belongs to. Although the information is thin, Patrick is amazed and immensely proud of his British Army contact for obtaining so much information so quickly.

The senior members of The Cartel deduce that Sarah is assigned to Interpol to investigate the whereabouts of their factory in Indonesia. Of all the information they have so far, Michael's smartphone number is the most useful, as they can use a special application to trace his whereabouts through his smartphone. Doing just this, they soon see that Michael has already returned to Manchester.

Rory contacts Richard in Indonesia and asks him to find out about Sarah through their contact at POLDA Metro Jaya, the territorial police force for the Greater Jakarta Area. Rory also tries googling Sarah's name, but it turns out lots of Indonesian women have the same name. He frowns as he checks them one by one.

16:32 GMT
Thursday June 4, 2026
Interpol Manchester
Central Park, Manchester, England

The team is now gathered in the meeting room. Liz and Matt, who are still in Ireland, report via video conference that all of the Gwilliam's bouncers are in the hospital, including the two that ran from the scene. In fact, the two who ran away are in worse condition than those beaten up by Michael and Sarah. As was predicted, none of the bouncers are naming their attackers.

Broussard reminds everyone that The Cartel will surely try to enact revenge. "All of you should remember your tradecraft and always employ counter-surveillance measures. Sarah, I urge you to carry more ammunition for your main sidearm and bring a backup."

This sounds like a suggestion, but Sarah knows it's an order. This is the third time someone has urged her to carry more ammo. She now must find out how to get her hands on more magazines for her HK P2000.

Michael presents the developments of the investigation by the Special Investigation Branch, Royal Military Police, who are still investigating the missing PE4s. As usual, Michael's passionate presentation style makes him look clownish and Sarah still can't imagine him as a squadron commander leading the finest special forces operatives in the world. It turns out the Special Investigation Branch has no suspects yet, as everyone in the army training area has easy access to the PE4. The investigators have had a difficult time investigating and everyone in the army training area has been uncooperative with them.

After work that day, as is now their habit, Michael takes Sarah for dinner. They go to the Nectar Bistro restaurant on Barlow Moor Road where they're welcomed by the friendly owner. In Arabic, Michael orders Moussakah for an appetizer and Dijaj Maheshi for the main course. Michael and the restaurant owner are surprised when Sarah also orders in

# THE POLICEWOMAN

Arabic. She orders Fattoush to start and Lahem Meshwi for her main. Michael is sheepish. He wanted to show off his skill in Arabic, but it turns out that Sarah's Arabic is far more fluent than his own.

"You speak Arabic very well," says Sarah after the owner left.

"Actually, British Army doctrine dictates that before we deploy to another country, we have to be somewhat proficient in the local language," says Michael, still sheepishly.

"So you've been deployed to the Middle-East?" asks Sarah with a raised eyebrow.

Michael only smiles at her and he's glad Sarah doesn't pursue it. Sarah isn't offended that Michael didn't answer her question, but she suddenly has an idea.

"Michael, most of The Cartel members are ex-army, right?"

"Indeed. So?"

"Is it possible they could have learned Indonesian *before* they deployed to Indonesia?" asks Sarah.

Michael eyes light up. "That's absolutely brilliant, Sarah! Why don't you call Paul and ask him to investigate any significant increases in people learning Bahasa these past few years?"

While they wait for their starters to arrive, Sarah calls Paul to tell him her idea. Paul also praises her thinking and will immediately follow up on it. If The Cartel really did study Bahasa Indonesia before they deployed, the team can interrogate their teacher. And who knows, maybe their teacher has some information on them. Michael and Sarah's food arrives and they sit back to enjoy their dinner.


19:09 GMT
Thursday June 4, 2026
Gwilliam's Bay
Derry City, County Derry, Northern Ireland

From Indonesia, Richard reports that their connection at POLDA Metro Jaya doesn't know anyone named Sarah Dharmawan and he doesn't recognize her photo. But there are rumours of a stunningly beautiful French woman working at the Densus-88 Building. Everyone at POLDA

Metro Jaya thinks she's one of the foreign instructors who train the policewomen of Densus, most likely from France. Like everyone from Densus, she always wears a balaclava outside the Densus-88 Building, so their contact cannot confirm whether this is Sarah or not. Rory concentrates on finding her on Facebook and after a couple of hours, he finally finds Sarah's account and shows it to his associates. Unfortunately, her account only displays Sarah's portfolio as a model. There's absolutely no personal information or any indication that she's anything but a model.

"I guess her legend is as a model then. This confirms that she was from Densus-88 before Interpol, most likely from their Intelligence Sub-detachment. With hand-to-hand combat skills like that, she probably has experience in their Strike Force also," says Rory.

"Any word yet from our contacts in the GMP?" asks Patrick.

Rory shakes his head. "They always deliver, but it takes time. It's powerful we have this much intel already."

Patrick smiles. The other senior members can see that their boss is fiercely proud of their British Army contact, who has quickly provided them with so much to go on.

They keep admiring Sarah's photos in her Facebook account. Niall is excited because his next victim is beautiful and sexy. Some photos show Sarah in a sports bra and gym shorts, displaying her athletic body. Niall really likes athletic girls because they can survive much longer than those who never work out. His latest female victim in Jakarta, although she was quite pretty, unfortunately died too soon. Niall only tortured her for a couple of hours before she fainted, never to regain consciousness. That was the second time he had tortured and killed an Indonesian girl but unfortunately, neither was satisfying. The first Indonesian girl he'd tortured died in the first hour because she was much too thin. He's tortured many women but Niall enjoyed torturing and killing Karen the most because she was in better physical shape than the others. She lasted over four hours! With a body as fit as Sarah's, Niall imagines that she could survive for more than ten hours, even with her guts slashed to bits. Niall can't wait to hear the Indonesian policewoman scream when he disembowels her.

That night, Rory finally receives word from their contact at the GMP that Sarah is assigned to the Interpol Incident Response Team under the leadership of Christopher Broussard. The Interpol team is a tight-knit team, meaning that they rarely socialize with the GMP. However, Sarah is well known. Besides being beautiful, she's also very nice. Their contact confirms that Sarah is a policewoman from Indonesia and she once said that she was a traffic constable before being transferred to Interpol. Like the other team members of the Interpol team, Sarah won't give them her smartphone number. She hangs out almost every night with one of her teammates, Michael. Their contact doesn't know whether they are a couple or not, but they always act professionally at work.

"I'll have at least twenty blokes from Swan's Mill sent to our HQ. We'll slot the SAS fella on the spot and snatch or slot the girl during one of their dates," says Patrick. "Tiny, ye're in overall command of this operation."

"I would like to go too if ye don't mind," says Steve.

"What the fuck for?" asks Tiny angrily.

"Hey, the girl is a handful and ye might need some help in controlling her during the snatch," says Steve, grinning.

"Ye can go as Tiny's 2 i/c," says Patrick.

Tiny looks angry while Steve only shrugs. Steve doesn't mind Tiny being in command of the operation as Steve's role in The Cartel is administration and accounting. He wants to be involved in this operation so he can meet Sarah. If they manage to snatch her, Steve wants to challenge her in hand-to-hand combat and then rape her a few times before turning her over to Niall.

Patrick calls his factory head at Swan's Mill to explain his plan. The factory head can send twenty-two men to England under the command of Seamus Fitzgerald and Declan Mulcahy. Patrick knows Seamus and Declan because they were both former Sergeants in the Royal Irish Regiment and they're both extremely reliable.

Once the men arrive at their HQ in England, they spend the next month planning and training. Pistol training, combat communication, and combat tactics, including close quarters combat. The training is led by Tiny, who was once a Staff Sergeant in the Army Ranger Wing. Although all of them have served in the infantry, they rarely practice with a pistol. Unfortunately, they cannot practice shooting with live ammo at their HQ and can only practice dry-firing their pistol. Tiny knows that this can't replace live fire exercises, but it's better than nothing. Besides small arms training, all the men are given refreshment training in hand-to-hand combat.

13:32 GMT
Tuesday, June 30, 2026
Interpol Manchester
Central Park, Manchester, England

A few weeks later, Paul and Arthur call everyone into the meeting room. Everyone can attend except Broussard.

"I've some canny news and some bad news about the new investigation angle Sarah brought up about a month ago," says Paul with his Geordie accent.

Paul tells them that the only institution in the UK teaching Bahasa Indonesia is the School of Oriental and African Studies (SOAS) at the University of London, which also offers language courses to corporate clients. A few years earlier, a company asked for intensive Bahasa Indonesia lessons for almost a hundred people. According to Paul's investigation, the company turned out to be bogus and they paid the hefty price tag in cash. Paul found the name of the person who taught them, a young lady from Bandung, West Java, called Rini Kusumo, who at the time was a SOAS post-grad student. Paul shows them photos of Rini from her Facebook account. She's attractive, but thin. Paul nods to Arthur, who takes over the presentation.

"During Niall Schroeder's reign of terror in London, one of his victims was Rini. She was disembowelled with her intestines slashed at her flat in London," says Arthur, showing them photos from the crime scene.

Rini's arms and legs are tied to her bed and she's wearing only her bra and panties. She was disembowelled and her intestines were shredded. Her eyes are open and her mouth full of blood. Sarah can't help but wince on seeing the photos. Arthur shows them other photos from the crime scene, including pictures of bags of pills.

Arthur continues. "We found a considerable quantity of MDMA in her apartment. At that time, we concluded that Rini was one of The Cartel's dealers who had angered them for some reason, although we had no evidence to support that besides the MDMA found in her apartment. The fact that she was Indonesian seemed irrelevant at that time because their dealers come from various nationalities. Now it seems like Niall planted the MDMA to conceal the fact that The Cartel has something set up in Indonesia. Scotland Yard will continue investigating this case from that angle, but I don't think we will find anything new."

"So we're back to square-one?" asks Sarah, disappointed.

"Indeed, Sarah, but it was brilliant nonetheless. We would never have come up with the language angle," says Arthur. "And if it's any consolation, you've also managed to clear Rini's name. Her parents were utterly devastated when we told them about the drugs found in her apartment and her suspected link to The Cartel. At least now we can tell her parents that the drugs were planted by The Cartel to cover up their operation."

Sarah nods. At least Rini's parents will be somewhat relieved to know their daughter was not involved in the drug trade and her good name can be rehabilitated. The team discuss other angles they might have missed until Sarah receives an e-mail from NCB Indonesia.

Sarah forwards the horrid crime scene photos to her teammates. "A known MDMA player was found murdered in his home in South Jakarta. He was beaten to death with a wooden board with some nails in it. A prostitute was also found dead beside him, disembowelled with her intestines slashed."

"Niall's in Indonesia!" exclaims Liz.

Sarah shakes her head in frustration. "This happened about two months ago. Niall could be anywhere by now."

"This means that The Cartel has already taken over production of MDMA from another player in Indonesia. Their next step is to take over the supply chain if they haven't done so already and then take over other players," says James. "After that, I'm afraid The Cartel will start narcoterrorism in Indonesia."

"Any suggestions on what I can do from here?" asks Sarah, frowning. Although the past month has been interesting, she still hasn't enjoyed relying on other people to do her job.

Paul suggests the INP keep an eye on the local MDMA players. One day, The Cartel will ask each of them to join up. If they refuse, The Cartel will eliminate them.

After dinner that day, Michael tells Sarah that starting next July, he must spend more time in Credenhill because his squadron is on standby for the next six months. Sarah is disappointed upon hearing the news and she doesn't even try to conceal her feelings, which makes Michael happy because it shows that Sarah has strong feelings for him.

Although they hang out every day, they're still not a couple and Sarah is frustrated that Michael hasn't made his move yet. Sarah has been really interested in Michael ever since Ireland. After thinking about it, Sarah realizes that this is the first time she's ever hoped that someone would make a move and she doesn't like worrying that Michael might not be interested in her. She's even spoken about this with her mum, telling her she'd found someone interesting in England, but they weren't a couple because he hadn't made his move yet. Her mum suggested that if Sarah were really that interested in him, *she* could make a move on *him*. Sarah told her that she is much too Asian to do something like that and her mum only laughed.

Sarah's mum is right. Michael has idolized Sarah for a long time, but he's taking things slowly as he doesn't want to risk losing her by going too fast.

05:30 WIB (GMT+7)
Friday July 24, 2026
PT. Horizon Turbines and Propulsions
Citeureup, Bogor, West Java

A container lorry has just left PT. Horizon Turbines and Propulsions, a turbine production manufacturer. The driver is tasked to deliver containers filled with turbines to the Kalibaru Port. The driver's paid below minimum wage by his company, which is a violation of Indonesian labour laws. He doesn't mind, though, because his side job generates much, much more money than his monthly wages. It's too bad that his side job only occurs every other month or so, but he's done it routinely for the past two years. The money from his side job enables him to buy a large house and with it, he can support his two wives and five kids comfortably.

Today, he's excited because last night he received a text from the foreigner who'd given him the side job. As usual, the driver was asked to stop by the factory to smuggle goods into the container headed for the Republic of Ireland. The factory is located nearby so the driver doesn't have to detour far from his itinerary. The driver briefly notices that the goods are much more plentiful than usual. He doesn't know that besides smuggling MDMA, they're now also smuggling raw materials for their factory in the Republic of Ireland. At the Kalibaru Port in North Jakarta, a port authority senior officer on The Cartel's payroll ensures that the container is loaded onto the ship without incident. The ship has an unusual name and the driver doesn't know how to pronounce it. It makes no difference to him anyway, as long as they keep putting money in his bank account.

After finishing his job, the driver goes to his bank to withdraw the tens of millions of rupiah already transferred to his account. After getting home, he splits the money with his two wives and many kids, who've been nagging him all month for money for this and that.

He doesn't give *all* the money to his family, of course. He saves some for himself to have fun in Central Jakarta.

19:17 GMT
Monday July 27, 2026
Old Trafford Stadium
Old Trafford, Manchester, England

Rory has studied Michael's movements through their sophisticated application. Once he exits the GMP HQ, he always executes counter-surveillance drills before having dinner at a restaurant. Tonight, The Cartel will execute their plan and they are now waiting at the FRV (final rendezvous) at the Old Trafford Stadium, southwest of Manchester.

"Heads up, the target is moving. Ye're on, Tiny," says Rory through his smartphone.

"Aye, we're on our way," answers Tiny, giving a signal to his men to deploy.

Steve and seven men are responsible for assassinating Michael and the snatching/assassination of Sarah. Tiny will guard the rear of the restaurant while Seamus and Declan guard the front to prevent them from escaping.

As Steve enters the restaurant, two men will enter from the back door to secure the kitchen so Steve and his men can escape the crime scene that way. If there's too much drama at the restaurant, Tiny, Seamus, and Declan can send in reinforcements from the front and rear. This tactic is called a 'hammer and anvil tactic' and they will use their personal smartphones to communicate with each other. Their strike force is twenty-four men strong; twenty-two men from Swan's Mill plus Tiny and Steve. This time, The Cartel is leaving no chance for their targets to get away.

There are a total of thirty men in six cars. The six drivers, who came from HQ, are not allowed to join in the fight and were drilled by Rory on how to exfiltrate from the crime scene. After the assassination/snatch, Rory needs them to conduct counter-surveillance measures before heading towards their factory at Liverpool. If they manage to snatch Sarah, they'll drop her off in Liverpool then head back to HQ. They'll return to Swan's Mill once the storm they've caused has died down. Rory has also determined the ERV (emergency rendezvous) for this operation, near the Audenshaw Reservoir, southeast of Manchester.

Patrick questions why his brother and not Tiny is the one leading their strike force. He nods in agreement when Tiny reminded him that he's much more conspicuous than Steve.

20:13 GMT
Monday July 27, 2026
Carluccio's
Spinningfields, Manchester, England

Michael and Sarah are having dinner at Carluccio's, near the River Irwell. The Italian restaurant is shaped in a half-circle and they're sitting in the middle of the dining area. The restaurant is quite busy and filled with office workers.

It turns out that the next day Michael has to return to Credenhill for a couple of days, so Sarah tries to enjoy this date as much as possible. Michael himself can't stop looking at Sarah, who looks lovely in a pink jumper and light blue jeans. They're talking while waiting for their food to arrive when Sarah notices a woman rise from her chair and walk towards the front door. Her Gucci bag is lovely and Sarah wants to buy the same one. While Sarah's observing the woman exit the restaurant, a group of men enter. The waiter directs them towards the middle of the room, but they insist on sitting on one side of the restaurant.

"Heads up! There are four men sitting next to the window, about twenty-five metres behind you. I think they're packing heat," says Sarah, keeping her eyes towards Michael's.

People who carry concealed weapons tend to behave differently than normal people. They're always jittery and unconsciously keep touching their weapons as if to assure themselves the weapons are still there. It's different for Michael and Sarah because they're accustomed to carrying concealed weapons. Michael wants to know what they look like, but he's too professional to turn around.

"Could you describe them for me?" asks Michael. He's smiling like a man enjoying small talk with his date.

"I don't recognize any of them from the files. All of them are wearing cheap clothes, jeans. One has red hair," says Sarah, also pretending to smile at him.

"Well, let's not jump to conclusions, but please keep your peripheral vision on them," suggests Michael.

"Of course," says Sarah. Her left hand is on her chin, but her right hand is hidden.

Their drinks arrive, but they only sip them. A few seconds later, four more men arrive wearing similar clothes and ask for the waiter to sit them on the opposite side of the restaurant.

Michael recognizes one of them. "Steve Dunbar just came in with three others. They're sitting at Red-3."

"What the devil are you talking about?" asks Sarah, a smile still on her face.

Michael forgot that Sarah is not one of his troopers. He explains what he meant. "They're sitting behind you next to the window. They're watching us from about twenty-five metres away. It seems like we're about to be ambushed from both flanks. I suggest you make ready your sidearm, but keep it out of sight."

"I've already done that," says Sarah, her heart is staring to race.

"Very good. Now if, and only if, they come for us, we will both stand, turn around, and counterattack the four X-Rays in our tactical area of responsibility. We will then try to find an exit through the kitchen. We will shoot-to-kill, is that clear?"

"Copy," answers Sarah. "The one with red hair has just told the waiter to bugger off and is taking out his smartphone."

"Indeed. It looks like Steve is calling him and they might be coordinating their moves. Okay, all four of them are starting to get up," says Michael.

"So are the ones I'm seeing. They're regrouping and slowly coming towards us in a close diamond formation on my left aisle," says Sarah. She tenses up and her heart is beating fast. Taking out four armed men in close quarters is absolutely no walk in the park!

"Same as what I see, on *my* left aisle," says Michael. He then gives Sarah some orders in a calm and assertive tone of voice. "On my signal, we will both stand and turn around to the right. The person at the back, Steve Dunbar, will be the assassin. He'll be hiding the gun behind the person in front. Steve is the immediate threat so you should take him out as soon as possible."

Michael's command voice calms her down. Sarah normally doesn't like being under the command of someone she hasn't trained with, but she's comfortable with Michael leading her through this ambush.

Michael continues. "They're now ten metres away. Standby for my signal… Standby… Standby… Go!"

Sarah jumps up, turns around, and goes forward, screaming at the top of her lungs! She can hear Michael doing the exact same thing. SCAN. As if in super-slow motion, Sarah sees four surprised, panicking men in front of her starting to reach for their pistols, while Steve, whose pistol is already drawn but hidden from view, pushes the man in front of him to get his sights on Sarah. ACQUIRE. Sarah aims towards Steve's centre mass. SHOOT. SHOOT. Sarah shoots him twice in rapid succession. ACQUIRE. Sarah makes sure both of her shots hit her target and sees Steve fall backwards before he's able to discharge his weapon. SCAN. Sarah sees the other three starting to react and she keeps moving forward, which really panics them. The one on the far right manages to draw his pistol. He's now the immediate threat. ACQUIRE. SHOOT. SHOOT. ACQUIRE. SCAN. Sarah sees one of them is so panicky that he accidentally drops his pistol while the other is having trouble drawing his pistol from his holster. That man's now the immediate threat. ACQUIRE. SHOOT. SHOOT. ACQUIRE. SCAN. The last man is bending down, trying to reach for his pistol. Sarah aims for his head, now at point-blank range. ACQUIRE. SHOOT. SHOOT. ACQUIRE. SCAN. Her ears are ringing as she changes magazines, all the time scanning around for more people trying to ambush them.

Everything is over in seven seconds, from the time Sarah rose from her chair to the time she finished changing magazines.

"Four Tangos down!" shouts Sarah.

"Four X-Rays down!" shouts Michael.

Sarah glances towards Michael and sees that he too managed to take all four of his attackers down, all shot in the head. Michael and Sarah calmly but quickly move towards the kitchen door. Sarah glances toward the dining area and sees the patrons starting to panic. Some of them throw themselves on the floor, but most try to escape through the front door. A group of men seem intent on entering the restaurant, but they are held up by patrons trying desperately to exit.

"Take point, I'll cover you," orders Michael, keeping an eye on the men held up at the front door.

"Copy," answers Sarah.

Sarah carefully opens the kitchen door with her pistol in a low ready position. SCAN. Sarah sees two men pointing their pistols towards the kitchen staff. One of them is facing the kitchen door. He instantly recognizes Sarah and starts pointing his pistol towards her. ACQUIRE. SHOOT. SHOOT. ACQUIRE. SCAN. The other Tango makes the mistake of turning towards her instead of taking cover. AQUIRE. SHOOT. SHOOT. ACQUIRE. SCAN. Sarah has succeeded in taking two more men down without even one of them able to return fire.

"Two Tangos down!" shouts Sarah. Everyone inside the kitchen is too scared to move. "Everyone! Keep your heads low and bugger off through the front door! Move! Move it!"

Everyone follows her orders except two women who can only crouch down and scream hysterically, both hands covering their ringing ears.

"Move it! Move it!" she orders again, grabbing them by the hair and directing them towards the door to the dining area. She does that while also scanning the area for more hostiles.

Michael does the same to the two women until they both exit the kitchen. The kitchen area is almost as spacious as the dining area. The rear exit is on the left corner and Sarah immediately heads towards it.

"Stand firm, Sarah!" orders Michael. "It's likely they have people guarding the rear exit."

"What do you suggest?"

"Let's barricade ourselves until the GMP arrives. Call Paul and have him call the North West CT Unit. Remind Paul to tell them to watch out for friendlies barricaded inside the stronghold," suggests Michael, turning off all the lights.

"Copy," answers Sarah.

The kitchen goes dark except, unfortunately, for light still coming from various appliances. While taking cover behind a heavy counter, Sarah tries to call Paul, but he doesn't answer his phone. She then contacts Arthur. When he answers, Sarah calmly reports what's happening to them. Arthur panics, but immediately contacts the commander of the North West Counter Terrorism Unit.

"Cover the rear exit and I'll cover the front," orders Michael.

"Copy," answers Sarah.

Sarah has to think like the opposition so she can anticipate their next move. She also has to keep asking herself 'what if?' For example, what if the Tangos manage to overrun Michael? What if her pistol has a stoppage? What if more than four men attack her from the rear exit? What if she runs out of ammo?

Sarah observes the rear exit and sees that the handle is on the left side and the hinges are unseen, which means the door opens outwards. This means that if men trained in CQB attack her from that door, the pointman will have to execute a move called a 'crisscross'. The pointman will try to secure the whole room from the back of the kitchen to the front while hugging the walls. The second man will have to perform a move called a 'buttonhook' in which, upon his entrance, he immediately heads towards the front of the kitchen. She takes a position so she can shoot the first two men who enter from the rear exit. Her position will be a blind spot for the pointman, who will most likely execute a crisscross.

Sarah takes a Glock 17 pistol from one of the Tangos she shot. Using firearms taken from the enemy is *not* recommended, but Sarah doesn't have a choice because she only has a total of six bullets left and she doesn't have a backup pistol. The comments of Michael, Matt, and Broussard on the amount of ammo she carries come back to haunt her, but there's no use regretting that now.

Sarah checks the Glock for a moment and sees it has sixteen bullets with one still in the chamber. She must rely on Michael to cover the front, just like he has to rely on Sarah to cover the rear. Sarah wants to take another mag from the Tango, but fears she doesn't have much time.

Sarah's decision is correct. Suddenly, both the front and back doors of the kitchen fly open at the same time. It looks like the opposition have once again coordinated their move. Sarah sees someone enter from the back door. As she predicted, the Tango performs a crisscross. He's hesitant entering the dark kitchen so Sarah can easily shoot him twice in his upper waist. The second Tango is stunned and can only freeze at the door when he sees his friend getting shot, which gives Sarah the opportunity to drill him twice in the head.

"Two Tangos down!" shouts Sarah.

"Two X-Rays down!" shouts Michael.

Sarah forces herself to wait for ten seconds to see whether there'll be more coming in from the back door while listening to the fierce battle raging behind her. After ten seconds, Sarah peeks behind her. She can see two Tangos on the floor with headshots near the front door but there are six Tangos shooting at Michael, who's shooting towards them from behind a counter with his pistol. Of the six Tangos, three are shooting from the door and the rest have already entered the kitchen, trying to flank Michael from his blind side. The three Tangos don't realize they're passing near Sarah's position.

Once they pass her, Sarah stands up and shoots two of them in the back with two shots each. Instead of dropping to the ground, all three Tangos turn around and point their weapons at her! Sarah immediately throws herself behind some cover, in time to hear four shots. She momentarily sees a couple of golf ball-sized exit wounds in the faces of the two Tangos when their heads are shot at close range from behind them.

"Two X-Rays down... Reload!" shouts Michael.

Sarah must act quickly so she can help Michael. She gets up again and gives the Tango a double-tap to his head, just as he was about to shoot

Michael. The Tango is dead before his body reaches the floor and Sarah drops to the ground when more shots are fired from behind her, riddling the tables and appliances all around her with bullets.

"Tango down!" shouts Sarah while moving from her position.

"Four X-Rays from Green-10!" shouts Michael.

"What the fuck are you talking about?" shouts Sarah angrily.

"Four X-Rays coming in from the back-left side of the kitchen!" shouts Michael once again.

Sarah peeks to the back-left, but she doesn't see anyone. She takes a plate and throws it towards the back-right side of the kitchen. Four Tangos suddenly stand up in the back-left side of the kitchen and shoot their pistols at the sound of the shattering plate. Sarah aims her pistol towards their heads, aware now that some of them are wearing body armour. Sarah's first two rounds find their target, but only one of her next two rounds does the same. Her next six rounds hit nothing as the two remaining Tangos have thrown themselves to the ground and are now hidden from view. Sarah's Glock is empty so she throws it away and reverts to her HK P2000, which she remembers still has four bullets plus two in the other mag.

Sarah rushes towards the Tangos before they can react, but there are shots fired from the front door. She empties her pistol that way to keep the shooters down while rushing towards the two remaining Tangos at the back-left side of the kitchen. The Tangos are nowhere to be seen and Sarah doesn't know where they went. She takes cover, changes mags, then makes her way towards the back of the kitchen. They're not there either, so she takes a right and slams into one of them who has just finished reloading his revolver. Both panic, but Sarah is faster and shoots the Tango through his chin and left cheek. Sarah's gun is now empty but the Tango is still alive, screaming at the top of his lungs. Sarah throws away her empty pistol, takes out her knife, and stabs him in the chest.

Reluctantly, Sarah takes the revolver from the Tango, who is still in his death throes. She shoots him twice in the head to ensure he doesn't get up again. Now she looks for the other Tango and finally sees him towards the front of the kitchen, starting to raise his pistol in Michael's direction. She rushes forward, shooting blindly. Although the Tango is huge, all her shots have missed. The Tango, who turns out to be Donald 'Tiny' Mullins, turns around and points his gun toward Sarah as she runs directly at him. Sarah knows she won't be fast enough so she throws herself into the air to deliver a flying kick to Tiny's chest. Tiny manages to squeeze the trigger and a single shot is fired at the same time Sarah's feet land on his chest.

Sarah's surprised to bounce right off. At first she thought that Tiny was wearing body armour, but it turns out he's only wearing a shirt. Sarah was bounced off just by his rock-hard pectoral muscles. Fortunately, Tiny was thrown off balance and he accidentally slams his hand on the corner of a counter, which makes him drop his pistol. Sarah stands up immediately before Tiny can reach his gun and gives him a powerful kick to the chin. Sarah's kick would've knocked out almost anyone, but Tiny doesn't seem to feel it. She's worried he might do the same to her so she kicks the pistol out of his reach and grabs a steak knife from a table. Meanwhile, she becomes aware that the firefight at the front of the kitchen has stopped. The enemy must be running out of men.

Tiny steps into a boxing stance as if he's in a boxing ring. Sarah remembers that he was a boxer and she knows that if he hits her in the head, it's game over. Tiny starts throwing some jabs, but Sarah keeps evading him. She manages to duck when he throws her a left-straight but he then suddenly moves forward and throws a right-uppercut smack into her solar plexus. Sarah clenches her abs and lets Tiny hit her. Tiny's punch is so hard that her body is lifted a few inches off the floor! Tiny's staggers a bit when his fist only bounces off of her, so Sarah takes the chance to move forward and stab the steak knife hard into Tiny's heart.

Unexpectedly, the thin knife breaks on contact with Tiny's chest. Without even the time to be surprised by that, Sarah kicks Tiny's right knee. He falls, but sends her a vicious left-straight towards her stomach. Tiny's punch is much harder than before because he used his whole body weight to deliver the blow. Sarah staggers back, but Tiny's fist again seems to bounce off her. Tiny's not the only one with rock-hard muscles. Sarah recovers her balance and moves forward to kick him in the neck. She connects and he falls on his back.

Sarah then grabs another sharp object nearest to her, which turns out to be a cheap pen from the waiters' station. She jumps on top of a counter and throws her body on top of Tiny. In the air, Sarah positions the back of the pen in the middle of her abdomen and the tip of the pen towards Tiny's chest. Just before she lands on top of him, Sarah clenches her abs so that her body weight is focused on the tip of the pen when it punches through Tiny's chest.

Tiny screams out loud when the pen goes into his chest! He throws Sarah away from him and struggles to pull the pen out. She ignores him for a moment to look around and sees Michael wrestling a couple of Tangos. Michael manages to kick one of them in the chest, which has him falling on his arse towards Sarah, who is only a couple of metres behind him. Sarah reaches for another sharp object, another steak knife, and throws herself onto the Tango, stabbing him in the soft tissue below his right ear. The steak knife slams into where she was aiming. The Tango drops like a sack of potatoes and starts convulsing on the floor. Sarah grabs his hair and begins slamming his head repeatedly until she finally hears his skull crack open and sees blood and grey matter spreading on the floor.

Sarah is on her knees, trying to catch her breath when she glances towards Michael, who has someone in a choke hold. Sarah can identify the choking man as Declan Mulcahy from James's file and Michael is in the process of breaking his neck. Although the kitchen is dark, Sarah can see the look of utter horror in Declan's eyes. His eyes are wide open in fear when he looks at Sarah, but they suddenly lose focus at the same time Sarah hears his neck snap. Looking into his eyes, Sarah sees Declan's soul leave his body, even though she knows she's only imagining it.

Michael throws Declan's dead body to the ground and takes another pistol from the floor. After checking it, he gives Declan's head a double-tap. Michael approaches the other slain or dying Tangos to finish them off with double-taps to the head as well.

A hand suddenly grabs Sarah's leg! She's jolted, but then she sees Tiny writhing on the floor behind her. Pink, oxygenized blood is frothing from Tiny's mouth, which means that his lung is punctured. Sarah steps away from him for a moment to do a 360. There are a couple of Tangos near the front door still writhing around and moaning. Sarah sees Michael go over to them to shut them up with his pistol.

Sarah crouches down to check on the big man. If Sarah can save him, he can tell her the location of their drug factory in Indonesia. It seems unlikely, though, as the pen looks to have also nicked his heart. Tiny seems to know that he's dying and he looks absolutely terrified. His hand is reaching out towards Sarah, as if he's trying to grab her hand. There's nothing Sarah can do for him except take his hand to keep him company when he finally meets the Ángel de la Muerte. Tiny cries when Sarah squeezes his hand and prays 'Padre Nuestro' to him. Sarah watches Tiny's tearful eyes looking back at her. His grasp grows weaker by the second until, once again, Sarah sees someone's soul leave his body. Tiny's hand goes limp and his eyes now empty of all expression.

Two shots are fired from behind her! At the same time, Sarah sees Tiny's right eye and nose suddenly look as though they are sucked into his head. Sarah looks back and sees Michael calmly step away to finish off the others.

Sarah finds Tiny's pistol. After checking it, she covers Michael as he finishes off the remaining Tangos. In the kitchen area alone, she counts fifteen dead Tangos, and that's on top of the eight they killed in the dining area. Between them, they've managed to kill twenty-three Cartel members including Donald Mullins and Steve Dunbar. Even with adrenaline still pumping, both Michael and Sarah can immediately figure out what went wrong with The Cartel's ambush. The Cartel attacked them in waves instead of all at once, enabling Michael and Sarah to pick them off one-by-one from concealed positions, even though the opposition had a twelve-to-one advantage. Also, like infantrymen everywhere, they were lousy pistol shooters. The darkened kitchen didn't help their aim either.

After making sure all Tangos have at least two bullets in their heads, Sarah hears Michael mumble to himself. "Stronghold secured."

Through their ringing ears, they finally hear the sirens of the GMP.

"Do you know anyone from the North West CT Unit?" asks Sarah. Her voice is calm although her heart is still racing and adrenaline is still surging through her body.

"Negative," answers Michael.

They both clear their weapons and throw them away. They kneel facing the front door with both hands behind their heads. Sarah feels some pain in her left forearm, but maintains the uncomfortable position.

"When they storm in, yell 'blue-on-blue' out loud," orders Michael. "Is that clear?"

"Copy," answers Sarah.

A few seconds later, both the front and back doors open simultaneously and black-uniformed police storm in, shouting 'armed police'. Michael and Sarah immediately answer with 'blue-on-blue', signalling that they are on the same side. As expected, the armed police consider them as suspects until proven otherwise. Some officers point their MP5s at Michael and Sarah's heads while others cuff them. They pick them up and slam them on top of a counter. A police officer gives Sarah a professional frisk, including her chest and groin area, and takes her wallet. Sarah is told to stand and another police officer flashes his torch at her face.

"Name and unit?" asks the armed police officer with his Mancunian accent.

"Inspector Sarah Michelle Dharmawan, Interpol Manchester," answers Sarah.

"Place and date of birth?"

"Jakarta, 30$^{th}$ of April, 2002."

"From Indonesia, eh?" asks the police officer, giving her a disbelieving look. "Now say 'I love you' in Bahasa."

"*Aku cinta padamu*," says Sarah.

The police officer is stunned for few seconds. "C-C-Could you... ehm... you know... ehm... look into my eyes and... ehm... s-s-say it again... please?"

"*Aku cinta padamu*," says Sarah, giving him a smile.

The police officer is stunned again for a few seconds and then starts scrambling for his smartphone. "Okay then... all I need now is your phone number..."

"Will you get on with it?" yells Michael, still face down on top of the counter. Unfortunately for him, the counter is covered in sliced and diced vegetables.

"Right, so who the *fook* are you?" asks the police officer.

He gives a signal to another officer to release Sarah and hauls Michael up. He takes Michael's wallet and takes out his ID card.

"Major Michael Adrian, British Army," answers Michael, his Irish accent more pronounced than usual.

"Where do you come from?"

"Ireland."

"I can hear that, you stupid mick. Which part of Ireland?"

"Belfast," answers Michael, starting to pout.

"Date of birth?"

"15th of December, 1997."

"Now say somethin' in Gaelic," orders the police officer.

"*Póg mo thóin!*" answers Michael without any hesitation.

"Yeah, right. I knew you were goin' to say that, you *fook*in' arsehole," says the police officer, taking off the handcuffs. "Now get the *fook* out of here while we sort your *fookin'* mess!"

"Wanker," mumbles Michael, cleaning his hair and face of bits and pieces of vegetables.

Michael and Sarah start walking toward the dining area when another police officer, kneeling near Tiny's dead body, asks from behind them. "Which one of you killed this *fookin'* monster?"

"I did," answers Sarah.

"How the *fook* did you manage to ram a pen into his *fookin'* chest?" he asks, giving her an incredulous look.

"You can read it in my AAR," answers Sarah curtly.

Michael leads Sarah out of the building. Arthur is waiting anxiously for them. He looks pale and dishevelled.

Arthur sees Michael and hurriedly goes over to him. "All right, mate?"

"We're fine, Arthur," answers Michael.

Arthur sees Sarah behind him and hugs her. "Oh thank God you're all right!" he says, his voice shaking.

"Hey, I could use a hug too, you know."

"Piss off, Michael," says Arthur without looking at him.

Arthur suddenly realizes that Sarah's returning his hug with only one arm. He sees blood on her left arm.

"Oh, fuck! Let's get you to a medic," says Arthur, panicking again and directing them to one of the ambulances.

They wait while Sarah is treated by a paramedic. The bullet has made a deep slash on her forearm, but hasn't hit any bones. It isn't that dangerous, luckily, as it has gone nowhere near her radial artery. The medic can treat her on the spot, but he urges her to go to the hospital for antibiotics.

"I'll clean the wound with antiseptics and close it with some Dermabond Advanced, but I want to give you some lidocaine beforehand. All right?" suggests the medic.

"No thank you on the painkillers," says Sarah firmly.

"Are you sure? It will be quite painful," the medic urges once again.

Sarah only shakes her head and the medic continues his treatment. The antiseptic really smarts when it touches her wound, but Sarah doesn't show that she's in pain and only closes her eyes. In the middle of Sarah's treatment, Broussard finally arrives with his team. All bar Paul. They're relieved when they see their teammates are still alive. Broussard and Arthur stay with them and the others are ordered to assist the GMP at the crime scene. Paul finally arrives, panting and looking quite pale, but is immediately ordered to go inside the restaurant.

Broussard talks to both of them, his voice shaking. "Thank God you two are all right! I will sort this one out, but I order both of you to return to HQ, re-arm yourselves, and to deliver the After Action Report immediately. After that, you have a twenty-four hour 'warm down period'. You two have been working almost seven days a week since the beginning of this and I really appreciate it, so I'd prefer both of you take the rest of the week off for some R&R. Stay away from Manchester, but please stay online at all times. I require both of you to be back at the office on Monday morning next week, is that clear?"

"Clear, Chief," they answer.

Broussard looks at Sarah's wound for a while before heading towards the restaurant. He has to report Sarah's condition to the Secretariat NCB Indonesia and Police Brigadier General Prasetyo.

The medic is finally finished treating Sarah. "You'll take a tetanus shot, right?"

Sarah nods and rolls her sleeve all the way up while the men admire her toned arm and shoulder. The medic gives the shot intramuscularly into her firm deltoid muscle. After that, the medic takes something out of his wallet.

"If you need anythin', call me at this number anytime. All right?" says the medic, giving her his business card.

Sarah smiles and thanks him. They head towards Michael's car in the car park. Michael briefly gives the medic a mean look before leaving him.

"How the fuck did they manage to find you?" asks Arthur incredulously.

Michael and Sarah can only shake their heads.

"Arthur, we're unarmed," says Michael. "Maybe you can help arrange an armed escort for us to GMP HQ?"

"Right, I'll handle it," says Arthur. He leaves them to make arrangements.

A few minutes later, a Land Rover Defender from the North West CT Unit arrives to escort them to GMP HQ.

# CHAPTER 6
# THE 22ND REGIMENT, SPECIAL AIR SERVICE

21:48 GMT
Monday July 27, 2026
Interpol Manchester
Central Park, Manchester, England

Sarah finishes filling out the AAR form, the After-Action Report, and sends it to her teammates. She and Michael have taken Glock 17 pistols and mags from the GMP armoury. This makes them feel slightly safer, but they won't be happy until they've broken in the new pistols and the GMP's indoor firing range is already closed. Sarah only sits, staring blankly at her tablet.

"All right, Sarah?" asks Michael from his desk. He has also finished sending his AAR.

"Not quite," answers Sarah, looking at him.

Michael can see tears in her eyes. He can clearly see that Sarah's suffering from combat stress, a condition that can affect anybody after a firefight, even special forces operatives. If left untreated, it could lead to Post Traumatic Stress Disorder (PTSD). Ironically, since the early 2020s, the best treatment for PTSD is MDMA-assisted psychotherapy, though Michael knows for sure that Sarah wouldn't even consider taking drugs to alleviate her stress.

"Well, there's a nice pub at the Holiday Inn across the street," says Michael, rising from his chair. "Come on. I think we both need a drink or two."

Sarah doesn't answer, but stands up and follows him. They take Michael's car across Oldham Road and enter the hotel's 888 Restaurant & Bar. The 888 looks comfortable and is perfect for their current mood. It's quiet and empty of patrons. The bar is well-stocked and the dining area in front of it is lit by candles on every table. Soft music plays throughout, and under other circumstances, the ambience would be fairly romantic.

A barman greets Sarah with gleaming eyes. "Good evenin', love. What would you like to drink?"

Sarah looks at the bottles behind him. "A triple Macallan please."

"And how about you, sir?" asks the barman, curtly. Michael is giving him a mean look.

"Guinness!" orders Michael, equally curt.

They don't talk as the barman prepares their drinks. It takes two minutes to pour the perfect Guinness and Michael is impatient waiting for it.

"Anythin' else, love?" asks the barman, serving her the whiskey.

"No, thank you," answers Sarah.

"And you, sir?" he asks curtly, handing Michael his Guinness.

"No… now piss off!"

The barman wipes the bar in front of them for a moment before returning to Sarah. "If you need anythin' else, love, just give me a yell," he says, giving her a wink before leaving them.

'Wanker!' thinks Michael, giving him a dirty look.

They drink in silence. Michael's first gulp of Guinness tastes like it's God-sent, especially after the day they've had. He enjoys it for a moment and then notices Sarah's eyes are moist again.

"Do you want to talk about it?" he asks gently.

Sarah still can't talk and her tears start flowing instead. She keeps silent for a couple of minutes before she's finally able to say something.

"I'm sorry," she says softly.

"For what?"

"You must think I'm weak… crying in front of you like this," she answers, wiping the tears from her eyes.

"What makes you think I won't be doing the same thing in a few minutes from now?"

"Well, it looks like killing people doesn't affect you. So what are you? A natural-born killer or something?" asks Sarah sharply.

Under different circumstances, Michael might've been offended by that question, but today he doesn't take it personally. This is an extraordinary day for both and he can also see that the whiskey is already starting to get the better of her. "I slot people because it's my job and I definitely don't enjoy it. I experience combat stress like everyone else, but usually a couple of hours after the action."

"Really?"

"The delayed shock, when adrenaline finally leaves the system, makes me feel nauseous. I'll probably start trembling and vomiting in about… fifteen minutes from now," he says, glancing at his Bremont.

They go silent again, trying to enjoy their drinks.

"Is this the first time you've ever slotted someone?" asks Michael.

Sarah only shakes her head and she suddenly remembers every time she's been forced to end a life. The first time she had to kill someone, she couldn't eat or sleep for two straight days. On that occasion, a cornered suspect suddenly drew a pistol and shot at one of her men. Fortunately, the policeman was unhurt because he was wearing body armour. Sarah remembers exactly how the suspect reacted when two bullets from Sarah's pistol went through his heart. After a couple of days trying to keep it to herself, she'd finally poured her heart out to her dad, who'd had plenty of combat experience. Her dad comforted her and told her that he also felt the same way after his first firefight, although he never did tell her the details.

Sarah doesn't mind roughing up criminals. She has no problem taking them down and breaking a few bones. Broken bones take months to heal, time for criminals to reflect on their lifestyles. Some of them actually repent and eventually become law-abiding citizens. This is different to criminals shot in the leg for 'escaping arrest', who tend to be proud of their scars and show them off to women and fellow criminals.

But killing someone is another matter. Although Sarah has taken the lives of quite a few criminals and terrorists, her conscience still bothers her and makes her remember every single person she has killed.

Sarah is silent for a few more minutes before she's finally able to speak. "I was looking straight into Declan's eyes when you broke his neck… I saw the sheer terror in his eyes just before it happened. The same thing happened with Tiny. I literally saw the Ángel de la Muerte take their lives away. How do you forget something like that, Michael?"

"You accept that you'll never forget it. It's a good thing, really, less you become desensitized to it. Taking the life of another human being is certainly not a natural act. You reacting like this shows that you're only human," says Michael, "and what you did for Tiny in his last few seconds of his life was very kind of you. You're a good person, Sarah."

Sarah finishes her drink and keeps silent for a few moments. Bad memories from this evening flash through her mind and tears start landing in her empty glass.

"Here, come with me," says Michael, taking her hand and directing her to the empty space behind them.

He puts her arms around his waist and presses her head toward his chest. He hugs her with his left arm and uses his right hand to caress her hair. As before, they feel jolts of electricity when they touch. Sarah feels so comfortable on Michael's hard chest that she cries unashamedly, covering his expensive tie with her tears. After a few minutes, she calms down and releases her head from his chest, although they're still hugging each other.

"I'm sorry for burdening you with this and for ruining your tie," says Sarah, smiling at him.

"It's the least I can do, Sarah. You did save my life back there," says Michael, returning her smile. "If you hadn't taken on those three who flanked me and then taken on Tiny, I would certainly be dead by now. Thank you... for twice saving my life."

Sarah smiles and blushes, making her so beautiful that Michael can't take his eyes off her. But Michael's own words remind him of today's events and he himself starts to tense up thinking about everything. Michael imagines that if Sarah had been just a few seconds late, he would be dead, or at least severely wounded, shot by the three men or by Tiny. Michael owes his life to Sarah, especially since she got wounded saving his neck.

"I didn't have the chance to read your AAR," says Michael, trying to change the subject. "How *did* you manage to ram a pen into Tiny's chest and into his heart?"

"After I knocked him on his back, I threw myself on top of him while putting the rear side of a pen I found against my abdominal muscles. My body weight then helped ram the pen into his chest."

"Wow! You literally have 'killer abs' then," says Michael, trying hard to smile at her.

Sarah laughs. She's now far less stressed than a few minutes ago. Michael, on the other hand, feels the opposite. As adrenaline starts exiting his system, he feels increasingly jittery and tense. His hands are starting to shake and he becomes nauseous. He's now feeling like someone who drank too much caffeine or someone having symptoms from drug withdrawal. He wants to throw up, but of course he doesn't want to do it in front of Sarah.

They now face each other with locked eyes. They can feel each other's heartbeat starting to speed up. The electricity between them feels so powerful... a feeling that makes them sometimes forget to breathe. Their breathing becomes heavier by the second... their lips getting closer... and closer...

"Sarah?" asks Michael softly.

"Yes?" whispers Sarah. Her eyes are watery, but not from stress this time.

"May I kiss you?" whispers Michael.

Sarah is briefly irritated. 'Our lips are literally millimetres apart and you're still *asking*?' she thinks.

"Yes..." whispers Sarah, closing her eyes. Her heart is racing and her lips are close to his, ready to be kissed.

Michael suddenly releases her. "Splendid... remind me to do that sometime. Come on, I'll drive you home."

He then goes to the bar to finish his Guinness and pay for the drinks while Sarah can only stand there, open-mouthed. She now feels so exasperated, frustrated, and irritated with Michael that she wants to wring his neck! She was really hoping that he'd kiss her and the timing was so perfect. Sarah hasn't realized yet that it's her turn to be a rock for Michael.

They exit the restaurant with Sarah fuming and pouting behind him. Inside the car, Michael only sits there for a while without starting the engine. Sarah can see that Michael's knuckles look pale, meaning that his hands are gripping hard onto the steering wheel.

"Is it starting?" asks Sarah.

"Yes..." answers Michael, half whispering.

"Do you want me to drive?"

"No! Let me handle this... please!" answers Michael curtly. He then turns on the engine.

Sarah doesn't take it personally and instead holds his shaking hand. Michael drives without talking and Sarah can see that his eyes are glassy. Sarah makes a decision.

"Come inside," invites Sarah when they arrive at her building.

Sarah leads him to her flat. Once inside, Sarah throws herself on to him and kisses him passionately.

After a couple of minutes, Michael releases his lips. "Are you sure about this?"

"Yes, Michael," answers Sarah firmly.

Sarah releases herself from Michael and takes off her jumper. She's now in a white bra and blue jeans. Michael can see that Sarah's body is far more ripped than the photo of her he keeps posted behind his office door at Credenhill. She has broad, athletic shoulders and a slim waist. Her breasts are the perfect shape and size. Most of all, Michael is impressed with Sarah's perfect six-pack abs. Sarah's skin is light-tan and looks silky-smooth and well-maintained, much more exotic than the pale, freckled British women he normally dates.

Michael also starts taking off his jacket, tie, and shirt. Sarah can now see Michael's broad chest and shoulders. There are numerous scars on his body, probably from a bomb, mortar, or grenade. Unfortunately, he's sporting a pot-belly. She also notices he's taking off his clothes with shaking hands.

Sarah takes both of his hands and looks at him. "All right?"

Michael only nods. It's not just combat stress that makes his hands shake. In the next few minutes, Michael will be intimate with someone whom he's idolized for the last couple of years and he's worried he might disappoint her.

"Nervous?" asks Sarah once again.

Michael can only nod again.

"Is this your first time?" teases Sarah.

"Of course not," answers Michael, returning her smile. "I've been nervous many times before."

Sarah laughs upon recognizing the 'Airplane!' quote and kisses him hard on his lips. They are now a couple.

23:54 GMT
Monday July 27, 2026
Audenshaw Road
Audenshaw, Manchester, England

After the battle, The Cartel's drivers conduct counter-surveillance measures and then meet at the emergency rendezvous. The remaining assault force had to abandon their colleagues because they'd run out of ammo and faced a big chance of getting killed or caught if they'd diddled around.

After all cars have shown up, they do another round of counter-surveillance measures, all the way to HQ. Everyone's waiting for them, looking pale. Their battle at Carluccio's is breaking news, but the reporters only said that dozens of people had been killed in the restaurant.

"How was the exfil? Did ye get away clean?" asks Rory.

"All of the drivers did the drills like ye taught them," answers Steve. He looks deathly white and Seamus is shaken and crying.

"What the fuck happened?" asks Patrick, relieved that his brother is one of the survivors.

"We tried to ambush them like we had planned, but they counterattacked just before we initiated the ambush. That fucking policewoman would've killed *me* if I wasn't wearing body armour!" says Steve, showing them the two bullets still embedded in his Kevlar vest.

"Are ye saying those two managed to slot twenty-two of our members by themselves?" asks Patrick incredulously.

"Fuck, Paddy! One of them was SAS, for Christ's sake!" says Steve. "And that girl is definitely no ordinary policewoman. The last time I saw her, she was taking on Tiny while Declan and another was fighting the SAS fella. I don't know what happened to them."

"Tiny's fucking dead! Our contact in the GMP said that that fucking policewoman rammed a pen straight into his fucking heart!" says Patrick.

Steve's jaw drops and he's speechless. Killing an ex-special forces operative with just a pen is definitely not an ordinary feat!

"We should've brought longs," says Rory.

Everyone can only nod in agreement. They're much more adept with assault rifles than pistols.

# THE POLICEWOMAN

"There were only two targets and ye couldn't hit even one of them?" teases Niall. He's frustrated that they didn't succeed in snatching Sarah and doesn't care that a lot of the men have been killed. "I thought ye're an expert with a pistol?"

"Why don't *ye* try shooting a fucking moving target after *ye* were almost fucking slotted!" snarls Steve, punching his finger into Niall's chest.

"Fuck off, Niall!" snaps Patrick. Niall only snorts and looks away. Patrick then asks Rory, "Any chance the coppers can find our HQ or Swan's Mill?"

"I don't think so but we should beef up security, especially for Swan's Mill," suggests Rory.

"We'll smuggle Swan's Mill a couple dozen more longs and all our PE4 with Seamus just in case they managed to trace it," orders Patrick.

"We've lost almost all the fellas from Swan's Mill, Paddy," says Steve.

"Better dead than apprehended. They won't be able to interrogate the dead fellas," says Patrick.

"When do we retaliate?" asks Carraig.

Patrick takes a long breath. He has lost too many men against those Interpol bastards and there are times he has to cut his losses... for now.

"I'll think of something," says Patrick, evading the question. "For now, ye fellas should go and get some rest."

Patrick makes a call to Swan's Mill. He can only accept his fate when his feisty factory head reams him a new arsehole for losing almost all the men from Swan's Mill.

After years of operations, this is the first time members of The Cartel have been killed.

06:35 GMT
Tuesday July 28, 2026
Stay Deansgate Apartments
Deansgate, Manchester, England

The next morning, Michael slowly opens his eyes. He's briefly disoriented, but then he remembers what happened to him the night before. He's now on his back, wearing only his undershirt and boxers. He's sore all over, but feeling relaxed. He doesn't see Sarah beside him, but hears scratching sounds on the floor on the right side of the bed. There's a nightstand on the right side of the bed and on top of it are Sarah's Glock, mags, and handcuffs. Michael keeps looking at the handcuffs and his fantasies go wild.

"You want me to wear them, don't you?" asks Sarah's voice from the floor on his right.

Michael is stunned. He shifts his body to the right and looks down. Sarah's doing her crunches. She has put on her jeans again, but is only wearing a white bra. The bandage is still on her left arm and a military watch on her right wrist. She's glistening with sweat, making the muscles of her six-pack stand out, especially when they're clenched.

"Good morning," greets Michael, evading her question.

"*Bonjour*," Sarah returns his greeting with sparkling eyes. "Why don't you come down here and join me?"

"No, thank you," answers Michael. "I'm getting knackered just watching *you*."

Sarah laughs, making her abdominal muscles even more pronounced. Michael absolutely loves athletic girls. He can't help but be mesmerized staring at Sarah's abs as she does her crunches. His hand comes down to caress her sweaty stomach.

"Come on, you could use some exercise," says Sarah.

"You already gave me one hell of a workout," says Michael.

Sarah laughs.

"Twice," says Michael.

Sarah laughs again.

"How many times do you do this every day?" asks Michael.

"Only a thousand times," answers Sarah proudly.

"Wow! Can your abs stop bullets?"

"Of course, but only small calibre rounds," answers Sarah, laughing.

"How long have you been doing this?"

"Since I was twelve years old."

"Really? Who inspired you?"

"I once saw a picture of a fitness model with such a perfect body. Her name is Jen Selter. Have you ever heard of her?" asks Sarah.

"I have indeed," answers Michael sheepishly.

Sarah's abs are as perfect as Jen Selter's and Michael can't stop touching them. He starts tapping her stomach with his finger, as if counting.

"What are you doing?" asks Sarah.

"I have a new hobby and it's counting your six-pack. One, two, three, four, five, six… one, two, three, four, five, six. I could do this all day long."

Sarah laughs. She keeps doing her crunches while Michael's finger finally finds Sarah's navel and starts snuggling deeply into it. Sarah is tickled but continues her crunches, crushing Michael's finger with her abdominal muscles as she does so.

"Ouch!" exclaims Michael, smiling.

Sarah laughs again. She suddenly lifts herself up, throws her arms around Michael's neck, and gives him a very hard kiss. She can't stand having her navel played with like that.

After a few seconds, Sarah releases him and looks deep into his eyes. "*Tu te sens comment*?"

"Spectacular!" answers Michael, smiling. "You?"

"*Fantastique! Merci… pour une nuit incroyable!*" Sarah returns his smile and gives him another hard kiss.

Sarah stands up and looks at herself through the mirror in front of her. She sees Michael admiring her as she checks her own six-pack. She turns towards him.

"How are my abs?" she asks with both hands on her hips.

Michael can now admire them from up close. Sarah's abs are as hard as the tyres on his bike and the ridges are cut very deep. He then starts kissing Sarah's abdomen, beginning from her sternum and going downwards. As they're a new couple, the electricity feels so powerful that Sarah starts breathing heavily. Michael uses his tongue to trace Sarah's stomach until he finally reaches her navel. He bites into the upper lip of her navel and then inserts his tongue into it. Sarah moans loudly when he does that and starts to pull Michael towards the ground. But Michael instead lifts her up, turns around, and places Sarah gently on the bed. He then sits on top of her thighs.

With an excited look, Michael takes the handcuffs from the nightstand, puts Sarah's arms above her head, and cuffs her wrists to the bedpost. Sarah has never done this before, but because she's so comfortable with

Michael, she becomes even more aroused. Michael gives her a lingering kiss and starts going down towards her neck. Sarah's breathing is already heavy when he starts kissing her chest and heads downwards to her stomach. Michael keeps tracing the muscles of her abs with his lips and tongue until Sarah gives another loud moan.

Unfortunately, Michael's own stomach growls in hunger because he hadn't eaten anything the night before.

"Sarah?" asks Michael, still kissing her stomach.

"Yes?" murmurs Sarah with her heavy breath and closed eyes.

"Are you ticklish?"

Sarah's eyes snap open. She sees Michael grinning at her wickedly. "Dare tickle me and I will kill you with my bare hands!"

"Really? With which hand?" asks Michael as his own hands start touching her slim waist.

"You don't believe me, do you?" she asks, giving him an evil eye. "Watch this!"

Two loud cracks are heard and the cuffs somehow fly off her wrists. Michael suddenly feels himself flying and then finds himself on his back. He doesn't even have the chance to realize what's happening when Sarah lands on top of his stomach and presses her forearm to his throat.

"How the devil... did you... do... that?" asks Michael, choking like a fish out of water.

"Densus taught all of us how to get out of handcuffs. Surrender?" asks Sarah, raising an eyebrow.

"Uncle... uncle!" gasps Michael, surrendering before he literally suffocates to death. He had completely forgotten that Sarah's bare hands are extremely deadly!

Sarah lets go and Michael can finally take a breath of relief.

"Now... what do you want for breakfast?" asks Sarah, still on top of him.

Michael rubs his throat for a while before answering her. "Hmm... I think I'll have pancakes, toast, grilled tomatoes, scrambled eggs, bangers and mash, loads of bacon..."

"Do you really expect me to cook all of that for you?" cuts in Sarah, giving him an incredulous look.

Michael only gives her his signature cheeky grin.

"Yeah, right! *Lekker eten zonder betalen!*" mutters Sarah in Dutch.

Michael laughs out loud. Sarah comes down from him and heads towards the fridge. She takes out a cantaloupe melon and starts cutting it into slices. Michael is still sore all over so he gets up slowly. He stretches for a few minutes and then walks toward Sarah. He hugs her from behind and kisses her on the neck. The kiss makes Sarah shudder and her breath starts to go heavy again. She tries to ignore him and keeps cutting the melon. After a few seconds, she stops and closes her eyes. She turns towards Michael to kiss him on the lips. After a while, Sarah releases him, takes a piece of fruit, and puts it into his mouth.

"Let's have breakfast," says Sarah, taking the plates of fruit to the dinner table.

Michael sits and starts eating while staring at the incredibly beautiful, sexy, and half-naked girl in front him. His heart races every time Sarah looks back at him.

"What do you plan on doing with your free time?" asks Sarah.

"I have a meeting today with the Director and my CO at the Barracks. Would you like to go with me to Herefordshire? The Regiment is currently doing Summer Selection and there's an open invitation to do the Fan Dance. It's tomorrow at dawn."

"Fan Dance?" asks Sarah, smiling to imagine Michael and his men doing a Korean fan dance.

"It's a fearsome twenty-four-kilometre run in full kit, up and down the Corn Du and Pen y Fan hills of the Brecon Beacons, which are the highest peaks in southern UK."

"That sounds lovely! But am I allowed to join?" asks Sarah hopefully.

"I'll sort it with the Director. I'm sure it won't pose a problem as almost all of the men, including the Director, already know who you are."

"How the devil could the SAS know who I am?" she asks, frowning.

"Oh, everyone knows your brother very well, but they'll recognize you also. No need to worry - as far as they know, you're just a constable in the INP."

"But how?"

"I'll show you when we get there," says Michael with a mysterious smile. "I have to do the Fan Dance in full kit like the other men, but you can wear anything you want."

"What kind of kit do you have to bring?"

"Oh, the usual. A bergen filled with food, water, bivvi bag, first aid kit, bayonet, ammo, and spare clothes. The bergen has to weigh at least fifty pounds before and after the Fan Dance."

"If you could arrange it, I would like to have the same kit as the others," says Sarah, wanting to challenge herself.

"Splendid! I'll have someone help us sort our kit. It's only a two-and-a-half-hour train ride from Manchester Piccadilly to Hereford and there's a train every bottom of the hour. I'll get the tickets and you can stay at my flat. How about we meet at Manchester Piccadilly Railway Station before 08:30?"

"Sounds good," says Sarah, taking their plates and putting them into the dishwasher. "It'll give me time to make my report for NCB Indonesia."

"Sod the report! We'll have time for another round," says Michael, standing up to give her a kiss.

Sarah returns his kiss. Michael's hand is trying to open Sarah's bra. He stops kissing her to look for the snap.

"How the devil do you open these stupid things?" he asks, frustrated.

Sarah rolls her eyes and opens her bra using the snap at the front. Michael observes that her breasts don't change at all; the shape is exactly the same whether she's wearing the bra or not. He squeezes them and they feel naturally firm, and his fingers start playing with her nipples, which immediately perk up. Sarah closes her eyes and enjoys the sensation. Michael keeps looking at her breasts until Sarah's hand raises his chin and she kisses him on the mouth. After a couple of minutes, Sarah releases him, although Michael's hands are still on her breasts.

"We don't have time for this. You should go and sort for the trip. I have to do the same," suggests Sarah.

"Oh, come on, you seem to want it also," says Michael.

"You could disembowel me and my breasts would still react this way if you keep doing that."

"Yeah... right," says Michael, eyes still mesmerized by her perfectly shaped breasts.

"My face is up here, Michael!" says Sarah, finally swatting his hands away.

"Right... of course," says Michael, struggling hard to divert his eyes towards hers.

"Go on and get into your clothes!" she orders with her hands on her hips.

Michael follows her orders as slowly as he can while staring at Sarah's magnificent body. Only the bandage on her arm mars the perfect image in front of him. Once he's finished, Sarah puts her arm through his and leads him to the door. At the door, Michael turns and kisses her passionately, a kiss she returns. A few moments later, Sarah releases herself, opens the door, and pushes him out.

"Are you sure we don't have time?" asks Michael.

Sarah smiles and pushes him out further. "Go, Michael!"

"Okay, okay," he says, finally getting out.

Sarah immediately closes the door. She must get rid of Michael right away before he manages to change her mind. She then takes her tablet and a pistol cleaning kit and sits down at the dinner table. She turns on her tablet and opens the latest Dragon Naturally Speaking software. While dictating her report, Sarah field strips her pistol. She's such an expert that she can field strip and clean any pistol without even looking at it. After the parts are cleaned and properly lubricated, she puts them back together again, also without looking. She dry-fires it a few times to make sure it works. The Glock pistol is extremely reliable, but she doesn't feel secure unless she's tested it.

It takes her an hour to finish her report. She checks it and revises it manually. Her report isn't that different to the contents of the AAR, but the quality of her writing is better because she completed it without stress. Sarah smiles to herself, remembering what Michael did to her last night to relieve the stress.

After sending her report by e-mail to the Secretariat of NCB Indonesia, she meets Michael at Manchester Piccadilly and they take the train to Hereford. Sarah looks fresh and beautiful in a white shirt and jeans shorts and Michael looks like a tourist in shirt, shorts, and sandals. It takes them almost two and a half hours to arrive.

"Will someone pick us up?" asks Sarah.

"Of course," answers Michael, his chin pointing towards someone near the exit.

The man's in his mid-thirties, a little shorter than Sarah, and looks like a bricklayer. He shakes hands with Michael and greets him in a thick Cockney accent. "All *roight*, old buddy?"

"I'm fine, Al. This is Inspector Sarah Dharmawan from the Indonesian National Police. Sarah, this is Al Spencer."

Sarah smiles and shakes hands with him. Al blinks a few times as if he's seen Sarah before, giving her a strong feeling of *déjà vu*. It's the same thing Michael had done on first meeting her.

"Isn't she...?" Al starts asking Michael, but gets cut off.

"It's her, Al," says Michael with a satisfied smile.

Unexpectedly, Al gives Michael a look of utter hatred. "You lucky bastard!"

Michael laughs out loud, leaving Sarah to wonder about the entire exchange.

"Have we met before, Al?" she asks while they exit the station.

"If we'd met before, you wouldn't likely forget me, lass," he answers with a raised eyebrow.

Michael and Sarah laugh, but she's still curious. They walk towards a Range Rover and Al insists Sarah sit in front with him. Michael explains to her that Al Spencer is B Squadron's SSM or Squadron Sergeant Major.

"To the SHQ, old buddy?" asks Al.

"Kremlin first, please. I have an appointment with the CO and the Director at 11:30," answers Michael.

Al goes through King's Acre Road and then A480 towards New Stirling Lines. The Regimental Headquarters, SAS Barracks moved from Hereford to Credenhill in 1999. Their original barracks is now a housing complex.

"How's everyone in the squadron these past few days, Al?" asks Michael.

"Roight, well, George's bicycle was ran over by one of our lorries when it was parked near the SHQ yesterday, so he's feeling fucking pleased roight now. He would throw a major eppie scoppie if someone asked him about his bicycle... so be sure *you* ask him about it."

Sarah tries to stifle a laugh, but fails. She knows that eppie scoppie means tantrum and suddenly remembers Tony when they were in primary school. He would always throw a tantrum whenever she beat him playing Scrabble. Al seems pleased at being able to make Sarah laugh and keeps on joking all the way to New Stirling Lines.

# THE POLICEWOMAN

11:26 GMT
Tuesday July 28, 2026
Regimental Headquarters, SAS Barracks
Credenhill, Herefordshire, England

The military police from the Military Provost Guard Service (MPGS), Royal Military Police check their ID and give Sarah a 'Red Pass'. This means she may enter the barracks, but must be accompanied at all times. Past the main gate and to her left, she can see a pink Land Rover 110, used by the SAS in the desert during World War II, Operation Desert Storm, and the War on Terror in Iraq and Afghanistan. The vehicle is called a 'Pinkie' and the pink colour is effective at camouflaging the vehicle in the desert, especially at night.

The RHQ is to the right of the main gate and resembles a deserted campus. There are only four men sitting around, eating ice cream in their T-shirts, shorts, and sandals. Their jaws drop when they see Sarah get out of the car and head towards the red-bricked building with Michael and Al. Before they reach it, a couple of men exit the building. One of them is the Director Special Forces (DSF) and the other is the CO of the SAS. Like everyone else Sarah's seen inside the barracks so far, except the military police at the main gate, they're also in mufti. In this case, though, they're decked out in business suits.

"Afternoon, Boss," greets Michael without saluting.

"Good afternoon indeed, Michael, you tatty old sod," answers Major-General Sir Charles Mountbatten, GCB, DSO in perfect King's English. "I'm afraid I have to postpone our meeting. I just received a call from Whitehall and they require my presence there this very afternoon. I shall return this evening."

The DSF looks more like a banker than a commander of a special forces unit. He's wearing a bespoke blue pinstriped suit from Savile Row with a white shirt and dotted blue tie that shows he has membership in the Army and Navy Club in London. He looks like the aristocratic version of actor Jason Isaacs and he's so distinguished that Sarah has to fight the urge to salute him.

Sarah has heard about the reputation of Major-General Sir Charles Mountbatten, GCB, DSO. He's the first royal to have passed Selection and has personally led the SAS in battle in Afghanistan, Iraq, and Syria. He became the Director Special Forces (DSF), leading the UK Special Forces (UKSF) Group, based on merit and military prowess, not because of his status as a member of the royal family.

Regarding the CO of the SAS, Sarah has absolutely no idea who he is because that information is qualified as Top Secret.

"Right, I guess we'll be going then," says Michael. "Before you go, may I present you Inspector Sarah Dharmawan from the Indonesian National Police?"

The Director's eyes sparkle when he sees Sarah and takes her hand.

"Ah, yes indeed... Tony's lovely sister," greets Major-General Sir Charles Mountbatten. He then kisses her hand in the manner of a British aristocrat. "It's a pleasure to finally meet you in person, Inspector Dharmawan."

Sarah can't believe Sir Charles knows who she is! "P-P-Please call me Sarah, Director."

Sarah also notices that the SAS commander, who looks like a bulkier version of the actor Benedict Cumberbatch, is staring at her with his mouth open in awe.

"And let me have the pleasure of introducing you to the bashful CO of the 22$^{nd}$ Regiment, Leftenant-Colonel Cormac McLaughlin," continues Sir Charles while giving a cheeky grin to Cormac, who hurriedly shuts his mouth, "who I know for sure is quite a big fan of yours."

Cormac and Sarah are both red in the face as they shake hands. Sarah is surprised to see that he tries to avoid her eyes. Behind her, Michael and Al can't help but giggle when they see Cormac release her hand as if he's trying to run away from her and hurriedly opens the car door for Sir Charles.

"Well, I guess we'll be on our way. Be sure to show her your squadron's Interest Room, Michael," says the Director, giving him a wink as he enters his car.

"Of course, Boss," answers Michael, trying not to laugh.

Their car heads towards an Agusta Westland helicopter, waiting on the helipad near their football field on the south side of the barracks.

"What the devil was that all about?" asks Sarah. "What does he mean by 'finally meet me in person'? And how could your CO be a big fan of mine? And what the bloody devil is an Interest Room?"

"She doesn't know about it yet?" asks Al, giving Michael a broad grin.

Michael can only shake his head, still trying hard not to laugh.

"Know what?" asks Sarah.

"Oh, I wish I could be there when she sees it. Ro*i*ght, well, I gotta go inside. I've prepared your kit and it's with Derek at SHQ. Here, take the keys," says Al, also stifling a laugh as he throws the car keys to Michael.

"Later, Al," says Michael.

Al waves his hand and enters the RHQ.

"Sees what?" asks Sarah, growing even more curious.

"Later," says Michael. "First things first."

Michael directs the car towards another building. They enter the building, which turns out to be an indoor firing range. They meet the range master, whose name is David Bancroft. Dave has just come out of his office without closing the door, wearing a shirt, shorts, and sandals. He's skinny and short, even shorter than Al. He doesn't look like someone from the special forces, but Sarah immediately disregards her first impressions of him because appearances can be misleading, especially in the special forces community.

"Going somewhere, Dave?" asks Michael.

"Yeah, going to the cookhouse for lunch," answers Dave, "and who's this?"

"Hi, I'm Sarah."

Unexpectedly, Dave seems to instantly recognize her, but he suddenly goes pale and his eyes pop open as wide as saucers. Dave hurriedly releases her hand and retreats to his office.

"Boss, you fucking berk!" shouts Dave angrily.

Sarah can only look at Michael in amazement as he tries hard not to laugh. Dave has retreated to his office door, which he locks so that no one can get inside.

"We'll be using the short range for a few minutes, Dave, and we'll be taking some of your ammo," says Michael.

"Yeah, all right," answers Dave, walking quickly towards the exit as if trying to escape from them.

Sarah sees Dave take out his smartphone before he's out of the building. Michael then directs her to the pistol firing range.

"What was that all about?" she asks, pouting at him.

"Later," answers Michael, putting on ear protection and taking out the Glock from his bum bag. "You said you wanted to test your Glock?"

After Sarah has put on her ear protection, Michael starts shooting towards his paper target, fifteen metres away. Sarah wants to hear an answer first but clearly none is forthcoming, so she takes out her Glock from her IWB holster and fires. Sarah notices that Michael uses the Weaver Stance, unlike her own Isosceles Stance.

After each empties a magazine, they clear their weapons, take off their ear protection, and press a button that pulls their targets towards them. They glance at each other's paper target and see they both have grouped all their shots in the "X".

Michael takes a box of 9x19mm Parabellum JHP from the armoire behind them and shares it with Sarah. Once their guns are loaded, Michael invites her outside again. He drives towards his SHQ with Sarah pouting all the way. He then asks her to follow him inside the T-shaped building.

Once inside, Michael pounds on one of the doors. "Derek, open up!"

A Lance-Corporal wearing a temperate barrack dress uniform comes out of the room. He's quite good-looking and it's obvious he has Asian heritage.

"Hi Boss, I have your kit in here. You said you wanted two of them?" asks Lance-Corporal Derek Sinclair in his King's English accent.

"Indeed. The other one is for my lovely friend here."

Sarah thrusts her hand towards him without saying anything and without smiling. She's surprised that even this doesn't work. Derek shakes her hand, his eyes slowly becoming as wide as dinner plates and his jaw as wide as the door behind him. Just like Dave, he suddenly turns around and shuts the door behind him. He then just stands there with a forced grin and face starting to turn red.

'I'm in a nightmare,' thinks Sarah, confused by the surreal experience so far.

Still trying not to laugh, Michael takes her hand and leads her towards the B Squadron Interest Room in the middle of the building. In the hallway, Sarah sees an interesting poster of a herd of sheep inside a pen with an open door. The words below it read, 'Make a decision! Either lead, follow, or get out of the way!' Sarah knows this is a quote from Thomas Paine.

"You will find your answer in here," says Michael. He hurriedly leaves as if running away from her.

Sarah is now alone in the Interest Room, which looks more like a museum. The first thing she notices is a huge head of a buffalo on the back wall above a large screen TV. There are Blu-Ray disc racks beside it and a whole rack dedicated to Monty Python films. A large sofa is in front of the TV and the walls are covered with plaques of special forces units from around the world. Besides plaques, there are also pictures of SAS troopers in various activities.

Sarah starts studying the plaques, looking out for a plaque from Satuan Bravo-90, as Tony would've surely given them one. She sees the plaque from Grenzschutzgruppe-9 (GSG-9) and Kommando Spezialkräfte (KSK) from Germany, Sayeret Matkhal from Israel, 1st Special Forces Operational Detachment – Delta, Naval Special Warfare Development Group, and the 24th Special Tactics Squadron from the US. When Tony had just joined Bravo, he was sent to the US to train with the 24th Special Tactics Squadron, as they have similar roles.

Below the plaque of the 24th Special Tactics Squadron, Sarah finally finds Bravo's plaque, a brass logo of the unit on a wooden frame. Underneath the plaque, there's a photo of Tony with his unit on top of a Welsh hill. Tony is flanked by Sersan Mayor Suprayitno, the unit's sergeant major and EOD specialist, and Sersan Kepala Pranoto, who happens to be one of Indonesia's top snipers. Sarah also recognizes Sersan Dua Zulkarnaen, the youngest but smartest NCO in Tony's unit; Sersan Satu Dedi Suhendri, probably the only person in the world outside their family who can defeat Tony in unarmed combat; and Sersan Satu Nyoman Sukarya, the combat medic. They all have longer hair than the average soldier. Anyone seeing the photo would never have guessed that they were looking at a special forces unit. And underneath that photo...

"What the bloody devil is my picture doing here?" shouts Sarah angrily, her face turning red.

In the large photo of her, Sarah's on a beach wearing a dark red string bikini. She's grinning, her right elbow on someone's shoulder, and her left hand on her hip. She has Oakley sunglasses resting on top of her head and she's barefoot. She remembers that Tony took the photo with her dad, but it looks like her dad has been cropped out. That photo was taken when her whole family were on vacation in Bali after she graduated from the Police Academy. She wasn't that muscular at that time, though her stomach shows a ghost of a six pack.

Although Sarah has been photographed hundreds of times by professional photographers and featured dozens of times in various magazines, Sarah has to admit that Tony's photo is her prettiest... and sexiest. There's a caption on the bottom part of the photo that reads 'Constable Sarah Dharmawan, Tony's sister.'

Sarah suddenly hears loud laughter behind her and she turns around. It turns out there are already some thirty people around her including Dave and Derek. Only Derek is wearing a uniform and he's recording her reaction with his smartphone. Michael is nowhere to be seen.

'*Verdomme!*' thinks Sarah. She then starts laughing with the others at how ridiculous this has become. She wishes Michael were here, though. Not to enjoy this moment together, but to beat the crap out of him.

"So, Dave, Derek, I presume you have a copy of this photo posted on the back of your office doors?" asks Sarah.

"As a matter of fact, we have your photo in *every* room," answers Derek sheepishly.

"That makes you all bloody wankers then," exclaims Sarah.

Everyone collapses in laughter. Derek laughs so hard he accidentally drops his smartphone.

"Now this is *definitely* Tony's sister!" exclaims Dave amid the laughter.

As the laughter dies down, those who haven't met her then introduce themselves to her. The last trooper is called George Hastings. He's absolutely huge like Tiny, who was as big and wide as a large armoire.

"Did you bring that red bikini with you?" asks George expectantly.

"No," answers Sarah. She laughs with the others and then strikes back. "Are you the chap who's planning to compete in the Tour de France?"

George is embarrassed while the others laugh at his expense.

"Do you have a photo of yourself wearing a constable uniform?" asks Derek, also expectantly.

"Of course... but I'm not showing it to you," she answers.

"Right, lads, fun's over. See you all here at five o' clock tomorrow," says Michael as he enters the room and takes Sarah by her arm.

"Be sure to save some energy for tomorrow, Boss," suggests George.

Michael gives George his middle finger, making the other troopers laugh hysterically, which Michael and Sarah can still hear even after they exit the building. Michael takes Sarah to Hereford to have lunch.

Michael notices Sarah smiling to herself as he drives on. "Why are you smiling?"

"Oh, I was just thinking about ways to murder you and Tony without getting caught," answers Sarah.

Michael laughs out loud.

"You owe me an explanation for how my photo got posted there, Michael."

"Well, first of all, your brother is such a handsome chap and we assumed, correctly, that he would certainly have a lovely sister. When he was here, we kept pestering him every day to show us a photo of you. One night, when we were all really pissed at a restaurant called The Nag's Head, he finally did. When *that* photo appeared, a couple of chaps jumped on him and took away his smartphone. There was… quite a bit of a scuffle and it took four of us to finally hold him down and knock him out while we transferred the photo to our smartphones. It was a good thing his men weren't there at the time, else there would've been major drama and most certainly an international incident," says Michael, smiling at the memory.

"How did he take it?" asks Sarah. She's annoyed with Tony, but somewhat proud of him because it took four SAS men to take him down, even if they were all really pissed.

"Tony was so pissed that night that he didn't remember anything about it the next morning. He kept wondering out loud why he and some of the other men had bruises on their faces. There were even a couple of men who had to be treated at the barracks hospital for severe bite marks! A few days later, just before he and his unit left for Hereford Railway Station to London, we took him to the Interest Room and showed him the good news. He threw a major eppie scoppie and cursed our bollocks off in Dutch! But then he took the stitch and laughed along with us after he called us 'bloody wankers'. However, he also made us promise not to share the picture outside the barracks because you work undercover. We've always honoured that request, of course," says Michael seriously.

Michael parks the car at the Maylord Shopping Centre and they walk to one of Hereford's best restaurants, a place called Saxty's.

"So… that photo's in *every* room in the barracks?" asks Sarah with a raised eyebrow.

Michael gets sheepish. "Indeed… and yes, that includes my office also."

Sarah laughs.

"There's one in The Kremlin too, you know," says Michael, grinning from ear to ear.

"Wankers!" exclaims Sarah.

Michael laughs out loud. "You know, the first few days after that photo was posted, we would just sit around the Interest Room and share our fantasies about you."

"Really? And what was *your* fantasy?"

"Well… there's one with you in a sexy Wonder Woman costume," says Michael, still grinning.

"Wonder Woman? I would've thought you'd prefer gladiatrix in bikini armour."

Michael eyes become unfocused, as if imagining Sarah being a gladiatrix… wearing a sexy, leather-bikini armour… her athletic body gleaming with sweat… fighting another gladiatrix similarly dressed…

Michael finally comes back to earth. "That's Dave's fantasy. But yes, you would look lovely in that also."

"You men are into cosplay, aren't you?" teases Sarah.

Michael laughs, but doesn't answer her.

"Your SAS culture and humour is certainly unique," comments Sarah.

"In The Regiment, humour revolves around slagging and stitching people. You're not allowed to take it personally or let yourself become too emotional," explains Michael. "Some three years ago, Dave had deployed to… a certain middle-eastern country. One day he had to shoot a mortar crew from a range of 1,900 metres. It took only four shots for Dave to slot all three of them from that incredible distance and he was quite proud of that… but he still took a severe slagging from us because he'd wasted a round."

Sarah is tickled imagining Dave's silly face as his teammates make fun of him, but she's also quite impressed with his marksmanship.

"You handled yourself with my troopers very well today," says Michael.

"Well, I'm used to it. Tony and I always do the same thing to each other," says Sarah.

Their food arrives and they both enjoy it. The quality of the food at Saxty's is excellent.

"What shall we do now?" asks Sarah after finishing her lunch.

"Fancy a bike ride to Hereford Cathedral? There's a unique Chained Library there and a Mappa Mundi."

"That would be lovely," says Sarah excitedly. She once heard that Hereford's Chained Library is the largest in the world.

They hire a couple of bikes and visit the Hereford Cathedral and other historical sites of the city. They ride their bikes in silence. Sarah feels that this is the most romantic date she has ever experienced and she has to admit to herself that she has fallen in love with Michael.

After returning their bikes, they go to Michael's flat in Orchard Road, which is in a region that before 1999 was the location of the SAS Barracks. Michael shows her around. There's only one bedroom with a queen-sized bed and a living room with a 46" TV. The living room looks as if it's often used by the troopers to hang out and Michael's bike is there. Despite this, the flat is neat and tidy. Sarah peeks behind the bedroom door, but doesn't see anything posted there.

"No photo of me?" she asks.

"Your brother requested it not leave the barracks, remember?" answers Michael.

Sarah smiles as she heads back towards the living room.

"So…ehm… did you bring that red bikini with you?" asks Michael hopefully from behind her.

Quick as lightning, Sarah throws a backhand punch towards Michael's nose. He can deflect it easily and even throws a counterpunch. Sarah catches his arm and tries to slam him to the ground, but Michael counteracts her move, which locks their arms. At the same time, Michael throws a kick to her belly with his knee, but feels his knee bounce back.

"You're holding back on me," accuses Sarah.

"Of course I am."

"Don't," says Sarah.

She suddenly gives him a head-butt, which makes his lips crack and bleed. Michael's head recoils from the blow but at the same time, he pulls her body with him, flips around, then throws her back to the wall behind her. Without stopping, Michael throws a hard punch to her stomach. A sickening thud is heard, but Sarah only smiles at him. To Michael's pleasure, Sarah takes off her shirt and she's now wearing a red bra and jeans shorts. She flexes her perfect six-pack.

"Harder!" orders Sarah.

Michael gives her a few more hard punches to her abs and his fists feel like they're hitting a silky-smooth brick wall. Michael's punches would've floored most people, but Sarah doesn't even flinch. Michael then delivers a powerful Muay Thay kick with his knee. A thunderous sound goes off but once again, Sarah only smiles at him. He then gives her an even more powerful kick, but she manages to grab his knee and tries to push him backwards. Michael has anticipated her move, so he grabs hold of her shoulders, flips himself to the left, and then slams her to the floor with Michael still on top of her. His knee was still on top of her stomach when he landed and the whole weight of Michael's body was transferred to Sarah's abs through his knee. Michael is sure that if someone else received the same treatment, they would've been knocked out for sure, but Sarah doesn't even flinch. Michael keeps his body over hers and holds her hands to prevent her from hitting him again.

"You're the only person who has ever defeated me in unarmed combat," says Sarah, smiling at him.

"What's my reward?" asks Michael.

"Whatever is on your mind, I guess."

Several fantasies flash through Michael's mind at the same time, but then he decides on a quickie.


18:11 GMT
Tuesday July 28, 2026
Oak Field Road, Saxon Gate
Hereford, Herefordshire, England


They've just finished an incredible round and their breathing's still heavy when Michael's phone goes off.

"Yes, Derek?" answers Michael, still trying to catch his breath. He listens for a while. "Yeah, right! Fuck off, you wanker!" he says curtly.

Sarah can guess what Derek has said and laughs.

"Right, I'll see him with Cormac and Al at nineteen hundred at The Kremlin. Thanks!" Michael disconnects the call and says to Sarah. "The Director wants to see me at The Kremlin at nineteen hundred. You can come with me and we can have some scoff after. Shower?"

Sarah showers with Michael and she carefully, softly washes his body with soap. Michael has never been treated like this before so he happily does the same to Sarah. They rinse each other and share a kiss.

"You do know that I'm in love with you, don't you?" asks Sarah.

"And I'm in love with you too."

"Really? Since when?"

"Since I first saw that photo," answers Michael honestly.

Sarah laughs and they both change into presentable clothes. Michael wears a jacket and tie and Sarah slips into a simple purple dress. Sarah's uncomplicated taste in clothes makes Michael even more in love with her. She doesn't need expensive dresses or even make-up to look lovely.

They drive towards the SAS Barracks and a few minutes later, Michael parks the car and they both enter the RHQ. Inside, they meet Al and Cormac, also in tie and jacket. The two men smile at Michael's bruised lips, but make no comment. Sarah waits in the RHQ's Interest Room while the three men meet with the Director.

The RHQ's Interest Room is a bit like the one at the SHQ. The pictures are mostly of famous SAS commanders, like Sir Archibald David Stirling, Sir Hugh Michael Rose, Sir Peter de la Billiere, and Sir Graeme Cameron Maxwell Lamb, to name a few. Sarah sees SAS members with the royal family and British Prime Ministers. His Majesty King William V, who a few years ago was Prince William, looks utterly charming, although his hair is almost gone. Queen Catherine looks lovely despite being forty-four years of age. Prince George and Princess Charlotte, who immediately became teen idols since they first appeared on the telly for their royal activities, both look adorable wearing MTP trousers. The royal family and British politicians are required to attend training with the SAS so they'll know what to do if they're ever snatched and know what the SAS will do to save them. The extraordinary thing about this is the use of live rounds during CQB training with the VVIPs acting as hostages.

There are several photos of Prince Harry, who looks dashing in his full dress ceremonial uniform. Although he's resigned from the British Armed

Forces since June 2015, Prince Harry is still active as Captain General of the Royal Marines and the Colonel-in-Chief of the Special Air Service, The Blues and Royals, and the Royal Gurkha Rifles.

Sarah is relieved not to find her own photo among these legendary people.

The Interest Room displays the UKSF Group organization and Sarah studies it intently. The United Kingdom Special Forces (UKSF) Group consists of Tier One Units, Tier Two Units, Reserve Units, and Supporting Units. The Tier One Units are the 22$^{nd}$ Regiment, Special Air Service (SAS) and the Special Boat Service (SBS), and the Tier Two Units are the Special Reconnaissance Regiment (SRR), the Special Forces Support Group (SFSG), and the 18 UKSF Signals Regiment. There are many units in the Reserve and Supporting Units, but one that catches her eye is the Joint Special Forces Aviation Wing (JSFAW), a joint unit which consists of the 657 and 658 Army Air Corps (AAC) and 7 Squadron Royal Air Force (RAF).

Sarah gets fairly lost looking at the many pictures and memorabilia until, after almost an hour, Michael finally enters the Interest Room. "All right, *mo ghile mear*?"

"*C'est-à-dire*?" asks Sarah. For some reason, she unconsciously reverts to French when she's close to somebody.

"It's Gaeilge and it means 'my gallant darling'," answers Michael, smiling.

Sarah feels her heart drop down to her stomach. Her previous lovers had given her various nicknames, but none that made her heart flutter like this one. Sarah even feels her knees weaken and her eyes tearing up and it makes her want to hug and kiss him right there. It's such a shame they're still inside an army headquarters and it would be inappropriate to do so.

"Do you like it?" asks Michael.

"It's lovely indeed," says Sarah. "So, where's my picture?"

"In Cormac's office," says Michael, giving her a wink.

Sarah laughs.

"Let's get some scoff," says Michael, taking out his smartphone.

Michael makes a reservation at the Castle House Restaurant and orders their famous Seven Course Meal for two. Sarah loves how Michael directs and makes decisions for her. All her previous lovers have always left all the decisions to her, as if they're afraid of making the wrong choice and disappointing her. They always say, 'whatever you want to do' on everything, from where to eat or where they want to hang out.

"How do like your vacation so far?" asks Michael.

"I'm loving it!"

"Do you miss Interpol?"

"Not really," admits Sarah. "How about you?"

"I prefer the army. I've always admired the traditions, especially the odd ones."

"Which regiment in the British Army do you think has the oddest tradition?" asks Sarah.

Michael thinks for a moment before answering her. "Well, the Royal Welsh infantry regiment has a Kashmir goat who's a ranking member of the regiment."

"How did that happen?"

"The story goes that during the Battle of Bunker Hill in 1775, a wild goat entered the battlefield and led the Welsh infantry regiment in their successful attack on Breed's Hill. Instead of stewing the goat, the regiment adopted him and made him the regimental mascot. They've adopted a goat as a ranking member of the regiment ever since. In 1837, Mohammad Shah Qajar, the Shah of Persia, presented a Kashmir goat herd to Queen Victoria as a gift upon her accession to the throne. Since then, the British monarchy has presented an unbroken series of Kashmir goats to the Royal Welsh from the Crown's own royal herd."

"Is the goat really a ranking member?" asks Sarah, smiling.

"Oh indeed. He even has his own Army number and ID card with his photo on it. The current goat is called William Windsor III and he's descended from the same royal bloodline as the original herd from Persia. William has a rank of Lance-Corporal, so all the Fusiliers have to 'stand to attention' whenever William walks past them."

Sarah laughs and this makes Michael pleased so he tells her some more.

"As a Lance-Corporal, William also has membership to the corporal's mess, where he's given a glass of Guinness and a daily ration of five unfiltered cigarettes."

"Don't tell me he smokes them," says Sarah.

"No, he eats them. His veterinarian said that the tobacco is good for his stomach."

Sarah laughs again.

"One of his predecessors, called Billy, was once demoted. On his first deployment to Cyprus and on a parade held to celebrate Her Majesty Queen Elizabeth II's eightieth birthday, he refused to obey orders. He failed to keep in line with the rest of the parade and even tried to head-butt the drummer in the arse a few times."

Sarah keeps laughing.

"After the parade, Billy was charged with 'unacceptable behaviour', 'lack of decorum', and 'disobeying a direct order', and had to appear before his CO. Following a disciplinary hearing, Billy was demoted from Lance-Corporal to Fusilier. The demotion meant that the other Fusiliers in the regiment no longer had to 'stand to attention' whenever Billy walked past, as they had had to when he was a Lance-Corporal."

"But he was only 'acting the goat'," protests Sarah, still laughing.

"Indeed. That's why a Canadian animal rights group sent a letter of protest to the CO of the Royal Welsh saying the same thing. They also said that because Billy couldn't possibly understand the charges against him and the court couldn't possibly understand his defence, the hearing should be considered unlawful and, therefore, his rank should be reinstated," says Michael seriously.

Sarah laughs louder.

"Fortunately, Billy regained his rank three months later after the Alma Day parade, which celebrates the Royal Welsh's victory in the Crimean War. The Colonel said that Billy had performed exceptionally well because he'd had all summer to reflect on his behaviour at the Queen's birthday, so his rank was reinstated, because he'd clearly earned the rank he deserved," continues Michael, still with a serious expression.

"How do you know all of this?" asks Sarah, still laughing at how ridiculous the story was.

"One of the EOD specialists in my squadron was a former Goat Major of the Royal Welsh. His name is Sinjin Williams and his job as Goat Major was to take care of William Windsor III. Even though the position is called Goat Major, William's handler has a rank of Corporal. You can imagine how bloody pleased Sinjin was when his CO, who happened to be an utterly sadistic bastard, appointed him Goat Major," says Michael, smiling. Although Michael pronounced the name as 'Sinjin', it's actually spelled 'St John'.

Sarah laughs out loud, imagining St John Williams being appointed by his CO to take care of a goat called William.

"One former Goat Major was court-martialed and demoted to Lance-Corporal when he was caught offering the goat for stud services to a local goat breeder. During his court-martial, the Goat Major's defence was that he had done it out of compassion for the goat, because it had appeared to him as if the goat really needed it," says Michael, seriously once again. "Unfortunately, the Goat Major's defence failed to impress the court."

Sarah laughs even louder and Michael is pleased that she can appreciate his dry sense of humour. After dinner, they return to Michael's flat. They change clothes before going to bed. Michael can't take his eyes off Sarah when she opens her dress, but he looks disappointed when she takes a shirt and a pair of shorts from her luggage.

"*Qu'est-ce qui te dérange*?" asks Sarah when she sees the look on his face.

"Well, it would be a shame to cover your body with clothes while you sleep," answers Michael, grinning.

Sarah laughs. "Unfortunately, I can't sleep without clothes on and I didn't think to bring my lingerie collection to England."

"You have a lingerie collection?" asks Michael. His face lights up as he pulls Sarah towards him.

"Indeed. I'm Victoria's Top Secret."

Sarah doesn't have any lingerie, but she enjoys teasing Michael. Sure enough, Michael's eyes fall out of focus as he imagines her in something black and lacy. He smiles and starts kissing her stomach.

"You would make a perfect belly dancer," he mumbles, his face buried deep in Sarah's stomach.

"Now *there's* an intellectual challenge!" exclaims Sarah, laughing.

"But do you know how to do it?" asks Michael, expectantly.

"Of course," says Sarah. "*Doucement*?"

Michael can only nod enthusiastically. Sarah takes her smartphone and tweaks it. Soft, slow Arabian music plays and Sarah begins her belly dance in her bra and panties. Michael's eyes go wide in disbelief that one of his ultimate fantasies is now playing out in front of him.

# CHAPTER 7
# THE FAN DANCE

04:24 GMT
Wednesday July 29, 2026
Regimental Cookhouse, SAS Barracks
Credenhill, Herefordshire, England

The next morning, Michael parks the car at the SHQ and they walk to the cookhouse, already full of troopers who plan on doing the Fan Dance today. Sarah looks really sexy in a black tank top and black pants from her days in Gegana. She feels like a celebrity because everyone recognizes her and wants to meet her. The food provided by the Royal Logistics Corps (RLC) looks greasy and starchy. The cookhouse's well-stocked and Sarah forces herself to take as much food as she can. They see Al Spencer and other men from B Squadron waving from one of the tables. All the thirty-odd troopers she met yesterday are there except Derek.

Everyone tries to eat as much as possible and then goes back in line for eggs and bread. They make egg banjos, which they intend to bring with them. This is a good idea and Sarah does the same as she will need a lot of energy today. After breakfast, they all walk to the SHQ to retrieve their bergens and load them into a lorry.

"Morning, everyone! Is this the celebrity everyone's all hyper about?" asks someone next to the lorry, thrusting his hand towards Sarah. He is really good-looking, tall, and muscular like a Greek god. Unfortunately, he speaks in a thick Birmingham accent that Sarah doesn't like. "I'm Captain Robert Covington. You must be Lara Croft."

"No, I'm Sarah," she answers, laughing.

"Right then, let's get you inside," he says as he helps her into the lorry.

The troopers prefer to sleep along the way and Sarah does the same. She puts her head against Michael's shoulder, already fast asleep.

## THE POLICEWOMAN

05:51 GMT
Wednesday July 29, 2026
Storey Arms Outdoor Education Centre
Brecon Beacons, Powys, Wales

Everyone wakes up when the lorry stops in the parking area of Storey Arms Outdoor Education Centre at the base of Corn Du. They meet Cormac and the Training Wing Sergeant Major, waiting near a red telephone box. Al gives Cormac a list of people partaking in the Fan Dance while the others put their bergens on a hanging scale to make sure they exceed fifty pounds. Sarah does the same and sees her bergen weighs 52.6 lbs, more or less the same as the other troopers. On top of the standard supplies, she's added several water bottles and egg banjos.

After they stretch and warm up, they put on their bergens. Sarah struggles with hers. It's as big as a fridge and it feels like she's carrying her sister Cindy, back when Cindy was six years old or so. There's an orange cloth on top of each bergen so Search & Rescue can spot them if they're lost. Everyone else has finished strapping on their bergens and they wait patiently for Sarah. They watch her struggling, but they don't offer to help. In any unit, there're always one or two people who are slower than the rest. Sarah's embarrassed because this time *she*'s the slowest. She hurriedly sorts herself and then puts on her Oakleys sunglasses to hide her blushes.

The Training Wing Sergeant Major checks his tablet. "The DS started with the volunteers at 05:45, G Squadron started five minutes after that and were followed by D Squadron only five minutes ago. B Squadron, standby... Standby... Go!"

Michael opens a wooden gate and they quickly walk up the steep hill. Within minutes, Sarah's heart is beating fast and her lungs are on fire. Unlike the troopers already in the SAS, volunteers for the SAS have to wear full MTP uniform and carry an SA80A3 assault rifle. The sling of the rifle is removed so they have to carry it as if they're on patrol, further hindering their movement. Sarah can't imagine having to carry more weight.

There's some relief after the first hill, as it starts to descend and they cross a small stream. Once it starts going uphill again, the troopers go at an even faster pace. Sarah starts to fall back, but she's determined not to be an embarrassment to the INP. Once the incline decreases, the troopers start running. Sarah tries to follow their pace. Ten minutes later, she starts to fall back, the distance increasing by the minute. She's only covered three-quarters of Corn Du, but Sarah fears she's reached her limit. She tries to maintain her pace for ten more minutes, but finally runs out of steam and has to stop. She has never felt this much pain in her life! She has given all she has, but she will fail to reach Corn Du together with the other troopers. Sarah has run for only four kilometres and she's suddenly worried because she must run six times that distance today!

"*Dios, ayúdame,*" mumbles Sarah in Spanish as she starts to jog again.

Sarah continues alone until she reaches the top of Corn Du. From the peak, she can see that B Squadron has already reached the top of Pen y Fan, which is about 350 metres from Corn Du. She continues her jog until she reaches the flat top of Pen y Fan. There's a tent there and someone standing beside it. Once she's closer, Sarah sees that the man is in his late forties with a face full of scars. He only has one eye and one arm. It turns out he's one of the Directing Staff (DS) from the Training Wing, called Fred, who is assigned to that checkpoint.

"Sarah... with B Squadron," says Sarah, panting. She takes off her bergen and puts it on the hanging scale.

"Good 'un, lass! *Yee* are only about three minutes behind the other blokes. Do *yee* know where *yee* are goin'?" asks Fred in his thick Yorkshire accent.

Sarah can only shake her head while strapping the bergen on her back.

Fred shows her the way. "Be careful descendin' Jacob's Ladder. Good luck!"

"Thank you, Staff!" says Sarah, waving goodbye to the friendly DS.

The view from the top of Pen y Fan is breathtaking, but Sarah doesn't have time to enjoy it. She goes to the northeastern part of Pen y Fan, an area called Jacob's Ladder. The top part of Jacob's Ladder is dangerous, especially for people carrying heavy loads on their back. There are steep steps which need careful footing and Sarah must suppress the urge to jump down. While descending Jacob's Ladder, she takes the opportunity to control her breathing, but becomes extremely worried when she realizes she'll have to climb up this difficult terrain on the way back. Once she's through the difficult part, Sarah runs at a faster pace to try to catch up with the others on the declining path. The path forks, the left goes to Cribyn and the right to the Roman Road, a road *not* built by the Romans. Sarah is determined to catch up with the others before they get to the Roman Road.

After a few minutes of fast running, she finally catches up with them, and even passes a few volunteers carrying the SA80A3. The path declines for the next five kilometres so B Squadron starts to run at an excruciating pace of fifteen kilometres per hour, making Sarah fall behind again. She sees the Neuadd Reservoir on her right and a forest block to her front. The rubbery path takes her parallel with the forest block for a few minutes before changing direction and cutting through it. Sarah meets first G Squadron and, some five minutes later, D Squadron, who've already reached the checkpoint at Torpantau and are now returning to Storey Arms. Five minutes after D Squadron, Sarah meets the DS running the Selection with the volunteers behind him playing catch up. She can only smile at them when they cheer for her to reach the checkpoint with the rest of B Squadron.

Several minutes later, Sarah finally arrives at the checkpoint, located approximately 200 metres from the ruins of Torpantau Railway Station. She reports herself to the DS manning the checkpoint while placing her bergen on the hanging scale. It turns out she's a little over six minutes behind B Squadron.

"Well done, Sarah!" says Al, shaking her hand.

The other troopers, especially Michael, are also impressed with her because she managed to finish the first stage of the Fan Dance only a few minutes behind the others. They all shake her hand and give her a pat on her shoulder. Sarah can only nod at them. She's too tired to even smile. She takes out her bottled water and drains it. They'll only stop for ten minutes at the checkpoint so she takes an egg banjo from her bergen and wolfs it down. The other troopers have already done the same. Sarah is in agony; her shoulders, back, legs, and lungs are killing her, but the words 'giving up' don't even begin to cross her mind.

"R*oi*ght, lads, rest is over," shouts Al after Sarah's only rested for three minutes. "We start again in a minute."

They all get up and put on their bergens, except Dave, who's still sleeping in a foetal position with his bergen as his pillow.

"Hey, Boss, let's shave him," suggests George, taking a bayonet out of his bergen.

Sarah straps on her own bergen while stifling a laugh.

"No time," says Michael, giving Dave a hard kick up the arse.

Dave wakes up, cursing his commander. Michael waves goodbye to the DS and then jogs back down the previous route. At the forest block, Sarah's left behind again, but this time she doesn't try to catch up with them. She now knows the terrain they will take and has a strategy to deal with it. When they reach the Roman Road, Sarah has fallen behind 200 metres from B Squadron and the distance is increasing, especially when the path starts inclining towards Pen y Fan. Sarah reaches the base of Jacob's Ladder, where she can see that the others have already reached the top of Pen y Fan.

Marathon runners always say that the *real* marathon starts at the thirtieth kilometre. Sarah feels like she's reached her thirtieth kilometre when contemplating the Jacob's Ladder. But she loves mountaineering and wall climbing so she powers herself up and takes the opportunity to close the gap between her and the others. Her lungs are on fire and her body is screaming for her to stop. Sarah once again can't imagine having to go up Jacob's Ladder with both hands carrying an assault rifle. With her bergen growing heavier by the second, she finally reaches the top of Jacob's Ladder and then reaches the top of Pen y Fan, maybe 150 metres behind B Squadron. She reports to Fred again while weighing her bergen on the hanging scale. The friendly DS once again cheers for her to catch up with the rest of B Squadron.

She starts running towards the mound-shaped top of Corn Du. She passes several volunteers carrying their rifles and sees that B Squadron has reached the DS leading several of the volunteers able to keep up with him. Once the path starts declining again, Sarah finally catches up with B Squadron. Michael and Al share a word or two with the DS before running past him. Further up ahead, they see D Squadron.

"Tally-ho, D Squadron 200 metres ahead!" shouts George.

"Fuck, let's do it! Let's do it!" shouts Michael from the front.

"Fucking yeah, let's do it!" shouts Al.

"Come on, lads! Let's do it!" shouts Robert.

Sarah doesn't know why they're shouting like that.

'I hope they don't plan on passing D Squadron,' she thinks, suddenly worried.

Sarah doesn't have enough energy to sprint and can only maintain her nine kilometre per hour pace, using all her reserve energy and mental toughness just to maintain that speed. She finally passes the DS leading the volunteers, but doesn't have the energy to greet him.

"Let's fucking do this!" shouts Michael. "Are you with me, lads?"

His squadron shout back.

"Yeah!"

"Let's fucking do it!"

"Fuck it, yeah!"

"Come on!"

"B Squadron… Chaaarge!" orders Michael with a thunderous voice.

They run down the last hill to Storey Arms as fast as they can. D Squadron look as if they don't want to be passed by B Squadron so they also kick it up a notch. Sarah is once again left behind. Further up ahead, G Squadron have finished and are waiting for them near the red telephone box with Cormac and the Training Wing Sergeant Major. From afar, Sarah sees all of B Squadron finish at the same time as D Squadron. A few minutes later, she hears G Squadron cheering her as she nears the finish line.

"Go, Sarah, go!"

"Come on, Sarah!"

"You can do it, Sarah!"

Sarah finally touches the wooden gate near the legendary red telephone box, to the cheering and applause of the troopers already at the finish.

"You have feathers in your bergens?" asks a trooper from D Squadron.

"Of course not. We just don't want to be caught up by a bloody policewoman," replies George, pointing his chin towards Sarah.

Everyone laughs. Sarah feels as if she's dying and is amazed that her friends still have energy to banter. This has been the most painful three-and-a-half-hours of her life! Her body is dripping with sweat, her shoulders and back are sore, her lungs are on fire, her heart's beating like it's about to explode, her abs are starting to cramp up, and her legs feel paralyzed. She takes off her bergen and now feels light enough that she can fly. She takes off her Oakleys and lets them rest on top of her head.

"Well done, Sarah!" says the Training Wing Sergeant Major, shaking her hand.

Cormac also shakes her hand, but looks embarrassed when Sarah looks him in the eyes. They all hang their bergens on the hanging scale to again ensure they weigh more than fifty pounds. Sarah's bergen weighs 51.3 lbs, more or less the same as the others.

"B Squadron, all of you, well done!" exclaims the Training Wing Sergeant Major. "You lot have smashed the regimental team record with a time of three hours and thirty-two minutes. And Sarah, you've done it in three hours and thirty-eight minutes. Very well done, lass!"

Everyone gives a round of applause and they all congratulate Sarah and B Squadron. The DS and five or so volunteers finally arrive at Storey Arms. Sarah's quite proud of her timing, but she has to admit that if she had to do the Fan Dance in full MTP while carrying an SA80A3, she'd probably need more than four hours to finish.

"Sarah, it would be an honour if you could join us for the Long Drag on the last day of Test Week," invites the DS leading the volunteers.

"The honour would be mine, Staff, thank you for the invitation," says Sarah with her remaining energy. 'I hope I don't die on it,' she thinks, genuinely worried.

Everyone seems happy that Sarah can join them on the last tab of Test Week. Although Sarah is not in Selection, she still wants to try it out to test herself. Michael finally comes up to her.

"That wasn't so bad, was it?" asks Michael, smiling at her.

"*Madre de Dios*," mumbles Sarah, still panting.

"Like those Para bastards at P Company like to say, 'pain is merely weakness leaving the body,'" quotes Michael.

Sarah can only smile at him. She's also envious that the others don't seem as tired as she is.

"You've pulled off an amazing accomplishment, *mo ghile mear*. I'm proud of you!"

Sarah's flattered, but still can't speak yet.

"Just remember every stage of the Fan Dance whenever you're enduring hardship in your life. You can always compare the situation with the pain and suffering you had to endure during the Fan Dance. Like when George ascended Mount Everest a few years ago. He said that facing the twelve metre Hillary Step was like facing the Jacob's Ladder on the way back to Storey Arms."

"How did Tony do on the Fan Dance?" asks Sarah, finally able to speak again.

"His team managed to stay with us most of the way, but they took their bloody time atop Pen y Fan just to grab some bloody selfies. But then they managed to catch up with us at Torpantau, just like you. They then stayed with us the whole time back to Storey Arms and we did it in three hours and thirty-four minutes."

"It's too bad I didn't have time to enjoy the scenery," says Sarah, annoyed that Tony once again beat her at something.

Sarah drains another bottle of water. She's dead tired but afraid that if she sits down, she won't be able to stand up again. She keeps moving, cooling down her body, her tank top drenched in sweat.

"Why don't you take your shirt off else you catch a cold," suggests Michael.

"You men would like that, wouldn't you?" quips Sarah.

Michael only smiles at her, but Sarah knows he's right. She could get hypothermia if she keeps wearing wet clothes in the mountains. Sarah takes off her tank top and uses it to wipe her body, still dripping with sweat. She's now wearing a black sports bra.

"Here, let me take some photos of you," says Michael, taking out his smartphone.

"Are you going to post them in the Interest Room?" asks Sarah with a raised eyebrow.

"Not unless you're wearing that red bikini under that sports bra…"

Sarah smiles and punches him in the chest. Michael photographs her smiling.

"There you go. Come on, model for me," says Michael.

Sarah is still too tired, but she does it for Michael. She poses like a covergirl with the Brecon Beacons as a beautiful background. Sarah might feel exhausted, but she still looks fresh and beautiful. Her body's still wet from sweat, which makes her look even more exotic. She can pose like a professional model, ignoring the drooling troopers around her. After a couple of minutes, all of B Squadron suddenly come forward and do some wacky poses with her, making the others laugh and forget their fatigue.

"Ro*i*ght lads, show's over. Load up in the lorries," orders Al.

Al helps Sarah into the lorry. She then hangs on intimately to Michael's arm.

"What's after this?" she asks when their lorry heads in the opposite direction to the other lorries headed for Credenhill.

"We're headed for PATA or Pontrilas Army Training Area, *mo ghile mear*, southwest of Hereford," answers Michael.

For some reason, all the troopers inside the lorry start sniggering when they hear their commander call Sarah by that nickname.

"Am I allowed to go inside?" asks Sarah.

"I've already sorted it with the Director," answers Michael.

"*Merci, mon amour*," says Sarah, giving him an adoring look and making the troopers even more jealous of their commander.

"Michael calls you '*mo ghile mear*', but you only call him '*mon amour*'?" quips George. "That's lame, Sarah. I know you can do better than that."

"What do you suggest I call him?" asks Sarah, smiling.

"I don't know… something Latin perhaps? Like Sillius Sodus? Or Nautius Maximus? Or maybe… Biggus… Dickus?" suggests George, trying hard to keep a straight face.

The troopers can't help but laugh.

Sarah smiles wider because she knows where this is heading. "Hmm… Biggus Dickus is appropriate for him… but then I don't want him calling me Incontinentia Buttocks."

Everyone rolls in laughter. It turns out that they're not the only ones who like 'Monty Python: Life of Brian'. As is always the way, one good joke deserves another. The wit and sarcasm keep bouncing off the canvas sides of the lorry until they finally reach Pontrilas, southwest of Hereford.

The lorry enters PATA without any problems and Sarah wonders what to expect inside. Tony told her that PATA is the training centre for counterterrorism for the UKSF Group and he and his men were invited to train there with B Squadron. Tony had told Sarah a little bit about what went on inside and now she's going to see for herself.

# CHAPTER 8
# THE KILLING HOUSE

11:48 GMT
Wednesday July 29, 2026
Pontrilas Army Training Area
Pontrilas, Herefordshire, England

They head towards the cookhouse near the front gate and across the football field. The food, provided by a private contractor, is quite delicious. Sarah helps herself to sirloin steak plus curry and rice, and she unashamedly takes as much food as the other troopers.

After lunch, they head towards the Killing House, officially called the Close Quarters Battle Building, a building used for Close Quarters Battle (CQB) training. PATA is home to several Killing Houses, including a number of underground facilities. Sarah and the troopers are heading towards the main Killing House, usually reserved for beginners. Before reaching the three-storey building on the northernmost part of the training area, they pass a football field, an indoor swimming area, several outdoor firing ranges, an EOD training area, a replica of a Boeing 747, and abseil training walls. From inside the lorry, Sarah watches the facilities pass by with mouth open in awe. She's especially impressed by the 747 replica. There's no way the Densus-88 training facility in Megamendung, Bogor could compete with PATA. What's surprising is the number of sheep, probably owned by citizens from the immediate area, grazing inside the military training area.

After they debus, Michael whispers to Sarah. "Just switch on, keep your trap shut, listen and do what Al says, and you'll be all right."

Michael enters the Killing House and leaves Sarah with Al and his squadron. Inside the three-storey Killing House, the walls are covered with ballistic rubber to absorb the bullets and prevent them from ricocheting. All training uses live rounds and each scenario is developed to be as close to reality as possible. Although they use live rounds, accidents during CQB training seldom happen.

Inside are rooms decked out to resemble a typical domestic residence, with furniture, toilets, TVs, lamps, beds, and the like. But each room has exhaust fans to clear out the smoke and CCTV cameras to record every move they make. The walls and partitions can be easily rearranged. They use steel targets, some of which are put on a special platform that can move around randomly and is programmed to stop once the target's hit.

Al gives Sarah a full CQB kit, starting with a black uniform called black kit, tactical gear including a respirator, a couple of flashbangs, and a set of plasticuffs. After she puts everything on, Al hands her a Sig Sauer P226 and a couple of mags. Upon receiving the pistol, Sarah checks the chamber, the most basic of firearms safety procedures, earning her a nod and a smile of approval from Al.

After everything's ready, Al gives her the mission. "R*oi*ght! Inside this unlocked room we have an X-Ray with a hostile High Value Target. Here's the photo of the HVT. This is a one-up snatch operation. You will shoot the X-Ray, snatch the HVT, and extract him outside. I say again, you will shoot the X-Ray, snatch the HVT, and extract him outside. Just remember the principles of CQB, which are speed, aggression, and surprise, and you'll be fine."

Al shows Sarah a picture of the HVT and she smiles when she sees that the High Value Target is Michael. One-up means that Sarah has to do this solo and X-Ray is the British Army term for terrorists. This is one way the British differ from the US and Indonesia, who prefer to use the term Tango. The SAS talk about utilizing speed, aggression, and surprise, a minor variation on the US's 'speed, surprise, and violence of action', although both mean the same. In this mission, Sarah must shoot an X-Ray and extract the HVT from a room. She's done this sort of training hundreds of times before so she doesn't feel anxious.

"Do remember that you're using live ammo and we would prefer our squadron commander in one piece, please," reminds Al seriously.

"Copy," says Sarah, also seriously.

"You may start when ready."

Sarah sees that the door handle is on the right side and the hinges are hidden from view, meaning that the door opens inwards. After she enters, she'll have to sweep left while clearing all the X-Rays inside the room. Al said that there was only one X-Ray, but he could easily be lying. She's used to these kinds of tricks during CQB training and even likes to do the same to her men. After all the X-Rays have been dispatched, she can finally handle the HVT.

Sarah first checks that the door is really unlocked, which it is. She stacks up by herself on the left side of the door while preparing her flashbang. She holds the lever with her right to prevent it from detonating and pulls out the pin with her left hand. As per SOP, she keeps the pin in one of the pockets of her black kit. She opens the door with her left hand and rolls the flashbang inside. She immediately closes the door and reaches with her right hand for the Sig Sauer, holstered on her right thigh.

After hearing the flashbang explode, Sarah makes her entry and everything seems to go in super-slow motion. SCAN. With a CQB move called 'slicing the pie', she clears the right-front area before sweeping left. She sees a target on the right-back side of the room. ACQUIRE. Sarah aims her Sig Sauer towards the centre mass of the target. SHOOT. SHOOT. Sarah fires twice. ACQUIRE. Sarah makes sure her two shots hit the target. SCAN. Sarah keeps sweeping left. She sees that the HVT is stunned by the flashbang but since he's not holding a weapon, she ignores him for the moment and keeps sweeping left. There's another target to the left of the HVT, which she also shoots twice. Sarah keeps sweeping left to clear the left-front side of the room, but sees no more targets. She does all of this while moving forward towards the HVT, who is already starting to react. All of this happened in only four seconds, from the time Sarah pulled out the pin of her flashbang to this very moment.

Sarah sees the HVT start to reach for his pistol. Quick as lightning, Sarah gives him a left hook to his jaw, flooring him down on his arse. With her pistol pointed at his face, she pulls on his hair with her left hand until he's face down on the floor and handcuffs him with the plasticuffs. She frisks him thoroughly and takes the pistol in his waist, a small pistol by his groin, and another on his right ankle. She must clear all the weapons she finds before storing them in her black kit. Then she pulls on his hair with her right hand and his arms with her left and drags him outside. She throws him face-first on the ground in front of Al and B Squadron.

"Two Tangos... I mean, two X-Rays down, HVT in custody," says Sarah, removing her respirator. "All clear and mission accomplished!"

Everything Sarah did had been taught by her instructors at Densus and it took her just thirty-two seconds, from pulling the pin of her flashbang until 'mission accomplished'.

Al stops his stopwatch and everyone seems impressed. She's done a flawless job, although the CQB tactics she used were outdated.

"Well done, Sarah!" says Al, cutting off the plasticuffs from Michael's hands. "You already have excellent CQB skills. You responded to the poor intel perfectly and handled the HVT extremely well."

Sarah smiles proudly at being praised by the CQB expert.

"Let's study the footage, shall we?" invites Michael, standing up. His right jaw is red from Sarah's punch, his face and lips are dirty and bloody from being thrown to the floor, and his hair is a mess.

Sarah doesn't feel remotely guilty because she was often treated the same way when she played the HVT role. She would even get angry if her men hesitated handling her or frisking her. She once had to recommend one of her men be kicked out of Densus because he absolutely refused to search her chest and crotch, citing religious grounds. Although Sarah respected his religious belief, there's no room for religion in the middle of an operation. That sort of behaviour could get him killed and endanger his teammates in a real operation.

Everyone goes up to the second floor, which makes Sarah feel like she's again climbing Jacob's Ladder. Behind them she sees a team of people in civilian uniforms, the word 'QinetiQ' emblazoned on their backs, rearranging the Killing House for the next round. On the observation floor, they all look at the footage, first in real time and then in slow motion. Sarah laughs when all of B Squadron shout and cheer each time they see the footage of Sarah flooring their commander with a left hook.

Al frequently stops the footage to give comments. "First, as you can see, the HVT is already reacting against you once you cleared the second target. Sometimes, it would already be too late for the assault team. That's why during overt entry, you should enter *with* the flashbang rather than enter after it explodes. The respirator you were using can significantly reduce the effects of the flash and sound released by the flashbang."

Sarah thinks hard for a moment. A flashbang grenade is designed to produce a blinding flash of light and an intensely loud 'bang' without causing permanent injury. The light and sound temporarily incapacitates the enemy so the assault force can dispatch them without much drama. The CQB instructors of Densus taught Sarah to throw the flashbang into the room and wait until it detonates *before* entering the room. Al's teaching her to enter *with* the flashbang. Sarah wonders how accurately one could shoot with a flashbang detonating next to them in an enclosed space, even when wearing a respirator.

"Copy," says Sarah, nodding even though she doesn't entirely agree with Al.

"Your aim was perfect. However, it's better to use controlled pairs and headshots instead of hammer pairs to the centre mass. Do you know the difference between controlled pairs and hammer pairs?"

"Indeed. Controlled pairs are 'Acquire, Shoot, Acquire, Shoot, Acquire', and hammer pairs are 'Acquire, Shoot, Shoot, Acquire'," answers Sarah.

"Precisely! Remember that most criminals and terrorists today use body armour and the 9mm doesn't have much stopping power compared to higher calibre bullets."

Sarah again thinks hard for a moment. The two shooting methods Al's described are both called double tap. The methods are a little different, but both have the same deadly purpose. Sarah has always been taught to use hammer pairs and aim for the centre mass. Controlled pairs are a bit slower (though much more accurate) than hammer pairs, and headshots are much more difficult than shots to the centre mass of the body. The purpose of the double tap is to have two bullets enter almost at the same place, killing the enemy as quickly as possible. This is because the 9mm bullet is not as powerful as higher calibre bullets. For the SAS, Sarah recognizes the problems with double taps to the centre mass, as sophisticated criminals and terrorists in Europe often wear body armour. However, for the INP, the Indonesian Human Rights Commission forbids Indonesian policemen from shooting criminals or terrorists in the head, even when they're armed. Sarah sometimes feels that KOMNAS HAM defends criminals or terrorists better than it does law-enforcement personnel.

Sarah then notices that all of B Squadron is also listening intently to Al, although she's sure they must have heard this many times before. She then decides to keep her opinions to herself. She's here to learn, not to debate tactics with the instructor from the most experienced counterterrorist unit in the world.

"Copy," says Sarah, nodding.

"Your handling of the HVT was also superb, though we prefer to force him to the ground than knock him out. Why drag or carry him when he can walk out on his own two feet?" explains Al, smiling.

"Copy," says Sarah, returning his smile.

"Ro*i*ght, overall it was an excellent job and expertly executed. Now, let us show you how we would clear a two-storey building. Could you please choose any four of us for the 4-man team?" orders Al.

In the SAS, the smallest unit consists of four men including the team leader and it's called a 4-man team or 4-man patrol. Sarah looks over B Squadron and smiles when they all raise their hands, eager to show off their skills to her. In a 4-man team, the pointman and the number two should be the most experienced in CQB, number three should be the leader, and number four the rear guard and Method of Entry (MOE) specialist, assigned to provide access into the stronghold for the others.

Now it's Sarah's turn to give them a hard time. "Right, the pointman is George, two is Dave, three is Robert, and four is Al," she says, smiling wickedly.

Al and Michael look at each other. Sarah has given them a less-than-ideal stack. George is absolutely huge and the pointman should ideally have a small frame so that the number two has a good view in front of them. Number three should be an experienced leader, something that the enormous Robert seems to lack. Dave, as number two, is going to look like a burger sandwiched between those two huge men. And Al, the most experienced operative, is in a position reserved for beginners. Sarah tried to choose the most hopeless team possible. However, she doesn't know that three of the four men she's picked are the most experienced operatives in B Squadron.

"Ro*i*ght then! You can watch us live here on the telly," says Al calmly.

The four men go downstairs and prepare themselves. A few minutes later, Sarah sees them stack up in their black kit, heavily armed. George, Dave and Robert, in front, carry MP5s while Al is holding a Remington 870 shotgun. Michael counts the men behind him to make sure everyone is accounted for.

"Killing House ready and I have control," says Michael into a microphone. "Standby... Standby... Go!"

The 4-man team start their assault. They enter randomly, which is quite different to Sarah's Densus training. She can't discern the pattern between the pointman and the number two. As pointman, George sometimes makes a move called a crisscross and sometimes makes a move called a buttonhook. A crisscross is when an operative crosses the entrance upon entering the doorway, moving diagonally and ending up opposite his original position during the stack. A buttonhook is when an operative steps *around* the doorframe to clear the front corner of the room. Dave, as number two in the stack, seems able to adapt to George's movement without hesitation and without George having to say anything. All four men move as if the assault was perfectly choreographed.

Just as Al had said, they enter the rooms with the flashbang, thrown by Dave. The flashbang detonates while they're entering the room and it doesn't seem to affect the accuracy of their controlled pairs. Sarah also observes that the SAS grip the MP5 differently to the way she was taught at Densus. Robert's voice is calm leading them, but Sarah doesn't understand some of the Voice Procedures (VP), like 'carry on to Green-9-0' or 'stand firm and cover Red-3-0 hallway'. Robert's codes remind Sarah of Michael when they both fought off The Cartel at Carluccio's.

The 4-man team reaches the base of the stairs and starts to ascend according to CQB procedures. Their feet go up sideways and raised high to prevent tripping on the stairs. Sarah doesn't see any difference between the SAS and Densus on the stair-clearing procedure and the team has executed it perfectly. They then start clearing the rooms on the first floor without any problems.

After the last room is cleared, Robert's distinctive Birmingham accent is heard on the speaker. "Stronghold secured!"

"Well? What do you think?" asks Michael.

"*Dios mío!*" exclaims Sarah, thoroughly impressed. "It's like watching poetry in motion!"

Michael smiles. "Any questions?"

"Your room-clearing procedures... I can't seem to find a pattern to them. We were taught that the first shooter should always do a buttonhook or a crisscross, depending on the layout of the room."

"That's an excellent observation, Sarah!" says Michael, giving her a wide smile. "In essence, the pointman's TAOR, Tactical Area of Responsibility, is not fixed, but based on the first threat they see. The pointman goes to the corner where he first sees the threat and then dominates it. The second shooter has to react to the movement of the pointman and then goes the opposite direction. The main principle is that the pointman's movement is never wrong. If the stack is on the left and he crisscrosses to the right, the second shooter should react and do a buttonhook to the left. If the pointman does a buttonhook to the left, the second shooter should react and crisscross to the right. The shooters behind them must react to the shooters in front of them. It's highly flexible and it's based on the Initiative-Based Tactics. So far, we think this is the best method for Immediate Actions with zero INT like the one you just witnessed, and also perfect against armed and dedicated X-Rays like the ones we are currently facing."

"Copy," says Sarah, nodding enthusiastically.

Densus-88 almost *never* conduct Immediate Actions. Almost all their assaults are meticulously choreographed beforehand. This is because law enforcement doctrine differs from military doctrine and Densus-88 is a police unit. Law enforcement doctrine dictates that they try to *apprehend* suspects to bring them to justice, not to kill them.

"What else did you notice?" asks Michael.

"Robert kept calling out colours and numbers. What is 'White-6-0', 'Green-9-1' and 'Red-3-0'? I didn't understand any of that."

"We call it the SAS Colour Clock Code," answers Michael, opening a file on one of the laptops.

On the large screen above them, Sarah sees a square divided into four, triangular segments. The upper segment is coloured black, the right red, the bottom white, and the left green. Outside the square, there are numbers from one to twelve like a normal clock.

Michael gives her the explanation. "Imagine the White side is the front side of any stronghold no matter which direction of the compass it is facing. It could be the front of any building, car, aeroplane, boat, et cetera. Black side would be the back side, Red would be the right side, and Green would be the left side. The clock is used for more accurate positioning. The second number indicates which floor unless the stronghold has only one floor. So when a couple of days ago I said to you 'four X-Rays from Green-10', it meant that there were four X-Rays coming in from the back-left side of the kitchen. This method is especially useful for snipers calling out positions of sighted X-Rays or Yankees. Let me give you an example; if you hear one of your snipers say 'X-Ray sighted, Red-4-0 window', what does that mean, Sarah?"

Sarah thinks hard for a moment while looking at the picture. "Does that mean that there is an X-Ray sighted on the right side of the building… towards the front of the stronghold… on the ground floor window?"

"Precisely! That's very good, Sarah!" says Michael. He then tosses his men a dirty look and some of the troopers get sheepish because they hadn't caught on as quickly as Sarah when they'd first learned about the colour clock code.

"But why do you need the colours? Why not just use the clock for positioning?" asks Sarah.

"That's a very good question, Sarah!" says Michael. "Sometimes there's confusion if you call out just the clock for positioning. If I say 'four X-Rays at ten o'clock', does that mean *my* ten o'clock? *Your* ten o'clock? Or the *stronghold's* ten o'clock? The colour makes it much easier. If someone says the word 'Green', you will automatically think about the left side of the stronghold no matter which way you are facing. This method is particularly useful during Immediate Actions where sometimes you don't have time to study the blueprints of the stronghold or rehearse the assault. Once you've cleared a room, for example on the back-left side on the first floor of the stronghold, all you have to say is 'Room cleared, Black-11-1' and everyone will know which room you meant."

"Copy," says Sarah, nodding enthusiastically.

"Let me show you another building," invites Michael.

Michael goes down the stairs and Sarah follows him. They see Al giving Robert, Dave, and George a debriefing on the ground floor. Hidden from Sarah's view, Al and the others smile and nod at Michael when he passes them. Michael returns their smiles and winks.

Michael and Sarah go to another building across the street. The small building only has two storeys and the upper floor is used for observation. In the middle of the room, there are two tables full of mags for the Sig Sauer pistol and the HK MP5A2 submachine gun. The room is surrounded by steel, head-sized targets, positioned according to the colour clock code. Sarah can immediately figure out the function of this building.

"This is the Colour Clock Building and we use it to practice the colour clock code," explains Michael. "Take all the mags for both weapons, wear your respirator, strap on the MP5 and sidearm, and ready your weapons. After you're ready, a recording calls out the colour clock code. Your job is to shoot according to the commands from the recording. So if you hear the words 'Red-2', give headshots using controlled pairs only at the Red-2 target. Is that clear?"

"Copy," says Sarah, picking up the mags.

Michael goes to the upper floor to observe her training.

Sarah readies her MP5 and puts it in the low ready position. "Ready!"

A voice recording says 'Black-12'. ACQUIRE. Sarah aims her weapon toward the target, dead ahead of her. SHOOT. Sarah fires her weapon. ACQUIRE. The MP5 has almost no recoil and Sarah immediately reacquires her target. SHOOT. Sarah fires again at the same target. ACQUIRE. Sarah confirms that both shots hit the target.

"White-6," says the recording.

Sarah turns around. SCAN. ACQUIRE. SHOOT. ACQUIRE. SHOOT. ACQUIRE. At first, the recording only calls out the primary positions, Black-12, Red-3, White-6, and Green-9. After a few hundred shots, the recording starts calling out the secondary positions, which are Black-11, Black-1, Red-2, Red-4, White-5, White-7, Green-8, and Green-10. Everything becomes doubly difficult when the recording starts alternating between the primary and secondary positions.

In the middle of Sarah's training, the CO of the 22$^{nd}$ Regiment suddenly joins Michael on the upper floor.

"How is she?" asks Cormac.

"She's fulfilling all my fantasies, mate," teases Michael, giving his CO a cheeky grin.

Cormac's eyes briefly become unfocused, but soon return to normal. "You know what I mean, you cheeky bastard!"

Michael lets out a satisfying laugh. "She's switched-on, a fast learner, and extremely fit. She's just as smart and tough as any rupert in The Regiment, Mac."

"Would you have her as a member of your patrol?"

# THE POLICEWOMAN

Michael gives him an incredulous look. "A member of my patrol? Didn't you hear what I just said? She's a born leader and commander, Mac. She has what it takes to command one of my troops. Right here and right now."

"Bollocks!" says Cormac, sceptically.

"She asks excellent questions and knows when to keep her gob shut. Everyone is impressed with her, including Al. And you know how hard it is to impress Al! Physically, she's in excellent condition. You saw for yourself that she almost kept up with us during the Fan Dance and we smashed the bloody regimental team record!"

"What about her aggressiveness and combat skills?" asks Cormac, still sceptical.

Michael gives his CO another incredulous look. "What kind of a bone question is that, you bloody wanker? I've already told you and the Director that I saw her slot fourteen fucking players without the slightest fucking hesitation! She even slotted a couple of them in unarmed combat, one with a knife and Tiny fucking Mullins, who was once a member of the Army Ranger Wing, with just a fucking pen! Don't you realize how hard it is to do that?"

"How about her ability to adapt and learn?" asks Cormac, visibly wavering.

"See for yourself!"

They observe Sarah enthusiastically fire controlled pairs towards the targets according to the instructions of the recording. She's holding the MP5 with the butt high on her shoulders, both elbows downwards, and her left hand on the magazine well. This grip is called the magwell grip, mostly used by the US Special Forces. Once she's exhausted all the ammo for the MP5, Sarah switches to the Sig Sauer. Cormac can see how she switches weapons and she executes the switch perfectly. He can also see Sarah change mags without even looking at her weapon. With the pistol, Sarah uses the Isosceles Stance, different to the SAS's Weaver Stance.

"Just send the Director the recording of her one-up snatch, you'll be surprised at how well she did it," suggests Michael, rubbing his sore jaw. Sarah almost knocked him out as he hadn't expected her to hit him. And it was one hell of a punch too.

"I'll do that," says Cormac. "Tell Al to teach her the Weaver Stance and our standard grip. Let's see how well she can adapt herself to new techniques. Then teach her our various entry methods. Give her the The Test and let's see how well she does."

"I'll wager you a hundred quid she'll do better than you," challenges Michael.

"You're on."

They keep watching Sarah train for a couple more minutes.

"So… you really think the Director's plan is all right?" asks Cormac.

"I've already told you a million fucking times that we'll need them in the squadrons for future operations, you bloody wanker," says Michael firmly.

"Fine," says Cormac, sighing.

Michael has frequently debated the Director's plans with Cormac, but Cormac always comes to the same conclusion. Thanks to Sarah, though, Michael can see that Cormac is finally starting to be convinced the Director's plan will work.

After observing Sarah for a few more minutes, Cormac seems to struggle with something. "Which fantasies?" he blurts out.

Michael smirks. "Yesterday morning, it was the handcuffs. Last night, she did a bellydance in her bra and panties. I plan on taking her to Soho after her training to shop for some costumes."

Cormac can see that Michael is telling the truth. He leaves the room, his eyes unfocused. A few minutes later, Sarah has spent all the ammo.

"All weapons unloaded," says Sarah.

Michael goes down to meet her. "All right, *mo ghile mear*?"

"*Oui. Merci pour les cours, mon amour!*" answers Sarah, her eyes gleaming.

"Let's continue tomorrow, shall we?"

"There are more lessons?" asks Sarah, enthusiastically.

"Of course," says Michael, giving her a water bottle. "We start tomorrow morning at eight."

Sarah puts her arm through his while draining the water. They exit the building and see Cormac from behind, briefing the rest of B Squadron.

"… and those who did not continue taking their NAPS pills after their recent deployment from Syria are obliged to continue taking them for a month after deployment. Those who fail to comply will be RTU'd," says the SAS commander in his Scottish burr.

### THE POLICEWOMAN

All the troopers complain.

"Are *you* still taking those pills, Mac?" asks George, giving his CO a hostile look.

"Of course I am," answers Cormac.

"They'll make you impotent, you know," says Dave, matter-of-factly.

"I've heard about those rumours and they are simply not true," assures Cormac, both hands in front of him. "I had a major stonker only a few minutes ago."

Sarah chokes on her drink as B Squadron collapses in laughter. On the ground, Michael is laughing so hard that no sound comes out of his mouth. Cormac finally realizes that Sarah is behind him and becomes extremely red-faced. He calmly goes to his Range Rover and exits the area while B Squadron is still on the ground, holding their stomachs. Only Sarah is still on her feet, coughing and laughing as hard as the others.


07:56 GMT
Thursday July 30, 2026
Pontrilas Army Training Area
Pontrilas, Herefordshire, England

The next morning, they arrive on schedule at PATA. Sarah looks fresh and beautiful in a plain white shirt and the green camouflage pants of Brimob. Al takes Sarah to the short range and teaches her the Weaver Stance for the pistol and the standard grip for the MP5. As expected, Sarah feels awkward at first, but everyone is impressed with how quickly she can adapt herself to the new shooting styles.

After Al's sure that Sarah has mastered the new styles, they go to the main Killing House again. They teach Sarah how they conduct the Overt Entry. First, Al introduces her to various Method of Entry (MOE) tools used by the SAS. The dynamic hammer, the Halligan bar, the hydraulic spreader-cutter, the Remington 870 shotgun with Hatton bullets made of hard plastic, and various frame charges used for blowing up windows, doors, and even walls. The frame charge can be used to make a hole the size of George in a wall so that the assault force needn't enter through a door or window, making their entry much more unpredictable. Sarah is already familiar with everything but doesn't mind the refresher training. They teach her everything about everything, from how to make a charge, how to detonate a charge, and how to disarm and dispose of a charge.

The SAS can easily acquire ammo and PE4 at PATA. This makes it easier for them during training. In fact, during the six months a squadron is 'On The Team', a single SAS Trooper can spend up to 100,000 rounds and hundreds of pounds of explosives. Even with rigorous supply checks, it's no wonder The Cartel can easily smuggle PE4s out from this place, especially if they have people in the UKSF Group on their payroll.

The next lesson is Covert Entry, in which Sarah must check the other side of the door before picking it. To do this, they use an endoscope camera inserted under the door. They can also use a thermographic camera to determine the location of someone by their body heat. Sarah must report her findings to her team by hand signals or by whispering through her headset. If she receives a signal to conduct a Covert Entry from the leader, she must conduct the entry stealthily. Sarah must lockpick the locked door without any sound, but since she's trained in lockpicking, this is no problem for Sarah.

Once Sarah has mastered her role as rear guard and MOE specialist, Al moves her to the role of pointman. Al emphasizes that Sarah must never stop for any reason and concentrate fully on dominating her Tactical Area of Responsibility based on the first immediate threat she sees. Sarah manages perfectly, although she's still more familiar with US Voice Procedures and still needs to get used to British Army VP. Sarah's also not yet used to the term 'X-Ray' and keeps saying 'Tango', although Al tells her not to worry about it because it's not important. Al tells her that the SAS use the term 'X-Ray' because they like to put an 'X' through pictures of all the terrorists they've killed.

Towards lunchtime, Al puts Sarah on the number two position. He emphasizes that Sarah must react to two things, the pointman and the layout of the room. The number two also has responsibility for throwing the flashbang inside the room during Overt Entry. Al reminds her that if the pointman crisscrosses, Sarah should buttonhook, and vice versa. She should do this automatically because the pointman won't give her verbal instructions. The number two and three must be extra careful because any mistakes from them can hurt the trooper in front of them.

After Al's happy that Sarah's mastered both positions, he turns off all the lights and gives her the latest Ground Panoramic Night Vision Goggles (GPNVG). Sarah's eyes go wide when Al gives her the state-of-the-art goggles. Unlike the NVG that Densus uses, which only has two tubes, the GPNVG has four tubes, doubling Sarah's field of view by up to 120 degrees. They then train in the Killing House in total darkness using the GPNVG. By lunch time, Sarah has mastered the art of assaulting a stronghold in total darkness and now she's absolutely starving.

All six of them go to the PATA cookhouse for lunch and Sarah sees four other women already there. Although her friends seem to know the women, they only glance at each other without exchanging greetings. The women, who are roughly Sarah's age, are wearing green sports bras, MTP pants, and army boots. One of them is extremely beautiful and all four are just as athletic as Sarah is. Three of the women have dyed their hair blonde, but the roots have started to grow back black. The last woman, the most beautiful, has long, red hair that looks natural.

Just like the other SAS troopers, those women seem to recognize Sarah when she passes their table. They don't greet her, but lean in close and whisper among themselves. Sarah hears one of them say 'Tony's sister', and without thinking she rolls her eyes.

Sarah suspects the women must come from the Special Reconnaissance Regiment (SRR), known as The Det. Basically, the role of the SRR is to seek and observe the target, laying out the groundwork before an assault by the SAS or SBS. To this day, SRR is the only unit in the UKSF Group that accepts women.

Sarah and the other five take their food and sit down. Robert, Dave, and George, who are still single, position themselves facing the table with the four women.

"Do you have any questions so far?" asks Michael.

"Indeed. Your training methods are different from what I'm used to. It doesn't feel like the military."

"What kind of training methods are you familiar with?" asks Michael, a satisfied smile on his face. He can see that Sarah is curious about those four women, but smart enough to keep her questions to herself.

"Our instructors usually give us a hard time if we don't learn fast enough or make too many mistakes. They give us punishments, yell at us, and even slap us around, especially if we repeat the exact same mistakes. You know, like drill sergeants," explains Sarah.

Sarah does the same to the policemen under her command. She treats the men of her unit very hard, especially those who are slow in learning. She has no qualms in slapping or even punching them for repeatedly messing up. She often curses at them, although they sometimes look baffled as she often curses in Dutch. This leadership style was taught to her by her instructors at Brimob, Gegana, and Densus-88. Tony used to have the same leadership style, but changed it after returning from England.

In stark contrast, during Sarah's training at PATA, Michael and Al have trained her patiently and praised her when she follows their instructions to the letter. If Sarah makes a mistake, and even if she makes the same mistake again, they patiently give her feedback and correct her without the need for yelling or punishing. Besides telling her how to do something correctly, they also explain *why* they do it that way. During training, they repeatedly had to stop when Sarah unconsciously reverted to the Isosceles Stance when using the pistol and the magwell grip when holding the MP5. They immediately corrected her and reminded her *why* they have to do it that way. They are patient with her because they know it takes time to change old habits.

This is 180 degrees different to her experience in Brimob, Gegana, and Densus-88. When she first joined those units, she was often yelled at, punished, and even slapped around by her instructors and senior officers. She expected that kind of treatment before she joined so she didn't mind being treated that way and has never taken it personally. But here, now, she's appreciating the SAS way.

"It still happens in the green army, but not in The Regiment anymore. The Brigade of Gurkhas is a lot like us also," explains Al. "Basically, why give a trooper a hard time if he's slower than the others? It'll just make him feel bad about himself and it won't help him learn faster."

"All the really slow ones get binned during Selection, but if someone needs extra training, well, we just give it to him. We encourage the other men in his troop to give him the extra training as well," explains Michael. "Anyhow, punishment is never a good reinforcement, especially in training. It's always better to have troopers seek rewards from instructors than have them only looking to avoid punishments. Right?"

Sarah thinks hard for a few moments. The people around her are recognized by the special forces community as the masters of CQB and this makes Sarah both happy and flattered every time they praise her skills. As a result, she's been trying hard to follow their instructions, to keep earning their praise. They don't need to yell or punish her because Sarah is already highly motivated to learn from them. Sarah now feels guilty about how hard she's been on her men at Densus and the security guards of her housing complex. In almost all cases, she realizes that she hadn't needed to treat them that way. Sarah feels that now is the time to change her leadership style.

"Copy," says Sarah, smiling. "In Indonesia, the tougher the unit, the tougher the atmosphere. Here, it's the exact opposite and your regiment is the toughest in the UK."

They only smile faintly upon hearing Sarah's praise.

"Unfortunately, that's not really true," says George.

"It's not?" asks Sarah.

The five SAS men shake their heads and look a bit deflated, intriguing Sarah.

"Then who do you, as members of the SAS, think is the toughest unit in the British Army?" she asks.

"That would be the Brigade of Gurkhas," answers Al. The others nod in agreement.

"The Brigade of Gurkhas is tougher than the 22$^{nd}$ Regiment?" asks Sarah, incredulously.

"Every single bloody Gurkha in the whole bloody brigade can do the bloody Fan Dance in under four hours," explains George. Sarah suddenly remembers the Interpol team teasing Michael about this. "They've all done it in full kit with fifty-pound bergens whilst also carrying the SA80A3 rifle and that even includes all the bloody female Gurkhas. All the bloody Gurkhas from the Royal Gurkha Rifles did the bloody thing in under three and a half hours. Physically, we're bags of shit compared to the Gurkhas of the RGR."

Sarah's jaw drops. "*All* soldiers of the Royal Gurkha Rifles did the Fan Dance in under three hours and thirty minutes in full kit plus rifle? How the devil did they manage to do that?"

"They ran every single step of the way and stopped only to give their names to the DS at Pen y Fan and Torpantau. Then they ran all the way back without taking a rest," says Dave. "They ran up and down Jacob's Ladder as if they were mountain lions. You wouldn't believe how tough they really are until you've seen them yourself. They really motored, especially on the uphill and downhill sections. They're so used to running up and down the mountains that they had trouble running on the flat terrain of the Roman Road. They're better at running up and down the bloody Brecon Beacons than running the bloody London Marathon."

Michael continues. "We only do the Fan Dance and the Long Drag twice a year. They probably do something like that in Nepal every day of their lives. One of the recipients of the Victoria Cross, Lachhiman Gurung, who lost an eye and an arm in World War II, had to walk three days up and down the mountains of the Himalayas just to collect his monthly pension. He then had to return back home the same way. He did it every month until he was seventy years old or so. When he couldn't make the trip anymore, one of his sons carried him on his back, just so he could sign the papers to release his pension."

Sarah can only listen to those stories with awe. The toughness of the Gurkhas is legendary and they're widely considered as the best infantrymen in the world. But Sarah didn't realize how tough they really were until she compared her timing at the Fan Dance with theirs. Sarah's proud of her fitness level, but it turns out to be nowhere near the level of the SAS. And the fitness level of the SAS in turn is nowhere near the level of the Gurkhas.

"So... the toughest unit of the entire *British* Army is the Brigade of Gurkhas, who are from *Nepal*?" teases Sarah.

The SAS men nod and look even more deflated.

"Well then, if that's the case," says Sarah, pretending to snort, "could you please remove my bikini photos from the SAS Barracks and have them posted instead in the RGR's Interest Room?"

The five SAS men laugh out loud.

"Good one, Sarah!" says Dave.

"Why aren't there any Gurkhas in the UKSF?" asks Sarah, still curious.

"The Gurkhas are the ultimate infantrymen, but not the roight personality for the UKSF," explains Al.

"How so?" asks Sarah.

"Well, the Gurkhas have a somewhat fatalistic attitude towards life and this doesn't fit with the UKSF mentality," explains Al.

"Fatalistic?"

"In Nepal, they have nothing because it's one of the world's poorest countries," explains Michael. "In the British Army, we give them food, clothes, money, a career, and a chance to become British citizens. In return, they're willing to give their lives for our King and Country. A Gurkha will do anything an officer orders them to do without question. Whilst in the UKSF Group, we prefer blokes who can show initiative, think on their own, and have a strong will to survive."

"They are absolutely fearless though," continues Al. "They have such a fearsome reputation that during the Falklands War, the Argies abandoned a strong defensive position on Mount William when they learned the Gurkhas were the ones going to attack them. The Gurkhas were disappointed because they took their objective unopposed as the Argies had already retreated."

"I've heard about their reputation, but are they really that good in battle?" asks Sarah, still curious.

"Well, during the War in Afghanistan in 2010, thirty or so Taliban fighters attacked a checkpoint post in the Helmand province that was being checked by Corporal Dipprasad Pun from the 1$^{st}$ Battalion of the Royal Gurkha Rifles," says Michael. "Corporal Pun found himself surrounded by the Taliban fighters armed with AK-47s and RPGs. Corporal Pun, alone and believing he was about to die, decided to slot as many of the enemy as possible. During the engagement, he reportedly spent all his ammunition, which was more than 400 rounds, used seventeen hand grenades, and a Claymore mine before battering a couple of Taliban fighters with the tripod of his machine gun. Queen Elizabeth awarded him the Conspicuous Gallantry Cross, which is the second highest medal for valour after the Victoria Cross."

"The thirty-to-one engagement wasn't considered a fair fight… for the Taliban, of course," says Dave. "A British Army general even commented that any battlefield commander who thinks he can take one Gurkha down with just thirty men is foolish."

"And that's not the only time a lone Gurkha defeated an overwhelming enemy force," continues George. "On a train ride from India, a retired Gurkha named Bishnu Shrestha, armed with only his khukuri knife, defeated around forty train robbers armed with pistols, swords, and knives when he saw that they had started raping a girl. Just like the Battle of Agincourt, in the narrow aisle of the train, a highly trained fighter like Shrestha had the advantage. Although some of the bandits had pistols, they were either fake or handled by someone who didn't want to get too close to an angry Gurkha armed with his fearsome khukuri knife. After about ten minutes of fighting in the train aisles, three bandits were dead and twenty or so of them were wounded. The rest had wisely decided to drop their loot and flee."

"That's incredible!" says Sarah, thoroughly impressed.

"But that's nothing, Sarah. We once saw a bloke successfully defend an Observation Point from an attack by 113 insurgents with just a machine gun in an open field," says Dave, grinning.

"How did you know there were exactly 113 insurgents?" asks Sarah, sceptically. "Did you take the time to count them when they attacked?"

"The same bloke then led the counterattack that slotted every single one of them and left exactly 113 dead bodies," says Dave. His grin turns into a wince when someone kicks his leg under the table.

"Wow! I'd really love to hear that story," says Sarah.

"You like to hear war stories?" asks Michael, seriously.

"Oh, indeed! It really turns me on," says Sarah, giving him a naughty wink.

"Then in that case, I'm sure one of us blokes will tell you about it someday," says George, grinning.

Everyone laughs except George, who gets his own leg kicked under the table and winces. Sarah hears the women behind her stand up. Three of them leave the cookhouse, but one comes up to their table.

"Hi, fellas! I noticed you have a new trooper today," says the beautiful red-head with her posh accent. She thrusts her hand towards Sarah. "Hi, I'm Sheila Neeson."

Sarah stands up to shake her hand. "I'm Sarah Dharmawan from the INP. Would you like to join us, Sheila?"

"I'm all right, thanks," says Sheila, still standing. She's the same height as Sarah.

Sheila looks even prettier up close, but has hard features and piercing green eyes. Her body is lean and shredded like Sarah's. Sarah sits down again, which brings her face to the same level as Sheila's stomach. Sarah's jealous of her six-pack, which looks like it could take repeated blows from a ballistic hammer. Sheila's perfect abs are adorned with an outie bellybutton, which makes her stomach look even sexier. Sarah glances at the others and sees that George, Dave, and Robert are looking at Sheila like she's one of the Seven Wonders of the World, making Sarah even more jealous of her.

"We missed you at the Fan Dance yesterday," says George, eyes gleaming.

"We planned to join, but we just got back from Brize Norton for our parachute wings," says Sheila. "Anyway, me and the girls plan on trying the Long Drag this time. Any of you coming?"

"We plan to do it also. We'll see you at the barracks beforehand," says Michael with a forced smile.

"Great! So how is Tony, Sarah? I absolutely loved him. Did he finally marry that gorgeous girlfriend of his?"

"Indeed. He got married soon after he got back from England. He has a son now."

"Oh, well, I guess the good fellas are always taken," says Sheila, glancing at Michael, who immediately looks away.

For some reason, Sarah feels even more jealous of her.

"There are still a lot of single, strapping blokes in The Regiment, you know… and some of them are right in front of you," says Dave, giving her a leery smile.

Sheila laughs, making her six-pack even more pronounced. "I think I've dated one too many Regiment blokes. Tony would've been perfect for me. It's too bad he's married. Anyway, I can't stay any longer and have to catch up with the other girls. Right then, see you during afternoon tea," she says, waving goodbye.

They return her wave and watch her all the way out the door.

"Wow, she looks really tough," comments Sarah.

"I'm pretty sure you can take her down. My money would definitely be on you," comments George, grinning.

"I would give up a month's pay to watch that fight," mumbles Dave as he drinks some water, his eyes unfocused.

Sarah can guess what he's thinking. "Especially if we took each other on in a gladiator arena wearing our bikini armour, right?" she teases, winking at him.

Dave chokes on his drink, making the others laugh.

13:03 GMT
Thursday July 30, 2026
Pontrilas Army Training Area
Pontrilas, Herefordshire, England

After lunch, Al places Sarah in the number three position, reserved for the team leader. Sarah has to implement everything she's been taught these past couple of days to lead Al, Dave, and George in assaulting a stronghold. At first, they do a simulation to see if Sarah has mastered the British Army's Voice Procedures. It's easier for her during Covert Entry because the hand signals are the same. After each simulation, Al gives Sarah a debriefing and feedback on her performance. While they conduct the debriefing, the civilian workers from QinetiQ rearrange the layout of the Killing House for the next round. Every time they enter the Killing House, the layout and furniture are entirely different.

After a few simulations, Al finally gives them live rounds. This is the last training for Sarah before they head for afternoon tea.

"Roight, Sarah, standby for Immediate Action. Inside this one-storey warehouse with an unknown layout, there is a Yankee with an unknown number of X-Rays. The X-Rays have threatened to slot the Yankee if they think they're being assaulted. Your mission is to secure the Yankee. I say again, your mission is to secure the Yankee. How will you do this, Sarah?"

Sarah observes the entry point. The door is now on the furthest right of the Killing House, opens outwards, and the handle is on the left side.

"We'll use Covert Entry. The stack will be on the left side of the entrance as follows; Al is number one as Alpha, George is number two as Bravo, I will be number three as Charlie, and Dave will be number four as Delta. All call signs, Charlie is in control. Please parade all equipment," orders Sarah.

Everyone checks their own kit. It turns out the batteries of her headset are almost depleted so she changes them and takes some more as spares. She then checks everyone's kit and their weapons. It turns out the batteries of their GPNVG and Dave's endoscope camera are also almost depleted so she asks them to change batteries and bring some extras for spares. After checking Dave's frame charges, Sarah notices that the wirings are wrong so she asks him to fix them. Once everything has been checked, Sarah checks everyone's kit once again.

"Make ready and stack up," orders Sarah when everyone is finally ready.

All four stack according to Sarah's instructions. At the rear of the stack, Dave squeezes Sarah's left shoulder, signalling that he's ready. Sarah immediately squeezes George's left shoulder, signalling to him that she and Dave are ready. A couple of seconds later, Sarah sees George give an exaggerated nod, so she knows that everyone in front of her is ready. Sarah then signals the MOE specialist to move forward to check behind the door.

Dave inserts his endoscope camera from underneath. After a few seconds, he signals that the door is unlocked, it's pitch black inside, there's no sign of X-Rays, and there's a hallway that turns to the left. Sarah signals that she copies and Dave returns to his original position.

"All call signs, use GPNVGs. We will enter and stack before the next hallway. We execute the entry in five," whispers Sarah through her headset.

All weapons are in a low ready position and Semi-Automatic Fire mode.

"Four."

"Three." Dave goes forward and stands on the right side of the door.

"Two."

"One." Dave starts turning the handle.

"Execute!" whispers Sarah.

Dave opens the door and lets the others enter the stronghold. As the MOE specialist and rear guard, his job is to give access to the others and guard the rear of the assault force. As instructed by Sarah, Al stops at the corner. They have to clear the next hallway before they can proceed. Sarah gives Dave the signal and he moves to the front to check on the hallway with a rod that has a mirror on its tip. Dave signals that no X-Rays are sighted and that there are six doors on the right side of the hallway. Sarah signals that she copies and Dave returns to his position.

"All call signs, standby to stack up on the first door. Standby... Go!" whispers Sarah.

With a move called 'slicing the pie' or 'pie' for short, they move forward as one towards the first door and stack up beside it. Sarah can see that, just as Dave described, there are six doors on the right side of the hallway. Sarah again orders Dave forward. He checks the door and inserts his endoscope camera underneath it. He gives the signal that the room is locked and completely empty. Sarah signals that she copies and Dave returns to his position.

"All call signs; standby to stack up on the second door. Standby... Go!" whispers Sarah.

Everyone moves at the same time and Sarah repeats the same procedure on the next three doors, which are also empty. On the fifth door, Dave signals that the room is a toilet with two stalls on the left side of the room, no signs of X-Rays, and that the door is unlocked. Sarah signals that she copies and Dave returns to his position. Even though Dave said the toilet is empty, Sarah knows that the toilet stalls still have to be cleared.

"Alpha and Bravo, bypass the door and cover Green side. Delta and Charlie will stack up and clear the fifth room. Acknowledge!" whispers Sarah.

Al and George signal that they copy and move forward past the door to cover the hallway in front of them. Now there's only Sarah and Dave stacking in front of the door.

"Delta, after opening the door, I will clear the second stall and you will clear the first. Acknowledge!" whispers Sarah.

Dave signals that he copies.

"Execute the entry in five," whispers Sarah.

"Four."

"Three." Dave goes forward and stands on the left of the door.

"Two."

"One." Dave starts to turn the handle.

"Execute!" whispers Sarah.

Dave opens the door and Sarah enters and immediately heads toward the second stall with Dave only half a step behind her. Dave's job is to clear the first stall while Sarah clears the second. Once they're in position, they simultaneously open the stall doors and Sarah sees an X-Ray on top of the toilet. She shoots a controlled pair to the head of the X-Ray with her HK MP5SD3. Her weapon has a built-in suppressor which is effective in suppressing the gunshots, meaning the sound of the bullets' impact is much louder than the sound of the gunshots themselves.

"Clear," whispers Dave.

"X-Ray down, fifth room clear," whispers Sarah, signalling Dave to exit.

## THE POLICEWOMAN

"Delta coming out," whispers Dave.

"Charlie coming out," whispers Sarah. True to CQB doctrine, they have to report every move they make to prevent any blue-on-blue.

Sarah makes sure Dave turns left to cover the rear. She then exits the toilet and turns right to stack behind Al and George, still covering the hallway.

"All call signs, standby to stack up on the sixth door. Standby... Go!" whispers Sarah.

Everyone moves forward and stacks up on the final door. Once again, Sarah orders Dave to move forward to check the door and what's behind it with his endoscope camera. After a few seconds, Dave gives the signal that the door is locked, opens to the middle of the room, and is heavily mined. A Yankee is sitting behind a desk at the back of the room and there are six X-Rays moving around. Dave also gives the sign that the room is shaped like an inverted 'L', doglegging to the right. This means that there must be another room at the back-right side of the main room. After Sarah signals that she copies, Dave goes back to his original position.

Sarah thinks hard for a few seconds before making a decision. "All call signs, standby to go noisy. Delta, prepare frame charge," she whispers.

Everyone switches their weapons to full-auto while Dave places the frame charge on the door. After it's ready, he gives the signal and returns to his original position. Once he's in position behind Sarah, he squeezes her left shoulder. Sarah then squeezes George's left shoulder, indicating that the people behind him are ready. George prepares a flashbang and shows the pin to Al, indicating to him that everyone behind George is ready. Al exaggeratedly nods and George does the same, signalling Sarah that everyone is ready. This takes less than ten seconds, from Sarah giving Dave the order to prepare his frame charge to George nodding.

"Execute the entry in five," whispers Sarah into her comm headset.

"Four."

"Three."

"Two." Al turns his body to shield himself from the blast of the frame charge.

"One." Dave flips off the safety and his thumb is on the detonator.

"Execute!"

What happens next is controlled chaos! Dave detonates the frame charge and George immediately throws the flashbang inside the room while Al enters. Al sees an immediate threat on the Green side so he crisscrosses to the left, shooting his weapon just as the flashbang goes off a couple of metres away from him. George notices Al crisscross to the left so he automatically buttonhooks to the right, also while firing his weapon. Sarah makes her entry and sees that the Green side of the room is clear. She buttonhooks and takes the right-middle to support George, who is shooting controlled bursts to multiple targets in his Tactical Area Of Responsibility (TAOR). At the same time, Sarah notices Dave take left-middle to support Al. The shouts of 'X-Ray down' are heard repeatedly, adding to the chaos.

SCAN. Sarah sees the Yankee, who turns out to be Michael, sitting behind a desk at the back of the room, which turns right into another room. A target moves inside her TAOR. ACQUIRE. Sarah aims toward the head of the target. SHOOT. Sarah squeezes off a round. ACQUIRE. Sarah recovers from the slight recoil and aims again toward the head. SHOOT. Sarah squeezes off another round to the target that has already stopped moving. ACQUIRE. Sarah reacquires her target to make sure both her shots hit the target.

"X-Ray down!" shouts Sarah, moving forward and making sure all targets are taken care of. "Alpha and Delta, stand firm and cover Yankee on Black-12."

"Roger that," reply Al and Dave.

"Bravo, standby to stun and clear Red-2 corner room, Charlie will Run the Rabbit," orders Sarah.

"Roger that," answers George.

Sarah notices Al and Dave have stopped and are pointing their weapons towards the Yankee and then she follows George towards the right corner to the next room. Sarah immediately stacks behind him.

"Charlie ready," says Sarah, slapping George's shoulder.

"Bravo ready," answers George.

"Execute!" shouts Sarah.

George throws a flashbang with his left hand to the back-right of the next room at the same time Sarah moves to the back and then to the right. She does this to draw away opposition fire so George can easily dispatch the X-Rays from cover. This CQB tactic is called 'Running the Rabbit' and perfect for an 'L' shaped room during Overt Entry. With his left knee on the floor, George fires his weapon at the same time the flashbang goes off. The flashbang explodes less than a metre from Sarah, but her respirator takes the brunt of it so she can clearly see two static targets in front of her, untouched by George. Robert is right between the two static targets and looks dazed by the flashbang. Sarah's briefly surprised to realize that George has missed all his targets. Moving forward, Sarah shoots the two targets with controlled bursts, making up for George's mistake.

"You! Get the fuck down on your face! Now! Move it!" shouts Sarah, pointing her weapon at Robert. "Alpha and Delta, secure Black-12 Yankee."

Robert follows her orders and drops to the ground and Sarah hears a 'roger that' from Al and Dave.

"Bravo, secure Red-2 Yankee," orders Sarah, keeping her weapon pointed at Robert.

"Roger that," says George, moving forward to follow her orders.

"Black-12 Yankee secured!" exclaims Al from behind her.

"Red-2 Yankee secured!" exclaims George after frisking Robert and cuffing him with a plasticuff.

"Stronghold secured!" exclaims Sarah, feeling relieved. "All call signs, unload and make safe all weapons."

Sarah turns around and sees Michael facedown with his hands plasticuffed behind him.

"Lights on!" shouts Al as he cuts off Michael's plasticuffs. George does the same for Robert.

The lights suddenly come on and they all turn off their GPNVGs. Sarah takes off her respirator and makes sure all weapons are on safe.

"Nice shooting, George," she says, her lips pouting.

George only gives her a sheepish smile.

"That was really fast, Al!" comments Michael, standing up.

They then wait for Al's debrief. Al looks as if he wants to say something, but then he shuts his mouth. He looks confounded.

"Congratulations, Sarah, you've managed to shut his gob!" says Dave, laughing.

The others laugh also, except for Al, who is red-faced.

"Al, are you all right?" asks Sarah. She's suddenly worried because Al still hasn't started his debriefing yet.

"I'm fine," says Al, waving her concern away. "It's just that you've done a textbook assault. For once, I have absolutely nothing to criticize."

"We deliberately sabotaged your comm headset, our GPNVGs and Dave's endoscope and frame charge to see how you'd react when things went wrong, but you managed to spot them before the assault. There aren't many ruperts as thorough as you, you know," says George.

Sarah's embarrassed being praised by George, but it turns out they're not finished with her yet.

"Too right! Almost all the blokes put too much trust in the MOE specialist. Most blokes would just take the specialist's word that there are no X-Rays in the fifth room and carry on. Even though I told you there were no X-Rays, you realized that the toilet stalls still had to be cleared. That was very well done!" says Dave.

"Your Running the Rabbit tactic was spot on. Even though most of the blokes would do the same thing, a lot of them would forget to order the other team to stand firm, and to use flashbangs," praises George once again.

"From my perspective, you were absolutely terrifying, Sarah," says Robert. "Anyone would've been shitting themselves if they'd seen you like that. You handled the second Yankee effectively even though Al told you there was only one."

Sarah is no longer surprised that Robert was in there also.

"Your aim was perfect, though I can't say the same to everybody," continues Robert, giving George a dirty look.

George grins sheepishly while Al finally finds his voice.

"Although we've shown you only a tiny fraction of our CQB methods, you've managed to excel in everything we taught you. One day, you could make an excellent troop commander in The Regiment, Sarah, and we would follow you anywhere," says Al firmly, closing the exercise.

"I second that," says George seriously.

"Too right," says Dave, also seriously.

Everyone gives her a round of applause, which makes Sarah even more embarrassed but also flattered.

"Right lads, let's bin it and head for afternoon tea, shall we?" invites Michael, his eyes gleaming with pride.

They all leave. Unbeknown to Sarah, Cormac has been in the observation room on the second floor the whole time and he saw and heard the entire thing. Without a word, he takes the recording of Sarah's exercise and slips it into his pocket.

16:06 GMT
Thursday July 30, 2026
Cookhouse, Pontrilas Army Training Area
Pontrilas, Herefordshire, England

The cookhouse is already full, mostly of B Squadron, but Sheila and her friends are nowhere to be seen. Sarah's group take their food and sit at the same table they sat at previously. They've just sat down when Michael's smartphone rings. It's from Broussard.

"Yes, Chief?" answers Michael. He's set his smartphone to speaker so Sarah can also tune in.

"Michael, my apologies but I have to cut short your vacation. There have been some developments and we need you here. Could you please return to the office tomorrow morning?" orders Broussard.

"Sure thing. Do you need both of us tomorrow?"

"Indeed. I'll call Sarah after this," answers Broussard.

"No need for that, Chief. She's here with me."

Broussard doesn't answer for a few seconds. "Have you two spent your vacation together?"

"Indeed, Chief," answers Michael, his signature cheeky grin on his face.

Broussard doesn't answer, but is heard letting out a long sigh.

"Don't get jealous, Chief," teases Michael. "You're married."

Sarah laughs.

"Fuck off, you bastard! You two better be here by 09:00 tomorrow morning," orders their commander curtly. "And wipe that stupid grin off your face!" He hangs up.

George suddenly waves his hand, grinning from ear to ear. "Hey, Sin! Over here!"

Someone tall and extremely skinny comes to their table and George introduces him to Sarah. It turns out to be St John Williams, the former Goat Major of the Royal Welsh infantry regiment. Sarah almost laughs out loud when she's shaking his hand because she suddenly remembers Michael's story about St John and the goat he takes care of, William Windsor III. St John has a silly looking face, sillier even than Dave's, and an odd figure, meaning he's easily recognized by everyone even from afar. St John looks embarrassed when he's introduced to Sarah, earning him an immediate slagging from his mates.

"What have you been up to, you old goat?" asks George, grinning broadly at his close friend.

"Just brushing up on my EOD, I am," answers St John with his Welsh accent and way of speaking. "And don't call me that!" He starts to pout, making him look even more ridiculous.

"I thought the head shed sent you here to take care of those goats outside, Goat Major," says Dave, trying hard to keep a straight face.

"Those aren't goats out there, you dickhead. Those are sheep!" says St John, looking exasperated. "And quit calling me 'Goat Major'!" His pout gets bigger, making the others start sniggering.

"Just grab a seat and join us, Williams," invites Michael.

"Thanks, but I gotta go back to my table," says St John. "And don't call me that either!"

"But your name *is* Williams, you muppet!" says Michael, giving him an incredulous look.

St John is taken aback and thinks a second. 'Oh... that's right, isn't it?' is written all over his face, making the others roll in laughter. Still pouting, St John returns to his table. Better that than to be ridiculed all throughout afternoon tea. A few seconds later, Robert, George, and Dave's faces suddenly light up at the same time. Sarah turns around and sees Sheila walk towards their table. She's wearing a black kit and her lovely hair is all a mess.

"Hi again, fellas! Michael, may I see you for a minute?" asks Sheila with her hand on his shoulder.

Michael looks extremely reluctant when he gets up from his seat. They go to a corner near the entrance so no one can hear what they are saying.

"This I gotta see," says Al, grinning broadly. He turns his chair so he can watch the unfolding drama.

Sarah sees everyone in the cookhouse do the same thing so she takes her chair and puts it next to Dave, who has already taken out his smartphone to record them. They all watch the drama unfold. Sheila is the one doing most of the talking while Michael's mostly keeping his mouth shut. Even from afar, Sarah can see that Sheila looks sad and her eyes are moist. Sarah is extremely jealous, but she doesn't show it.

"What's the story on those two?" asks Sarah, with a voice that sounds just a bit too cheerful for the occasion.

"They dated each other after Michael returned from... some place. It was more than a couple of years ago," says Dave, "but then they broke up."

"The blokes from her unit said that she took it really hard. A few times she dated blokes from B Squadron just to annoy him. I don't think it worked, but none of us minded being used like that, though," says George, giving her a cheeky grin and a wink.

Sarah guessed that George was one of the men Sheila had gone out with, which makes her laugh.

"It's a sin for Michael to date her anyway," says Al dryly, making George and Dave laugh out loud.

Sarah doesn't understand why it's considered a sin so she doesn't join in the laughter.

"What about Tony?" asks Sarah.

"Oh, she came on to him very strongly, but he didn't take the bait. He was always nice and polite to her though, which made her want him even more," says Dave, still recording the drama with his smartphone. "Anyway, Tony showed us a photo of his girlfriend at that time and his girlfriend was much better looking, so we couldn't blame him for turning her down."

"Lydia is his wife now," says Sarah.

"Lucky bastard," mumbles Dave.

"Tony's wife is much better looking than Sheila?" asks Robert. He can't imagine anyone prettier than Sheila... except for Sarah, of course.

Everyone at the table nods in agreement. Sarah suddenly remembers her dad, who was immediately smitten with Lydia, the former Miss Indonesia, when Tony introduced her to him.

Sheila starts crying, but she and Michael keep talking for a while. After a couple of minutes, Sheila takes hold of Michael's hands and comes forward to give him a kiss on his lips. Michael suddenly turns his face, evading Sheila's kiss and making her lips land on his cheek. Sheila's taken aback by Michael's sudden move. She then gets so angry that she gives Michael a spectacular slap across his face!

Everyone in the cookhouse, mostly men from B Squadron, cheers out loud! They all give a standing ovation as if appreciating the drama being played out in front of them. Sheila quickly shoots everyone an evil eye and storms out of the cookhouse. Michael is stunned and can only stand there for a while before walking, like a man about to be hanged, back to his table. As he passes some of the tables, his men shake his hand and give him a pat on his back, all the while laughing their arses off. Michael sits down at the table, the left side of his lip bleeding.

"Right, lads, let me have it," says Michael, accepting his fate.

They all start slagging him mercilessly.

"Now *that's* what I call an 'eppie scoppie'!" says Sarah, laughing. "Or is it called an 'eppie *slappie*' in this case?"

"Yesterday, you took a left hook from Sarah. Today, you took a right slap from your old girlfriend," says Al. "What the fuck will you be getting tomorrow?"

"I can see the headlines in the next edition of Soldier Magazine: squadron commander of the famed 22$^{nd}$ Regiment slapped around stupid by a couple of his girlfriends," says George. "What the fuck would the other regiments think about us then?"

"I think this deserves to be replayed in The Kremlin's Interest Room, eh?" says Dave, grinning from ear to ear as he shows them his video. He managed to record Sheila's spectacular slap in close-up, and has already edited it to loop and keep replaying. Michael looks as if he's being slapped over and over again by Sheila.

They all have to stop taking the piss out of Michael for a few minutes because they can't stop laughing after seeing Dave's super-silly video. Once they're able to control themselves, though, they go right back to making fun of Michael and he can only accept his fate, his ears turning red from all the slagging. Some people from other tables go over to their table just to join in the slagging, including St John, who looks absolutely delighted. Sarah can only collapse in laughter until her stomach hurts and tears stream from her eyes seeing Michael's deflated expression when St John makes full use of this golden opportunity to give his boss the most severe slagging ever! Only Robert doesn't join in the piss taking, but laughs just as hard as the others. Towards the end of afternoon tea, Michael's smartphone rings.

"Yes, Derek?" Michael listens for a few seconds. "Right, we'll see him at The Kremlin at 20:00, thanks!" He disconnects the call and says to the others. "The Director wants to see us all at 20:00. We should bin it and RTB."

They try to finish their cakes and tea, but keep choking on their food. Dave can't stop replaying his video and the others can't stop laughing at it. In the car, they keep taking the piss out of Michael all the way to Hereford.

19:59 GMT
Thursday July 30, 2026
Regimental Headquarters, SAS Barracks
Credenhill, Herefordshire, England

After taking a shower together and packing for their return trip to Manchester, Michael and Sarah are now waiting with everybody else in the Interest Room at the RHQ. Everyone has dressed smartly for their meeting with Sir Charles. Sarah's wearing an elegant black dress and the others are in jacket and tie. Right on time, Lance-Corporal Derek Sinclair enters the Interest Room, also in jacket and tie.

"The Director will see you now, please," says Derek formally, his eyes gleaming on seeing Sarah.

Derek escorts them into a meeting room. Sir Charles Mountbatten and Cormac are already inside, also in jacket and tie. Derek, for some reason, takes out his smartphone and starts recording.

"Good evening, Sarah, how has your training been?" asks the Director warmly.

"It was extremely insightful, Director. But I would like your permission to pass on what I learned at PATA to my unit in Indonesia."

"You don't need my permission for that, Sarah, but thank you for confirming it with me anyhow," says Sir Charles. "Actually, I would be disappointed if you didn't pass on the knowledge. The UK, like the rest of the world, is now at war with narcoterrorists. We would like as many allies from around the world as we can get in the fight against them."

"On behalf of my government, I thank you very much for this, Director. The lessons I've learned will be invaluable in our country's war against narcoterrorists. I would also like this opportunity to thank you for letting me use your facility at Pontrilas and B Squadron for training me. It was an honour being trained by the SAS, Director," says Sarah.

What Al taught her was only a small fraction of CQB, but what she has learned was insightful, especially for Immediate Actions. However, no one in the room could ever imagine that within the next couple of months, Sarah would need to implement everything she's learned these past couple of days when she fights against The Cartel.

"It's the least we could do for you, Sarah," says Sir Charles, accepting a parchment from Cormac.

Sarah looks happy because it appears to her that the Director is going to give her some sort of CQB certificate.

Sir Charles reads the parchment. "Inspector Sarah Michelle Dharmawan of the Indonesian National Police,

"On Monday July 27, 2026, Inspector Sarah Michelle Dharmawan along with an officer from the British Army, who were both on secondment to Interpol Manchester, were assaulted by armed members of the Irish Drug Cartel at the Carluccio's Restaurant at 3 Hardman Square, Spinningfields, Manchester. She identified the threats when the first fireteam entered the premises and immediately alerted her teammate, who in turn noticed another fireteam. With excellent coordination and teamwork, both Sarah and her teammate eliminated the first wave of the assault, in which eight narcoterrorists tried to ambush them from two flanks. Both Sarah and her teammate then retreated into the kitchen area, where Sarah identified two more narcoterrorists and immediately dispatched them, undoubtedly saving the lives of the kitchen staff of Carluccio's in the process."

"In the kitchen area of the restaurant, both Sarah and her teammate were once again assaulted from two flanks. Thanks to their superior tactics, skill, and determination, they repelled the assault and killed almost all the attackers. It was during this stage when, without any thought for her own safety, Inspector Dharmawan saved the life of the British Army officer, not once but twice, in the process sustaining a wound to her left arm. Disregarding her wound, she killed two more narcoterrorists in hand-to-hand combat. A total of twenty-three members of the Irish Drug Cartel were killed that day, with an incredible fourteen kills attributed to Inspector Dharmawan."

"It was probably to no small extent due to her combat skills and determination in holding an unfavourable position under adverse conditions that the rest of the criminals, after taking heavy casualties, were soon forced to withdraw. Her actions that day dealt a severe blow to the Irish Drug Cartel, an enemy of both the people of the United Kingdom of Great Britain and Northern Ireland and the Republic of Indonesia."

"Inspector Sarah Michelle Dharmawan of the Indonesian National Police, for exemplary gallantry in saving the life of a highly decorated British Army officer during active operations, His Majesty King William the Fifth is graciously pleased to approve the award of... the Military Cross," says Major-General Sir Charles Mountbatten.

The Director is investing her with a medal! Sarah's jaw drops when she receives her citation and medal in a blue box, to the cheerful applause of everyone in the meeting room.

"Congratulations, Sarah," says Sir Charles, shaking her hand warmly.

"I... thank you very much for this, Director," says Sarah. She really wants to say something else, but wonders whether it would be appropriate.

"Do you have anything you wish to express, Sarah?" asks Sir Charles, smiling.

"Well, Director, it's just that Michael... Major Adrian... was with me the whole time and he was the one who led me through the ambush. He was in command at that time, Director, and he deserves this medal just as much."

The Director smiles even wider. "What you just said speaks volumes about your character, Sarah, and I expected no less from you. But rest assured that Major Adrian has more than enough medals to ensure an excellent career in the British Army. He will be well taken care of."

"So long as he doesn't step on his own bloody Hampton on his way up the career ladder," comments Dave dryly, to the sniggering of the others in the room.

"Thank you, Dave," says Sir Charles without looking at him. "Very well, you may carry on then. I'm sure you have things to sort out before you return to Manchester. Once again, Sarah, I thank you for saving the life of one of my squadron commanders."

"Thank you for everything, Director," says Sarah.

Sarah snaps to attention in the INP manner, which Sir Charles returns in the manner of the British Army. Sarah really wants to salute him, but she's afraid he won't return it because she's a civilian. Sir Charles is prohibited from returning it anyway, because he's not wearing any sort of headdress. British Army regulations prohibit its members to give or return a salute if they're not wearing a headdress.

After Sarah is congratulated by everyone present, Michael invites them all to celebrate. "I guess it's time for a piss-up. The Nag's Head, shall we?"

"Hear, hear!" says Dave happily.

Michael takes some notes from Cormac as he leaves the room. The DSF and Cormac stay behind while the others take the Range Rover to head towards The Nag's Head, a restaurant in the north of Hereford. This time, Michael is driving and Sarah is riding shotgun. Michael explains that Sarah is now entitled to have the letters 'MC' as post-nominal letters, indicating to other people that she has been invested with the Military Cross and recognized as a certified British hero. All the way to the restaurant, it's Sarah's turn to be slagged off by her friends. George teases her that her name now sounds much cooler, Inspector Incontinentia Buttocks, MC.

Michael parks the car and they all debus. Robert, George, Dave, Derek, and Al enter the restaurant first, while Sarah waits for Michael. Michael opens the door for Sarah so he's the last person entering.

Once inside, Sarah sees a fight between sixteen people in the pub area. A couple of them are moaning and writhing on the floor, and the barman is crouching behind the bar, looking terrified. No weapons are seen but plates, glasses, and furniture are flying around. Sarah glances at Michael, but he only grins with gleaming eyes looking at the chaos in front of him. The other men only stand there, watching the fight without any expression.

"Squad, squaaad 'shun!" orders Michael suddenly, his thunderous command voice echoing throughout the pub.

Just like Pavlov's dogs, Sarah unconsciously stands to attention in the INP manner. She senses her friends do the same, but in the manner of the British Army, in which they raise their left leg and then strike it to the ground, both feet forming a 'V', and both hands clenched.

Sarah is surprised that the fight suddenly stops and they all immediately stand to attention, including the two men who were writhing on the ground. The sound of dozens of feet striking the floor echoes throughout the pub. Sarah glances toward her friends and they are all giving Michael an incredulous look.

With a satisfied smile, having seen his order executed by everyone, Michael leads the others to the dining area. He opens the double door to the dining area and lets the others go in first. A waiter escorts them to a table and they immediately order food from the menu. Sarah's heart is still beating hard, not because of the fight, but because Michael's command voice is still ringing in her ears. She has never heard a command voice that powerful before!

"Who were those men?" asks Sarah.

"Fucking Mobility Troop from A Squadron. They just got back from… abroad," answers Al, frowning. "They're always fighting each other."

"One time, they fought each other just before a big football match just because they couldn't agree on who should go get the bloody football," says Derek, laughing.

After a few minutes, their food arrives and it's quite delicious. The waiter leaves and returns again, bringing them a nice bottle of red wine.

"Compliments of the owner, Major Adrian," says the waiter, pouring the wine into their wine glasses.

"Please send our thanks to Fred for us, Blake," says Michael, giving him a friendly smile.

"Of course, Major," says the waiter, bowing.

Michael stands and raises his glass, followed by everyone else.

"My lady and gentlemen! The King!" says Michael.

"The King!" say the others, including Sarah.

Everyone seems appreciative of Sarah for participating in the Loyal Toast, even though King William V is not her king. They then take a sip of wine.

"Fallen comrades!" says Al, a new toast.

"Fallen comrades!" says the others.

They again sip their wine, remembering their fallen friends.

"And finally, to Sarah," says Dave, grinning. "If it weren't for you, we would probably have to break in a new OC by now."

Everyone laughs, especially Michael, who then orders multiple pitchers of beer, which are drained in minutes. As the most junior among them, Robert is appointed as designated driver.

Sarah pays for everyone's dinner, subsidized £100 by Michael, who got it from Cormac for winning a wager between them. They then stagger towards their car. Robert takes them to Hereford Railway Station and they all help Michael and Sarah with their luggage. Before they part, Derek has some surprises for Sarah.

"Sarah, we have some things for you. These two are for you and the other is for Tony. I hope you don't mind taking it to him," says Derek, giving her three wrapped gifts.

"Why, thank you, Derek," she says, hugging and kissing him on his cheek.

Sarah does the same to the other SAS men and they all look happy. They exchange e-mail addresses and smartphone numbers.

"Do keep in touch, Sarah," says Dave, waving goodbye to her.

"Of course I will. Thanks again for everything!" says Sarah, returning their wave. Her eyes are moist because she will miss her new friends.

Sarah can't know that, during her days in Herefordshire, she has already met The Cartel's British Army contact.

And just before she returns to Indonesia, Sarah will have to attend the military funeral of a member of the UKSF Group...

# CHAPTER 9
# KGM

23:40 GMT
Thursday July 30, 2026
Hereford Railway Station
Hereford, Herefordshire, England

Sarah sits next to Michael and looks out the window for a couple of minutes, tears streaming down her cheek.

"All right, *mo ghile mear*?" asks Michael, smiling.

"Thank you for introducing me to your men, *mon amour*," says Sarah, wiping her eyes with a tissue. "I'll miss those silly buggers."

"It was an honour for them to meet you as well, you know," says Michael seriously.

"Robert is awfully quiet, isn't he?"

"Oh, we were all exactly like him during our first year in The Regiment, including myself. Like I told you when we first arrived at PATA, if you just switch on, keep your mouth shut, and listen to everyone, you'll be all right. No one likes to hear him talk anyhow… if you catch what I mean," says Michael, giving her a wink.

Sarah laughs. A lot of Brits would agree that the Brummie accent is the most unpleasant to hear compared to other British accents.

"One time, Robert was caught singing in the shower. So we recorded it and used it as our ringtone for a few weeks. He was never heard singing out loud again," says Michael.

Sarah laughs even louder, imagining Robert being stitched by the others. Michael knows how to instantly cheer her up, making Sarah really hope that he is serious with her. She's also still curious about Michael's squadron.

"Was Robert from the Royal Marines or a Para like you?"

"Only George was from The Paras and he's Senior NCO for Air Troop.

Robert was from the Coldstream Guards. He used to be an Olympic swimmer so we placed him in Boat Troop after his Selection last year."

"How about the Director and your CO? Which regiment did they come from?" asks Sarah.

"Sir Charles was originally from the Princess of Wales's Royal Regiment and was once the OC of G Squadron. Cormac was from the Royal Scots Dragoon Guards and used to be the OC of B Squadron before I took it over."

"What about Dave and Al?"

"Dave is the Senior NCO for Mobility Troop and he was from the King's Royal Hussars. Al was from The Rifles and besides being the SSM, he's also handling Mountain Troop because no one in that Troop is senior enough to become Senior NCO."

"You have really good men under your command, Michael," says Sarah.

"They are indeed," Michael agrees. "So, what did they give you?"

Sarah opens the first package and just as she'd expected, she sees an SAS plaque. After opening the second package, Sarah laughs. It's a framed picture of Sarah and B Squadron doing silly poses at Storey Arms after the Fan Dance. It's filled with funny comments and a caption on the bottom says 'Train hard, fight easy. Train easy, fight hard – and die', which is the Training Wing's motto.

Michael also laughs after seeing the photo. "Derek asked me to send a photo of you with the men of B Squadron. So that's what it's for."

"Anyhow, thank you for the most amazing week I have ever experienced, *mon amour*," says Sarah, giving him her adoring eyes.

Michael feels his heart drop down to his stomach being looked at by Sarah like that. He doesn't answer and only kisses her lips softly.

"I think George is right. I *should* call you something else besides '*mon amour*'," says Sarah, smiling.

"What do you have in mind?"

"How about if I call you '*sayang*'?"

"*Sayang*? Does that mean Biggus Dickus in Bahasa?" asks Michael with his cheeky grin.

Sarah gives him a hard pinch on his arm, but Michael laughs happily instead. "It means 'my dear', *sayang*."

"It sounds lovely, *mo ghile mear*," says Michael.

Sarah returns his smile, but then turns dead serious. "Michael, why?"

"Why what?" asks Michael, pretending to be confused.

"Why did the SAS give me lessons?"

"The Director gave you the reason. And you *did* save my life…"

"I don't think that's enough reason," says Sarah, staring deep into his eyes.

"You even got a medal for it," says Michael, obviously trying to evade her.

"The Military Cross is eligible only to members of the British Armed Forces, Commonwealth countries, and allied forces… Indonesia is not a member of the Commonwealth nor an ally," says Sarah carefully.

"The Cartel's drug factory is in your country and we're fighting the same people. Whether it's official or not, Indonesia is our ally in the war against narcoterrorism," says Michael, still trying to evade her.

"And I'm police, not military."

"I'm sure there are always exceptions. I guess that's one of the plus points of having a member of the Royal Family as the DSF," says Michael, shrugging. "Anyhow, you should know that everyone has been quite impressed with your performance these past few days, including the Director."

"Really?" asks Sarah. She's flattered, but can sense that Michael is trying change the subject.

"Like Al said, you would make an excellent troop commander someday and I agree with him," says Michael.

"How do you know that?" asks Sarah.

"The men followed every command you gave them, right?"

"Indeed they did."

"There you have it. It's not easy commanding the very best chaps in this business, but they seem to follow your orders without question. You're a natural born leader, Sarah!" praises Michael once again.

Sarah is happy being praised by her lover, who also happens to be a squadron commander of the finest special forces unit in the world… but there's still something bothering her. She's grateful for the training, but is curious *why* they gave it to her so readily.

"So… are there any reasons behind my training that you're not telling me?"

Michael is exasperated with himself for not being able to change the subject. He thinks for a moment before answering her.

The Special Reconnaissance Regiment (SRR) is the only unit in the UKSF Group that accepts women. Those female special forces operatives are especially effective in intelligence operations, but unproven in combat operations. Future combat operations will need them in the front lines, so the Director has plans to open all positions in the UKSF Group, including the Tier One Units, to women. In this case, His Majesty's Armed Forces are behind other European armed forces, which already have women in their special forces units.

The Director's plan met heavy resistance from most officers and Senior Non-Commissioned Officers in the UKSF Group, especially from the two Tier One Units, the SAS and SBS. They don't believe that women could ever pass Selection, follow their rigorous training, adapt with the men, or be aggressive in battle. They think that women in the Tier One Units would be liabilities instead of assets. Sir Charles needs someone who can prove them otherwise and found that someone in Sarah when Michael debriefed him regarding their actions in Ireland and Manchester. The Director was impressed knowing Sarah managed to kill fourteen narcoterrorists on her own. He was thoroughly impressed when Michael told him that Sarah managed to kill Tiny Mullins with just a pen! Sir Charles once knew Tiny Mullins when Tiny was still active in the Army Ranger Wing because they routinely train with the SAS. The Director then ordered Michael and Al to train Sarah to see whether she could keep up with them. Basically, these two days have been a kind of Selection for Sarah, even though she doesn't have to know it.

Sir Charles was extremely satisfied when Sarah far exceeded their expectations. Sarah managed to finish the Fan Dance faster than anyone predicted and could follow Al's instructions better than most. He watched the footage that Cormac took from PATA and was impressed with her performance. There were quite a few female soldiers tough enough to pass Selection, but so far, they had all failed to adapt themselves to the SAS culture. Only Sarah seemed able to adapt herself easily and had been well-received by the men.

Although Sarah will *not* be invited to join the SAS, the Director has at least proven that one day, women can be accepted by the ranks of the SAS.

If an Indonesian policewoman can do it, the Director is sure that one day, a British female soldier can do it also. Sir Charles has reminded Michael and Al that his plans are still confidential and forbidden them to tell Sarah about it. Michael wishes he could tell Sarah, but he cannot. He must be careful with what he says, because Sarah is nobody's fool.

Michael decides to take a chance. "There are other reasons indeed. However, the Director has made it clear to me that his reasons are strictly confidential," he says, looking deep into her eyes.

Sarah gives him an understanding smile and Michael looks relieved. Sarah understands because she herself has lots of secrets. She has several times conducted special operations unknown by the media that she cannot discuss with anyone, including her family. Densus-88 is mostly an antiterrorist unit, which tries to prevent terror acts *before* they happen. Whereas counterterrorist units are deployed *after* a terror act has happened, antiterrorist units like Densus-88 pre-emptively try to arrest the terrorist suspects and 'handle' them *before* they commit their terror. Antiterrorist operations must be kept classified so that the methods of Densus-88 and other intelligence units in tracking and 'handling' terrorist suspects are not uncovered by the media and the public.

Sarah realizes that Michael, as a member of a special forces unit, must have lots of secrets like herself. She can accept Michael's answer and is glad he hasn't lied to her. This turns out to be the best for both of them.

'Right, that's it! I am definitely in love with this woman,' thinks Michael, taking a deep breath. "Sarah, I am very much in love with you. H-H-How about... ehm... how about if I invite you to my house in Belfast sometime... so I can introduce you to my parents?"

"That would be lovely, *sayang*!" answers Sarah, her eyes gleaming.

"Splendid," says Michael, looking relieved.

The train inspector approaches them and asks for their tickets. After the he leaves, Sarah finally begins her interrogation. "And what's the story with you and Sheila?"

Michael can't help but tense up again on hearing Sarah say the name of his ex-girlfriend.

"We broke up a long time ago, but she wouldn't let go of me for some reason. This afternoon, she told me that she still loves me very much and wants me back. She's also willing to resign from the military so she can be with me. But I told her that I'm already very much in love with you," answers Michael seriously.

"Why would she have to resign from the military?" asks Sarah, frowning.

"Well, I'm an officer and she's a Lance-Corporal. In His Majesty's Armed Forces, it's considered a sin for officers to have relationships with the ranking members," explains Michael, giving her a cheeky grin.

Sarah nods and she finally understands what Al meant a few hours ago. Romance between an officer and the ranking members is strictly prohibited. Even dating is not allowed. But Michael's explanation only makes Sarah extremely jealous because it turns out there's a beautiful woman still in love with her partner!

"Did you love her?" asks Sarah, giving Michael a look so deadly that it makes him almost fear for his life!

"I... ehm... wasn't actually in love... but I felt a sort of tender curiosity," quotes Michael, giving her a forced smile.

"That's a load of bullshit, F. Scott Fitzgerald!" says Sarah sharply, but then tries hard not to laugh.

Michael grins sheepishly. He should've known better than to try to bluff his way out of the situation by quoting something from 'The Great Gatsby'.

"I once had feelings for her, *mo ghile mear*, but she's now ancient history," says Michael, smiling. "You don't have to worry about her."

"But she's very pretty and very sexy," says Sarah.

"Indeed, but she's a bit of a bitch. As you saw yourself, she's also a drama queen. She's also high maintenance, demanding, possessive, artificial, and she asks too many questions. She has unsophisticated tastes, so I didn't really connect with her when we were dating."

"She has a perfect body," comments Sarah.

Michael has to admit that Sarah is right, but he doesn't know how to respond to that so he wisely keeps his mouth shut.

"I would've loved to kiss those abs and bite into her delicious outie though..." continues Sarah.

Michael is so shocked that his jaw drops to the floor! For a few seconds, he can only swallow and clear his throat a few times.

"S-S-Sarah... ehm... h-h-have you... you know... mmm... ever d-d-

# THE POLICEWOMAN

done it… ehm… w-w-with another w-w-woman… b-b-before?" stammers Michael.

"Of course I have," answers Sarah, sounding as though it's nothing unusual.

Michael's jaw drops once again and his eyes become unfocused. Sarah tries hard not to laugh because her lover looks like a complete dickhead.

"Do you want me to tell you about it?" asks Sarah, teasing him even further.

It takes a while for Michael to react. "I don't think I would be able to survive that story right now."

Michael takes Sarah and kisses her passionately. Unfortunately for Michael, they can't do it inside the train and must wait until they reach Sarah's flat.

08:57 GMT
Friday July 31, 2026
Interpol Manchester
Central Park, Manchester, England

The next day, they enter the Interpol area and everyone gives them a standing ovation. Sarah is embarrassed, but Michael takes it in his stride. They walk towards their commander's office, shaking hands with their teammates.

"I'm so sorry I couldn't pick up the phone, *pet*," says Paul while shaking her hand. "I was in the shower."

"No problem, Paul," says Sarah, smiling. Already the experience in Carluccio's feels like a lifetime ago.

Broussard's secretary immediately lets them into his office after shaking their hands.

"Good morning, Chief," they greet.

Broussard looks much better than the last time they saw him. He rises from his chair to shake their hands. "Good morning indeed. I didn't have the chance to thank you both for a job well done," he says, motioning for them to sit down. "How's your arm, Sarah?"

"Optimum, Chief," answers Sarah.

"That's good to hear. Anyhow, both of your AARs coincide with the action captured by Carluccio's cameras. They have CCTV cameras in the dining area and in the kitchen. Although the two of you initiated the firefight, the authorities have all cleared you both of any wrongdoings and has judged your actions to be 'lawful killing'. Here are your weapons," says Broussard, giving them back their weapons.

Sarah is happy receiving her Smith & Wesson knife and HK P2000 pistol. Michael also looks happy receiving his two Sig Sauers. Although their pistols are obviously empty, they both do a chamber check before stowing them.

"Of the twenty-four people that tried to assassinate you, two of them got away and twenty-two were killed..."

"I beg your pardon," cuts in Sarah. "Was it not twenty-three people?"

"You killed thirteen, Michael killed nine, and two men got away. A few minutes after you shot Steve Dunbar, he got up and joined the fight at the kitchen door. He and Seamus Fitzgerald then buggered off after they ran out of ammo. This happened just before you took on Donald Mullins."

"*Verdomme!*" curses Sarah in Dutch. "Steve must've also been wearing body armour."

"Indeed, Sarah. Anyhow, Paul managed to identify all the other players you killed and they are all core members of The Cartel. We have never apprehended any core members of The Cartel but you two have, incredibly, managed to kill twenty-two of them in a single night. This incident is a major blow to their organization as this is also the first time one of their senior members has been killed. We have to be on the alert for further possible retaliation so please remember your tradecraft and bring extra mags this time," orders Broussard sternly to Sarah.

Sarah can only smile and nod. She has already sent a text to her dad and he has promised to send her four more HK mags by way of diplomatic courier. She has also decided to hang on to the Glock as her main sidearm.

"James said that he and Paul have just finished analyzing the phones the players carried, so you should see them right after this, all right?" orders Broussard.

They both nod.

"The unanswered question is how they managed to locate you at Carluccio's. They didn't immediately take the bait from your reconnaissance by fire tactic, but they somehow tracked you to Carluccio's and then ambushed you there. They're good and I want to know how they did it. The worst-case scenario is that there's a leak in our team, which is unlikely, or from your parent units or the GMP, which is maybe the most likely. This is the main reason I have asked everyone to limit your interactions with the GMP. Now, though, I have no choice but to involve the GMP's 'Y' Department so they can help investigate this."

Michael frowns when Broussard tells them the leak is most likely from their parent units. He seems uncomfortable with the fact that someone from the SAS could betray him. Sarah also can't imagine someone from Indonesia leaking her identity to The Cartel, but understands that they must investigate every possibility.

"Contact your respective commanders and ask them to investigate this. All right?" orders Broussard.

Both nod and make notes on their tablets.

"We have to assume the worst, that The Cartel now knows your name, address, and smartphone number. Remember that if someone has given your phone number to The Cartel, they can easily track you with it. As an extra precaution, I recommend both of you change your phone numbers and move into new flats."

Both nod again.

"Now, the two of you also saved many lives that day, so I have recommended both of you for a George Medal. As expected, my superiors have downgraded this to a King's Gallantry Medal, which has been expeditiously approved by the Home Secretary. Even though it's not the medal I think you deserve, it's still a great honour, and Sarah's investiture by His Majesty King William the Fifth is scheduled for next year at Buckingham Palace."

Sarah is happily surprised that she will be invested with another medal and gets the chance to meet King William V. She imagines taking her whole family and, who knows, maybe Cindy can meet Prince George.

"However, due to complications regarding Michael's status as a member of the SAS, his medal will be sent to his Colonel-in-Chief, which happens to be Prince Harry. Michael's investiture by Prince Harry will be held at a different time and place. Both of you are entitled to use the post-nominal letters of KGM."

Sarah's now disappointed she won't receive the medal with her partner. It turns out that this is impossible because investitures to the SAS are always done in secret, just like when the Director invested her with the MC. Sarah gives Michael a disappointed look, but he doesn't seem to care and only shrugs. As a highly decorated British Army officer, he must be used to being invested with medals.

"Which do I put first after my name?" asks Sarah to Michael. "KGM or MC?"

"MC?" asks Broussard.

"The Director Special Forces has invested her with a Military Cross for saving my life at Carluccio's, Chief," explains Michael, his eyes gleaming with pride.

"That's bloody marvelous! Congratulations, Sarah!" exclaims Broussard, very much impressed.

"Thank you, Chief," says Sarah proudly.

"And to answer your question, you should put MC first and then KGM," explains Broussard further.

"Like George said, you have a cool name now; Inspector Incontinentia Buttocks, MC, KGM," says Michael, giving her his cheeky grin.

Sarah gives him a hard punch to his shoulder and pouts at him.

"Pardon?" asks their commander, pointedly.

"Nothing, Chief," they both answer.

Broussard frowns at their behaviour. The two people in front of him are from Gen Z, the latest generation to enter the workplace. They are usually descendants of Gen X-ers, like Broussard. Gen Z-ers like Sarah and Michael are mostly raised by affluent Gen X-ers, which has enabled those Gen Z-ers to choose a career that fits their talent and passion. Because of this, they're not particularly concerned about the salary they receive as long as they love what they're doing. This also tends to mean they're extremely skilled in their chosen profession.

Gen Z-ers are also notoriously hard to control and they have their own way of doing things. They can be, and often are, insolent towards the older generations. What's worse is that Gen Z-ers *know* that the older generations need *them* more than the other way around.

"And now I must insist both of you seek an appointment with the GMP's inhouse psychologist for counseling. That incident at Carluccio's must have been quite traumatic and the last thing I need is my team members having PTSD," suggests Broussard.

"We're all right, Chief. We have our own way of dealing with combat stress," says Michael.

"Really?" says Broussard sceptically.

"Oh, indeed. Alcohol, exercise, and sex, not necessarily in that order, always helps," answers Michael with his cheeky grin. "You should try at least one of them, Chief."

Sarah tries hard to stifle her laugh, but fails miserably.

"Fuck off, you cheeky bastard!" curses Broussard, glowering at him. "I know you two spent your vacation together, but I trust both of you to keep your relationship professional on this mission. Is that clear?"

"Sure, Chief," answers Michael, still grinning.

Sarah only nods sheepishly.

"Now bugger off... both of you!" says Broussard, curtly dismissing them.

They both exit the office, giggling all the way out, making Broussard roll his eyes. They pass Paul and James on the way to their cubicle, and invite them to a meeting room.

"The Chief said you've analysed their smartphones," says Michael.

"Aye and it seems that their calls converged at a place in Inishowen, County Donegal, Republic of Ireland," answers James.

"Right, how about we assemble the team to propose a plan of action for the Chief?" invites Michael.

"I'll call the others," says Sarah.

After the other team members arrive, James and Paul present their findings. Basically, all call and text records from their smartphones have been analysed by the Government Communications Headquarters (GCHQ). The calls and texts can be traced to a place called Buncrana, Inishowen, County Donegal in the Republic of Ireland. It turns out that Liz knows the place because she was originally from Inishowen before moving to Dublin.

"That place in Buncrana was once called Swan's Mill and it was used to generate electricity for the city. The Town Council must have sold it to The Cartel. I'll check with Garda HQ," says Liz, already texting on her smartphone.

"Is there any way we can get confirmation without alerting them?" asks

Arthur. "Remember, we have to assume that they have the local politicians and Garda members under their control."

"How about a recce by the Garda intelligence unit?" suggests Matt.

Liz shakes her head. "I could contact the head of the Garda NSU, but I don't think they will want to do this one. Too many of their members have been compromised, snatched, and then killed by The Cartel."

"*Hoo* about Clive and the Garda ERU?" suggests Paul.

"Same thing, Paul. Look, the Garda can handle the dealers, but not The Cartel with their army training and automatic weapons. They will most likely take heavy casualties," says Liz.

"Any suggestions?" asks Matt.

"I would suggest the Chief recommend the Irish government initiate MACP. The Irish Defence Force, or maybe the British Armed Forces, could then conduct the recce and/or the assault. That decision, however, is up to the politicians," says Liz.

Everyone nods in agreement. If this place is the Cartel HQ, the Garda would be in over their heads. Even the Army Ranger Wing probably can't handle them, given their lack of experience in special operations. Liz is right, there's a big chance that the Irish government will ask military assistance from His Majesty's Government.

Liz's smartphone suddenly goes off, indicating an incoming text. "Right, Swan's Mill was sold five years ago to a person called Finn Langely."

"And we all know that Finn Langely is one of Rory Hanrahan's aliases. Good job, Liz!" says Arthur. "Right, does everyone agree that this place is their headquarters?"

"It could be their headquarters, a drug factory, or just a distribution centre. And we can't assume anything unless we do a recce, which will have to be conducted by the military," says Michael. "For the military to have authority to conduct a recce, the Chief should first recommend the Irish government initiate MACP. Now, do we have enough evidence for the Chief to submit this recommendation to the Irish government?"

Everyone thinks hard for a moment and then they all nod in agreement. Paul invites Broussard into the meeting and James presents their findings. Once they've answered all their commander's sharp questions, he approves all their recommendations. Broussard then must coordinate with his superiors to suggest to the government of the Republic of Ireland that they initiate MACP.

A couple of weeks later, the Government of Ireland becomes the second country in the world to initiate the MACP during the War on Narcoterrorism.

# CHAPTER 10
# CLOSE TARGET RECONNAISSANCE

20:18 GMT
Friday, August, 7, 2026
City Hotel – Derry
Derry City, County Derry, Northern Ireland

After negotiations, His Majesty's Government and the Irish government reach an agreement. If Swan's Mill really is the Irish Drug Cartel's HQ, a drug factory, or an MDMA distribution centre, then the recce and DA (Direct Action) assault will both be conducted by the UKSF Group. Before the assault is greenlighted, the recce will have to prove that Swan's Mill is at least one of the above.

Even though the Irish Defence Force have their own special forces (Army Ranger Wing), their experience in special operations is nothing like as complete as the SAS, so it's decided that they will replace the Special Forces Support Group (SFSG) as the supporting unit. The Army Ranger Wing will be tasked to cordon the immediate area during the assault. Cormac will be in overall command of the mission and Michael will be the field commander during the recce and assault. The recce phase of this mission is codenamed Operation Rowman, and if they manage to prove that Swan's Mill is part of the Irish Drug Cartel, the assault phase will be codenamed Operation Crankshaft. Cormac appoints Sarah as liaison between the Interpol IRT and the SAS for both operations.

It's only a twenty-five-minute drive from Derry to Buncrana so they'll set up their Forward Operating Base (FOB) in Derry. Because there are no military bases in County Derry, they book the Presidential Suite at the City Hotel, Derry. A few minutes after Michael and Sarah enter the suite, the doorbell rings. It turns out Al came with George, Dave, and Robert, pushing great heaps of luggage on the hotel trolley. They all look utterly exhausted, but are delighted to see Sarah. Sarah is happy to see her new friends again too.

"Michael told us a few days ago that the Home Office has recommended you a KGM. Congratulations, Sarah!" says Al, shaking her hand. The others join him in congratulating Sarah on her medal.

"Thanks, Al," says Sarah, embarrassed. "Michael will get one too, you know."

"Yeah, we know," says George. "We already took the piss out of him for getting the same medal as you, since you slotted thirteen of the buggers and he only got a piddly nine."

Sarah laughs, although killing more men than her lover isn't something she's especially proud of. "How was the Long Drag?" she asks Dave.

"We didn't break the record," answers Dave. "It's too bad you weren't there to spur us on."

Michael and Sarah help them sort out their kit. While helping them, Sarah notices that all of them are dirty and smelly, as if they haven't showered in over a week. She doesn't say anything, but makes a mental note not to stand downwind from them. A few minutes later, another person arrives, and it turns out to be the CO of the Army Ranger Wing. He looks like Broussard, but muscular and completely bald.

"*Dia dhuit*, Michael, *conas atá tú?*"

"*Tá mé go maith*, Alwyn, *go robh maith agat*. This is Sarah from Interpol."

"Leifteanant-Choirnéal Alwyn Buckley, Army Ranger Wing," he introduces himself in his Munster-Irish accent.

"Inspector Sarah Dharmawan, INP," answers Sarah, shaking his hand.

"Aren't ye Tony's sister?" asks Alwyn.

Sarah rolls her eyes and her friends laugh at her expense. She invites Alwyn to the dinner table, where they've already laid out satellite photos and the blueprints of Swan's Mill. As the UK doesn't have its own reconnaissance satellite, MoD has enlisted the US's National Reconnaissance Office (NRO) to take satellite images of Swan's Mill.

Swan's Mill can be viewed by Google Earth and Google Street View, so the images from those programs are also used as reference. Headquarters, Planning & Intelligence Section of the SAS has a blueprint for almost all of the buildings in the UK and all of them have been converted into 3D. The blueprint for Swan's Mill provided by the Irish government has also been converted into 3D. Now they can see the interior of Swan's Mill in 3D with a special tablet the size of the dinner table. Swan's Mill looks impressively majestic and everyone can see that it will be quite a challenge for the assault force to secure it. During the past week, Al, George, Dave, and Robert have conducted a recce of Swan's Mill and installed dozens of surveillance cameras. They present their findings while uploading their photos to the TV by Bluetooth.

Swan's Mill is between the Mala an Mhuilinn road and the River Owenkillew in the city of Buncrana. Swan's Mill looks like a four-storey apartment complex with three connecting buildings forming the letter 'J'. The third building is the smallest and, according to the blueprints, is only used as a stairway. All three buildings have a shield roof, making an assault from on high almost impossible. On the north side of Swan's Mill, there's an old, abandoned train bridge called Mill Bridge that crosses the River Owenkillew. Across the river from Swan's Mill is a forest block. The 4-man team have set up their Lying Up Point (LUP) inside the forest block.

What's most curious is that the three buildings only have one entrance between them, in the first building facing the tight parking space. During the recce, Al and the others have discreetly surveyed the buildings' surrounds, but they can't find another entrance besides that one. All the windows are covered with plywood, preventing anyone seeing the interior. Outdoor CCTVs are installed everywhere, pointed out towards the surrounding areas, including the river.

They observed that four men and four men only go out for shopping every day, and return with enough food for up to a hundred people. Their thermographic cameras counted more than ninety people inside the buildings. Each night around 21:30, around a hundred women arrive and enter the building and most go home the next morning. Al has asked other troopers to follow some of the women, who turned out, predictably enough, to be prostitutes from Buncrana and the surrounding cities. They've also observed that after breakfast, lunch, afternoon tea, and dinner time, fifty or so men exit the building to smoke by the river. They've installed video cameras to observe the target and now there's another team continuing the recce.

"Have you seen any of the senior members?" asks Sarah.

They shake their heads and start showing pictures of the men smoking by the river. There are hundreds of pictures and they've successfully taken close-up pictures of most of their faces.

Sarah suddenly recognizes someone. "That's Seamus Fitzgerald!"

"That's him indeed," says Michael. "Very good job, lads! Now go take a shower before you stink up the room."

Al and George head to the spacious bathroom and Robert and Dave prepare several TV monitors to catch the live streaming from the OPs. Sarah orders food for twenty people through room service while Michael uploads all the pictures and sends them to their teammates and also to MoD. Although Seamus is not a part of the top echelon, his presence indicates that the Irish Drug Cartel has activities in the building.

"What do you think, Alwyn?" asks Michael.

"I'm sure glad ye poor sods will be the ones doing the assault," comments Alwyn, looking at the 3D rendering from the blueprints.

Despite his words, Sarah can clearly see that Alwyn is frustrated his unit hasn't been trusted with this mission.

"Indeed. You might have to deal with something like this in the future, so how about we both come up with an assault plan?" asks Michael.

"Sure. Let me have a copy of all the intel ye have and I'll discuss this with my men," says Alwyn.

Michael sends all their intelligence data to Alwyn. Meanwhile, Al and George have finished washing and now it's Robert and Dave's turn to shower.

"I'll have a draft for ye tomorrow afternoon," Alwyn promises. He steals a glance at Sarah before leaving.

"In case we decide to execute an assault, let's have all the airlines to and from the Derry Airport fly low above the target. This will distract them and get them used to the noise. Al, could you please call the head shed and have him take care of that?" orders Michael.

"Sure, old buddy," answers Al.

"The target is on the way to a Coyles Arro warehouse on An Rorybhóthar road. I would love to have their lorries drive around a few times at night." Coyles Arro is a home and garden store in the heart of Buncrana, but their warehouse is on An Rorybhóthar road, which passes the Mala an Mhuilinn road.

"I'll contact Liz and have her discreetly ask the company to do that," offers Sarah.

"Thank you, Sarah. Does anyone have any suggestions for now?" asks Michael.

"How about if I 'interrogate' a couple of their lady friends?" suggests George, grinning broadly.

"You'd really enjoy that, wouldn't you?" quips Michael.

Sarah starts to smirk, but she then has a thought. "Wait a minute! We have been assuming *all* of them are prostitutes, right? Some of our intel suggested that The Cartel has female players, but we never had any confirmation. What if some of them are players or distributors?"

Al and George are taken aback for a moment, but they then nod in agreement and give Sarah a smile. Making assumptions is a rookie mistake when conducting a recce, and they should've known better.

"Good one, Sarah! However, I don't want the local coppers involved in the investigation. Could you please call Liz and Matt and see whether Garda HQ and PSNI HQ can help us with background checks on all of the women? You should call Paul as well, in case the NCA has additional info. Please don't have the Garda and PSNI follow anybody or pick them up - we don't want to alert the players," says Michael. "In the meantime, I'll send the files to MoD to see if any of the girls have military experience."

Sarah nods and conducts a conference call with Paul, Liz, and Matt in Dublin, while Michael sends the women's pictures to his contact at MoD. Matt will go to Derry and Liz to Letterkenny to investigate the women in each city. Liz will also meet with the owner of Coyles Arro to follow up on Michael's request.

"We should follow the girls, starting tonight, and try to establish their status. Al, could you please take the lead on this and deploy Mountain Troop for the surveillance?" orders Michael.

"Shouldn't The Det be doing that?" asks Al.

"I've been asking the head shed right from the start for them to help us on the recce, but he won't allow it for some reason. He said that all intelligence operations will be conducted by B squadron, who are 'On The Team'. It must be politics or something," explains Michael, shrugging.

Michael isn't that good at lying. Al gives him a disbelieving look, but Michael just ignores him. Their food finally arrives and is immediately swarmed on by the starving SAS men.

11:18 GMT
Saturday, August 8, 2026
Tower Museum
Derry City, County Derry, Northern Ireland

Michael and Sarah wake up late and have brunch together.

"Fancy a stroll around Derry?" invites Michael.

"That sounds lovely, but shouldn't you focus on planning the assault?" asks Sarah.

"Let me worry about that," says Michael, winking.

They walk south and soon arrive at the Tower Museum, inside the City Walls. At the museum, they see an exhibition called 'An Armada Shipwreck – La Trinidad Valencera', which tells the story of a ship called La Trinidad Valencera, one of the largest ships of the Spanish Armada. In the year 1588, it sank in a storm at Kinnagoe Bay, County Donegal. It was found 400 years later by divers from the City of Derry Sub Aqua Club.

Michael enthusiastically starts telling Sarah about the Naval Battle of Gravelines that took place in Dutch waters in 1588, in which the English managed to defeat The Spanish Armada. The English lost less than a hundred men, but the Spanish Armada lost up to 5,000, forcing them to retreat towards Ireland. One of the escaping ships was La Trinidad Valencera. The English gained a decisive victory because they absolutely refused to use the normal tactics of that period. The only reason the English didn't sink the whole Spanish Armada is because they ran out of ammo and were also forced to retreat. That victory is considered one of England's greatest victories since the Battle of Agincourt in 1415. Michael is a history buff and it's fun to watch him enthuse about British victories.

After the museum, they walk on the City Walls, adorned by twenty-four cannons that were used to defend the city during the siege in 1689. Sarah really enjoys walking around the city with Michael like this, but she knows that Michael's mind is focused on his mission. Soon, it's time for them to return to the hotel.

15:38 GMT
Saturday, August 8, 2026
City Hotel – Derry
Derry City, County Derry, Northern Ireland

When they return to the hotel, everyone has already gathered at the dining table and their friends are conducting another debriefing with Cormac. The CO of the SAS has doubts about the single entrance and the four men of B Squadron are trying to convince him that that's really all there is. This is confirmed by the blueprints of Swan's Mill.

Cormac is still not convinced. "Look, you're assuming the blueprints are correct. Who's to say they built it according to the blueprints? Who's to say they haven't renovated it in secret? Remember that most of these chaps are ex-army and follow the same doctrine as we do. If this was *your* headquarters, would *you* want to be stationed in a stronghold with only one exit?"

They fall silent because Cormac is right.

"Let's just assume for now that this place is *not* their headquarters, but a drug factory or a distribution centre and those girls are the distributors. How do they supply the raw materials? You haven't seen them receive any supplies through the front door except groceries, right?" Cormac challenges once again.

They can only remain silent.

"What if they built an underwater access tunnel to smuggle their supplies from under the river?" Robert suddenly asks in his thick Brummie accent that makes everyone wince. "The only place we haven't checked is the river itself. How about if we conduct a recce in the river near the target?"

"That's brilliant, Robert!" says Michael. "Let's do it. Please check also whether it's possible to smuggle supplies from Lough Swilly directly to the target by using the river."

Lough Swilly is a sea inlet west of Buncrana and only about 200 metres from Swan's Mill. The River Owenkillew passes beside Swan's Mill and flows towards Lough Swilly and eventually connects to the North Atlantic Sea. Robert calls the Senior NCO of Boat Troop, who is currently at Hamworthy Barracks.

"I'll check with James to see whether it's possible to smuggle the drugs from Indonesia through Lough Swilly," offers Sarah.

"Thank you, Sarah," says Michael.

After Sarah briefs James, the doorbell rings. Sarah opens the door and Alwyn arrives with his Battalion Sergeant Major. Alwyn immediately joins the others while the Sergeant Major introduces himself to Sarah.

"Maor-Sáirsint Cathláin Emmet Liammhóir, Army Ranger Wing," he says, shaking her hand.

"Inspector Sarah Dharmawan, INP," says Sarah.

"It's an honour to finally meet ye in person, Sarah," says Emmet, grinning.

Sarah laughs. "Does the Army Ranger Wing have my picture at your camp also?"

"Unfortunately, the SAS blokes wouldn't give us a copy for some reason. A couple of my Rangers even had their smartphones smashed for taking pictures of the one in the Interest Room," says Emmet.

Sarah is happy that the SAS has kept their promise not to spread her picture. At the dinner table, Alwyn is given a quick briefing and asked to present his assault plan. Sarah listens carefully and looks enthusiastic being involved in the planning stages of a military assault.

As expected, Alwyn's plan is simple, with an assault from both sides of the buildings. Twenty-four Rangers will cross Mill Bridge and assault the first building and forty-eight Rangers will come by lorry and assault the second building from the road. All Rangers will enter through the windows with frame charges from the ground floor and then go upstairs to assault the upper floors through the third building. The upper floors will be assaulted simultaneously after each team is in position. If there really is a basement, Alwyn will add another team to assault the basement from the ground floor.

Sarah sees everyone nodding on hearing Alwyn's plan and Michael looking dead serious noting everything in his tablet.

Cormac suddenly looks at Sarah. "What do you think, Sarah?" he asks, smiling at her.

Sarah has her own opinion about Alwyn's plan, but she is hesitant to speak out.

"You might have to do this yourself someday when you finally find their factory in Indonesia so feel free to voice your opinion. This is what we call a 'Chinese parliament' session in The Regiment, in which everyone is free to voice his or her suggestions and opinions," explains Cormac.

"Well, I think Alwyn's assault plan is simple with minimum risks during entry," answers Sarah.

"But?" asks Cormac, still smiling.

"But... isn't it a bit... predictable?" asks Sarah carefully.

Sarah sees Cormac's smile widen, but Alwyn goes red-faced. He doesn't like having his work criticized, especially by a civilian. Now it's Michael's turn to present his own assault plan. Sarah knows that Michael hasn't prepared anything yet and she is worried that her lover will look silly... or sillier than usual, anyway.

It turns out Michael has made a plan on the spot and his plan is 180 degrees to Alwyn's plan. Michael suggests using Air Troop to assault the upper floors of the first two buildings using helicopters. They'll place frame charges on each window of the third floor and then secure the third floor of both buildings simultaneously. After the third floor is secured, they'll go downstairs to secure the lower floors. The main principle behind Michael's plan is that it will be much safer for the assault force to go downstairs than up. If Swan's Mill does have an underwater access, Boat Troop will assault the basement from there. Meanwhile, Mobility Troop will provide suppressing fire from the road and Mountain Troop will provide suppressing fire from across the river. The ground floor will eventually be secured by Air Troop while Boat Troop concentrates on the basement.

"And what do you think about Michael's assault plan, Sarah?" asks Cormac.

"It's different to Alwyn's plan and much more complicated. It's more audacious during the entry and much more dangerous, especially with that kind of roof. Air Troop would have to abseil directly into the stronghold by helicopter. That carries risks, of course. However, it will be much safer to clear downstairs than up."

"Which plan would *you* pick, Sarah?" asks Cormac once again.

Sarah thinks hard for a few moments. There's no effective way to counter a situation if an X-Ray throws some form of explosives, like grenades, to an assault force going upstairs. This is every field commander's nightmare scenario when leading an assault upstairs. To prevent large numbers of casualties, one team member has to throw themselves on top of the explosives and pray that their body armour can withstand the blast and prevent it from killing and wounding the others. Nobody wants to do that, obviously. Theoretically, as the commander, Sarah is the one who would have to sacrifice herself. She has practiced this scenario hundreds of times, and in training Sarah automatically and without hesitation would throw herself on top of the explosives, allowing the others to run as fast as they could to the next floor. In a real-life situation, the blast would most likely kill her. At the very least, it would maim her. But that's the risk every special forces operative faces.

On the other hand, X-Rays tend to *not* throw explosives towards an assault force going downstairs because there's a big chance the explosives could go right back to them. This is one of the reasons why special forces units prefer to assault from the roof than from the ground floor.

Both plans carry risks. Alwyn's plan is simpler during the entry, but carries high risk when the assault force has to storm upstairs to secure the upper floors. Michael's plan carries high risks during the entry, but is safer for them during the assault. The most critical phase of an assault is during the entry and Michael's entry is risky indeed, but if there really is an underwater access from the river, Michael's plan has an additional element of surprise.

"I would pick Michael's plan," answers Sarah, looking straight at Cormac.

"I agree with Sarah," says Cormac without any hesitation. "We will fully go with Michael's assault plan."

Alwyn is offended when he realizes that his ideas are completely ignored. "What the fuck, Mac? Michael asked me to plan a fucking assault and ye haven't implemented even one of my fucking ideas! What the fuck am I here for?" he says while standing up.

"Calm down, Alwyn, and we'll explain it to you. This is a Chinese parliament session, remember?" says Michael.

"Fine! But this is supposed to be a covert *military* operation. Why the fuck is this fucking policewoman in here?" asks Alwyn, his chin pointing towards Sarah.

Everyone goes silent and Sarah can clearly see that her friends are getting angry. Only Michael is expressionless, but Sarah knows him well enough to see that he's angry. She also understands that he's in no position to defend her.

Sarah decides to save everyone from this awkward situation and starts to stand up. "If you don't want me here then I'll just step outside. I'll be at the gym downstairs."

"Stand firm, Sarah!" orders Cormac. He stands up to face Alwyn, and he's red-faced from anger. "That fucking policewoman slotted thirteen of the fucking Cartel in a single fucking day! In all this time, Alwyn, how many of the fucking Cartel has *your* unit managed to slot?"

Alwyn and Emmet are surprised, but look sceptical. The Garda ERU and the Army Ranger Wing have never succeeded in killing Cartel members. There's absolutely no way an Indonesian policewoman could kill thirteen of them on her own.

"She also managed to slot Tiny fucking Mullins all by herself with just a fucking pen by ramming it through his fucking chest! Could *you* have done the same thing, dickhead?" asks Al, giving Alwyn a frightening look.

Al's fists are clenched as if he's gearing up to punch Alwyn out, which makes Alwyn take a step back. Emmet's jaw drops upon hearing that. Tiny used to be one of his men and he'd heard rumours during his funeral that Tiny was killed with a pen through his heart. Emmet had dismissed the rumours because that feat would've been impossible, especially to someone like Tiny.

"The Home Office has recommended her for a fucking KGM and the Director has already invested her with a fucking MC! I strongly suggest you treat our national fucking heroes with respect, you arrogant fucking piece of shit!" shouts Robert, standing up and slamming the table with his fist.

The sound of it echoes throughout the suite and Sarah is stunned. She has never seen a special forces commander being brought down like that. She is also touched because she didn't expect her friends to defend her so fiercely. On the other hand, Alwyn looks repentant. He didn't know that Sarah was a British hero and the guilt is almost overwhelming him.

"Right, I was out of line and I am truly sorry. Please accept my most sincere apologies, Sarah," says Alwyn, thrusting his hand toward her. He looks so regretful that he can't even look her in the eyes.

"Sure, Alwyn," answers Sarah without hesitation.

Emmet also thrusts his hand toward Sarah. "Tiny was one of my Rangers and he has been a thorn in my side these past few years. Thank ye for getting rid of him."

Sarah only smiles at Emmet. Killing Tiny is not something she's proud of.

"Now that this is settled, let's get back to work, shall we?" orders Cormac. He has calmed down, but his eyes are still giving Alwyn a hard look. "The reason we've asked you to do this, Alwyn, is because of Donald Mullins. We must assume the worst, that he has helped prepare the defence of their stronghold and devised some countermeasures to counter any assault from us. He will most likely have assumed that you and the Army Ranger Wing would be the ones doing the assault and his countermeasures will probably be based on what you proposed a few minutes ago."

"Think of this like the Naval Battle of Gravelines, Alwyn. The opposition expect us to do one thing, but we go completely the other way," explains Michael.

Sarah suddenly realizes why Michael took her to the Tower Museum.

"Ye could've just told us about this, Michael," says Alwyn, defensively.

"But then your fucking plans would've been entirely different to the ones you just fucking proposed! R*oi*ght?" asks Al sharply. He hasn't really forgiven Alwyn for treating Sarah the way he did.

Alwyn and Emmet fall silent. They have to admit that Al is right.

"You've done us a great service, Alwyn. Now let's figure out what countermeasures Tiny would have made to counter your assault and then let's all work together to build upon Michael's draft, shall we?" orders Cormac.

Throughout the night, the nine people work hard together perfecting Michael's assault plan. After midnight, Robert picks up his Senior NCO at the airport and conducts a recce with him at the River Owenkillew.

10:28 GMT
Sunday, August 9, 2026
City Hotel – Derry
Derry City, County Derry, Northern Ireland

The next morning, Sarah receives word from James that there is only one Irish-flagged ship, called MV Báinigh, that routinely goes between the Kalibaru Port in Jakarta and the Killybegs port in County Donegal. The mixed specialist cargo ship is currently at the Arctic Circle and plans to arrive in Killybegs on August 22, 2026. Sarah contacts NCB Indonesia and asks them to discreetly investigate the manifest of MV Báinigh.

A unit from the Royal Corps of Engineers are currently building a mock-up of Swan's Mill at RAF Odiham in Hampshire, England for B Squadron to train on. Cormac didn't tell anybody, but he also asked QinetiQ to build another mock-up of Swan's Mill at a remote area in PATA so that the Army Ranger Wing can train there. Robert arrives with his Senior NCO after conducting the recce. His name is Pierce McGregor and he's even better looking than Robert. The two men debrief the others.

There's a large tunnel inside the river that heads towards Swan's Mill. They've entered it and noticed that it heads under Swan's Mill. There is a watertight pressure door between the tunnel and Swan's Mill, and since this was more than ten metres underground, there's a big chance the Swan's Mill's basement has two storeys. Everything they did they recorded on video and the rest of the team can see the same things they saw and reach the same conclusion. Michael orders Robert and Pierce to think of ways The Cartel might smuggle the narcotics from MV Báinigh to Swan's Mill while the other men from Boat Troop place sensors in the tunnel and the river itself. If there are any movements in either the tunnel or the river, they can monitor them from the FOB.

Matt asks to meet Michael and Sarah at the Thompson's Restaurant on the ground floor of the hotel. They sit near the window facing the River Foyle. Matt tells them that all the women from Derry have been investigated by PSNI HQ. Most of them are prostitutes, but some have criminal records for distributing drugs.

"Some of the girls are most likely distributors for The Cartel. PSNI could pick them up and interrogate them about Swan's Mill," offers Matt.

"Negative, Matt. That would compromise the operation," says Michael.

"How about we put surveillance on them?"

"We already have a team following them, Matt," says Michael.

"Oh, well," says Matt, looking deflated. "Is there anything else I can do while I'm in Derry?"

Sarah looks toward the River Foyle and her mind starts wandering, thinking about the time she fought in the river. That gives her an idea. "Matt, could you discreetly check all the members of the City of Derry Sub Aqua Club?"

"What are ye thinking?" asks Matt.

Sarah explains that The Cartel is likely to smuggle the MDMA from under the River Owenkillew. "Diving gear is difficult to maintain. Unless The Cartel have divers on retention and have diving gear and maintenance equipment, they might be using outside divers to smuggle the MDMA into Swan's Mill. If that's the case, there's a good chance they'll have hired people from the club."

Michael and Matt think hard about Sarah's idea.

"They could be hiring club members, or divers from The Cartel could be renting gear from the club. For a start, I'll check with the club whether their diving gear is available for rent. If not, then I'll do a thorough background check to see whether there are club members with a criminal record. Let me get right on this. Good idea, Sarah!" says Matt as he stands up to leave them.

"I'll check with MoD and Paul whether they know of any Cartel members with diver's qualifications," says Michael.

While Michael makes a call, Liz joins them.

"I met Matt outside and he told me ye were in the restaurant," says Liz. "I've checked the girls ye sent me. All of them have criminal records except one and she looks interesting."

Liz shows her one of the pictures. The woman looks to be in her forties and has long, red hair. She's tall and fearsomely fit, though not very pretty.

"Who is she?" asks Sarah.

"That's the question. Paul, Matt, and I don't have anything on her," says Liz.

"Wait a minute!" says Sarah, suddenly remembering a picture.

She opens one of James's files that show Rory Hanrahan talking to a tall, fit, red-headed woman with her back turned towards the camera.

"Do you think this is the same woman?" asks Sarah.

Sarah and Liz study the picture for a while. The two women have similar features, but of course they can't be a hundred percent sure, so Liz sends the pictures to the Garda Technical Bureau for photo analysis. They discuss other things until Michael finally finishes his call. He looks satisfied.

"MoD has identified one of the girls using their face recognition software and they will send me her file in a few minutes. She's an

Irishwoman named Muireann de Buitléir and she used to be an MCDO or Minewarfare and Clearance Diving Officer based in Scotland. She resigned from the Royal Navy for personal reasons in 2004 and her last rank was Le*f*tenant-Commander. Of all the people in The Cartel, this is the only person we know whose background is as a rupert from the Royal Navy, so there is a high chance she's a senior member of The Cartel. It seems like the rumours there's a female in their top echelons are correct."

"MCDO? Is that something like the SBS or the Yank's Navy SEALs?" asks Liz.

"No, they don't have a combat role. They're basically EOD specialists who mostly work underwater, which is quite a fearsome location to perform EOD if you really think about it," explains Michael.

"The Royal Navy has female divers?" asks Liz.

"Sure, women may join any unit in His Majesty's Armed Forces as long as they're given a non-combat role… for now," says Michael, giving Sarah a meaningful smile.

A couple of e-mails enter Michael's mailbox, but he sends Muireann's file to his teammates before he opens them. Liz and Sarah study the file on their tablets. The tall, fit, red-headed woman at Swan's Mill turns out to be Muireann. She resigned from the Royal Navy because she wanted to marry an NCO from the British Army. She had to resign because she was an officer and he was just an NCO. Unfortunately, it doesn't say who she married.

Michael starts forwarding his e-mails. "MoD has also stated that almost all of the chaps from the photos from Swan's Mill have military backgrounds, including a significant number from the Royal Irish Regiment. Paul said seven of them have civilian diving certifications and one of them is Seamus Fitzgerald. Paul also said that Muireann has a dive boat under her name called Swan's Tide, currently moored in the Lough Swilly Marina at Fahan, County Donegal. This means that they can use her boat to transport the MDMA from MV Báinigh into Swan's Mill."

Michael asks Robert and Pierce to come down and join them. Liz's eyes light up when she's introduced to the two men of Boat Troop, both of whom are tall, sexy, and good looking. Michael tells them about Muireann de Buitléir and they in turn tell the others about their supposition. There's a chance that members of The Cartel onboard MV Báinigh dump their cargo overboard when they arrive at the mouth of Lough Swilly and Cartel members from Swan's Mill pick it up using Muireann's boat. Once the boat reaches the mouth of the River Owenkillew, they smuggle the goods in from under the river. Their supposition sounds good, so Michael orders Robert and Boat Troop to conduct a recce and place bugs and Active Radio Frequency Identification (Active RFID) on Swan's Tide, allowing them to track her if she ever leaves the marina.

Matt calls and says that tourists can rent diving gear from the City of Derry Sub Aqua Club. Muireann de Buitléir and seven other people from Swan's Mill are listed as members and Muireann likes to rent diving gear for herself. She and the seven men currently have plans to rent diving gear for three days, from August 19 to August 21, 2026. Those dates are well within the timeframe of MV Báinigh entering the UK and Irish borders.

Sarah also receives a report from NCB Indonesia that MV Báinigh has turbines in its cargo, produced by PT. Horizon Turbines and Propulsions, a company located in Citeureup, Bogor. The turbines are produced for oil & gas companies, operating in the North Atlantic Sea. Sarah then asks NCB Indonesia to investigate the company.

The Interpol team members, except for Michael, gather in Dublin to discuss the new developments. They conclude that Muireann is part of the top echelon, in charge of production and distribution of MDMA for Ireland, and Swan's Mill is a drug manufacturing plant and a distribution centre.

The next few days, the Interpol team is busy presenting their findings to various agencies of the government of the Republic of Ireland and His Majesty's Government. Both governments agree with Interpol's assessment and the assault by the UKSF Group is finally given a green light. The mission is a go. Cormac will need police support on the scene so he appoints Liz as liaison between the UKSF Group and An Garda Síochána.

The Director decides that B Squadron, SAS will assault Swan's Mill and Swan's Tide, and M Squadron, SBS will assault MV Báinigh. Both will be done simultaneously on Thursday August 20, 2026 at 01:30 in the morning. This means that they have less than two weeks to prepare and train for the assault. Once the mock-ups of Swan's Mill have been built, Cormac orders the Army Ranger Wing to train at PATA and B Squadron will train for their assault at RAF Odiham. M Squadron will train for their assault at Portland Harbour with a ship called RFA Sir Tristram, and a 4-man team from 6$^{th}$ Boat Troop will train at Hamworthy Barracks in Poole, Dorset.

Unfortunately for all, The Cartel's British Army contact is a member of the UKSF Group… currently training at PATA.

# CHAPTER 11
# FISH & CHIPS

12:02 GMT
Wednesday August 19, 2026
Pontrilas Army Training Area
Pontrilas, Herefordshire, England

In a remote area of PATA, an accurate mock-up of Swan's Mill stands majestic. Alwyn and the Army Ranger Wing have been training there since it was built. In the upcoming operation, they will replace the Special Forces Support Group securing the target's immediate surroundings. Their job won't be too complicated, but Cormac has asked Alwyn to train for the assault based on his original assault plan. Cormac said that because Michael's plan carries enormous risks, the Army Ranger Wing must be ready to assault Swan's Mill as a contingency.

An assault should always have a Plan B, a Plan C and so on to ensure mission success. Alwyn's delighted his Rangers are being given a more significant role than merely cordoning the target. They train hundreds of times, perfecting their entry until they've convinced themselves they could pull off the assault with or without the SAS.

Rumours of the Army Ranger Wing training for an assault have spread throughout PATA. A day before the assault, everyone at PATA is invited to the mock-up to watch the Army Ranger Wing train. They execute the mock assault flawlessly, but Cormac orders them to keep on training until otherwise directed. Alwyn and Emmet don't see the point in this and think it's a waste of time. Nevertheless, Cormac is the boss. Alwyn and Emmet fly to RAF Odiham to attend the final briefing and half of the Rangers fly to Derry, leaving the other half to continue training at PATA.

The Cartel's contact also watches the mock assault and instantly recognizes the three distinct buildings of Swan's Mill, and worries Swan's

Mill is about to be assaulted by the Army Ranger Wing. Everyone watches the mock assault until their lunch break is over.

"Let's head back to the demolition range, shall we?" invites the contact to a teammate.

"Sure, Sin," answers the teammate, looking at his friend quizzically. For some reason, his friend suddenly has an Irish accent.

The contact wants to tell Patrick the news immediately, but can't. First everyone must go straight to training.


13:22 GMT
Wednesday August 19, 2026
Lough Swilly Marina
Fahan, County Donegal, Republic of Ireland

Muireann de Buitléir, Seamus Fitzgerald, and six other men are preparing to pick up their goods in the North Atlantic Sea. Once her boat is on her way to the RV (rendezvous), Muireann takes off her clothes to sunbathe on the boat's deck wearing a blue bikini. As usual, her men find places to sit around nearby and watch her sunbathe. Muireann likes being stared at by her men and it's good for her ego. They wouldn't dare touch her anyway.

Muireann has a husband and a step-child from her husband's first wife. She has no kids of her own and that's the way she prefers it. She's immensely proud of her step-child and the two of them love each other very much. Muireann is almost fifty, but has a body that's firmer and fitter than most women half her age. Her stomach is lean and flat, thanks to the diving. If she weren't so busy with her factory, she would do nothing but dive around Lough Swilly and hang out with her distributors. Her previous job in the Royal Navy suited her hobby but, unfortunately, it didn't pay as well as drug smuggling.


13:38 GMT
Wednesday August 19, 2026
Four Seasons Hotel – Hampshire
Dogmersfield, Hampshire, England

Michael and Sarah are in bed in the Grand Manor Room of the Four Seasons Hotel in Hampshire, near Odiham. Sarah is lying on her back wearing nothing but denim shorts. Michael can't stop his hands from touching his lover's firm body. Sarah ignores him as she watches BBC on the telly with her hands behind her head.

Although he tries not to show it, Sarah knows that Michael is anxious about the mission. Sarah understands because she often feels the same way before a mission. A commander of a unit bears a lot of responsibility. Besides being responsible for the success of the mission, a commander is also responsible for the safety of their men. For a commander, no feeling is worse than failing a mission and/or losing someone under his or her command. Fortunately, this has never happened to Sarah. She has never failed a mission and has always brought all her men back in one piece.

On the other hand, there's nothing more satisfying for a commander than successfully accomplishing a mission without casualties. Sarah's always proud of herself and her men when they apprehend suspects without injuries on either side. Successes like that require meticulous planning and hard work, and Sarah's at her happiest when everything goes exactly as planned.

Even though Michael is going into harm's way, Sarah is not too worried. She was involved in the planning stages and can clearly see that they've done everything that can be done to ensure a successful operation. Sarah remembers her mum and feels sorry for her, for having to watch Sarah's dad deploy on missions without any idea what to expect.

Sarah glances towards Michael, who looks lost in thought. She feels sorry for him because he's getting tenser by the minute. Sarah guides Michael's head towards her abs and he kisses her there, but without the usual enthusiasm.

Sarah decides to help him relax. "You know, this reminds me of the time I did it with another woman…"

Michael makes a choking sound and looks at Sarah. Now he's all ears! "How did the story go?"

Sarah smiles. Her plan is working. "Well, the team at Densus came up with a plan to infiltrate the drug trafficking operations in the entertainment business using undercover policewomen posing as models. They selected some of the better-looking girls from the unit and sent us to a hotel to attend a modelling class, to learn how to look the part."

"That sounds like an excellent plan," comments Michael.

"Anyhow, we had to be quarantined at the hotel throughout the week-long course to maintain our cover, and the budget only stretched so far, which meant we were sharing rooms. My roommate was unbelievably attractive. Such a gorgeous girl. And we happened to have the same exercise routine, so we got in the habit of doing our daily crunches together."

"You crunched together? That's good. It's important to stay fit."

"One night after class, we had a contest to see who could do the most crunches. We were both similar, very competitive, and we had to stop after about 2,000 crunches as it became evident that neither of us were going to quit. My roommate then proposed something else, an abs-punching contest, to see who could last the longest."

"Ahh... A girl-on-girl fight... Dave would've loved that..."

"So we took off our shirts and started pounding each other in the abs a few hundred times. I can't remember exactly what happened next, but we were so hot and high from all the exercise that we started kissing."

"What was that? C-C-Could you say it again?"

Sarah laughs. "We started kissing. So, of course, one thing led to another, and then it finally happened."

Michael keeps looking at Sarah with wide eyes. "D-d-did you... both of you... y-y-you know... ehm... enjoy it?"

"Of course we did. I loved kissing her abs and she loved doing the same to me. The 69 position seems the best way to do this sort of thing. From there, we started kissing the... ehm... more erogenous parts of our bodies."

Michael gulps and almost chokes to death when she says that.

"We were both very fit girls so the orgasms were never-ending. We just kept coming and coming and coming." Sarah has to work hard not to laugh. Michael's face is changing colour! "We repeated it every night until we had to return to our unit but then we both agreed there was something missing from the experience." Of course, the truth of the affair was less exciting, less dramatic. But Michael seems to have enjoyed the story.

A few minutes later, Michael has already forgotten why he was feeling so anxious just a short while earlier.

14:30 GMT
Wednesday August 19, 2026
Joint Special Forces Aviation Wing HQ, RAF Odiham
Odiham, Hampshire, England

The final briefing is at the HQ of the Joint Special Forces Aviation Wing (JSFAW). Everyone in B Squadron is excited because it's rare for a special operation to require a full squadron.

The scale of this operation also involves the entire M Squadron and elements from Z Squadron of the Special Boat Service. M Squadron specializes in maritime counterterrorism and ship-boarding operations. They're also experts in helicopter assaults. These skills will be needed to secure MV Báinigh. Sarah and Liz's eyes open a little wider when they're introduced to the OC of M Squadron, Major Mark Johnston, a handsome man who looks like Il Divo singer Sebastien Izambard.

Besides the SAS and SBS, who are already in their black kit, no one in the room is wearing uniform. Everyone has arrived ahead of the designated time so Cormac starts the briefing.

"Ladies and gentlemen! For the Preliminaries: Operation Rowman, the recce of the target to determine its status, has concluded. We've determined that the stronghold is a DMP and distribution centre of MDMA for the Irish Drug Cartel. We can now proceed with Operation Crankshaft, which is the assault phase. Operation Crankshaft will be a textbook 'fish and chips' operation involving the entire B Squadron, who are currently 'On The Team', the entire M Squadron and elements from Z Squadron of the SBS, the Irish Navy, the usual support elements, and the Army Ranger Wing, who will be replacing the role of SFSG for this operation..."

Cormac continues the Preliminaries, the Situation, and finally the Mission.

"Our Mission is to 'shoot-to-kill' all members of the Irish Drug Cartel at Swan's Mill, Swan's Tide, and MV Báinigh. I say again, our Mission is to 'shoot-to-kill' all members of the Irish Drug Cartel at Swan's Mill, Swan's Tide, and MV Báinigh."

After Cormac states the Mission, its Michael's turn to continue. The Execution is presented in phases, but the gist of the plan is as follows:

Swan's Mill is codenamed Bravo, Swan's Tide is Charlie, and MV Báinigh is Delta. All three targets will be assaulted almost simultaneously. Operation Crankshaft will commence at 01:30 GMT, which is the same time a 737-700 aeroplane from Ryanair is scheduled to pass low right over Bravo. The sound of the low-flying aeroplane can mask the sound of the two Chinook HC6 helicopters that will deliver Air Troop.

Half of Air Troop, under the direct command of Michael Adrian, will enter through the windows of the top floor of the first building. At the same time, the rest of Air Troop, led by George Hastings, will assault the second building. The shield roofs of Swan's Mill prevent them from landing on the roof, so Air Troop will use the Special Patrol Insertion/Extraction (SPIE) method when dangling below the heli to place the frame charges.

These past few weeks, every morning at 01:30 GMT, a convoy of lorries from Coyles Arro has passed Swan's Mill. On the day of the assault, they will be replaced by four Land Rover 110s, each containing members of Mobility Troop, led by David Bancroft, the Senior NCO of Mobility Troop. Alwyn Buckley and the Army Ranger Wing will escort Mobility Troop from the front and rear of the convoy. Mobility Troop will stop in front of Bravo to secure the road-side of the buildings. Each 'pinkie' will be equipped with two General Purpose Machine Guns and they're tasked with providing suppressive fire from the road. Across the river, twelve men from Mountain Troop will infil from the forest and they're tasked with providing suppressive fire from across the river. Mountain Troop will also be led by Dave. Al Spencer, the most experienced EOD specialist in B Squadron, will abseil into Swan's Mill and lead the rest of Mountain Troop, with their EOD adquals, to dispose of any explosives found in Swan's Mill.

A 4-man team from Boat Troop, led by Pierce McGregor, will assault Swan's Tide once the assault on Swan's Mill is underway. Swan's Tide location is unpredictable and when the assault on Swan's Mill commences, Pierce has to be ready to assault her anywhere. Twelve men of Boat Troop, led by Robert Covington, will enter from the underwater access tunnel. They must be in position before 01:29 GMT, because everything needs to coincide with the low-flying aeroplane at 01:30. They have a tough job because they need to swim upstream toward Bravo laden down with weapons and ammo. Unfortunately for his team, river conditions make it impossible to swim downstream towards their target.

## THE POLICEWOMAN

Michael's briefing is supplemented by Mark. All of M Squadron and four sniper teams from Z Squadron, both under the command of Mark Johnston, will assault MV Báinigh once Swan's Tide has been secured. The SBS squadron consists of the 4 Troop, 5 Troop, 6 Troop, and HQ Troop. HQ and 5 Troop will assault MV Báinigh from the air (helicopter assault). At the same time, 4 and 6 Troop will assault the ship from the sea (seaborne assault). Four sniper teams from Z Squadron led by their SSM, each in an AW159 Wildcat heli, will cover M Squadron during their assault. M Squadron has the most challenging job because they need to search every inch of the ship to kill The Cartel members inside it. They will receive intel on what The Cartel members look like when they throw their goods overboard towards Swan's Tide.

Once Mark is finished, Michael continues the briefing. All assault troops will use the Colt Canada C8 CQB carbine. The rifles will contain 5.56×45mm NATO FMJ (full metal jacket) ammo that can penetrate body armour, which they're expecting the X-Rays to use. FMJ ammo can easily penetrate body armour, so nobody need worry about making headshots in the heat of the battle. They can save headshots for finishing them off.

They must assume that the X-Rays will be using assault rifles (longs) to defend their factory, so all assault troops are obliged to wear body armour and ceramic plates, capable of stopping high velocity rifle rounds. During the Chinese parliament a few days ago, Robert and Pierce protested that ceramic plates would be too heavy for them to carry during the dive. But Michael insisted and finally ordered them to wear it. Despite his direct order, Robert and Pierce still don't agree with him, and they considered *not* following his order. During the assault, Michael won't know whether they're wearing one or not anyway.

Michael is giving everyone a thoroughly professional briefing. As Sarah predicted, there are absolutely no signs of anxiety or doubts in his presentation. Quite unlike his previous presentations at Interpol, which tended to be clownish, Michael has presented the Execution and Command for the mission with such authority and power that Sarah's heart starts racing. Sarah has never seen Michael like this before! Now she can finally appreciate that her lover is truly a squadron commander of the finest special forces unit in the world. She can't take her eyes off him and even feels herself getting aroused, especially when Michael looks particularly dashing in his black kit.

Sarah suddenly realizes why women are easily attracted to Michael. She's seldom known anyone who has the aura, charisma, and voice of a leader. Those men who can portray that much power certainly attract women, who can imagine them as generals, CEOs, or even presidents. This aura is called command presence, and Sarah has never witnessed someone with a command presence as powerful as Michael before.

After almost an hour, Michael finally starts to brief the Support, which reaffirms the role of the supporting units for this mission. Sarah is still looking at her partner with awe and his voice is having quite an effect on her.

"Graham!" says Michael.

Wing Commander Graham Mitchell stands to attention. "Sir!"

"Your call sign is Juliet. The Air Troop, a 4-man team from Mountain Troop, four sniper teams from Z Squadron, and the HQ and 5 Troop from M Squadron will directly deploy from RAF Odiham. Could the JSFAW please provide heli transport for the respective teams to assault Bravo and Delta?" orders Michael.

"Yes, sir!" answers the CO of JSFAW. He stands at ease.

"Nigel!"

Leifteanant-Cheannasaí Nigel O' Tierney stands to attention in the manner of the Irish Navy. "Sir!"

"Your call sign is November. The 4 and 6 Troop from M Squadron will deploy from LÉ Niamh. Could you please provide transport and have the crew of LÉ Niamh halt and inspect Delta after M Squadron has secured it?"

"Aye aye, sir!" answers the liaison officer from the Irish Navy. He stands at ease.

"Alwyn!"

Leifteanant-Choirnéal Alwyn Buckley stands to attention in the manner of the Irish Army. "Sir!"

"Your call sign is Romeo. The Army Ranger Wing will substitute the SFSG on this mission and you will also provide sniper support for the assault on Bravo. Could you please escort Mobility Troop and cordon Bravo to make sure no X-Rays escape, and to ensure no civilians, especially the media, enter cordon areas immediately before, during, and after the assault?"

"Aye, sir!" says the CO of the Army Ranger Wing. He stands at ease.

"Simon!"

Major Simon Stilwell stands to attention. "Sir!"

"Your call sign is India and you will be stationed at the FOB. We have just received intel that three crewmembers of Delta are currently throwing bags of goods overboard and these goods are being taken aboard Charlie by their crew. During the assault, could you please provide real time intel support on all three targets using UAVs before and during the assault?"

"Yes, sir!" says the officer from the 21$^{st}$ Regiment, Special Air Service (Artists Rifles). He stands at ease.

"Des!"

Lieutenant-Colonel Desmond Aldridge stands to attention. "Sir!"

"Your call sign is Zero-Alpha and you will be stationed at the FOB. Could you please lead the other scaleys in providing signals & IT support for the whole operation?"

"Yes, sir!" says the CO of the 18 UKSF Signals Regiment, Royal Corps of Signals. He stands at ease.

"All right then. We will also need the Interpol team to provide INT support for the slimes at the FOB using the fixed cameras installed during the recce and to monitor the Active RFID and the bugs at Charlie. Sarah, please support India on this. Your call sign is Echo. After Bravo, Charlie, and Delta have been secured, could you please immediately lead the Interpol team in conducting the SSE for all three targets?" asks Michael.

Unconsciously, Sarah stands to attention in the INP manner. "Yes, sir!" she says in a husky voice.

Sarah tried to sound assertive, but sounded instead like a woman almost having an orgasm. Her eyes open wide as saucers and she immediately closes her mouth with both hands while everyone in the room starts laughing. Michael briefly looks as if he is stifling a laugh, but then his face hardens up again.

"Right, lads, you can take the piss out of her all you want after this is over. For now, let's concentrate on our mission, shall we?" orders Michael, giving his men a piercing stare.

The laughter immediately ceases, which is harder for some than for others. Sarah's face is so red that she's worried it can't return to normal.

Michael continues the briefing. "We know it would be better if we involved the local coppers on this right from the start, but we cannot risk a leak from anyone before the assault. Liz, could you please contact and brief the local Garda *after* all strongholds have been secured? We will also need Clive and the Garda ERU to support the Army Ranger Wing once Bravo and Charlie have been secured."

"Sure, Major," answers Liz, still trying hard not to laugh.

"Splendid! This concludes the mission briefing. Any questions?"

No one asks anything because the Five Paragraph Order ensures that everyone knows what their role is during the operation.

"Right, then, let's do this the way we rehearsed it, but without the cock-ups. Carry on, lads," orders Michael, closing the briefing.

Everyone scatters to take their positions. Liz and some of the others look Sarah's way and try hard not to laugh. Sarah sighs to imagine the kind of slagging she's going to have to suffer once this operation is over.

Everyone assigned to the Forward Operating Base flies to Derry. On the way there, Liz is still curious about something. "Mac, what the devil is a 'fish & chips' operation?"

Cormac smiles. "It's an acronym for 'Fighting In Someone's House & Creating Havoc In People's Streets'."

Sarah and Liz laugh at their silly acronym, but it's perfect for this operation.


16:02 GMT
Wednesday August 19, 2026
Pontrilas Army Training Area
Pontrilas, Herefordshire, England


During afternoon tea, The Cartel's contact calls Patrick to tell him what's going on. Patrick almost panics and asks his contact to tell him *how* the Army Ranger Wing will conduct their assault on Swan's Mill. Patrick is relieved to find out their assault plan is exactly what Tiny predicted when he designed the defensive measures for Swan's Mill. The Rangers will be slaughtered and everyone inside can escape easily. They'll even get away with all their goods.

Patrick tells his contact to keep an eye on things and to immediately call him once training stops. Patrick then starts calling Muireann, but she

# THE POLICEWOMAN

doesn't answer. He knows that Muireann is currently smuggling their goods and unavailable, but he has to keep trying. To protect the members of the top echelon, only Patrick has Muireann's number and Muireann in turn has only his. Under normal circumstances, this keeps things safe for their operation, but it really hinders things if one of them can't be reached. Patrick keeps trying to call Muireann and sends her text messages, but receives no reply.

Patrick gets extremely worried for Muireann.

19:49 GMT
Wednesday August 19, 2026
City Hotel – Derry
Derry City, County Derry, Northern Ireland

Sarah's in the suite with Cormac, Liz, Des, Simon, and three men flying the UAVs. Sarah's tasked with observing the live streaming from the Observation Posts to support Simon's team. Her job is quite boring, but its importance is not and she does it with full concentration.

Sarah can see that the people of Swan's Mill are going about their business as usual. Four men go out to shop and fifty or so men go out to smoke as scheduled. Through the bugs planted by Boat Troop, Swan's Tide is anchored at Lough Swilly near the mouth of the River Owenkillew. Through a Thales Watchkeeper UAV, remotely flown by one of Simon's men, they can see three people and Muireann resting on the boat. Through the underwater sensors planted by Boat Troop, they can trace the other four men as they smuggle their goods. Those four men are now nearing the boat. All this information is conveyed to Cormac, who forwards it to the field commanders. A few hours earlier, the UAV tracking MV Báinigh photographed the three men on board who threw the goods overboard to Swan's Tide. The pictures have been sent to Mark, who has forwarded them to all his men. Every member of M Squadron and the sniper teams from Z Squadron must memorize the faces of the three men, and they'll have to search the whole ship to take them out.

Seamus and three of his mates start climbing on board their boat. Their conversation can be heard through the bugs planted by Boat Troop.

"That's the last batch of Mandy, Guv'nor," says Seamus.

"Powerful," says Muireann. "Ye know what to do."

Seamus nods and starts the engine. Muireann dives into the water and heads towards Swan's Mill. Seamus and his six mates head towards Lough Swilly Marina to moor the boat. Seamus and his six mates can have fun at Fahan before returning to Swan's Mill.

21:12 GMT
Wednesday August 19, 2026
Swan's Mill
Buncrana, County Donegal, Northern Ireland

After her dive, Muireann finally enters the basement of Swan's Mill. She takes off her diving suit and walks up to her room in her bikini. She likes being stared at by her men as she passes them. She's dead tired but feels satisfied, which is what she always feels after a long dive. This night, the River Owenkillew is more rapid than usual, meaning she's more tired than usual. In her room, her smartphone keeps ringing but she ignores it for a while. She puts on a pair of jeans shorts before taking the call, which turns out to be her husband.

"Goddamnit, Muireann!" curses Patrick.

"What the fuck, Paddy?" protests Muireann.

"Swan's Mill is about to be raided by the Army Ranger Wing, damn it!" shouts Patrick.

"Fuck! Do ye have any intel?"

"It's exactly the way Tiny predicted it would be," says Patrick.

Muireann is a little relieved. "Do ye know when?"

"As of today, they're still rehearsing the assault in a training area at Pontrilas. Soonest the assault could take place is tomorrow night," says Patrick.

"Powerful! We have time to evacuate with all our Mandy," says Muireann.

"Fuck the Mandy! Get out of there while ye still can!" orders Patrick.

"We've got millions of quids' worth of Mandy from Indonesia and ye want me to leave it? Fuck, Paddy, we've rehearsed for this!" yells Muireann.

Patrick is quiet for a while. "Fine! Just get yer arses to Sandalwood Farm by tomorrow noon."

"Aye," answers Muireann.

She hurries to the dining room on the first floor. Her men have just finished dinner and some are doing the dishes. Some are about to go out for a smoke.

"Heads up!" shouts Muireann. "Our home is about to be raided by the Army Ranger Wing! Take out the longs from the armoury, grab yer body armour, activate the defensive measures, and start packing!"

Her men can only freeze in shock.

"Move yer fucking arses!" yells Muireann.

Everyone starts to do as they've been ordered to do, while Muireann sends a text to her distributors and to all the prostitutes not to come today. Muireann starts destroying documents showing the location of their HQ and their other factories, including the one in Indonesia. She then starts activating the defensive measures designed by Tiny. Muireann's experience as an MCDO means she's able to do this quickly and efficiently. She's sure that the Rangers will be annihilated if they assault Swan's Mill and everyone inside will escape easily with all their goods. After checking that everything is being prepared for their evacuation, Muireann finally calls Seamus.

"Aye, Guv'nor?" answers Seamus. His boss prefers being called 'governor' to 'boss'.

"Get yer arses back in position on the mouth of Owenkillew. We're evacuating!" orders Muireann.

"Wha…?"

"No time to explain! Make ready yer long, wear yer body armour, and move yer fucking arse!"


21:40 GMT
Wednesday August 19, 2026
City Hotel – Derry
Derry City, County Derry, Northern Ireland

"Boss, Charlie has just reversed course," reports Simon.

Everyone looks toward the large screen in front of the intelligence officer. Through the cameras of the Unmanned Aerial Vehicle, they see Swan's Tide reversing course, though she'd almost reached the marina.

Sarah suddenly realizes several things at once. "Mac, something's wrong!"

"What is it?"

"Half the men always come out for a smoke around this hour, but today – no one," says Sarah. "No distributors or prostitutes have arrived either."

Cormac and Simon look at each other, but don't say anything.

Sarah continues. "Aren't these signs that the operation is compromised?"

One clear sign that a special operation has been compromised is that the opposition suddenly have a change in habit. If The Cartel knows that they are about to be assaulted, it can endanger the assault force. The Cartel might be ready for them. If a special operation is compromised before it's initiated, it's better to abort the mission to prevent casualties. But Cormac only nods and says nothing.

"Shouldn't we abort?" asks Sarah, amazed at Cormac's lack of reaction.

"We've anticipated this, Sarah. Don't worry, but go ahead and inform Michael," answers Cormac.

Sarah is connected by Des to Michael, still at RAF Odiham, with his satellite communication terminal. Cormac asks Des to put the call on speaker so everyone can tune in.

"Yes, Sarah?" answers Michael.

"Michael, we have reason to believe that the operation is compromised. Charlie has just reversed course and the men never came out for their evening smoke," says Sarah. "Also, no distributors or prostitutes have arrived. This has never happened before."

Michael falls silent for a few moments. His worst nightmare has come true. "Have you spoken to Cormac about this?"

"Of course."

"And he told you not to worry, right?"

"Indeed..." answers Sarah, frowning.

"We've anticipated this, *mo ghile mear*," says Michael, trying to calm her. "Don't worry about it, all right?"

"Just be careful, Michael," says Sarah, trying to ignore everyone in the room when they started sniggering.

"Of course," answers Michael.

Everyone is still giggling when Des disconnects.

"Michael calls you '*mo ghile mear*' now?" asks Cormac, grinning from ear to ear.

"Indeed," answers Sarah, starting to blush. "Why?"

"Nothing... sounds appropriate," answers Cormac, still grinning.

"What do *you* call him, Sarah?" asks Des, sipping his coffee.

Sarah wants revenge on Michael for all the embarrassment she felt today.

"Biggus Dickus," she answers.

Everyone collapses in laughter... except Des, who chokes on his coffee, spilling it onto his shirt.


01:28 GMT
Thursday August 20, 2026
First Basement, Swan's Mill
Buncrana, County Donegal, Republic of Ireland


Muireann has just finished checking all of the Claymore mines and IEDs on the ground floor. They can be triggered remotely or by pressure plates. After the Rangers enter the ground floor, all of the explosives will detonate, turning the Rangers into mincemeat. Rangers still outside will be slaughtered too, as some of the Claymore mines face towards the Mala an Mhuilinn road and the River Owenkillew. Muireann's men have practiced evacuating hundreds of times and Muireann's feeling confident. A few hours before, she sent a third of her men to take a rest on the upper floors. The entire first floor of Swan's Mill is used for dining and recreation, and the second and third floor are their sleeping quarters. While awaiting the siege, everyone must wear body armour and be fully armed at all times, even when resting. Now Muireann orders another third of her men to replace the ones resting on the upper floors.

Muireann doesn't realize that her last order has doubled the people on the upper floors of Swan's Mill, just as Michael and Air Troop are about to make their entry...

01:29 GMT
Thursday August 20, 2026
3rd floor, Swan's Mill
Buncrana, County Donegal, Republic of Ireland

Just above Swan's Mill, a 737-700 from Ryanair is flying low, heading towards the City of Derry Airport. It makes an almighty racket. At the same time, hidden by the noise, two Chinook HC6 helicopters arrive and hover above the first and second building of Swan's Mill. The men of Air Troop are hanging from the helicopters. Once they're in position, they place frame charges on the windows. Before the charges are placed, Michael hears Sarah's voice in his headset.

"One, this is Echo. Be advised that there are currently twice as many X-Rays on the third floor as anticipated," reports Sarah, looking at the thermographic camera installed during the recce.

"One roger," answers Michael. Everything will now be twice as dangerous, but they must proceed as planned. "This is One in position."

"One, this is Two-Alpha in position," reports George.

"One roger. Zero, this is One, Alpha team in position," reports Michael.

"Zero roger," answers Cormac. This means that Michael and George and their respective teams are in their Final Assault Position (FAP). "You may initiate the assault at your discretion."

"One roger," answers Michael, tensely. He needs to wait until the other units are in position before he initiates the assault.

Cormac and Michael are worried because Robert and his team were supposed to be at their FAPs long before Air Troop was in position, and they're still not there.

01:29 GMT
Thursday August 20, 2026
River Owenkillew
Buncrana, County Donegal, Republic of Ireland

Robert and his Boat Troop are still underwater in the River Owenkillew. The river's pace has picked up hugely and they're having to fight their way upstream towards Swan's Mill, carrying loads of weapons and ammo. Robert's extremely worried because they should've been at the FAP inside the underwater access tunnel several minutes ago. The success of the mission depends on everything happening together.

01:29 GMT
Thursday August 20, 2026
Lough Swilly
Buncrana, County Donegal, Republic of Ireland

At the mouth of the River Owenkillew, Pierce and three men from Boat Troop are underwater, nearing the enemy boat - target Charlie - currently facing south. This means that the River Owenkillew and Swan's Mill are on the port side of the boat. Based on intelligence from the UAVs, Simon has told him that all seven men on board are wearing body armour and carrying AK-47s. Pierce and his team will not take any chances.

"Zero, this is Two, Sierra team in position," whispers Pierce.

"Zero roger," answers Cormac.

01:29 GMT
Thursday August 20, 2026
Mala an Mhuilinn, Swan's Mill
Buncrana, County Donegal, Republic of Ireland

At the same time, Dave and Mobility Troop have arrived in front of Swan's Mill in their modified Land Rover 110s. Mobility Troop is escorted by the Army Ranger Wing in their Ford F350 Special Reconnaissance Vehicle, which immediately blocks all access towards Swan's Mill. The Rangers then debus to cordon the surrounding buildings of Swan's Mill. Snipers from the Army Ranger Wing, already deployed the day before, are covering everybody.

"One, this is Romeo in position," reports Alwyn.

"One roger," answers Michael.

At the same time, Mobility Troop have debussed and are placing frame charges on all windows on the ground floor facing the Mala an Mhuilinn road. After the frame charges are ready, they all return to their vehicles.

"This is One-Golf in position," reports Dave to his team.

"One-Golf, this is Two-Golf in position," reports one of the NCOs of Mountain Troop. This means that they have placed frame charges on all windows on the ground floor facing the River Owenkillew and are ready in their positions across the river.

"One-Golf roger," answers Dave. "One, this is One-Golf. Golf team in position."

"One roger. All call signs, this is One. Ten seconds, out," orders Michael in his command voice, calming the men under him and instilling them with confidence in their commander's ability to lead them into battle.

Everything is done in only twenty seconds, from Air Troop placing their frame charges to Michael giving the ten-second warning.


01:30 GMT
Thursday August 20, 2026
First Basement, Swan's Mill
Buncrana, County Donegal, Republic of Ireland


The people inside Swan's Mill on the first, second, and third floor can hear nothing but the loud roar of the plane descending towards the City of Derry Airport and the convoy of lorries from Coyles Arro passing by on the way to their warehouse. These are the same sounds they've heard every day at the same time for weeks now. Everyone inside has gotten used to the noise and can ignore it. The only unusual sounds they hear are the 48 frame charges simultaneously detonating and blowing up all the windows on the third and ground floor.

BOOOOOM!

Muireann is below the tremendous blasts, on the first basement, used as a warehouse to store the MDMA.

"Guv! They're fucking here!" shouts one of her men.

Muireann forces herself to wait ten seconds to give every Ranger time to enter the ground floor. "Fire in the hole! Fire in the hole! Fire in the hole!" she shouts, slamming on the clacker three times to detonate all the

# THE POLICEWOMAN

Claymore mines and Improvised Explosive Devices (IEDs) on the ground floor.

BOOOOOM!

The dozens of Claymore mines and IEDs detonating on the ground floor shake the whole complex. The explosion warps the steel balls inside the Claymore mines into shapes similar to a .22 rimfire projectile. The explosion fires the projectiles outwards towards Dave and Mobility Troop on the Mala an Mhuilinn road and Mountain Troop across the River Owenkillew…

01:30 GMT
Thursday August 20, 2026
3rd floor, Swan's Mill
Buncrana, County Donegal, Republic of Ireland

Several seconds earlier…

At exactly 01:30, Michael can no longer wait for Robert and his team. The mission must begin now or lose the cover provided by the low-flying aeroplane. "All call signs, this is One and I have control. Standby… Standby… Go!"

BOOOOOM!

All of the windows are blown inwards, wounding or killing those inside. Michael abseils into the room and sees two X-Rays on the floor, moaning and bleeding to death. Without hesitation, Michael shoots them in the head with his carbine. Their heads practically disintegrate under the high velocity rounds from his Colt Canada C8 CQB. Michael releases his carabiner as everyone under his command reports that they're complete.

BOOOOOM!

A tremendous explosion is heard and felt from the ground floor, shaking the whole complex like an earthquake. They've anticipated this so they can ignore it.

"Juliet, this is One. Alpha team complete," reports Michael.

"One-Juliet roger," answers Graham. The CO of the JSFAW is personally flying the Chinook that brought Michael and his team.

"Two-Juliet roger," answers the pilot of the second Chinook.

Both Chinooks immediately fly away from the target.

"Zero, this is One. Two X-Rays down at Bravo-1-3-Papa," reports Michael.

"Zero roger," answers Cormac. He then asks Des to put him through to Pierce. "Two, this is Zero, standby. You may initiate the assault at your discretion."

"Two roger," whispers Pierce.

"One-Golf, this is One. Commence fire," orders Michael.

"One-Golf roger," answers Dave.

All the men of Mobility and Mountain Troop shoot their weapons towards all windows, from the ground floor to the second floor, from both sides of the buildings. No one in Mobility Troop is hurt because after placing the frame charges, they'd hidden themselves inside their armoured pinkies, which are now riddled with dents and small holes. Something similar happened across the river, where Mountain Troop hid behind the thick trees before the explosion from the ground floor. Not a single soldier has been hurt by Muireann's Claymore mines and IEDs.

Michael exits the room and his team does the same. The number of X-Rays was double their original estimate, but Air Troop easily handled them with speed, aggression, and surprise of entry. After securing the third floor of the first and second buildings, Michael and the sixteen men of Air Troop make their ways towards the third building, clearing the stairway to the second floor.

"Zero, this is One. Third floor secured, Alpha team in position," reports Michael.

"Zero roger," answers Cormac.

"One-Golf, this is One. Check fire on Bravo-2-2," orders Michael.

"One-Golf roger," answers Dave.

The shots on the second floor of the second building of Swan's Mill immediately cease. Two men throw flashbangs into the hallway and everyone enters before the flashbangs detonate. Michael and his team head towards the first building while George and his team start clearing all the rooms in the second building of Swan's Mill.

"One-Golf, this is One. Check fire on Bravo-1-2," orders Michael as they near the first building of Swan's Mill.

"One-Golf roger," answers Dave.

The shots on the second floor of the first building of Swan's Mill immediately cease. The number two on Michael's team throws a flashbang into the hallway and everyone on Michael's team enters before the flashbang detonates. Michael and his team start clearing the rooms of the first building of Swan's Mill. Michael is assigned to clear the room on the furthest left. After preparing a flashbang, he kicks open the door, throws the flashbang inside, and enters with it. There's only one X-Ray inside, face down and with both hands covering his head. Michael doesn't know if he's still alive or not. He doesn't waste time checking and shoots him in the head at the same time the flashbang detonates.

"One, this is Two-Alpha. Bravo-2-2 secured," reports George.

Michael listens to other reports of X-Rays killed before answering him. "One roger. Zero, this is One. X-Ray down at Bravo-1-2-Hotel. Bravo-1-2 secured."

"Zero roger," answers Cormac, helping Simon put an 'X' through all the rooms with killed X-Rays.

Michael and Air Troop head towards the third building and descend towards the first floor.

"Zero, this is One. Second floor secured, Alpha team in position," reports Michael.

"Zero roger," answers Cormac.

"One-Golf, this is One. Check fire on Bravo-2-1," orders Michael.

"One-Golf roger," answers Dave.

The shots on the first floor of the second building of Swan's Mill immediately cease. Four men throw flashbangs into the large room at the same time everyone enters. There are ten men inside and all are on their bellies, trying to take cover from the heavy fire from outside. They're shot where they lie and Air Troop starts clearing the rest of the first floor, normally used as a dining and recreation area.

01:31 GMT
Thursday August 20, 2026
Lough Swilly
Buncrana, County Donegal, Republic of Ireland

A few minutes earlier…

Seamus and six of his mates are guarding the boat, smoking and fingering their AK-47s, when the first blast from the direction of Swan's Mill surprises them. Instinctively, they all go to the port side of the boat to watch the explosion, some 200 metres away. They can clearly see two Chinooks flying away from Swan's Mill, but that's the last thing they see. High-velocity rounds from assault rifles riddle their bodies from the starboard side, passing easily through their body armour. Although Seamus and his mates will never get up again, Pierce and the three men of Boat Troop finish them off with shots to the head, blowing their heads apart.

"Zero, this is Two. Seven X-Rays down at Red-3. Stronghold secured!" reports Pierce.

"Zero roger," answers Cormac. "Three, this is Zero, standby. You may initiate the assault at your discretion."

"Three roger," answers Mark.

As planned, Mark and M Squadron will commence their assault on MV Báinigh, now in Irish waters. Pierce takes Swan's Tide back to Lough Swilly Marina while his three men conduct the SSE.

01:34 GMT
Thursday August 20, 2026
Second Basement, Swan's Mill
Buncrana, County Donegal, Republic of Ireland

While Air Troop is still securing the first floor, Robert and his team finally arrive at the underwater access tunnel. Still panting heavily, they stack beside the watertight pressure door and Robert signals his MOE specialist to place the frame charge.

"One, this is Three-Alpha in position," whispers Robert, anxiously. This is his first time going into battle.

"One roger!" answers Michael curtly. About bloody time!

01:35 GMT
Thursday August 20, 2026
First Basement, Swan's Mill
Buncrana, County Donegal, Republic of Ireland

Once Michael and Air Troop have secured the first floor, they return to the third building and start descending. They can safely bypass the decimated ground floor and head straight towards the first basement.

"Zero, this is One. First floor secured and ground floor bypassed, Alpha team in position," reports Michael.

"Zero roger," answers Cormac.

"Three-Alpha and Four-Alpha, this is One, standby. Go!" orders Michael.

"Three-Alpha roger," answers Robert.

"Four-Alpha roger," answers Al.

Al leads three men from Mountain Troop and abseils into the third floor from an Agusta A109 helicopter. They head to the ground floor to clear it from explosives. At almost the same time as Al's entry, the whole complex shakes again from the blast in the second basement. This means that Robert and his team has made their entry.

"Ready frags," orders Michael.

Michael, George, and two of their men throw fragmentation grenades into the first basement. "Frag out!"

BOOOOOM! BOOOOOM! BOOOOOM! BOOOOOM!

Michael and his men can hear the screams amid the blasts. They enter the first basement and finish them off. After securing the first basement, Michael and Air Troop enter the third building again and guard it against X-Rays from the second basement who might use it to escape.

"Zero, this is One. One-Three X-Rays down, first basement secured. Alpha team in position," reports Michael.

"Zero roger."

Michael and Air Troop have reached their Limit of Exploitation (LOE) and to prevent blue-on-blue, they will go no further. They've managed to secure four out of six floors in Swan's Mill in less than five minutes. Michael now must count on Robert and his team to secure the second basement, and Al and his team to secure the ground floor.

01:35 GMT
Thursday August 20, 2026
Second Basement, Swan's Mill
Buncrana, County Donegal, Republic of Ireland

Less than a minute earlier…

Muireann is sure that all the Rangers of the Army Ranger Wing have been slaughtered so she orders her men to evacuate through the river. Once she reaches the second basement, she sees one of her men start to open the watertight pressure door. It suddenly explodes!

BOOOOOM!

Muireann sees her man shatter to pieces before her eyes. Six fragmentation grenades fly into the second basement, the MDMA production area.

Before taking cover behind a pill-making machine, Muireann glimpses the limbs of her men flying away from their bodies in the explosions. The assault troops start entering the second basement, firing their assault rifles as they enter. Muireann notices that their rounds pass easily through her men's body armour.

BOOOOOM! BOOOOOM! BOOOOOM! BOOOOOM!

Four blasts are heard from the first basement above her. It turns out the assault force have pinched her, so she and her men are trapped. Muireann wonders how any of the Rangers survived her Claymores and IEDs. She's surprised too, because she hadn't thought that they were smart enough to find her underwater access tunnel.

As a senior member of The Cartel, Muireann knows she can't allow herself to be captured. She destroys her smartphone and SIM Card with the butt of her rifle so they can't trace her calls. This is the end for her, but she hopes to kill at least one Ranger before she dies.

The FMJ ammo the Rangers must be using is designed to pass through body armour, but is less effective hitting bare flesh, so she steps out of her body armour. Now she's just in her jeans shorts and bikini. As long as they don't hit her directly to the head, spine, or vital organs, their rounds will pass clean through her body with minimal damage. Muireann then decides to step out of her jeans shorts and bikini, hoping she can startle the Rangers and buy herself a few precious seconds of shooting time. She's now stark naked, except for her belt kit, which she straps around her waist. She then dry-swallows a couple of ecstasy pills. The adrenaline she's experiencing will mean the pills kick in fast, and both together will help reduce the incredible pain she's about to experience.

'Fuck… This is going to hurt…' thinks Muireann as she comes out of her hiding place.

As she expected, everyone is surprised by her appearance! Muireann knows that no matter how highly trained a special forces operative is, they will always hesitate to shoot a woman… especially a woman who's naked. This gives Muireann time to shoot one of the lead soldiers with a three-round burst from her M4 Carbine.

Robert is floored by the three high-velocity rounds to his centre mass. Muireann immediately aims her M4 towards his head and starts squeezing the trigger to finish him off…

01:36 GMT
Thursday August 20, 2026
Ground Floor, Swan's Mill
Buncrana, County Donegal, Republic of Ireland

Al and three of his men are checking every inch of the ground floor. They can't even imagine what the Rangers would look like now if they had used this entry. The only UXO, or Unexploded Ordnance, they find is an IED still attached to the front door. EOD specialists from around the world know that disposing of an UXO is one of the most dangerous jobs in the world, so Al asks his team to stand down and take cover. Al Spencer will personally disarm the extremely dangerous UXO. Any distraction could prove fatal, so he turns off his comm headset to fully concentrate on his task.

01:37 GMT
Thursday August 20, 2026
Second Basement, Swan's Mill
Buncrana, County Donegal, Republic of Ireland

Before she can finish squeezing the trigger and shooting the downed soldier in the head, Muireann feels several bullets pass through her torso. She decides to ignore the soldier on the ground and turns to shoot the others, who pose more of an immediate threat to her. Unfortunately, none of her rounds hit her targets. However, more bullets pass through her body. Because of the drugs and adrenaline rushing through her system, she feels little pain. Instead of falling to the ground and dying, she empties her mag.

While changing mags, Muireann sees the downed soldier suddenly rise and give her a short burst from his assault rifle. She feels a couple of rounds pass through her right chest, shattering some of her ribs and collapsing her right lung. She's still able to stand and fires towards the huge soldier. Unfortunately, he's already taken cover behind a pill-making machine. At the same time, shots from several different directions pass through Muireann's body. It seems to have little effect on her, although pink blood is starting to flow out of her mouth from her collapsed lung. Once again, Muireann empties her rifle, but the soldiers have already taken cover.

Muireann has just finished changing mags when the huge soldier appears from cover and empties his rifle at her in full-auto. The bullets hit her lower belly and start to go upwards. None of the rounds hit her pelvis or spine, so Muireann can still stand and return fire, even though her stomach has more holes than Swiss cheese and her guts are starting to spill out. A couple of bullets take off most of her left arm, so now she can shoot only with her right arm. Muireann struggles to shoot the huge soldier, but the last bullet hits her in the sternum. No matter how tough someone is, if they're hit in their sternum, they will always go down. This is the shot that finally takes Muireann down. She's been indefatigable, but at last she's now on her back.

Muireann sees the soldier she shot walk warily towards her. He changes mags and kicks her M4 away from her hand. He points his rifle at Muireann's face. She's still alive, even though her torso is a bloody mess.

"Good… bye… Paddy…" murmurs Muireann. She then looks sharply at the soldier who's about to end her life, daring him to finish her off as she looks him in the eyes.

Robert shoots her full in the face, shattering Muireann's head to pieces.

"One, this is Three-Alpha… B-B-Basement s-s-secured!" stammers Robert, completely shaken.

01:37 GMT
Thursday August 20, 2026
Second Basement, Swan's Mill
Buncrana, County Donegal, Republic of Ireland

"One roger," answers Michael.

They now must wait for Al and his team to secure the ground floor from explosives. Michael looks at his watch and frowns. Al should've been done by now.

BOOOOOM!

What was that? Unlike the previous explosions, nobody expected that blast from the ground floor!

"Four-Alpha, this is One. Radio check," says Michael.

Al doesn't answer.

"Four-Alpha, this is One. Radio check, goddamn it!" shouts Michael.

There is only silence. Michael and George can only share a look of utmost concern for Al…


01:37 GMT
Thursday August 20, 2026
MV Báinigh
North Atlantic Sea, Republic of Ireland

M Squadron will conduct a simultaneous helicopter and seaborne assault on target Delta. Mark and half of M Squadron will board using the Fast Rope Insertion/Extraction System (FRIES) from a Chinook, while the rest will use Rigid Inflatable Boats (RIBs) to go alongside target Delta and use hook-and-pole assault ladders to board the ship. M Squadron will have to secure all cabins and eliminate the three Cartel members. They must be careful not to accidentally shoot innocent crewmembers. The UKSF Group has executed this kind of operation before, on a ship called MV Nisha in 2001.

However, they don't need to do any of that. Looking through the camera of the UAV, Simon tells Mark that the three Cartel members are on the ship's deck, smoking and leaning on the starboard rail. Mark orders his sniper teams from Z Squadron to take them out. There is a delay because the four sniper teams fight over who gets to shoot the three X-Rays. The SSM of Z Squadron, leading the sniper teams, finally steps in and orders the most junior and least experienced among them to stand down and act as backup in case the other snipers miss their targets.

Once the SSM gives the order, the three snipers hit their targets in their centre masses, almost simultaneously from a range of 600 metres.

"Three, this is Two-Zero-Zulu. Three X-Rays down at Green-9," reports the Squadron Sergeant Major of Z Squadron, a look of utter satisfaction on his face.

"Three roger. November and Four-Juliet, this is Three. Please proceed with Phase Three," orders Mark.

"November roger," answers Nigel onboard LÉ Niamh.

"Four-Juliet roger," answers the Chinook pilot.

Mark and his men fast-rope on board the ship to finish off and secure the three dead X-Rays while the captain of LÉ Niamh orders target Delta to heave to. Once all ships are at full stop, those on board the RIBs are ordered to return to LÉ Niamh.

"Zero, this is Three. Three X-Rays down, stronghold secured," reports Mark, sounding disappointed. The assault on MV Báinigh by his unit is anticlimactic.

"Zero roger," answers Cormac.


01:37 GMT
Thursday August 20, 2026
Ground Floor, Swan's Mill
Buncrana, County Donegal, Republic of Ireland

A few minutes earlier...

Al sees that the IED is beyond disposing so he decides to just blow it up with the PE4 he is carrying. He and his team take cover.

"Fire in the hole! Fire in the hole! Fire in the hole!" shouts Al. As per SOP, those words must be said three times before an EOD specialist blows something up, to give the other teams fair warning that an explosion is about to take place.

BOOOOOM!

"One, this is Four-Alpha. Ground floor secured!" reports Al.

Al wonders why Michael doesn't answer. He suddenly remembers why and turns on his comm headset.

"One, this is Four-Alpha. Ground floor secured!" reports Al, properly this time, ignoring his men's sneers.

01:38 GMT
Thursday August 20, 2026
City Hotel – Derry
Derry City, County Derry, Northern Ireland

Through the Satellite Ground Terminal, Michael's command voice echoes throughout the FOB. "One roger. Zero, this is One... For King and Country, stronghold secured!"

"Zero roger. All targets secured and mission accomplished," says Cormac, smiling broadly. "Good job everyone!"

The Forward Operating Base erupts in loud cheers and celebration! The men and women inside shake hands and hug each other and clap each other on the back. Sarah feels extremely relieved, proud, and ecstatic at the same time. This is what she always feels after leading a successful operation and it's almost orgasmic! Her respect and admiration for Michael and the SAS have gone through the roof and from now on, she won't just consider him as her partner... he's also her hero.

Liz calls the Sáirsint in charge of Buncrana Garda Station to tell him what's happening in his area. They arrange to meet face-to-face at the Buncrana Garda Station. Liz also calls Clive to deploy the Garda ERU to Swan's Mill and to coordinate with Alwyn, who is already at the site. Liz then contacts the Garda National Drug Unit (NDU) to secure the MDMA at Swan's Mill.

Sarah sends a text to the rest of the Interpol team to board the heli at the hotel's helipad. Before Sarah enters the heli, she receives a text from Michael. 'I need to see you. Could you please convince Mac to let you join our debrief?'

'Echo roger,' writes Sarah, smiling broadly.

Michael returns her text with a smiley. Sarah, Broussard, Matt, and Arthur are dropped off at Swan's Mill to conduct the Sensitive Site

Exploitation (SSE), an activity to gather intelligence immediately after a special operation. Paul is dropped off at Lough Swilly Marina and James is taken to MV Báinigh.

Michael and B Squadron have already left Swan's Mill when they arrive. The area surrounding Swan's Mill has been secured by the Army Ranger Wing and the Garda ERU so the Interpol team can enter it without any trouble. Before entering Swan's Mill, Sarah sees Alwyn and Emmet talking outside. They are inspecting the building and both look quite pale. Sarah decides to meet with them first.

"Is everything all right, Alwyn?" asks Sarah.

"Ye were fucking right, Sarah!" says Alwyn, pale and wide eyed.

"About what?"

"The ground floor was a fucking killing zone! My Rangers would've been wiped out if *we* were the ones doing the assault," says Alwyn.

"Aye... and it would've been Tiny that had killed us," says Emmet, shuddering.

Sarah only nods and they continue talking while inspecting the buildings. Sarah has studied the blueprints of Swan's Mill hundreds of times, but this is the first time she's seen it first-hand. Swan's Mill looks much more impressive in real life than in its picture.

"The fucking SAS secured a fucking stronghold like this without sustaining a single fucking casualty. And in less than nine fucking minutes," says Alwyn, shaking his head. "No wonder they're the best in the world."

Sarah smiles proudly when Alwyn praised her partner. From afar, she recognizes Clive in his Garda ERU black kit, waving at her. Sarah smiles at him and returns his wave, making Clive happy. Only half of the soldiers on location are Army Ranger Wing and the other half are Garda ERU personnel, some whom are taking turns grabbing selfies with Swan's Mill as a majestic background.

"Where are the rest of your men, Alwyn?" asks Sarah.

"Cormac ordered half of my Rangers to continue rehearsing the assault at PATA for some reason," answers Alwyn, shrugging. "He ordered me to have them stand down only a few minutes ago."

"Wait a minute! I thought the mock-up was at RAF Odiham. There's another mock-up of Swan's Mill at PATA?"

"Aye, my Rangers rehearse there whilst the SAS rehearsed at another mock-up at Odiham," says Alwyn.

"When Cormac made us rehearse our assault, I was sure we would be given a more active role in this assault. I'm sure glad Cormac ordered us to stand down," says Emmet.

"Rehearse what, Emmet?"

"Cormac made us rehearse our entry as a back-up plan. He said that this was just in case Michael's entry went to shite," says Emmet.

Sarah suddenly has an idea. "Did anyone at PATA see you rehearse your assault?"

"Everyone at PATA was invited to see our rehearsal yesterday," answers Alwyn. "How did ye know that?"

"Just a wild guess," answers Sarah. Alwyn and Emmet give her quizzical looks so she tries to evade them. "Right, I guess I'll be going in then. I'll see you at the debriefing, and thank you for the support of the Army Ranger Wing on this mission," she says, giving them her sweetest smile.

"Ye're welcome, Sarah," says Alwyn and Emmet, both somewhat stunned by her perfect smile.

Sarah hurriedly enters Swan's Mill. Broussard is handling the third floor, Matt is on the second, and Arthur on the first. There's nothing on the ground floor so Sarah heads towards the second basement. In the middle of the basement, there's a dead body of a woman, most likely Muireann's. The body looks odd because it is completely naked except for a belt kit, drenched with blood and full of bits and pieces of her guts. Her head and torso are shattered, with her entrails hanging out. Her left arm is missing and shards of white bone are sticking out of the bloody stump. Sarah has seen quite a few dead bodies and in various stages of decomposition, but Muireann's condition makes her feel nauseous. Sarah calls Cormac.

"Yes, Sarah?" he answers.

"Are you alone, Mac?"

"Simon's still with me at the FOB and we were just about to RTB. What's up?" asks Cormac.

"When will you conduct the debriefing?"

"The men are in a 'warm down period' for twenty-four hours, so probably tomorrow noon."

"Who will attend?"

"This is a Scale-A Meeting so the whole UKSF Group and all the support personnel are required to attend," says Cormac. He can clearly sense that Sarah wants to join in, but this activity is classified as Top Secret and for UKSF personnel only. "Why? What's up?"

"Just wondering if you've managed to identify the traitor at PATA," answers Sarah. "It would seem quite awkward to have him invited to the debriefing of an operation that wiped out a lot of his mates…"

Just as she expected, the CO of the SAS falls silent. Inside the FOB, he looks at Simon, his face slowly turning pale. "Did Michael tell you about this?"

"Of course not!" says Sarah, clearly offended.

"I need to speak to you about this, Sarah. How about coming with us to the barracks for the debrief?" orders Cormac. "You can learn quite a few more things from us during the debriefing, you know."

"I thought you'd never ask, Mac," says Sarah, grinning.

"How about you return to the FOB so we can fly together to Credenhill?" orders Cormac.

"I'll be there ETA thirty-five mikes," answers Sarah.

Sarah quickly counts the dead bodies in the basements. This isn't as easy as it seems because their body parts were scattered everywhere by blasts from the grenades. She then goes to the third floor to see Broussard, who's enthusiastically conducting the SSE in Muireann's luxurious bedroom.

"Chief, there are a total of twenty-nine bodies in the basements, including that of a woman I suspect is Muireann de Buitléir. However, the SAS have invited me to their barracks for the debrief. I have to return to the FOB."

"Go," orders her commander.

Sarah exits the building to see Clive. She asks him if one of his men could take her to the City Hotel in Derry, but Clive happily takes her there himself. He uses this golden opportunity to hit on her, of course.

04:13 GMT
Thursday August 20, 2026
Regimental HQ, SAS Barracks
Credenhill, Herefordshire, England

Once they arrive at the RHQ, Sarah, Cormac, and Simon go into one of the meeting rooms.

"How did you find out we have a traitor?" asks Cormac.

"PE4s were used to blow up the International Liaison Building at Dublin and Michael told us a few months ago that the Special Investigation Branch had investigated the missing PE4s at PATA. We think someone in the UKSF Group is working for The Cartel and smuggled the PE4s out for them. This person most likely gave them Michael's old smartphone number so they could've easily traced him to Carluccio's. You ordered QinetiQ to build another mock-up of Swan's Mill at PATA so the Army Ranger Wing could be seen rehearsing *their* assault using *their* entry and you made sure your suspects saw them doing it. This was to ensure the opposition was looking the other way when Michael and his Air Troop assaulted Swan's Mill from the air. It also meant you ensured that no distributors or prostitutes entered Swan's Mill during the assault, so the assault teams needn't worry about Yankees. Correct me if I'm wrong, Mac," says Sarah. She already knows the answer from the look on Cormac and Simon's faces.

Cormac takes a long breath before answering her. "You are correct, Sarah. Someone in the UKSF Group is working for The Cartel and Simon is helping me identify who it is. We have narrowed it down to a handful of suspects, but we still don't know who it is yet."

Simon continues. "We're soldiers, not detectives. We have no clue on what to do next so it'll probably take some time before we finally identify this person."

"Why not cooperate with the Special Investigation Branch of the Royal Military Police?"

They don't answer. Sarah can conclude that they want to investigate this without involving anyone outside the UKSF Group.

"Is there anything I can do to help?" offers Sarah.

"Thank you for the offer, but this matter is strictly confidential. We would appreciate it if you keep this information to yourself," says Cormac.

"No problem, Mac," says Sarah. "If I may suggest, though, you should closely observe your suspects during the debrief. If any of them are acting oddly or out of place - for example if one of them looks sad or angry because of the success of the operation - he could well be your traitor."

"Good idea, Sarah!" says Cormac. He gives a nod to Simon, who also nods appreciatively.

They exit the meeting room and Cormac invites them both into the Main Briefing Room. In the room, loud music is blasting away, but it's drowned out by the cheers of everyone inside when the door opens and they see Cormac, Simon, and Sarah.

Everyone involved in the operation is partying and getting pissed. The Main Briefing Room, called the Blue Room, is surrounded by tables packed with food and bottles of beer. They're ecstatic because the extremely complicated operation was executed perfectly without casualties. This is the best achievement for B Squadron since Operation Nimrod in 1980. Everyone wants to shake the hands of Sarah, Cormac and Simon, and give them a pat on the back, but Sarah is interested in one person only. She finally sees her partner across the room and, exactly like a cheap romance flick, she runs towards him, leaps into his arms, and gives him a long, hard kiss on his lips. This to the cheers and whistles of everyone in the Blue Room.


06:02 GMT
Thursday August 20, 2026
Sandalwood Farm
Nether Alderley, Cheshire, England


At The Cartel's headquarters, Patrick is suddenly awoken by Steve, Rory, and Carraig, tears in their eyes. They turn on the telly to watch the BBC headline news reporting that earlier this morning, Swan's Mill was assaulted by a joint operation between the Army Ranger Wing and the Garda ERU. Everyone inside has been killed, including a woman named Muireann de Buitléir, considered to be a senior member of the Irish Drug

## THE POLICEWOMAN

Cartel. The Garda NDU seized hundreds of tons of MDMA and raw materials and the Garda ERU seized hundreds of assault rifles, pistols, and explosives. A talking-head spokesperson praises the Rangers and the Garda ERU for securing Swan's Mill in an operation that sustained no casualties. The reporter clearly states which units assaulted Swan's Mill, but the senior members of The Cartel are having none of it. They know exactly who was responsible for assaulting their factory.

Patrick curses out loud, then cries hysterically for the loss of his wife. The others try in vain to calm him down.


13:29 GMT
Friday August 21, 2026
Main Briefing Room, Regimental HQ, SAS Barracks
Credenhill, Herefordshire, England

Everyone in the UKSF Group currently in the UK is obliged to attend the debriefing. Prince Harry, as Colonel-in-Chief of the $22^{nd}$ Regiment, is supposed to attend, but he is currently abroad. There's now a stage at the front of the Blue Room and a large screen behind it.

Everyone is in uniform except Sarah, making her stand out even more, especially when she's asked to sit at the front next to Cormac and Sir Charles Mountbatten. Before the debriefing begins, Sarah briefly notices Al, George, and Dave sitting behind her. George is laughing his arse off after taking the piss out of St John, sitting behind them with a huge pout on his face. Sarah also notices around fifteen women of the Special Reconnaissance Regiment sitting in the back row. Sheila's among them, looking especially gorgeous in her SRR uniform. At the back of the room, Derek is frowning, struggling to operate a video camera. Sarah also notices that few soldiers wear medals on their uniform. Like her own medals from the INP, Sarah is sure that there are many among them whose medals are classified.

The debriefing finally starts and it's important that it be delivered as honestly as possible, so that mistakes can be prevented in future operations. Michael looks especially dashing in his SAS uniform and sand-coloured beret when he delivers the results of their recce during Operation

Rowman and the Execution phases of Operation Crankshaft. Sarah's excited to see her partner in action again, especially as this is her first time seeing him in his temperate parade uniform. Operation Crankshaft was executed as planned and everyone can see the action from the CCTV recordings taken from Swan's Mill and their own cameras at the Observation Posts.

Pierce goes on stage after Michael. The 4-man team from Boat Troop also conducted a textbook assault on their target, so he's on stage for less than ten minutes. Next up is Mark, who's done in just five. The last person to come on stage is Robert. Sarah's getting a headache from watching her partner standing up front next to three men who are all tall, sexy, and good looking.

Robert admits that his entry didn't go smoothly. He and his men were stunned when they saw the naked Muireann de Buitléir. They froze and she counterattacked them. Robert himself was shot by a three-round burst from Muireann's M4 Carbine, but luckily all the bullets were stopped by his body armour and ceramic plates. Robert praises Michael's command decision, ordering everyone to wear ceramic plates, even though the same plates almost drowned them when they were infiltrating from the river. The plates and the rapidness of the river were responsible for their lateness reaching their Final Assault Position.

He points out that the 5.56×45mm NATO Full Metal Jacket rounds, designed to pass through body armour, were ineffective deployed on Muireann's naked body, passing through her flesh and barely even slowing her down. If one of his bullets hadn't have hit her sternum, there's a big chance Muireann would still be fighting now. Robert and his team admitted that none of them had thought to try to shoot her in the head. He suggested that because there are an increasing number of female terrorists, all Killing Houses should have more female targets, so the men could get used to shooting at them. Robert also suggested that, even when using carbines with FMJ rounds, they should still aim for headshots. Robert also praises the SAS style of standard grip for holding the rifle. If he had used the magwell grip, there's a big chance one or both of his elbows would have been shattered by Muireann's M4. Sarah enthusiastically notes everything and notices that everyone else is doing the same thing.

After Robert's presentation is a Q&A session, moderated by Cormac. Everyone can ask questions, and give feedback and ideas for similar operations. Sarah learns a lot in this session and furiously tries to note everything on her tablet. A young trooper asks how Muireann could still fight after being riddled with bullets. Cormac answers that that sort of thing is not uncommon. During Operation Iraqi Freedom in 2007, Senior Chief Petty Officer Mike Day, a US Navy SEAL, was shot twenty-seven times by four Al Qaeda fighters armed with AK-47s while clearing a house in the Anbar Province. A grenade then exploded only ten feet away from him. Not only did he survive, he managed to kill the militants who shot him and then cleared the rest of the house with his teammates. After the house was secured, the tough Navy SEAL then walked, unaided, to the medevac heli despite being severely wounded in the abdomen, in both legs, and both arms.

The Q&A session lasts into the evening. The Director goes centre stage and praises Cormac, Michael, and Mark for their excellent leadership, successfully completing a highly complicated operation without sustaining a single casualty. He also announces that the Irish Defence Force will invest medals to the assault forces and supporting elements, which wins a few cheers. Cormac will be invested with An Bonn Míleata Calmachta Le Dearscnacht (The Military Medal for Gallantry with Distinction), the second highest medal in the Irish Army, and Michael will receive An Bonn Míleata Calmachta Le Tuillteanas (The Military Medal for Gallantry with Merit), the third highest. All the others will receive An Bonn Seirbhíse Dearscna (The Distinguished Service Medal). Cormac and Michael are now entitled to use BMC post-nominally and the others can use BSD. Sarah is proud of her friends and grows even more proud of Michael.

Cormac goes centre stage and thanks all members of the supporting units, and asks their representatives to go on stage, beginning with Graham, Nigel, Alwyn, Simon, Des, and Sarah. Everyone in the Blue Room starts cheering when Sarah's name is called. Cormac hands over the stage to Michael, who again thanks B Squadron, M Squadron, the sniper teams of Z Squadron, and all the supporting elements for their support during the operation.

"On a special note, I would like to thank the Interpol Incident Response Team for their intel support on this mission, and especially Inspector Sarah Dharmawan from the INP for her input and support during Operation Rowman and Operation Crankshaft," says Michael.

Everyone cheers again when Michael calls her name and Sarah can only look down, embarrassed. For some reason, Cormac starts pushing her towards where Michael is standing.

Michael's voice tenses up when Sarah stands beside him. "After the success of the operation and during the flight back to Credenhill, I caught a glimpse of Mount Earagail and it made me remember the first stanza of an old Irish song called Gleanntáin Ghlas' Ghaoth Dobhair. The song is in Gaeilge, but the translation of the stanza is as follows:

"Farewell to the noble mountains of Donegal,
And twice farewell to tall Earagail,
When I passed by Dunlewey lake, lying quietly in the glen,
Behind me were the little green glens of Gaoth Dobhair,
And it had nearly broken my heart."

Before continuing, Michael takes a deep breath. He looks extremely nervous. "Well… it nearly broke my heart, because I was leaving Ireland once again and I had no idea when I will return. Fortunately, my broken heart was short-lived… as there is someone here in England who I love very much and cannot live without."

Everyone cheers again and Sarah starts to wonder how long she'll have to endure this embarrassment. The next thing Michael does makes Sarah's jaw drop! Michael goes to one knee and opens a box containing a beautiful diamond ring. The Blue Room erupts in whoops and hollers when they see what's about to happen.

"Sarah… I love you very much and I cannot imagine living my life without you… I can only hope that you consider me to be good enough for you… and I really hope that I deserve the honour of being at your side for the rest of our lives," says Michael, dry-mouthed and pale as a ghost. "Inspector Sarah Michelle Dharmawan, MC, KGM of the Indonesian National Police… m-m-my gallant darling… w-w-will you… m-m-marry me?"

Sarah is so stunned that she covers her mouth with both hands and her knees feel weak… but there's no hesitation at all when she answers him.

"Yes, Michael!" she says, happy tears pricking her eyes.

Michael looks relieved and puts the ring on Sarah's finger. Sarah's embarrassed for crying in front of everyone, but notices the women of SRR in the back row also crying. Everyone claps and cheers happily for them.

"Kiss… Kiss… Kiss… Kiss… Kiss…" shouts everyone repeatedly.

Michael stands up and Sarah gives him a long kiss on the lips. Everyone finally gives them a standing ovation. Sir Charles is the first to congratulate them, followed by everyone else. The last person to congratulate them is Sheila, who looks absolutely gorgeous in her SRR uniform and beret.

"Congratulations," says Sheila, shaking Michael's hand and then hugging him.

"Thanks!" says Michael, smiling.

"Congratulations, Sarah," says Sheila, shaking her hand and then hugging her too.

"Thank you, Sheila," says Sarah, holding both of her hands. Everyone can clearly see that Sheila is on the verge of crying, making Sarah feel sorry for her. "I hope you're all right…"

"I'll be all right," says Sheila, trying to smile at her.

Everyone claps their hands and cheers. Sarah has never felt this happy before.

# CHAPTER 12
## SNATCH OPERATION

19:21 GMT
Friday August 21, 2026
Regimental HQ, SAS Barracks
Credenhill, Herefordshire, England

After congratulating Michael and Sarah, The Cartel's contact exits the RHQ and heads toward the main gate, hoping to catch a ride to Hereford. The debriefing hadn't explained why there was another mock-up of Swan's Mill at PATA and why half of the Army Ranger Wing were still training there when the assault commenced, but there's only one possible explanation. The UKSF Group must have figured out that someone at PATA is a Cartel member and hoped to misinform The Cartel that Alwyn and the Army Ranger Wing would enter from the ground floor when assaulting Swan's Mill. This misinformation enabled the SAS to secure the upper floors of Swan's Mill without any drama. The contact now feels extremely guilty for providing the wrong information to Patrick, which resulted in the massacre of Swan's Mill without a single SAS casualty.

The contact was close to Muireann and when the CCTV recording showed Robert blowing her head off, the contact got emotional and almost shouted out in anger. This didn't happen, thanks to the Resistance to Interrogation (R2I) training everyone in the UKSF has had to attend. Now is the time to avenge Muireann and everyone at Swan's Mill. Now is the time to desert from the military and fully join The Cartel.

"Going somewhere, Sin?" asks George from behind, grinning from ear-to-ear.

"Why do ye ask? Are ye offering me a ride to Hereford?" asks The Cartel member. "And quit calling me 'Sin'!"

George laughs out loud on seeing his friend's pout. He also knows that his close friend's accent always reverts to Irish whenever stressed out, which is hilarious. "Cormac's taking us for some scoff and a piss up at the Grafton Restaurant, but we all have to head back to our flats to change into mufti before we go. I'm really hungry now, so how about we grab some scoff at the cookhouse before I drop you off at your flat?"

The contact's flat is right next to George's, so it makes sense to go with him. While walking to the cookhouse with him, the contact sends a text to Patrick.

19:22 GMT
Friday August 21, 2026
Sandalwood Farm
Nether Alderley, Cheshire, England

Patrick receives a text from his British Army contact, saying that one of the SAS men who assaulted Swan's Mill will drive his contact home. His contact wants to snatch George and hand him over to Niall as revenge for his part in killing Muireann and her men. Patrick immediately responds, ordering his contact to stand down. The Cartel will avenge Muireann, but this is *not* the way to do it. They won't touch anyone from the SAS.

Feeling overwhelmed by rage and hatred, the contact decides to ignore Patrick's order.

20:21 GMT
Friday August 21, 2026
Grafton Restaurant
Hereford, Herefordshire, England

After changing into mufti, Cormac treats Sarah, Michael, Robert, Al, Mark, Pierce, and Dave to dinner at the Grafton Restaurant, not far from Michael's flat. George was invited too, but he excused himself first to take their friend home. He will join them later at the restaurant for drinks.

All through dinner, they give Michael a slagging for his cheap, public proposal and for the terrified look on his face. After dinner, they make their way through several pitchers of Brains beer while waiting for George, who still hasn't arrived yet. They keep glancing at Sarah as they drain their beer.

"Come on then. You numbskulls look like you're about to burst," says Sarah, accepting her fate. "Just let it out and let me have it."

"Oh, we'll definitely take the piss out of you in a minute, Sarah, but we're not quite finished with Michael yet," says Dave.

"That's right," says Cormac. "So, Michael, what's this 'for King and Country' shit you said after the operation?"

"Yeah, I've never heard you say shit like that before," says Pierce in his Scottish burr. "And why not add '*Éirinn go Brách*' while you're at it?"

"Oh, I bet he said it just because he wanted to sound heroic for Sarah. We all know how orgasmic she finds his voice," quips Mark. "Isn't that right, Sarah?"

Sarah's face turns red and her friends laugh out loud. Her husky 'Yes, sir' from during the briefing is coming back to haunt her. It's lucky that George hasn't arrived yet, as she knows he'd be the worst of the lot.

'Here we go...' thinks Sarah, preparing herself for the onslaught.

"You were at the FOB, Mac. Did Michael's command voice make her writhe in ecstasy?" asks Robert.

Cormac snorts. "You can bloody imagine what she went through when Michael said 'for King and Country, stronghold secured' in his posh accent... She almost came just watching him conduct the bloody briefing!"

Sarah gets so embarrassed she has to cover her face with both hands, making her friends roll with laughter. Knowing this lot, they will never let her live that down. The only answer is to give as good as she gets. She has an idea, but she must wait for the right moment.

Dave continues. "There's nothing to be ashamed about, Sarah. Watching our gallant OC conduct a briefing arouses all of us, you know."

Everyone howls with laughter.

George suddenly arrives, so Sarah grits her teeth. He seems to know instinctively what they're all talking about and jumps right in. "I bet as foreplay, Michael gives Sarah the Five Paragraph Order for what he'll do to her in bed," he says, pouring himself a pint of beer.

"Does that make you 'stand to attention', Sarah?" asks Pierce.

"If Sarah 'stands to attention', I'm sure Biggus Dickus does the same," says Mark, grinning from ear to ear.

"And if you salute his Biggus Dickus, is it able to return it?" asks Al.

Everyone laughs out loud, including Sarah this time.

"No briefings are necessary, you muppets," says Michael, "because every one of them were Immediate Actions. Sarah uses the colour clock code and she says things like, 'that's enough of my Red-3 and Green-9, *sayang*. You may now execute the entry at White-6.'"

Everyone can imagine what Michael meant and they all laugh hysterically... except for Sarah, who is giving her fiancé a nasty look.

'Watch it, Michael!' she thinks, although she has to admit that Michael's joke is really funny.

"Wait, wait, wait!" says George as the laughter finally starts coming to an end. "We have to be absolutely clear on this one. Is your White-6 the bottom part of the stronghold or the top part, Sarah?"

"Whichever turns you on, you bloody wanker!" answers Sarah. "Feel free to use your bloody imagination."

"I'll drink to that!" says George, laughing loudly.

They all drink their beer and this is the golden opportunity Sarah was waiting for. "Did Michael get the chance to tell you about the time I had sex with another woman?"

Everyone chokes on their drinks and spouts beer from their mouths. As she'd expected, their beer drenches Michael, who is giving them a dirty look.

Sarah gives everyone a satisfied smile. "Ah, well, it's too bad you wankers won't get to hear that story today."

The men can only look at Sarah with open mouths as she grabs Michael's arm and exits the restaurant. They look like they really want to hear that story right this instant.


01:08 GMT
Saturday August 22, 2026
Sandalwood Farm
Nether Alderley, Cheshire, England


A few hours earlier, the Cartel's contact ate dinner with George and thought about snatching him. Unfortunately, George is a jap-slapping instructor and has the muscles and ability to match. The contact realized that snatching him without drama would be almost impossible and wisely dropped the plan. The contact's now driving a sports car towards The Cartel's HQ in Cheshire.

It takes almost four hours to get there. The leaders of The Cartel are waiting as a welcoming committee. They all embrace, to say hello and to mourn fallen comrades. They share a bottle of whiskey during the debrief. The contact describes everything, from the mock-training drill designed to trick The Cartel, to the debriefing of Operation Crankshaft. All gathered (except Niall) grow emotional hearing Muireann's fate. No one blames their contact for the misleading information and Patrick is still immensely proud of the ex-UKSF member. He assures everyone that this time they will avenge Muireann and the men of Swan's Mill. Niall finally looks excited when Patrick tells them that he plans on snatching Sarah.

13:11 GMT
Saturday August 22, 2026
Sandalwood Farm
Nether Alderley, Cheshire, England

That afternoon, the senior members plan for Sarah's snatch. Through their contact at the GMP, they receive intel that Sarah run-commutes every day, but no one in the GMP knows where she lives. Sarah is unpredictable in her routes going home from work and it's impossible to follow her leaving GMP HQ. They've checked the 3Towers Apartment, but Michael has already moved and didn't leave a forwarding address or phone number. Michael's old number is already inactive, though they still have his Range Rover Evoque's Vehicle Registration Number.

The ex-UKSF member told the others that Michael is still 'On The Team', meaning that he's on twenty-four hour standby from Saturday to Tuesday evening and has to stay within thirty minutes of the Credenhill barracks. He has Wednesday to Friday to spend time with Sarah. Every Saturday morning, he leaves his car at Manchester Piccadilly and takes the train to Hereford. The Cartel decide that following Michael's car to his new flat when he returns from Hereford is the only way to find out his new address. Someone will standby at Manchester Piccadilly until he returns from Hereford, at which point he'll give the others a heads up. The others will then take turns following him. If they know where Michael's staying, they'll know where to find Sarah.

The intelligence operation to tail Michael will be quite challenging, considering that he's a pro. Patrick doesn't want to take any chances so he will deploy everyone from HQ to follow their target from Manchester Piccadilly to his address. They're all trained by Rory and the ex-UKSF member in surveillance and counter-surveillance, giving them the skills to follow Michael without being spotted and to avoid GMP detection after they've snatched Sarah. The ex-UKSF member also trains them in CQB.

The day of the snatch comes. Michael returns from Credenhill on Tuesday evening and members of The Cartel start tailing him. Michael conducts counter-surveillance drills on leaving the station, but The Cartel members were expecting that and it doesn't give them any problems. They take turns following him to avoid detection and follow him all the way to Stay Deansgate Apartments. Rory confirms that Sarah is living there by getting her flat number from the apartment's administrator. They plan on snatching her on Saturday when she runs to work and after Michael leaves for Hereford. This will give them the maximum possible time before Michael and the SAS can realize she's been snatched.

Niall and the ex-UKSF member want to snatch Michael too, but Patrick, Steve, Rory, and Carraig insist on leaving him alone. The SAS would surely take things personally and with the MACP still in effect, they wouldn't need authorization from the civil authority to hunt the rest of The Cartel down. This would be bad for business.

Unfortunately, Rory can't lead the operation because he has to go to Jakarta to prepare Phase Five. Patrick will join him once this operation is over. Steve volunteers to lead the mission, but Patrick forbids him and picks Carraig instead because of his IRA experience. He makes the ex-UKSF member Carraig's 2 i/c. Gwilliam, who has abandoned his clubs since the assault on Swan's Mill, will take over their factory in Liverpool while Carraig leads this operation. Niall will also be waiting at Liverpool.

06:51 GMT
Saturday September 26, 2026
Stay Deansgate Apartments
Deansgate, Manchester, England

Since August, Michael has been living in Sarah's flat. They decided Michael's flat would be too risky. If there's a leak, the leak's in the UKSF

Group. Michael admits that some of his friends in the UKSF know he stays at the 3Towers Apartment during his work in Manchester. But nobody knows where Sarah lives, not even Densus or NCB Indonesia, which makes her flat the more secure of the two.

They're now living together, but they will have to wait until their assignment is over before getting married. Broussard would surely ask one of them to withdraw from his team if they were married any earlier. Although Broussard knows they are romantically involved, he doesn't know and doesn't have to know that they're engaged.

This morning, Sarah does her daily crunches while Michael watches her exercise from the bed. Watching Sarah do her exercise is much better than watching the telly, especially when she does it with her shirt off.

"Come down here and join me, *sayang*," asks Sarah for the umpteenth time.

Michael only grins as he caresses his fiancée's perfect body, which seems to feel harder every day.

"Come on, Michael. My mum has three children and she has better abs than you," says Sarah, pouting at him.

"Your mum has a six-pack?" asks Michael, intrigued.

"Of course she does. Now come down here and exercise with me!"

"Only after you've managed to defeat me in our run to the office," says Michael with his signature cheeky grin.

Sarah's pout gets bigger. Despite his pot belly, Sarah has to admit that Michael is actually in better shape than she is. Whenever Michael is in Manchester, they always run-commute together and once they reach Oldham Rd, they always race to GMP HQ. Michael wins every single time.

Sarah's almost finished her workout when she notices Michael's expression. "*Qu'est-ce qui va pas, sayang?*"

Michael is silent for a moment before answering her. "Have you ever thought about what we will do after we get married?"

Sarah continues her crunches and doesn't immediately answer. Although Sarah's parents know that she loves her job in Densus, they've always hoped that one day she will build a family like her brother. Sarah once thought about this and had decided she would be willing to give up her career if she ever found someone she could be proud of and look up to. Sarah's finally found that person in Michael and, in fact, she even considers him her hero and her idol. For Sarah, being in the same room with Michael feels like being in the same room with a rock star or a famous Hollywood actor. Although Sarah loves working at Densus, she can't imagine living without Michael by her side. She feels lonely and can't sleep well whenever he's away for a few nights on the 30 Minutes Team at Credenhill.

"I guess I'll have to resign from the INP and move to Hereford with you," says Sarah, sadly. "Who knows? Maybe the West Mercia Police needs someone with my background?"

"But you have an excellent career in Densus. Why would you want to sacrifice that for me?" asks Michael.

"Sacrifice my career for you?" asks Sarah, looking deep into his eyes. "*Je mourrais pour toi*, Michael."

Michael can see that Sarah is serious and he's touched. He then decides something. "What if I resign my commission and move to Indonesia with you?"

Sarah is shocked! She hadn't expected Michael to offer to sacrifice his career for her. None of her previous partners would do that and they had even asked her if she would resign from the INP in the event they took their relationship to the next level. She finally finishes her workout and looks deep into his eyes. She can see that he's serious too.

"Why would you want to do that?" asks Sarah.

"I want you to be happy, *mo ghile mear*," answers Michael.

"But what would you do in Indonesia?" she asks, her eyes getting moist.

"You once said your mum needs someone to run the family business, right? Well, I don't mind running your family business. If your mum would let me, of course," says Michael. "If not, well, I'll just have to find another job or start a business of my own."

Sarah thinks hard for a moment. Michael's offer is interesting and she's sure that her mum would entrust her company to Michael. He's willing to sacrifice his career in the British Army for her and she loves him even more for that. On the other hand, no matter how well Sarah does in her own career, she realizes that she will never be the Chief of the INP (Kapolri). There would be too many political factors standing in her way, protesting her gender or her religion. Compared to much of the rest of the world, Indonesia is still primitive in these aspects. For the same reasons,

Sarah can't even imagine herself becoming the commander of Densus-88. Her career in Indonesia will only ever go so far.

Michael, though, is a highly decorated British Army officer, and Sir Charles once said that the British Army would surely look after his career. Michael could reach Director Special Forces one day and Sarah is sure that he could eventually become the Chief of the General Staff. With his achievements so far, Sarah can even imagine him as a future Chief of the Defence Staff.

Sarah makes a decision. "No, Michael, it doesn't make sense for you to come to Indonesia. I will submit my resignation when all of this is over."

Michael doesn't say anything and Sarah can tell he has mixed feelings about this.

"I really love my job at Densus, *sayang*, but I love you even more," says Sarah, firmly once again. She will fully support her future husband until he reaches the pinnacle of his career.

Michael smiles at her and gets down from the bed. He kisses her on her hard, sweaty stomach, the same way he always does after she finishes her crunches. But then he lies down beside her and starts doing sit-ups. Michael absolutely hates doing sit-ups, but he knows it's something that would mean a lot to Sarah and there's nothing he wouldn't do for her.

Sarah gives him a broad smile. She can't even imagine she could love him more than this. In the end, Michael has only done a few sit ups when Sarah suddenly jumps on top of him and gives him a loving kiss on his lips.

"*Je t'aime tellement*, Michael," says Sarah, eyes moist as she looks deeply into his eyes.

"*Aku cinta padamu juga, mo ghile mear*," answers Michael, smiling back at her. *I love you too, my gallant darling.*

09:23 GMT
Saturday September 26, 2026
Deansgate St
Deansgate, Manchester, England

"They're fucking late," says Carraig.

"Patience, Frag," replies the ex-UKSF member.

"What if she's taking the day off this weekend?" asks Carraig.

"She *never* takes a day off," says the ex-UKSF member, trying to be patient with all the amateurs in this operation.

Michael usually leaves at eight and Sarah starts her run to work not long after that. They've been waiting since seven in the morning, but Michael hasn't left the flat yet.

One of The Cartel members assigned to the Observation Post at the Deansgate Hot Food Bar suddenly sees Michael's Range Rover Evoque pass by the bar at high speed.

"Zero, this is Delta. Heads up! Target Mike is mobile to the North," he says through his smartphone in conference call mode.

"Zero roger," answers Carraig. "All call signs, standby for the snatch."

All they have to do now is wait for Sarah to come out of her flat.


09:55 GMT
Saturday September 26, 2026
Interpol Manchester
Central Park, Manchester, England


"Sorry I'm late!" says Sarah, red-faced as she enters the meeting room. Today's the first time she's ever been late to work, even though she took Michael's car instead of run-commuting.

Broussard and her teammates don't seem to mind. This Saturday, the Interpol team, except for Michael, plans to discuss the SSE results. Michael's schedule changed starting today, meaning he will now be in Manchester from Saturday till Tuesday and in Credenhill the rest of the week. Michael took temporary leave from his Interpol duties so he could organize the routine amendments that accompany a change in schedule.

As Sarah came in, Paul had been presenting the results of his investigations these past few weeks. Since the assault on Swan's Mill, the price of MDMA has tripled in the Republic of Ireland and Northern Ireland. However, Arthur's investigations indicate that the price remains stable in Great Britain. They can safely conclude that Swan's Mill must've only supplied Ireland, meaning there are probably more drug factories in Great Britain. James and Paul's investigation shows that The Cartel have successfully smuggled MDMA from Indonesia routinely every two months for almost two years.

James presents the SSE results of MV Báinigh. According to the manifest, the ship was carrying turbines for oil & gas companies operating in the North Atlantic Sea produced by PT. Horizon Turbines and Propulsions, a company in Citeureup, Bogor, West Java. Inside the containers, they found residue of MDMA and raw materials for processing MDMA. The INP must discreetly investigate the turbine company to determine whether or not they are involved with The Cartel. If the company turns out to be clean, Sarah has a suspicion that the lorry carrying the turbines took a detour to another company to pick up the goods before finally heading for the Kalibaru Port.

With so little information available on The Cartel's presence in Indonesia, Sarah needs to follow up every possible lead. Unfortunately, because Swan's Mill is no longer active, The Cartel will probably change their previous MO, so Sarah can only investigate the standard route the lorry would've made towards the Kalibaru Port and have the Bogor Police Precinct investigate all companies, especially foreign companies, close enough to be possible pick-up points. The Bogor Police also have to locate, apprehend, and interrogate the driver from PT. Horizon Turbines and Propulsions.

Matt and the PSNI have apprehended all of the prostitutes and all of the distributors seen entering Swan's Mill. PSNI are still interrogating them. The distributors, who are all female, had been disguising themselves as prostitutes to visit Swan's Mill and each day they'd taken thousands of MDMA pills to be distributed to dealers at Gwilliam's clubs all around Ireland. Now they have enough evidence to apprehend Gwilliam O'Donnel but, unfortunately, he's disappeared.

Liz presents Garda's investigation results. There were ninety-four dead bodies at Swan's Mill, including Muireann de Buitléir. The number of bodies, weapons, and MDMA pills has overwhelmed the Buncrana Garda Station, forcing them to ask assistance from Garda HQ. Among the most surprising things uncovered are wedding pictures of Muireann and Patrick Dunbar, confirming that Muireann is a senior member of The Cartel. Unfortunately, there is absolutely no information showing the location of their HQ or other factories, including the one in Indonesia. Muireann successfully destroyed all documents and destroyed her smartphone before getting killed.

Towards lunch time, Broussard emphatically reminds his team to always follow tradecraft. The Cartel will surely try to avenge the death of their leader's wife. Broussard also announced that because Michael was still seconded to Interpol team during the assault, the Home Office has decided that his KGM will be upgraded to a George Medal (GM) for his role in combating narcoterrorism. The George Medal is the second highest medal for civilians, but soldiers may be invested with it also. Sarah is immensely proud of her fiancé and sends him a text.

Michael immediately returns her text. 'Can you come home for scoff?'

'See you in 30 mikes, sayang,' writes Sarah.

Michael replies to her text with a smiley. First she was late to work and now, for the first time ever, she wants to skip out early. This is quite a day of firsts for Sarah…

12:10 GMT
Saturday September 26, 2026
Stay Deansgate Apartments
Deansgate, Manchester, England

"Fuck!" curses the ex-UKSF member. "I guess you're right, Frag, she's taking the day off today. We'll just have to go in and snatch her."

After having waited for five frustrating hours, Carraig agrees – it's time to go into Sarah's flat and complete the mission.

"All call signs, this is Zero and I have control. We're going in her flat for the snatch. We deploy in five, four, three, two, one, go!" orders Carraig into his smartphone.

Twelve people debus from their cars and ascend in the lift towards Sarah's flat.

12:13 GMT
Saturday September 26, 2026
Stay Deansgate Apartments
Deansgate, Manchester, England

Michael receives a text from Sarah saying she's on her way home. As per SOP, Michael immediately deletes the text. He's just finished making some sandwiches for his fiancée when there's a soft knock on the door. Michael is about to look through the peephole when the door suddenly slams into his face! Michael is floored, blood gushing out of his nose and mouth, and twelve people clad in balaclavas storm in. Michael can only cover his bloody nose and mouth with his hands when a boot slams on his chest, pinning him to the floor. A pistol is pointed towards his head and somebody gives him a thorough frisk.

From the corner of his eye, Michael can see four people pointing their pistols at his head, preventing him from escaping. If a soldier has been captured by the enemy, the time to escape is as soon as possible. Unfortunately for Michael, his ambushers seem to be aware of this.

"X-Ray secured!" says the person who frisked him.

"Clear!" says the person tasked to secure the bedroom.

"Clear!" says the person tasked to secure the bathroom.

"Stronghold secured!" says the person pointing a pistol at his head.

Michael can immediately identify that voice. "You…"

Michael doesn't get the chance to finish when a vicious kick lands on his mouth.

"Where the fuck is she?" asks the ex-UKSF member, angrily.

"Not here… obviously," says Michael, sarcastically.

As he'd expected, Michael receives another vicious kick to his face. While his ambushers are distracted, Michael discreetly writes three letters on the floor in his own blood. He has just finished when someone binds his hands together with duct tape. Another of his ambushers twiddles with his smartphone.

"Yer choice is simple, ye dickhead. Give us her fucking phone number or ye'll take her place!"

"Are you seriously planning to snatch a squadron OC of The Regiment, Sin?" asks Michael, cynically.

The ex-UKSF member gets angry and gives Michael an extremely powerful kick, fracturing his cheekbone. "Give us her fucking phone number! I won't ask ye again!"

"You're wasting your time. You can just slot me on the spot or snatch me. Make a decision, you muppet!" says Michael. He has to provoke them into making a quick decision because Sarah will be here at any moment. No matter how good Sarah is, Michael knows that she can't possibly take on twelve Cartel members by herself... especially when one of them is a special forces operative!

The ex-UKSF member falls silent for a moment before giving Carraig an order. "Take him!"

"Paddy said not to touch him!" protests Carraig.

"I know what he fucking said. Take him!"

"I'm in command of this fucking operation!" shouts Carraig.

The ex-UKSF member points the gun towards Carraig's head. "Take him or I'll shoot yer fucking head off!"

Carraig's not happy, but he can't do anything about it. He curses out loud and orders the others to bring Michael. Although Michael is anxious about his fate, at least he's prevented them from snatching someone he loves very much.

12:17 GMT
Saturday September 26, 2026
Stay Deansgate Apartments
Deansgate, Manchester, England

As usual, Sarah takes the stairs to her flat. As soon as she enters, she senses something's not right. She sees blood on the floor and pulls out her pistol from her IWB holster. Sarah locks the door to her flat and starts securing the rooms. There are no signs of Michael, so she has to assume the worst has happened. Sarah calls her commander.

"Yes, Sarah?" answers Broussard, chewing on his lunch.

"Chief, I'm at my flat. Michael was supposed to meet me here for lunch, but there are signs that he's been snatched. There's blood on the floor," says Sarah.

'Oh, please, not again,' thinks Broussard, worriedly. "I'm coming over with Paul and the GMP. Lock the door, wait for us, and make ready your sidearm, is that clear?"

"I've already done that," replies Sarah.

"Good! In the meantime, James will try to trace Michael's whereabouts using his smartphone number. When we get to your flat, I'll say a number and then you will say a number. The sum of those two numbers should add up to the number eight. This is our password before you open the door. Is that clear?"

"Clear, Chief!" Her commander has given her a simple password so they can ensure Sarah is behind the door to her flat.

"Stand firm until we get there!" orders Broussard, hanging up.

Sarah takes the initiative and calls Cormac. His phone is busy so she calls Derek Sinclair.

"Yes, Sarah?" asks Derek, pleasantly surprised.

"Lance-Corporal, heads up and write this down," says Sarah in her calm and assertive voice.

Derek is taken aback by Sarah's command voice and follows her orders without question. "Ready to copy."

"I'm at my flat. Michael was supposed to be here, but there are signs that he's just been abducted. We have to assume the worst case, that he was snatched by members of The Cartel. Could you please inform your CO about this immediately, Lance-Corporal?" orders Sarah.

Derek is silent for a few seconds, stunned from what he's just heard. Criminals would never dare do something like this – not to a member of the SAS!

Sarah's about to repeat her order when Derek finally answers her. "Right, let me contact the head shed and we'll get right back to you." He hangs up.

Sarah finally hears the sirens of the GMP. While waiting for them, she examines the blood on the floor and notices the letters 'N', 'I', and 'S'. She's about to take a picture with her smartphone when it suddenly rings.

It's Cormac. "Sarah, I'm at The Kremlin and Derek is here with me. Could you please send your sitrep?"

Sarah tells him everything and her report takes a minute. "MI5 is trying to track Michael via his smartphone number and I'm currently waiting for my teammates to arrive."

Like Derek, Cormac goes silent for a few seconds. "Be on high alert before your reinforcement arrives. Let me brief the Director and I'll get back to you. Thanks for the heads up!" He hangs up.

A loud knock comes from the door. Sarah immediately stacks next to the door with her pistol at low ready.

"Sarah, this is Christopher Broussard with Paul Elliot. Open the door, please. The number is three."

"This is Sarah and the number is five," says Sarah. She opens the door and lets Broussard and Paul in.

"Right, we will consider your apartment a crime scene and this will be the GMP's jurisdiction," says Broussard. "Paul, please coordinate with the GMP Criminal Investigation Department when they arrive."

"*Reet*," answers Paul, crouching to examine the blood on the floor.

"Let me contact Michael's commanding officer," says Broussard, taking out his smartphone.

"I've already updated Cormac. He will contact me again after he has briefed the Director."

"Very good, Sarah," says Broussard.

"There's some writing on the floor with the letters 'N-I-S'. Michael's probably trying to tell us that Niall Schroeder snatched him," says Sarah. She remembers that his full name is Niall Iollan Schroeder.

"Is it 'N-I-S'," says Paul, "or 'S-I-N'? I'll have the GMP Crime Scene Investigators immediately find out what it says by analysing the strokes of the writing."

Sarah suddenly feels incredibly stupid! She gets angry at herself for assuming the letters are 'N-I-S' and not spotting that upside down they read 'S-I-N'. Paul notices Sarah's reaction and gives her a wink and a smile, calming her down. She takes a deep breath and finally returns his smile. Meanwhile, the GMP arrive at her apartment.

"Any news from James, Paul?" asks Sarah.

Paul shakes his head in frustration. "Michael's smartphone is already inactive."

"Sarah, please return to GMP HQ and be on high alert *en route*," orders Broussard. "I'll have one of the GMP constables escort you there. Could you please coordinate with the others and try to figure out what this bloody 'N-I-S' or 'S-I-N' means?"

"Right, Chief!" says Sarah as she's leaving her flat.

They arrive at GMP HQ in under ten minutes and Sarah immediately briefs her team. From the crime scene, Broussard and Paul have asked the GMP to deploy all assets to search for Michael. The GMP immediately send police officers to set up Vehicle Check Points (VCP) on all roads heading out of the city. Sarah suggests to Broussard that Cormac be appointed as Michael's temporary replacement so that the military can also be deployed to help find him. Broussard immediately agrees and Sarah calls Cormac to tell him about it. Cormac has no problems with that, but he will first have to ask permission from the Director.

Paul sends a text to the team and tells them that the GMP Crime Scene Investigators' preliminary analysis indicates the letters are 'S-I-N', not 'N-I-S'. The letters have Michael's fingerprints on them. Paul also sends them the CCTV recordings from the building, on which they can see twelve people in balaclavas entering Sarah's flat. They snatched Michael within three minutes and took him down by the lift, where they pushed him into a black Range Rover parked outside. The police at the VCPs are ordered to be extra careful when stopping that kind of car. Unfortunately, no CCTV cameras caught sight of the Range Rover's plate number.

The CCTV shows that there were only thirty seconds between Michael getting snatched and Sarah entering her flat. Sarah is stressed out thinking she could've saved Michael. If only she'd been quicker up the stairs or had used the lift. But her team remind her that she would've been killed or snatched along with Michael if she'd shown up during the snatch. Her teammates consider it lucky she didn't show up in the middle of the attack. Sarah knows that her teammates are right, but she still feels guilty and frustrated for not arriving sooner. At this point, there's nothing more the team can do except try to find out what Michael meant by those three letters.

"Is there anyone in The Cartel with those initials?" asks Arthur.

"None of them. Nor do any of them have a name or surname that starts with Sin," says James, studying his file.

"Can we determine whether it is 'S-I-N' or 'Sin'?" asks Matt.

They all look at the picture, but it could be either.

"Are we sure it's Michael's handwriting?" asks Liz.

"Has anyone seen his handwriting?" asks Arthur.

Everyone shakes their heads. Nowadays, everyone uses their tablets or smartphones to write.

"It could be The Cartel playing mind games with us," says James.

"It's better not to write anything at all, James. Why take a chance and leave evidence behind?" asks Matt. "Michael's fingerprints are on those letters anyway."

"But there's no one in The Cartel with those initials!" says James, frustrated.

"No one we know," says Arthur, frustrated as well.

Cormac texts them and tells them that he's temporarily replacing Michael in the Interpol team. Every member of the UKSF Group has been deployed throughout the UK in the search for Michael, except for B Squadron, who are 'On The Team'.

It's getting dark outside and Sarah can't do anything but study the CCTV footage. While studying the footage, she suddenly has an idea, because the body of one of the attackers reminds her of someone in the UKSF Group.

"Wait a minute! This team isn't the only team Michael's on. Maybe his friends in the SAS know what 'S-I-N' means," says Sarah.

"Let's give it a shot," says Arthur.

Sarah calls Cormac.

"Yes, Sarah?" answers Cormac.

"Michael wrote a clue for us at the crime scene. We can't figure it out, so maybe you could help us?"

"Sarah, I'm at B Squadron HQ and I have Robert, Al, George, and Dave with me and you are now on speaker. What can you tell us?"

"Let me send you a picture. Before Michael was taken, he wrote the letters 'S-I-N' in his own blood on the floor of my apartment. We think he was trying to identify one of the attackers. Do these letters ring any bells for you?" asks Sarah.

Cormac, Al, George, and Dave go dead silent and look at each other. Without looking at the picture, they know exactly what Michael meant when he wrote 'S-I-N'. Robert looks confused by the reaction of his teammates.

"Hello?" asks Sarah when no one says anything for a few seconds.

"Sarah, this is George. Are you sure Michael was writing 'S-I-N'? I'm looking at the picture you sent and it could be 'N-I-S'."

"The thought crossed our minds, George, but the GMP Crime Scene Investigators who analysed the strokes said that it's 'S-I-N'. Why? Does 'S-I-N' mean anything to you?" asks Sarah, expectantly.

The SAS men are silent again and only look at each other except Robert, who's still confused.

"Sarah, we have to discuss a few things," says Cormac. "We'll call you back, all right?"

It's Sarah turn to be silent. She's intrigued by their reaction, but she doesn't want to pressure them.

"Right, thanks. I'll wait for your call," says Sarah, hanging up.

Her teammates look at her expectantly.

"It seems 'S-I-N' struck a nerve when I said it, but they won't tell me about it yet," says Sarah.

"At least there's some progress," says Matt.

Everyone nods and tries to go back to work. They find it hard to concentrate as they're extremely worried about their teammate.

19:24 GMT
Saturday September 26, 2026
B Squadron HQ, SAS Barracks
Credenhill, Herefordshire, England

Back at Credenhill, the four men debate heatedly. As the most junior among them, Robert can only watch his teammates, not sure what's going on.

"But it just can't be, Mac!" argues George.

"We've had our suspicions for a while, George," says Cormac.

"Do you have any proof?" asks Dave.

"Look, what I will say is off the record because it's still an ongoing internal investigation and this is strictly confidential. All right?"

Cormac continues after he sees each one of them nod. "We have reason to believe that at least one member of the UKSF Group is involved with The Cartel. At PATA, there are eighty kilograms of PE4 that are unaccounted for and Sin was at PATA when it went missing. Most of that PE4 was then used to blow up the International Liaison Building in Dublin."

"But hundreds of people have easy access to PE4 at PATA, Mac!" protests George.

"I'm not finished! We had two mock-ups with two different assault plans before the assault on Swan's Mill. We gathered all the suspects and let them see the mock assault by the Army Ranger Wing. At least one of them alerted The Cartel. That's why they were ready for us when we assaulted it. Sin was one of the suspects who saw it."

Everyone is stunned as they hadn't expected to find out there was a traitor in their midst.

"Furthermore, Sin hasn't been seen for the last thirty days and is already considered AWOL."

George is still not convinced, especially since he's close to that person. "Being AWOL doesn't mean Sin's a member of The Cartel, Mac."

"Does Michael know about this?" asks Al.

"I told him a few months ago and he agreed that Sin could be one of the prime suspects. For now, let's just ask Sarah and hear what she thinks, all right?" asks Cormac.

"Don't tell Sarah about Sin at first. Let's hear whether Interpol has any suspects or any suspicions," suggests Dave.

Everyone nods and Cormac calls Sarah, who picks up on the first ring.

19:27 GMT
Saturday September 26, 2026
Interpol Manchester
Central Park, Manchester, England

"Mac, you are on speaker and I have the Interpol team with me."

"Sarah, could we speak in private?"

Sarah becomes silent for a few seconds. "Do you want me to step out of the room?"

"Please," says Cormac.

Sarah looks at her teammates who nod, understanding. Sarah goes into another meeting room, closes the door, and resets her smartphone to handset.

"I'm alone now, Mac."

"Michael may have been referring to someone in the UKSF Group. Before we tell you who it is, does Interpol have any suspects?" asks Cormac.

"We have bugger all, Mac!" says Sarah, starting to get frustrated.

"Right, now bear with us for a minute, Sarah, because you have met this person before. If I asked you to guess who Michael was referring to, who would you suspect?"

Sarah is silent once again. She doesn't like accusing someone without hard evidence.

"I think it's Sheila," she answers at last.

"Do you have anything to support that?" asks George sharply.

"I don't have any evidence, but let me send you some files."

Sarah finds the picture of Rory Hanrahan with a tall, fit, red-headed women with her back towards the camera, and sends it to Cormac. She also sends him the CCTV footage from her flat. "Just to remind you, that man is Rory Hanrahan and he's the 3 i/c of The Cartel. At first, we thought the woman was Muireann de Buitléir, but the results of the photo analysis came out negative. We don't have a positive ID on her, but both this photo and one of the snatchers from my apartment feels a lot like Sheila wearing a balaclava."

"Michael has seen this photo too, right?" asks George.

"Of course."

"Don't you think Michael would've recognized his ex-girlfriend?" asks George sharply.

"I don't know what to say, George. What about you? You've dated her, right? Don't you think that's her?"

George becomes silent and he has to admit that the girl in the picture looks a lot like Sheila. However, George knows that the picture can't be considered evidence of Sheila's involvement.

"It could be someone who look likes her from behind. Even if it is her, talking to the 3 i/c of The Cartel doesn't make her guilty. Remember, we're running on gut feelings and razor thin evidence here," says George.

"Mac, you said that S-I-N refers to someone at UKSF," says Sarah. "Was that Sheila? Michael's clue can only mean that she's involved with his abduction."

Cormac takes a deep breath before answering her. "You are correct, Sarah. Michael once said that dating her felt like committing a sin, because officers are not supposed to be in a relationship with ranking members. We all call her Sin as a joke after Michael dumped her, because it also happens to be the initials of her full name, Sheila Iona Neeson. Anyway, during Operation Rowman, when I told Michael that Sin... Sheila... was one of our suspects for involvement with The Cartel, he immediately agreed. He said she was far too wealthy for someone with her background.

He also told me that one of the senior members of The Cartel was photographed talking to a woman matching her description, though they couldn't identify her. Michael told me that he suspected Sheila had given The Cartel his phone number so the assassination team could track him and then finally attempted to assassinate both of you at Carluccio's. She's also one of the suspects for nicking the PE4 at PATA and leaking the assault plan of Swan's Mill to The Cartel. She is currently AWOL and we don't know where she is."

Sarah's response is immediate. "That's more than enough for us to bring her in for questioning. But since she's military, we'll have to go through proper channels and have the Special Investigation Branch of the Royal Military Police follow this up. I'll ask Liz to contact them immediately after this. Her husband happens to be in that unit."

The CO of the SAS becomes silent. He sees Al slowly shake his head. "Is there any way we could keep this matter within the UKSF family, Sarah?"

It's Sarah's turn to be silent. She can guess what they'll do to Sheila if she's found guilty. Sarah's afraid that one day, Sheila will just 'disappear'. "You want to… take care of her yourself, don't you?"

"Please," answers Cormac.

Sarah is silent again for a moment. "This is against my oath as a law enforcement officer and Interpol agent, Mac… but the answer is yes."

"Thank you for letting us do this," says Cormac. "What's the catch?"

"Let me in on your operation, Mac," says Sarah.

"Deal!" says Cormac without having to think about it. "Even better, since we don't have any experience in police investigation and detective work, *you* will have to lead the men on this and in finding Michael. What say you?"

Sarah is stunned. The CO of the SAS has just asked her to lead a team of the finest special forces unit in the world! She is flattered, but also extremely terrified of failing and disappointing them. "Mac… are you sure about this?"

"Michael and Al once told you that you would make an excellent troop commander someday, right?" asks Cormac curtly, starting to get impatient.

"I think so."

"Well, the Director and I disagreed with them…"

"Oh…" says Sarah, disappointed.

"… because we think you have what it takes to be at least a squadron commander."

Sarah is so flattered that she's unable to say anything.

"Now, will you take command of this mission?"

"I'll take it, Mac," answers Sarah, confidently.

"Very good! I'll have the Director contact your chief for your secondment to The Regiment. Your mission is to lead the team and do whatever it takes to save Michael. I say again, your mission is to lead the team and do whatever it takes to save Michael. Is that clear?"

"Clear, Mac."

"Now, what do you need from us?"

"I need info. What can you tell me about Sheila?"

"Let me go to The Kremlin to brief the Director about Sheila and about your secondment to The Regiment. I also have to coordinate with your chief regarding the secondment of His Majesty's Armed Forces to the civil power. For now, George will brief you on Sheila," says Cormac, giving George a sharp look.

George is still not convinced that his close friend in the SRR is involved with The Cartel. However, George does as he is ordered.

"So, what can you tell me about Sheila, George?"

"Sin was born in Newtonabbey, County Antrim, Northern Ireland. She joined the army when she was sixteen and immediately signed up for Selection for The Det after three years in the service. She has been with The Det ever since and was just recently promoted to Lance-Corporal."

"What was her previous regiment?" asks Sarah, noting everything down on her tablet.

"The Royal Irish Regiment… but you can't hold that against her! There are plenty of other men in The Regiment formerly from that unit," says George.

"What do you know about her family?"

"She's an only child. Her dad left her when she was two or three years old and her mother died just after she joined the army. Sin has her own car and a nice flat in Hereford."

"What kind of car does she have?" asks Sarah.

George is silent for a moment before answering her. "An Aston

Martin… but I once asked her how she could afford it and she told me she owns a warehouse that she leases to other people."

"How did Sin get the money to buy a fucking warehouse?" asks Dave, incredulously.

"How the fuck do I know?" retorts George, starting to get angry.

"Enough!" snaps Sarah. "When was the last time anyone saw her?"

"Sin hasn't been seen for more than thirty days," answers Al. "Someone from her unit checked her flat and she wasn't there and neither was her car. The Det have already listed her AWOL."

"The last time *I* saw her was after the debriefing of Operation Crankshaft," says George. "We had dinner at the cookhouse and then I dropped her off at her flat before I joined you blokes at the Grafton Restaurant."

"Do you still have her smartphone number, George?"

"No… she changes it all the time. I don't know why and I don't have her latest number."

"Does she own other property besides her flat and warehouse?" asks Sarah.

"The last time we met, she told me she was going home to her house in…" George suddenly stops.

"George?"

"Her house is in Cheshire," says George, starting to get a nasty feeling in his stomach.

Cheshire is an affluent area south of Manchester, about a thirty-minute drive from Deansgate.

"Right, this is the only lead we have. Do you have her address in Cheshire?"

George reluctantly gives her the address. Sarah can sense that George still doesn't entirely believe that Sheila is involved with The Cartel.

"I can get there within the next forty-five mikes to conduct a one-up recce on Sheila's house," says Sarah. "In the meantime, could you please bring all the necessary kit and RV with me at her house? Be sure to bring some kit for me also."

"Hold on a minute here!" snaps George. "We're now accusing a member of the UKSF of being involved with The Cartel *and* snatching a squadron OC of The Regiment. Are we sure we want to go through with this?"

"This is the only lead we have, George, and we will act upon it. They could be torturing your squadron commander to death, *por el amor de Dios*! Now make a decision, *eikel*! Lead, follow, or get the fuck out of the way!" yells Sarah, unconsciously reverting back to her role as an Indonesian special forces commander.

The four men of the SAS are stunned by the assertiveness of their new commander, especially George, who looks shocked. Sarah briefly regrets yelling at George in front of his teammates, but she feels that he's starting to hold her back. The four men are silent.

"I'm with you, Sarah. What about you blokes?" asks Al, giving his men a sharp look.

The three men nod, although George is still hesitant.

"Sarah, all four of us are with you on this. This 4-man team will drive directly to her house with all the necessary kit. ETA in about three and a half hours," says Al.

"One more thing, Al. Could you please send me the blueprints and the 3D rendering of her house?" asks Sarah.

"Sure, I'll send a request to The Kremlin and we'll send it to you by e-mail."

"How about satellite imagery?"

"We'll have to go through MoD for that and they'll have to make a request to the Yank's NRO. I'm afraid it would take too much time, old buddy," says Al.

"How about we have Simon fly a UAV over to Sheila's house?" suggests Robert.

"Good idea, Robert!" says Sarah.

"I'll ask the head shed," says Al. "In the meantime, good luck and be careful when you conduct the recce, all r*oi*ght?"

"Of course, Al, thank you."

"And don't worry about Michael. He's big and ugly enough to endure anything they throw at him," says Al, trying to calm her down.

Sarah laughs in spite of the situation.

Robert adds, "Once we save Michael, you can imagine the severe slagging he'll get for letting himself get snatched and needing his fiancée to lead the team to rescue him."

Sarah laughs again imagining just that. She loves the way these men use dark humour in dealing with bad news.

"And please don't take Sin down before we get there," says Dave, grinning. "I'd like to watch you do it."

Sarah laughs louder while George gives Dave a cuff on his head.

"Of course, Dave. I'll see you at Sheila's house," says Sarah. She hangs up and goes to her teammates. "This conversation is off the record, all right?"

Her teammates are curious, but they all nod.

"The SAS knows who Sin is, but they want to handle this matter themselves. They have seconded me to the SAS and they want me to lead them in handling this, but we need your full support on this mission. What do you think?"

The Interpol team is surprised and debate heatedly for a while because what Sarah and the SAS propose doing is against the law. However, their priority is to rescue Michael and the MACP is still in effect anyway, so the team quickly agree to help. Sarah calls Paul to ask him to check Sheila's address. James gives Sarah a small camera for her recce that can upload pictures directly to an MI5 server. The pictures will be available for Cormac, Al, and the Interpol team to access on their tablets.

Sarah receives a text from Paul. The NCA reported that the house belongs to someone named Sheila Iona Neeson. It's clear someone on Sheila's UKSF salary could never afford a house so luxurious, so this substantiates the evidence against her. The NCA is now searching for other property under her name.

Cormac informs Sarah that the 4-man team has deployed to Sheila's house. The rest of B Squadron will be deployed once Michael's location has been confirmed and they'll be led directly by the CO of the SAS. He sends the blueprint of Sheila's house, already converted to 3D by The Kremlin, and tells her he has ordered Simon to fly a UAV to recce the house from the air.

Sarah studies the blueprint of Sheila's house while James drives her home. Sheila's house is on a six-and-a-half hectare property with its own lake. The main house has three floors - two above ground and one below. The stairs to the first floor are near the entrance hall. The first floor is solely for living quarters. There's a master bedroom with two private bathrooms and changing rooms, and five other bedrooms, each with their own bathroom. The basement is mostly used for recreation and there's also a plant room used for the central air conditioning and heating system.

The opulence of Sheila's property doesn't end there. Outside the house, there's a garage big enough for four cars and, in the middle of the lake, there's an island with its own summer house.

Sarah reaches her apartment, still full of crime scene investigators, and briefs Broussard and Paul on the plan. She then changes into a jumper, jacket, jeans, gloves, and boots, all black. She takes almost all her kit, including her Glock as her main sidearm, her HK P2000 with the extra mags sent by her dad for backup, a balaclava, handcuffs, and her Smith & Wesson knife. She also brings her lockpicking kit and a roll of black duct tape. Every special forces operative in the whole world knows not to forget duct tape on any type of operation. She must leave her telescoping baton behind because it makes a rattling sound whenever she moves and she can't risk discovery.

Sarah's driven by James again and she hides herself in the back seat, wearing her balaclava. She sends a text to Cormac and Al that she'll be online with them throughout the recce. She puts the Bluetooth earset on her ear and makes a conference call with the two men plus James. All three of them can monitor Sarah's movement through a UAV flown directly by Major Simon Stilwell.

It only takes them twenty minutes to arrive in Cheshire. Sarah and James agree to an ERV (emergency rendezvous) point, for which they pick the crossroad between Congleton Rd and Bollington Lane. The ERV can be used by Sarah if she's compromised and needs a place to escape. James will standby a little further away from the ERV and he can get there within two minutes to pick her up. The ERV location is also conveyed to Cormac and Al.

James will drop Sarah some 500 metres from Sheila's house at Bollington Lane. As she was trained to do, Sarah debusses from the car when it slows down turning towards Bollington Lane. Once out of the car, she immediately enters the treeline. Sarah does this flawlessly, and if someone was tailing their car, there's no way they would have seen her debus.

"I'm foxtrot," reports Sarah, meaning that she's now on foot.

"Roger that," answer Cormac, Al, and James through her Bluetooth earset.

According to the Google Earth images Sarah looked at before leaving Manchester, Sheila's property is surrounded by trees that Sarah can use to approach her target. It's already dark when Sarah enters the trees, so she forces herself to sit quietly and do nothing for five minutes. It takes up to forty minutes for eyes to fully adjust to the darkness, but she can see quite well within five. What she observed after she debussed and what she sees after those five minutes are almost entirely different. If her eyes are exposed to just a small amount of light, she'll have to readjust all over again. Besides Sarah, her surroundings also have to adjust to her presence. After a couple of minutes, the sound of various insects start playing again, meaning that they no longer consider Sarah a threat.

After five minutes, Sarah closes her right eye and checks her position using Google Earth on her smartphone with just her left eye. This is so that her shooting eye, her 'master eye', won't be exposed to the light from her smartphone. If she's compromised, at least her master eye can still see in the dark.

Sarah stealthily walks towards Sheila's house until she reaches the treeline that surrounds the property. She starts taking pictures of the house. She observes that The Cartel don't place men on stag to guard the house, but dozens of outdoor CCTV cameras are installed everywhere. Assuming somebody's watching the CCTV images, Sarah won't be seen as long as she moves as slowly as possible. Besides taking pictures of the CCTV camera locations, Sarah also has to take pictures of possible entry points, like doors and windows. All the pictures she takes are directly uploaded to MI5's server and Cormac, Al, and James can immediately study them. Sarah's recce will be extremely useful in case the SAS needs to assault the place.

Sarah takes almost one-and-a-half hours to recce the whole property, including the main house, garage, and summer house. There are noises from inside the summer house, meaning that there are people inside and she conveys this to her team. Sarah can see two black Range Rovers in the open-door garage, but Sheila's Aston Martin is nowhere to be seen. Sarah takes pictures of the number plates of both cars and James will coordinate with Paul to check on them.

Sarah's now near the entrance to the property, around a hundred metres from the main entrance of the house. She notices that the door to the main entrance has an electronic lock. There's no door lock and the occupants only have to enter a password to open the door. James asks

Sarah to zoom-in with the camera and take close-up pictures of the electronic lock so he can identify the brand. Only a few minutes after the picture was uploaded, James can send them the master password from the manufacturer. It turns out MI5 has all the master passwords for all electronic locks of every brand in the world.

Paul reports that both Range Rovers belong to Sheila, which is odd. Why would she need two exact same cars? The NCA can't determine if one of them was the vehicle used in Michael's abduction.

"We are ETA one hour and thirty mikes away, Sarah," reports Al.

"Copy," whispers Sarah.

There's nothing more Sarah can do except wait. For a few minutes, Sarah can only shiver from the cold and watch the entrance. After ten minutes of doing nothing, her worry for Michael is almost overwhelming her.

A sports car suddenly roars on Bollington Lane and enters the property. It's a blood-red Aston Martin. Sarah takes pictures of it and slowly goes to a position where she can photograph the driver. Sarah sees Sheila exit the garage and head towards her house. Sarah wonders why Sheila doesn't have a shirt on and is only wearing a white bra, light blue jeans, and army boots. Sarah takes pictures of her walking unevenly towards her house. Sheila enters the password and disappears inside. Less than a minute later, Sarah sees the lights on the right side of the house on the first floor turn on. Sarah can safely assume that Sheila has just entered that room.

"Heads up! Sheila has just arrived. She looks quite odd and I think she's on the piss," whispers Sarah.

"Roger that," says Cormac, Al, and James, studying her photos.

"There are some stains on her jeans," says James. "I'll have MI5 analyse the photos."

Sarah closes her right eye again and studies Sheila's pictures.

"It looks like blood, James," whispers Sarah, anxiously.

"It could be, but we can't be sure without some photo analysis," says James.

Her anxiety has reached its peak and Sarah suddenly makes a rash decision! She jumps out of the property and walks towards the entrance. She takes off her balaclava and wears it again as a cap, bundling her long hair into it. Sarah walks leisurely to the front door as if she belongs there.

From the UAV camera, Simon can see Sarah move towards the house and immediately reports to Cormac. "Boss, Sarah is foxtrot!"

"Sarah, what the fuck do you think you're doing?" asks Cormac angrily.

"I'm going in for the infil," whispers Sarah.

"Stand down and wait for us, damn it!" curses Al.

"Don't risk it, Sarah!" says James, almost panicking.

Sarah ignores them and everyone starts cursing her all the way to the front door. When she reaches the door, Sarah holds her breath as she enters the password. The password is correct and Sarah can enter without any problems. The inside of the house is quite warm and comfortable, especially compared to the cold outdoors. Sarah can hear loud sounds of the telly from the family room and music blaring from the basement. Fortunately, the entrance hall isn't visible from the other rooms, but there's a CCTV camera pointed directly towards the front door. She heads for the stairs as if she has done this hundreds of times before.

"I'm complete," whispers Sarah. "Lots of activity heard on the ground floor and basement."

"Roger that!" says Cormac, fuming. No one in The Regiment is as reckless as Sarah's being right now!

Once she reaches the first floor, Sarah remembers from the blueprint that the main bedroom is on her left. She can faintly hear a woman crying inside. Sarah must secure the other rooms before securing the main bedroom.

"I'm on the first floor," whispers Sarah.

"Roger that. Al, step on it!" orders Cormac.

"Roger that!" answers Al curtly. They're already driving way past the speed limit.

Sarah doesn't see any CCTV cameras on the first floor so she covers her face with her balaclava again and takes out her knife. She moves stealthily like a ninja and, till now, no one seems to have realized that someone has infiltrated the house. Sarah heads toward the room she wants to clear first, which is located on White-6-1. She puts her ear next to the door and tries to hear if there's any activity inside. She then carefully checks the knob to see if it's locked. It isn't, so Sarah enters to clear it. The bedroom and bathroom are empty so she exits and turns left. She must do the same thing in all the other rooms.

"Bedroom cleared, White-6-1," whispers Sarah.

"Roger that," says Cormac, his heart racing as he puts an 'X' on the blueprint.

"What the devil do ye mean by White-6-1?" asks James, looking confused studying the blueprint.

Sarah ignores him.

"Stay off the net, James!" orders Cormac.

Sarah walks towards the Green side. The next two doors are closets and she gives them both a quick look inside to clear them. There are now two doors facing each other in front of her. She checks them and both rooms are empty.

"Bedrooms cleared, White-7-1 and Black-11-1," whispers Sarah.

"Roger that," says Cormac, sounding increasingly tense.

Sarah goes to the next room. When she places her ear on the door, she can faintly hear someone snoring. Sarah remembers from the blueprints that beyond the door there is a hallway with a bathroom on the left. Sarah has no choice but to secure the bedroom first before securing the bathroom. Once she enters, the sound of snoring grows louder. Sarah starts walking slowly towards the sound. Sarah passes the door to the bathroom and when she reaches the end of the hallway, she sees someone sleeping on the bed, his torso covered by a blanket. Sarah carefully approaches the bed with her knife in a reverse grip.

A couple of metres from the bed, Sarah recognizes the sleeping person as Steve Dunbar, the little brother of Patrick Dunbar, and one of the leaders of The Cartel. Sarah's job as a police officer is to apprehend Steve and bring him to justice. He can also tell her where the remaining factories are.

Very carefully, Sarah opens her bum bag. She's just about to take out her handcuffs and duct tape when Steve suddenly wakes up. Steve's eyes go wide when he sees someone dressed like a ninja in his room! Without hesitation, Sarah jumps on top of him and covers his mouth with her left hand, just before he screams in terror. Sarah immediately slams her knife into his chest. Steve's face contorts in pain as the blade goes into his heart. With both of his hands, he tries to grab hold of Sarah. At the same time, an object drops loudly to the floor. Steve struggles furiously and they both fall to the floor. Sarah manages to clamp his mouth shut.

Steve grows weaker by the second and, once again, Sarah sees into someone's eyes as his soul is taken by the Ángel de la Muerte. Steve's eyes, that a few seconds ago looked surprised, terrified, and in pain, finally go blank. As with all the other criminals and terrorists Sarah has killed, this event will probably haunt her for the rest of her life.

After checking Steve's pulse to confirm that he's dead, Sarah pulls out the knife from his chest and cleans it with his shirt. She checks the object that fell to the floor and it turns out to be his pistol. In a way, it is lucky Steve woke up. If she'd tried to apprehend him as she'd planned, there's a big chance he would've shot her with the pistol he kept beneath his blanket. Sarah regrets not being able to arrest him, but decides that from this moment on, she's not a law enforcement officer. She's now a soldier. A soldier's job is to kill the enemy, not apprehend him.

Sarah clears the bathroom she'd passed. Although the bathroom is most certainly empty, she still has to clear it. After that, she forces herself to wait one minute to ensure no one's coming to check on them. This gives her time to calm herself down.

"X-Ray down, bedroom cleared, Green-10-1," whispers Sarah.

"Jesus fucking Christ!" curses Cormac.

"Fucking shit!" curses Al.

"Bloody hell!" curses James.

The three men curse simultaneously, making Sarah's eardrums ring.

"Are you compromised?" asks Cormac, worriedly.

"Negative… I took him out with my knife."

The three men curse again and even louder this time, making Sarah wince from the pain from her eardrums.

"How the fuck do ye know he's an X-Ray?" asks James, emotionally.

Sarah doesn't immediately answer him. She takes pictures of his dead body and sends them to the team. She then closes Steve's eyes, lifts his body, puts him face down on the bed, and covers his waist with the blanket. Steve now looks as if he is sleeping.

"It's Steve Dunbar and I've sent you his picture," whispers Sarah. "This place could well be The Cartel's headquarters."

"Are you saying you've managed to slot Steve fucking Dunbar with just a fucking knife?" asks Cormac.

"Affirmative," answers Sarah.

"Fuck!" curse Cormac and Al, sounding impressed.

Sarah suddenly remembers that the British Army doesn't give soldiers knives other than bayonets. They've not been taught how to kill someone with a knife. Only James is unimpressed by Sarah's actions.

"Bloody hell! We could have used the fucking intel from him. Ye're a fucking police officer, for God's sake! Ye're supposed to apprehend him and bring him to justice, not kill him in cold blood!" says James angrily.

"Negative!" answers Sarah, suddenly feeling angry at James.

"Let's discuss this another time, shall we? The team is ETA twenty mikes. Stand down until they get there!" orders Cormac.

"I still have two more rooms to clear and the last one is the Master Bedroom at Red-3-1. There's a big chance Sheila's in that room. We also need to know Michael's location. Let me try to get a confession before you conduct a DA and kill everyone in the house," she whispers.

They all go quiet. The SAS have enough evidence to conduct a Direct Action assault. However, Sarah's also right. They should try to get information on Michael's whereabouts from Sheila before they assault the building.

"The rest of B Squadron and I can carry out a full assault within the next forty-five mikes by heli. Al, set up OPs when you get there," orders Cormac.

"Roger that," answers Al.

"Sarah, you may proceed with caution," orders Cormac.

"Copy!" whispers Sarah curtly, starting to get impatient.

Sarah clears the room across from Steve's. No problem there. "Bedroom cleared, Green-8-1."

"Roger that," answers Cormac.

Sarah heads towards the master bedroom. She remembers from the blueprint that the door leads to a hallway and there's another door to the right, leading to the changing room, which itself has another door leading to the bathroom. She'll have to ignore those rooms to handle Sheila, the immediate threat.

"I'm going in the Master Bedroom at Red-3-1 to confront Sheila," whispers Sarah.

"Roger that," answer the three men, sounding far tenser than Sarah.

"Be careful and try to arrest her if she confesses," reminds James.

"Copy," answers Sarah in a noncommittal manner.

Sarah holsters her knife and takes out her Glock. She takes off her balaclava and sets her smartphone to record her conversation with Sheila. Very slowly, she turns the knob and enters the master bedroom. For some reason, Sarah feels much more anxious than she did taking on Steve Dunbar. There's something that just doesn't feel right.

What Sarah doesn't realize is that when she set her smartphone to record the conversation, the setting on her smartphone automatically set it to speaker...

# CHAPTER 13
# HOSTAGE RESCUE

23:47 GMT
Saturday September 26, 2026
Sandalwood Farm
Nether Alderley, Cheshire, England

Sarah enters the room and sees Sheila cowering in the corner, her head in her arms. She hasn't put on a shirt and doesn't seem to have realised there's someone else in the room. Sarah clears her throat and Sheila finally raises her head. She doesn't seem too surprised by Sarah's presence.

"*Dios mío*, Sheila! Why the devil would you do something like that?" says Sarah, as if she already knows what Sheila has done.

"Put that thing away," says Sheila in her posh accent. "If you were going to shoot me, you would have done so already."

"I have to apprehend you for what you've done," says Sarah, throwing her handcuffs in Sheila's direction. "Put these on!"

"What makes you think I'll go quietly?" says Sheila, standing up unevenly.

Sarah sees that the stains on Sheila's jeans are indeed blood stains. Probably Michael's blood. Sarah can't shoot her as the noise would certainly invite her friends upstairs. If she takes her down, it will have to be some other way. Sheila looks intoxicated and Sarah's confident she can overwhelm her easily, although she knows not to underestimate a UKSF operative.

"We've captured Steve Dunbar and he told us everything," says Sarah.

Sheila doesn't say anything.

"He admitted your house is The Cartel's HQ. Your choice is simple. You can confirm that and make up some story about what you're doing here, or you can admit that you're also a member of The Cartel. We'll consider your cooperation during your trial. What do you say?" offers Sarah.

An experienced interrogator will often offer a suspect the choice of two incriminating options. Choosing one automatically admits guilt. It's a trick, but an effective one for getting a confession out of a suspect. Normally, Sarah would have saved this kind of tactic for the end of an interrogation session, but she doesn't have much time. Though she's intoxicated, Sheila's still sharp enough to recognize the trap and throws Sarah a sharp look.

"Do you think I'm that stupid?" she says, curtly.

"Your HQ and warehouse have been decommissioned. B Squadron is here and everyone downstairs and in the Summer House is dead. You're in enough trouble already so don't make things more difficult. Surrender yourself!" orders Sarah.

"Sounds like I don't have anything else to live for, do I?" says Sheila, eyes starting to moisten as she walks slowly, unevenly towards Sarah. "Go ahead and shoot me!"

Sheila hasn't admitted that her house is the Cartel's HQ, but nor has she denied it. Sarah imagines the SAS have more than enough evidence to assault this place and kill everyone inside. Now she must force Sheila to reveal Michael's whereabouts.

"I won't shoot you, but I will give you the same amount of pain you have given Michael," she says, holstering her pistol and taking out her knife.

Sheila stops some three metres from Sarah and Sarah can see a glint of anxiety in her eyes. Sarah's knife only has a three-inch blade, but that's more than enough to puncture all major organs. Sheila looks sad hearing Michael's name spoken aloud, which makes Sarah even more worried for him. And angrier, too.

"I thought you loved him, Sheila?"

Sheila doesn't answer.

"How the devil could you do something like that to someone you love?" asks Sarah, as if she already knows what's happened to him.

Sheila keeps silent and only looks down sadly.

"You do realise that you can't snatch an SAS squadron commander and torture him without dire consequences, don't you?" says Sarah.

"We had planned to snatch *you*, but that stupid bastard was there instead!" says Sheila angrily.

She's just admitted to snatching Michael! Now it's Sarah turn to stay quiet and let Sheila continue.

"Niall and I were disappointed to snatch him instead of you," says Sheila.

Sarah stays silent.

"I would've enjoyed watching Niall disembowel you," says Sheila, giving her a look of utter hatred.

Sarah is still silent.

"But that dickhead wouldn't give us your fucking phone number!" says Sheila.

Sarah keeps a straight face. She's getting even more worried, but she's also touched. Michael is protecting her.

"How do you plan on getting rid of him?" asks Sarah, deciding now's the time to talk.

"There's a pig farm in Dudley, West Midlands," answers Sheila.

Sarah suddenly feels weak in the legs, knowing they plan on feeding her fiancé to the pigs. "Where is he now?"

"At my warehouse," answers Sheila without thinking. She then frowns because Sarah's question sounds odd. Hadn't Sarah said they'd already taken the warehouse?

"Right, we have more than enough for a confession. Good job, Sarah!" says James's voice from her smartphone, accidentally set to speaker.

Sarah's stunned! She can't believe she's made such a stupid mistake and hurriedly tries to reset her smartphone back to Bluetooth.

"We are ETA two mikes and will immediately set up OPs for B Squadron's assault," says Al.

"B Squadron and I will deploy within five mikes," says Cormac, just before Sarah manages to reset her smartphone.

Sheila finally realises she's been tricked. "You fucking bitch!"

Sheila rushes forward and tries to kick Sarah's knife from her hand. Sarah moves her hand just before Sheila kicks it, but Sheila immediately does a roundhouse kick with her other leg straight to Sarah's abdomen. Sheila's boot hits the target, but Sarah clenches her abs so Sheila's boot merely bounces off. Sarah goes forward, stabbing her knife towards Sheila's stomach, but she manages to catch Sarah's hand. Sarah's momentum pushes Sheila back. Sarah trips Sheila's feet and she falls on her back with Sarah landing on top of her. Sheila successfully prevents the knife from entering her body, but Sarah can now use her body weight to push the blade down.

While this is going on, Sarah hears Cormac frantically ordering Al to immediately conduct an assault. He's sure Sarah can easily defeat Sheila, but he's extremely worried that Sheila's friends will go to her room to find out what all the ruckus is about. Al tells Cormac that they can't assault the main house until they've first secured the summer house and garage. Even after that, they'll still have to secure the ground floor and basement before he can send someone to help Sarah. James wants to go in to help them out, but Cormac orders him to stand down to prevent blue-on-blue. Al hangs up his phone and switches to his comm headset to lead his team.

The tip of the knife is pointed towards Sheila's abdomen, just above her navel. Sarah uses all her strength and the tip finally starts piercing Sheila's stomach. Sheila clenches her muscles and Sarah struggles to push the knife through her incredibly tough abdominal muscles. As the blade slowly goes in, Sarah feels her opponent getting weaker by the second. Sheila suddenly gasps when the knife pierces her intestines! Sarah pushes the knife all the way in and Sheila finally lets go of Sarah's hands when the knife is up to its hilt. Sarah releases her knife and leaves it embedded deeply in Sheila's stomach.

Both women are panting and for a moment do nothing but lie on top of each other like that. Sarah stands up and takes out her pistol. She moves to a position where she can cover the door and Sheila. As she's looking towards her opponent, Sarah's distracted by the hypnotic movement of the knife going up and down in time with Sheila's breathing. Not much blood comes out, but Sarah wonders why Sheila doesn't appear to be in any pain.

Sarah's jaw drops when Sheila stands up and slowly, calmly heads toward a mirror. Sheila smiles seeing the knife embedded deeply in the middle of her six-pack, making Sarah astonished and at the same time, terrified. Sheila then turns to face Sarah, both hands on her waist.

"I never would have thought I'd be bested by an Indonesian policewoman," says Sheila, smiling at her. "Congratulations, Sarah. It seems ye've succeeded in slotting me."

Sarah is too surprised to say anything. Sheila has dropped her posh accent and is now sounding Irish. She's now an entirely different person. Sarah finally understands what Michael meant when he said that Sheila is artificial.

"My *daidí* always said that we would most certainly die by the sword. It looks like I'll die by yer knife today," says Sheila, still smiling.

She looks back towards the mirror, as if she's admiring the knife embedded deep in the middle of her abdomen. Blackish blood slowly oozes out, indicating her liver's punctured. Blood also starts coming out of her mouth.

"Your father said that to you? I thought he left you when you were little?" asks Sarah.

"Neeson is my mum's surname. My *daidí* is Paddy Dunbar. *Daidí* recruited me into The Cartel when he became the leader," says Sheila calmly. Blood slowly flows from her mouth as she talks, looking like something from a horror movie. "Michael and the SAS slotted my stepmother and now *ye* have slotted me. Mark my words, Sarah. Once *daidí* finds out that ye did this, he'll take his revenge on ye and yer family in Indonesia."

"It doesn't have to end this way, Sheila. You could still survive this. Give yourself up and let us take you to a hospital," pleads Sarah.

"Would *ye* surrender?" asks Sheila with a raised eyebrow.

Sarah doesn't answer.

"I thought so," says Sheila, giving her a smile and a wink.

Sheila holds her breath and grabs the hilt of the knife with both hands. As she pulls it out, her face hardens and her lips go tight, finally revealing some pain. Once the knife is out, Sheila's intestines start peeking out, as if trying to force their way out of the small opening in her abdomen.

Sarah's paying attention to the hole in Sheila's stomach and not to the rest of Sheila. She suddenly snaps out of it when Sheila kicks her pistol out of her hand, sending it flying across the room. Sheila rushes her, holding the knife in a reverse grip, aiming to stab Sarah in the face. Sarah evades to the right and sends a punch into Sheila's stomach with her left fist. Sheila gasps in pain when the hard punch catches her right on the knife wound. The jab opens the wound a little wider and a stretch of Sheila's intestines bursts out. They're dangling from the wound and more blood is spurting from her mouth and stomach. Even so, Sheila keeps on fighting. She tries to slash and stab at Sarah, who manages to evade all her thrusts. Sarah is sure she can defeat Sheila, so long as no one comes into the room to help.

The two tough women start circling each other. Sarah can't help herself getting distracted by Sheila's hanging intestines and Sheila takes a chance to throw herself at Sarah, slamming her to the wall behind her. Sheila uses both hands to try to stab Sarah in the face, but Sarah grabs a hold of Sheila's wrists, the tip of the blade literally millimetres from her left eye! Sheila's putting all her effort into pushing the knife further and the strain pushes her intestines spilling out even more, until they finally slap on the floor.

Sarah knees Sheila in the lower belly, making her gasp in pain. Sheila retreats a few steps and finally drops to one knee. Sarah takes the opportunity to take out her backup pistol from her ankle holster, her HK P2000, even though she still daren't fire. At some point during the struggle, her Bluetooth earset has fallen out and she has no idea what's happening with Al and his team.

Sheila's eyes never once leave Sarah. Even down on one knee with bits of her insides dragging on the ground, she still looks hell-bent on killing. Sheila starts moving towards Sarah to attack her again, but suddenly stops with a loud gasp as more blood gushes out of her mouth. Both women look down and see that Sheila has accidentally stepped on her own intestines! Sheila calmly moves her foot away and starts inching towards Sarah again. Sarah's so shocked that for a second she forgets to do anything. Sheila finally sees an opportunity to kill her.

The door suddenly flies open! Sarah snaps out of it and points her pistol towards the person entering the room. George comes through the door and points his own pistol towards Sarah. They recognize each other at the same time and then point their pistols towards Sheila, who is already facing George.

"George..." gasps Sheila.

George hesitates aiming his pistol at his friend's face. But then his face hardens and he fires a controlled pair. One round enters Sheila's left cheekbone and the other enters her left eyebrow, the thickest part of the skull. Sheila drops on her back and starts convulsing. Both her eyes are still open and blood is gushing from her mouth and nose. George and Sarah move forward as one and empty their pistols in Sheila's face. The ex-UKSF member's beautiful face is now a complete mess. She'll need a closed casket at her funeral.

George and Sarah change magazines. When Sarah sees George's face, it's cold, expressionless, and frightening to look at. Sarah doesn't realise it, but she always displays the exact same expression during an operation.

"All right?" asks George.

Through her ringing ears, Sarah can still hear the ice in his voice. "I'm all right. Could you please clear both bathrooms? They haven't been cleared yet."

Although both bathrooms are most certainly empty, they still have to clear them. Without answering, George does as he's ordered while Sarah takes her knife from Sheila's hand and wipes the blood off on Sheila's jeans. Sarah finds and holsters her Glock. She also finds and puts in her Bluetooth earset.

"X-Ray down, master bedroom cleared, Red-3-1," says George to his headset. He listens for a couple of seconds. "Al said 'stronghold secured', Sarah."

"Mac, James, the stronghold is secured," says Sarah through her earset. "James, please update the Chief and have him send the rest of the team over here. After that, could you please get over here to assist me with the SSE?"

"I'll do that," answers James, sounding relieved. He hangs up.

"Good job, Sarah! We're standing down and I'm going to brief the Director," says Cormac. He too hangs up.

"George, could you please ask Al to meet me at the Entrance Hall?" orders Sarah as she exits the room, followed by George, who forwards her order to Al though his headset.

Sarah is down the stairs in no time and when Al shows up, she asks him to debrief her.

"Roight," says Al, "we entered the premises at approximately 00:03..."

Sarah listens intently. Al led the assault, even though Robert outranks him. This is quite normal in the SAS, where new officers are required to *learn* from their men, not *lead* them. The 4-man team was led by Al in the number three position, with Dave as pointman, George as number two, and Robert as MOE specialist.

They parked outside the complex and first secured the Summer House and garage. The Summer House turned out to be a warehouse with ten men inside, whom they dispatched without any problems. They entered the house with the same password James had given them and secured the ground floor. They killed six people watching telly in the family room. The drawing room and study room had been converted into living quarters, and they took out a dozen people sleeping there. The whole basement had been converted into a drug factory and the team shot around twenty people where they stood. Inside the plant room, they found various assault rifles, ammo, explosives, and Claymore mines. While the others were finishing off the X-Rays, Al sent George to the first floor to help Sarah.

The 4-man team of the SAS successfully killed more than fifty narcoterorrists of the Irish Drug Cartel! Unlike their assault on Swan's Mill, none of the X-Rays were armed and most were shot while sleeping or resting. The 4-man team used the HK MP5SD3, which has a built-in sound suppressor, meaning the enemy didn't realise they were being assaulted. Solid proof that speed, aggression, and surprise from a special forces unit can defeat a much larger force, so long as they can keep their momentum.

Al ends his report. "Assault rifles were kept near the X-Rays, but none of them managed to grab them, much less fire them."

"Proper job, Al! Please place the men on stag covering all the entrances to the stronghold. There's a friendly on the way here - James Hicks from our Interpol Incident Response Team. Please send him upstairs to assist me with the SSE. The rest of the Interpol team is on the way here and they'll probably arrive within the next forty mikes. Carry on," orders Sarah.

Sarah must now concentrate on finding Sheila's warehouse. She goes into Sheila's room again and frisks her dead body. The left pocket of her jeans holds a plastic bag half full of ecstasy and Sarah suspects this helped Sheila ignore the pain and continue fighting with her insides out. A smartphone peeks out the pocket of Sheila's jeans, but Sarah has to move aside the intestines covering the pocket before she can retrieve it. Sarah sees the wallpaper on the smartphone and is taken aback - it's a picture of Michael hugging Sheila from behind. They look happy and Sarah briefly feels jealous until she sees again what Sheila looks like now. But Sarah is suddenly saddened when she realises she has no photo of herself together with Michael. Sheila's smartphone has a password so she'll need James's help to open it. Sarah doesn't find anything else in her pocket with any significance so she starts searching the closets in her bedroom. James walks into the room and steps back again when he sees Sheila's dead body.

"Bloody hell," he mumbles. Sheila's messy face and sprawling intestines turn him pale and nauseous.

"I'll exploit this room for intel on Michael's location. Could you please do the same for Steve's room?"

James nods and hurriedly leaves to look through Steve's room. Sarah searches behind the paintings on the wall and finds nothing hidden behind them. She's growing frustrated – there's nothing here! Barely a minute passes by before James calls her and asks her to come into Steve's room. Inside, Sarah sees stack upon stack of documents and she suddenly feels incredibly stupid!

'Steve's in charge of accounting and administration. What the fuck was I doing wasting my time in Sheila's room?' thinks Sarah, extremely angry at herself.

Sarah hands Sheila's smartphone over to James and starts studying the documents. James calls his teammate at MI5 to help him hack into the smartphone, but he keeps getting distracted. Steve's lying there, looking more asleep than dead, and James can't shake the feeling he's going to wake up any second. Paul calls Sarah and says that the NCA have found a warehouse in Liverpool under Sheila's name. Sarah must confirm it's the right place with the documents in front of her before SAS can carry out an assault.

James gets into Sheila's smartphone at the same time Sarah finds the deeds and blueprints to her warehouse, at 63 Kempston Street, Liverpool. There's a phone number on the deed and James finds the same number in Sheila's smartphone. They agree that that warehouse is the place they're looking for.

"Right, let me brief the team downstairs," says Sarah, taking the documents with her.

"I'll continue the SSE here," says James.

Sarah meets with Al, on stag in the drawing room. He's facing the door, accompanied by the dead bodies of the narcoterrorists they'd killed a few minutes ago.

Sarah calls Cormac and sets her smartphone to speaker so Al can tune in. "Mac, Sheila's warehouse is in Liverpool. We've found the deeds and blueprints to her warehouse and it's under her name. The telephone number for the warehouse is one of the contact numbers in her smartphone. You also heard her say that Michael is being held there. Do you think this is sufficient evidence for another direct action?"

"Indeed it is," answers Cormac. "Send me the address and blueprints so B Squadron and I can study it. We'll deploy in the next two hours."

Sarah winces and Al shakes his head in frustration. Cormac would need two hours to plan and prepare for the assault. Although they can deploy by heli, that doesn't mean they'll go directly to the warehouse and make entry from the roof. It'll probably take them at least three hours to finally secure the warehouse. Michael is in the hands of Niall Schroeder and Sarah can't imagine what her fiancé will endure in three hours. They must save him *now*, before Niall starts hitting him with his board.

Before Sarah can answer him, Al angrily interjects. "Bollocks, Mac! Five of us can get there within the next forty mikes! We don't have two hours, for fuck's sake!"

"Negative! This is *not* an Immediate Action and I won't let you conduct a fucking rescue on a stronghold like a fucking warehouse with just five men!" says Cormac.

"We've just assaulted their fucking HQ and slotted more than fifty of them!" says Al.

"Slotting fifty players while they're sleeping and assaulting a fucking warehouse while it's active are entirely different scenarios! You're experienced enough to know that!" retorts Cormac.

"You heard Sheila, *eikel*, they're torturing him!" snaps Sarah. "We can't wait another two hours!"

"Negative, Sarah! I can't risk you or the team," says Cormac firmly. "Stand down and send me the address so I can plan the fucking rescue!"

Sarah is silent and shares a look with Al. Cormac has made the right decision and they both know it.

"Wait one, Mac," says Sarah. She hangs up. "Al, could you please call the others to the Entrance Hall for a head shed meeting?"

Al calls the others to the entrance hall with his headset. George is on stag there. While waiting for Robert and Dave, Sarah notices George's thousand-yard stare and he's shaking. Sarah knows that he's experiencing combat stress. George has killed someone close to him, someone he even dated for a while, and Sarah understands the negative impact this is having on him. As his commander, Sarah must keep an eye on him, especially since they'll have to work together again shortly.

After everyone is gathered, Sarah briefs them. "Sheila's warehouse is in Liverpool and we can get there within forty mikes, but your CO has ordered us to stand down. Our choice is simple; we can try to save Michael ourselves and risk a court-martial for disobeying a direct order, or we can stand down and have your CO and the rest of B Squadron try to rescue him which will take at least three hours, which may or may not be too late for him. I know what I think we should do, but I want to hear what you think."

The three SAS men look at Al, their Squadron Sergeant Major, who gives them an almost imperceptible nod.

Dave breaks the silence. "Let's go and save him!"

"Yeah!" says George. "Let's fucking do it!"

"We're wasting time here. Let's go now, damn it!" says Robert. He looks at Sarah. "Give us an order, Boss!"

Everyone looks at Sarah, who is somewhat taken aback by Robert calling her 'Boss'. They're all waiting for her to give them an order.

"Right, standby for Immediate Action," orders Sarah. "Here are the blueprints for the warehouse. Let's study them *en route* and plan for the rescue. Let me brief James before we deploy and I'll meet you in the car. Carry on!"

Sarah gives the blueprints to Al and goes upstairs to meet James. She briefs him.

"Are ye out of yer fucking mind?" yells James, eyes as wide as saucers.

"Do you have any other suggestions?" asks Sarah, trying to be patient.

James goes silent. He's extremely worried for Michael, but also for Sarah if she has to go to lead the assault. "No, but ye can't just leave me here all alone. What if someone else comes home?"

It's Sarah's turn to be silent because James is right. He won't be able to confront a Cartel member if one of them turns up. "What's the ETA on the rest of the team?"

James glances at his watch. "About twenty minutes."

"How about you call Paul and have him send the Cheshire Constabulary over here right away? At this hour, they should be able to get here within five minutes."

James thinks for a second and nods. He calls Paul to have the Cheshire Constabulary send every copper on hand to the crime scene. Sarah boards the Q car, the Range Rover the SAS men came over with. Robert is driving and the others are in the back. Al, Dave, and George study the blueprints and discuss how to conduct the assault. This is called a Chinese parliament, in which everyone can give input and ideas on the best way to conduct the assault. Their leader, in this case Sarah, provides input of her own and agrees or disagrees with their plan.

Without hesitation, Sarah removes her clothes and puts on the black kit the SAS provided for her. She then puts on her body armour, ceramic plates, tactical holster, and belt kit. Sarah's friends don't even glance at her when she's stripped to her bra and panties, so focused are they on the job at hand. Once she's ready, Sarah finally accepts Cormac's call, who's been ringing her all the way from Sandalwood Farm. She sets her smartphone to speaker so everyone can tune in.

"Goddamn it, Sarah!" yells Cormac.

"Mac, you are on speaker. We are mobile to Sheila's warehouse in Liverpool, ETA twenty mikes," says Sarah.

"Sarah, you are taking too many risks! We must assume the worst - that the X-Rays at the warehouse already know you assaulted their HQ and they will be ready for you! You *do not* have the manpower or firepower to do this properly! Please stand down!" orders Cormac.

"Negative, Mac," answers Sarah.

"This is *my* team you are risking and I'm giving you a direct fucking order! Stand down and let the rest of B Squadron take care of this! Stand down... now!"

"Negative, Mac," answers Sarah once again.

"Al! Stand down, goddamn it! That's a direct fucking order!"

"Negative, Mac," answers Al.

"Stand down now or I guarantee all four of your arses will be RTU'd by the end of next week! I'll also fucking court-martial the lot of you for disobeying a direct order if you're still alive after all of this!" shouts Cormac, barely in control of himself.

"Sarah's in command of this fucking operation and you're being a dickhead! We're just following her orders like *you* ordered us to," answers Al curtly.

Cormac's lost for words.

"You gave her a mission to do whatever it takes to save Michael. Now let her finish it, goddamn it!" yells Al.

Cormac is still silent so Sarah continues. "I'll send you the address, Mac, but I would like you to send us the 3D rendering of the stronghold. Either you support us on this and send us the information we need within the next five mikes... or you can have us go in half-blind for the assault. Your call, Mac."

Cormac has been cornered. Sarah can ignore his orders because she's not under his command. She's not even a member of His Majesty's Armed Forces and can't be threatened with a court martial for disobeying a direct order. The four men with her can also evade him because he himself has placed them under Sarah's command. The CO of the SAS suddenly realises that he doesn't have any choice but to support their incredibly reckless plan.

"Fucking shit! Very well... send me the address and I'll send you the 3D rendering. But brief me on your assault plan beforehand. Are we fucking clear on this?" orders Cormac, curtly.

"Clear, Mac, I'll text you the address right away," says Sarah, relieved.

"I owe you one, Al!"

"You already owe me a lot," says Al, a look of satisfaction on his face.

Cormac is heard cursing loudly before hanging up, making everyone in the car smirk. Sarah immediately sends Cormac the address and blueprints. She then looks at the blueprint, while the others study images of the building from Google Street View and Google Earth. In a matter of minutes, they receive the 3D rendering from Cormac. The CO of the SAS also sends the address to Simon and orders him to fly the UAV there.

Sheila's warehouse is located on the corner of Kempston Street and Gildart Street. It has three storeys and each floor is five by forty metres. There are three entrances on the ground floor; the main entrance at White-6, a delivery entrance at Green-10, and a corner entrance at Black-11. There's a lift at Black-12 and a wooden stairway at White-5. There's an office area on the White side of the second floor, facing Kempston Street. There's a complete bathroom at Green-8 on each floor.

Sarah will have to lead the assault because she's the most secure, meaning that she can't be court-martialed for disobeying a direct order from Cormac. The four SAS men absolutely don't mind being under Sarah's command, as they've long considered her as smart and tough as their commander. This says a lot, considering that Michael is one of the best OCs to ever command B Squadron. Sarah has shown them incredible courage by conducting a one-up recce and infiltrating a Cartel stronghold, killing two members with her knife, including Steve Dunbar. George told Al that Sarah deserves credit for slotting Sheila since all he did was deliver a *coup de grâce*. If George hadn't entered, Sheila would've died by Sarah's hands.

Unlike all the other times she's killed people, Sarah doesn't feel anything and this worries her. Is it because they're responsible for Michael's abduction? Is it because today she's a soldier, not a law enforcement officer? Is it because she's killed so many people that now she's numb to it? Sarah tries to ignore these thoughts and concentrates on her next mission.

Sarah appoints Al as Alpha and pointman, George as Bravo and number two, herself as Charlie and team leader, Robert as Delta and 2 i/c, and Dave as Echo and MOE specialist. The stack is similar to the stack Sarah used in The Test, back at PATA a lifetime ago. The only difference is placing Robert as Delta and 2 i/c. Once Cormac has arrived, his call sign will be Zero. Call signs are supposed to be random, but Sarah wants to avoid confusion.

An assault by a special forces unit usually involves an assault from the roof because that's the most unpredictable entry. With no heli, they could climb up the other rooftops and walk stealthily towards the roof of the target and abseil into the windows of the second floor. But as with the assault on Swan's Mill, they must assume that Tiny Mullins has designed the defensive measures for the warehouse, so they have to plan an assault that's the opposite of their standard practice.

They'll park the Q car in front of the door at Green-10 and conduct their Covert Entry on the door at Black-11. After securing the ground floor, they'll have to ascend the stairs at White-5 to secure the upper floors. They'll need more firepower than the HK MP5SD3 can offer so they all switch to the Colt Canada C8 CQB with sound suppressor. Just as Robert suggested during the debriefing of Operation Crankshaft, all assault rifles will be set to semi-auto and they'll aim for headshots with controlled pairs.

The use of assault rifles in a hostage rescue operation is rare because it could endanger the Yankee with secondary penetration. They must be extra careful on the second floor, which is where they assume Michael is being held. They present their plans to Cormac and he agrees to everything. Cormac will arrive by Chinook with the rest of B Squadron and he will send reinforcements from the ground floor.

Sarah orders her men to parade all kit and weapons. All their kit and weapons are at optimum state, but they still recheck them anyway. Grinning, George reminds Sarah to reset her smartphone to silent. Sarah answers by giving him her middle finger. The others laugh and briefly forget the anxiety they're all feeling. Sarah can see that George's eyes are focused again and she knows she needn't worry about him anymore. She's confident that she can fully rely on him in their next mission.


00:48 GMT
Sunday September 27, 2026
Kempston Warehouse
Islington, Liverpool, England


The area looks completely deserted. As planned, they park right in front of the door at Green-10-0. A CCTV camera is on top of the door and they can only hope that no one is watching. Dave debusses accompanied by Al while the others cover them from inside the Q car.

Dave checks behind the door with his endoscope camera. Seeing no one, he disarms the alarm and picks the lock. Once the door is safe for entry, the others debus and stack behind Al on the left side of the door. They already have their respirators on, their GPNVGs turned on, and weapons at 'low ready'.

"All call signs, this is Charlie and I have control. Standby... Go!" whispers Sarah.

Dave opens the door and lets the others enter the stronghold. Because the ground floor is completely empty, Al buttonhooks and takes the left wall. George reacts to Al's movement and takes the right wall, heading towards White-7-0. Sarah goes left as she enters and then turns right towards White-6-0 and Robert goes slightly further than Sarah before turning right towards White-5-0. Dave is the last to enter and covers their rear.

Once on the White side, Al secures the bathroom. After it's secure, they head towards the stairs at White-5-0 and stack behind Al. They start to ascend the wooden stairs according to CQB procedures. Their feet go up sideways and raised high to prevent tripping on the stairs. They must go slowly because the wooden stairs make a creaking sound whenever they step. When Al has almost reached the next floor, he suddenly fires his rifle!

"Contact front!" shouts Al.

"Go noisy!" shouts Sarah.

They hurriedly climb the stairs, no longer mindful of the noise they're making to reach the next floor. Sarah's worried because they've now lost the element of surprise and the X-Rays must surely outnumber them many times over. Cormac's words about their lack of manpower and firepower are ringing in her ears.

"*Dios nos ayude*," thinks Sarah.

00:52 GMT
Sunday September 27, 2026
Kempston Warehouse
Islington, Liverpool, England

On the second floor of the warehouse, Carraig and Gwilliam are doing some dirty work when they hear gunshots on the first floor. Gwilliam runs to get his assault rifle and Carraig sends a Cartel member down to investigate.

00:52 GMT
Sunday September 27, 2026
Kempston Warehouse
Islington, Liverpool, England

On reaching the next floor, Sarah sees Al's rifle take three X-Rays down and George's take two more. However, three X-Rays take cover behind bags upon bags of goods. While her teammates are handling the X-Rays, Sarah fires her rifle at the lights, darkening the whole floor. Pistol shots from the X-Rays sound deafening in the enclosed space, but then fall silent when her teammates' rounds go through whatever they're hiding behind. Even after the X-Rays are down, her team still have to move forward to finish them off and clear the rest of the area. From behind her, Sarah hears Dave shoot his rifle. Once they've cleared the area, they turn around and head back towards the stairs. Sarah sees two X-Rays down with their heads blown off, one near the stairs and one just coming out from the now-empty bathroom. They stack and run upstairs towards the second floor. Since they've 'gone noisy', they don't care what kind of racket they make. As they're running up the stairs, Sarah's worst nightmare suddenly rolls towards them…

"Grenaaade!" screams Al, panicking.


00:53 GMT
Sunday September 27, 2026
Kempston Warehouse
Islington, Liverpool, England

Several seconds earlier…

Carraig hears the distinct not-really-silent sounds of suppressed rifle shots. He waits until he hears them on the stairs and pulls the pin from his fragmentation grenade. If the blast doesn't immediately kill whoever's assaulting them, the wooden stairway will surely collapse all the way to the ground floor, killing them anyway.

He peeks down the stairway and rolls the grenade he's been carrying since his IRA days…


00:53 GMT
Sunday September 27, 2026
Kempston Warehouse
Islington, Liverpool, England

Al gives the X-Ray a long burst from his rifle, blowing his head into a million pieces. George tries to kick the grenade downstairs, but misses and falls down instead. The grenade finally comes to rest less than a metre from George's head. George can only close his eyes and wait for the inevitable…

Sarah knows what she must do. She jumps over George and throws herself on top of the grenade. "Man down, White-5 stairway!"

"Delta in control! All call signs, go!" screams Robert, falling over himself to help George stand up and jump over Sarah.

Her teammates all start running upstairs without hesitation. Sarah realises she won't survive this explosion. She closes her eyes and accepts her fate, even though her heart is pounding like a jackhammer, as if realizing that these are the last beats it will ever make. Sarah has never been this scared before in her life, but at least she will die saving her fiancé and her teammates. She can't even think of a better reason to die than this.

Sarah's been on the grenade for two seconds and knows that most grenades explode within five. Even though she's wearing body armour and has a ceramic plate covering her torso, Sarah knows that they won't stop a grenade blast at point blank range. The ceramic plate will probably even prolong her misery. Her body will shatter, but the explosion probably won't immediately kill her. The blast will sever her arms and legs, unprotected by body armour, and she'll probably die from blood loss. Even if she does survive, SAS CQB doctrine means her teammates won't be able to immediately help her and must first secure the stronghold. Meanwhile, the wooden staircase will collapse, finally finishing off whatever little's left of her. Sarah glances up in time to see Dave reach the next floor. She's relieved to know all her teammates have made it, but unsuppressed rifle shots are heard from the second floor, giving her fresh cause to worry. Flashbangs are going off repeatedly, making her flinch every single time.

With these thoughts, Sarah suddenly realises that she's still alive, even after ten seconds. Cautiously, she starts to get up, trying hard not to move the unexploded grenade that looks like a steel pineapple. Still carefully, she makes her way up to the second floor. Sarah can finally breathe again when she's almost reached the second floor.

"B-B-Blue-on-b-bluel!" she shouts, her voice shaking.

"Boss?" asks Dave, guarding the rear.

"Affirmative! Check fire, *g-g-godverdomme!*" orders Sarah, still finding it hard to believe she's alive.

"Checking fire, Boss," says Dave, relieved.

Through her GPNVG, Sarah sees pill-making machines and chemical reactors on the second floor. X-Rays are taking cover behind barrels of chemicals on the Black side of the warehouse, firing their M16A2 blindly towards the office area, which her teammates have just finished securing.

"Yankee secured, White office area c-c-cleared!" says Robert.

"Charlie roger," says Sarah. "All call signs, this is Ch-Ch-Charlie and I have c-c-control!"

"Roger that," answer her teammates, also with shaking voices.

Although she's completely shaken by the experience, she's also relieved her team have secured Michael. As per SAS CQB doctrine, they'll have to secure the stronghold before helping him. The faster they secure the building, the faster they can help Michael. Her teammates exit the office area and take cover behind some pill-making machines. They look towards Sarah for her next order. Sarah hopes her men still believe in her leadership as they can clearly see that she is badly shaken. She needs to calm herself down, and fast.

Sarah glances towards the Black side and thinks hard for a moment before issuing some orders. "All call signs, standby to pepper-pott. Alpha and Bravo will assault, Charlie and Delta will go firm, Echo will stand firm and cover White-5-2 stairway. Acknowledge!"

Her men are stunned by her orders. From behind their respirators, they can only look at Sarah with wide eyes and open mouths. They are frozen.

"All call signs, acknowledge!" orders Sarah with a stronger voice.

They finally snap out of it and set their assault rifles to full-auto.

"Let's fucking do it!" shouts Al.

"Fuck! Yeah!" shouts George.

"Let's do it!" shouts Robert. "Let's do it!"

Pepper-potting, officially called fire and manoeuvre, requires a lot of aggression and the men are psyching themselves up.

"Delta, suppress fire! Alpha and Bravo, go!" shouts Sarah.

Sarah and Robert empty their mags in the direction of the X-Rays, forcing them to take cover while Al and George rush forward as fast as they can for about ten metres. Al and George take cover on the left side of the floor while Sarah and Robert change mags. Al and George give a sign that they've 'gone firm' and are ready to cover Robert and Sarah. On her command, Al and George provide suppressing fire as Robert and Sarah rush forward.

"Coming through! Coming through!" shout Robert and Sarah as they pass through Al and George's position.

Robert is on Sarah's left and because he can run faster than her, Sarah falls half a step behind him. Sarah suddenly sees an X-Ray on her front-right, aiming his rifle straight at Robert's head. Robert doesn't seem to realise the immediate threat facing him!

00:55 GMT
Sunday September 27, 2026
Kempston Warehouse
Islington, Liverpool, England

Gwilliam readies his M16A2 and aims at the head of the tall lead man. He starts to pull the trigger…

00:55 GMT
Sunday September 27, 2026
Kempston Warehouse
Islington, Liverpool, England

"Contact right!" yells Sarah as she deliberately trips Robert's feet and floors him face first.

The X-Ray fires at the same time Robert collapses. Sarah doesn't know if Robert's hit or not. She goes to one knee and fires a burst at the X-Ray, who's also firing his rifle at her. Sarah can feel the air pressure from the bullets on her head and shoulders, meaning that the rounds have missed her by mere centimetres. All her rounds, though, hit the X-Ray right in his throat, severing his neck and making his head roll horrifically towards her. On pure instinct, Sarah empties her mag into the rolling head, making it literally explode!

All the while, Al and George keep screaming at them to take cover. Sarah drags Robert's huge body towards some cover. Sarah counts at least eight X-Rays on the Black side, still firing blindly at them.

"Are you hit?" asks Sarah worriedly.

"N-N-Negative," says Robert, shaking badly, finally realizing how close his head came to being blown off.

"Ready frags!" orders Sarah.

Robert nods and they both pull the pin from a fragmentation grenade.

"Alpha and Bravo, suppress fire!" shouts Sarah.

Sarah and Robert throw their grenades towards the X-Rays while Al and George provide suppressing fire from behind them.

"Frag out!" yell Sarah and Robert as they take cover.

BOOOM! BOOOM!

Both grenades detonate almost simultaneously and they can hear the screams of the X-Rays amid the blasts. Less than a second after both grenades detonate, Sarah and Robert rush forward, firing their rifles to finish off the X-Rays. As she does this, Sarah has to remind herself that today she's a soldier, not a law enforcement officer. She's sure no one has managed to escape from the lift as it was open on the second floor the whole time.

"Black side clear," says Robert.

"Stronghold secured," says Sarah, sounding relieved.

After catching their breath for a few seconds, Sarah and Robert start walking towards the White side and remove their GPNVGs and respirators. Through her ringing ears, Sarah can hear someone's smartphone ringing.

"How's Michael, R-R-Robert?" she asks as they walk towards the office area.

Robert doesn't answer and Sarah can clearly see that he's also shaking. This is the second time this evening he's almost been killed.

"Robert?" asks Sarah once again.

Robert doesn't say a word and only looks down.

"Answer me, *klootzak*!" yells Sarah as she gives him a hard cuff on his head.

Robert looks shocked being hit by Sarah! He can only look at her with his mouth open, but no words come out. Sarah briefly feels remorse for striking an officer in front of the other ranks, but her worry for her fiancé has reached its peak.

"He's in the White-7-2 office, Boss," says George, almost inaudibly.

Sarah immediately heads there, but Al grabs her arm.

"Please don't go in there, Sarah," he says, softly.

"Take your fucking hands off me, Al!" yells Sarah, giving the SSM of B Squadron a frightening look.

Al's taken aback and immediately lets go of her arm. Even during his basic training, he's never been yelled at like that before. Sarah finally goes into the office room where her fiancé's being held.

Michael is still handcuffed to his chair. He is recognizable only by the clothes he was wearing when she last saw him. His face looks as if it was clawed off by a large animal... almost all the bones in his body are shattered... and both of his legs have been hacked off... a wood-saw is embedded halfway into his left shoulder... and two small gunshot wounds are barely visible in the middle of his forehead.

She has failed.

# CHAPTER 14
## LAST POST

14:43 GMT
Saturday September 26, 2026
Kempston Warehouse
Islington, Liverpool, England

Several hours earlier...
Michael is handcuffed to a chair with a pillowcase covering his head. He doesn't make a sound, as if he's already resigned himself to his fate. He's fully aware of his surroundings, though. His snatchers are flapping when they realize they've snatched an SAS squadron commander. They're panicking after violating Patrick's order and all the while, Niall is throwing a tantrum because they've failed to snatch Sarah.

Despite his situation, Michael's relieved knowing that his fiancée's safe. He'll die a horrible death, but at least Sarah will be all right. The thought crosses his mind that he should've accepted Arthur's ring. If he had, he would've swallowed it before his hands were immobilized by duct tape.

The pillowcase covering Michael's head is taken off. He can finally see that he's in an office with Niall and Sheila standing in front of him. Niall looks frustrated and Sheila looks sad.

"Tell us where she is or give us her number!" orders Niall.

Michael doesn't answer and instead looks at his ex-girlfriend. Niall punches him in the face and Michael feels his mouth fill up with blood.

"Please, Michael, just do what he says," begs Sheila in her posh accent.

Michael spits at Sheila's face, but his saliva and blood only go as far as her shirt. Sheila gets angry and starts hitting his face repeatedly. Blood from Michael's face is spouting everywhere, painting Sheila's clothes red. Michael is in agony as Sheila repeatedly hits his fractured cheekbone. He knows that this is just the beginning. He knows that the Interpol team and The Regiment will most likely be too late rescuing him... if they ever find him. Once Sheila's finished, Michael just stares at her through his swollen eyes.

Sheila's suddenly disgusted by her ex-lover's blood and saliva all over her shirt, so she takes it off. Niall is immediately aroused seeing Sheila's bare flesh. He has never seen his boss's daughter without a shirt on. Niall imagines her screaming as he guts her, but he suddenly receives a slap across his face.

"Don't even think about it!" threatens Sheila.

"Think about what?" asks Niall

"If you want to think about disembowelling someone, think about disembowelling Sarah!"

Sheila seems to know exactly what Niall's thinking about. Reluctantly, Niall diverts his eyes away from her.

"Please, Michael, save yourself. Just give us Sarah's phone number," says Sheila.

Michael doesn't say anything and keeps looking at Sheila. His ex-girlfriend is now wearing a white bra, light-blue jeans, and army boots. She reminds him of Sarah, the morning after they first had sex. Michael has idolized Sarah since long before he met her and the real Sarah far exceeds his wildest dreams. Many of the women who know Michael have tried to win his heart because of his title and privileges, but Sarah is the only woman who loves him for who he is. Sarah is the only woman that Michael truly loves and no amount of pain would make him betray her, especially as she twice saved his life at Carluccio's.

"I love you, Michael. Please don't let Niall do this to you," says Sheila.

Michael stays silent and Niall punches him again. Michael doesn't react. He doesn't want to give them the satisfaction of seeing him in pain. Just this morning, Sarah told him she would die for him and Michael believes her. The only thing Michael can do now is prove to Sarah that he's not just willing to die for her, but also willing to die a long and torturous death for her. Michael hopes that somehow, someway, Sarah will know about this ultimate sacrifice for her. The only regret Michael feels is that he can't say goodbye in person to Sarah, his gallant darling.

'*Slán go fóill… mo ghile mear*,' mumbles Michael as he closes his eyes, imagining that Sarah is in front of him.

Sheila starts to get angry.

"How the fuck can ye call her *'mo ghile mear'*? That nickname was supposed to be for me and for me only!" snaps Sheila, in an accent that suddenly sounds Irish.

Michael stays silent.

"She's not even Irish, for heaven's sake! Why would ye even *consider* calling her that?"

Michael's still silent.

"*I'm* supposed to be yer *'ghile mear'*!" yells Sheila, getting even more emotional.

Michael keeps silent.

"Everyone gave me a slagging when they heard ye'd started calling her that too, ye know!" yells Sheila.

Michael doesn't react, but in her anger, Sheila thinks she sees him smirk. She finally loses it.

"Do yer worst, Niall!" orders Sheila.

Niall's instantly excited. "Open yer eyes!"

Michael doesn't react.

"I won't ask ye again!"

Michael's closed eyes don't even flicker. Niall takes out his Gerber knife and sticks it into Michael's left eye. He then pulls it out and blood flows from the hole as if Michael is crying bloody tears. Michael opens his remaining eye and sees that Sheila has started crying.

"Do ye have any last words before ye're unable to gob off?" asks Niall, grinning sadistically.

Michael looks around with his remaining eye and sees a board with nails hammered through and a wood-saw that they're probably going to use to cut him up. He then looks at the small knife in Niall's hand. There are a few things he could say, but he finally chooses to quote Lord Henry William Paget, The Earl of Uxbridge, the commander of the Anglo-Allied Army Cavalry Corps during the Battle of Waterloo. One of the last cannon shots of the battle hit Lord Uxbridge's right leg, necessitating its amputation. There's an anecdote that he said something in the middle of that dreadful surgical procedure.

"The knife appears somewhat blunt," quotes Michael.

Niall laughs, but Sheila cries and leaves the room. Niall then turns on heavy metal music. He likes listening to something loud while he does his 'job'. He wipes his knife on Michael's shirt before stowing it and then puts on a pair of brass knuckles. He starts hitting Michael repeatedly.

Not long after, Michael starts screaming…


21:48 GMT
Saturday September 26, 2026
Kempston Warehouse
Islington, Liverpool, England

Several hours later…

That night, Patrick finally arrives in Liverpool. He can faintly hear heavy metal music when he steps out of his car and takes the lift to the second floor. His men won't make eye contact with him when they see him walking by towards his office. From afar, Patrick can see Sheila cowering outside the office. He wonders why his daughter doesn't have a shirt on, but is even more surprised when he sees Niall's using his board. Patrick knows that Niall only uses a board to finish off men, so he runs towards him. Michael's barely alive, but unconscious. Before Niall hits him again, Patrick takes out his pistol and gives Michael's head a double tap. Patrick's S&W Model M&P22 pistol has a suppressor and he uses Eley Subsonic Hollow .22lr bullets, used by professional assassins all over the world because they're the most silent.

"What the fuck do ye think ye're doing?" yells Patrick, furiously pointing his pistol at Niall.

"What the fuck, Paddy?" asks Niall angrily. His whole body is covered with Michael's blood and bits and pieces of his face.

"I specifically told ye *not* to snatch the SAS bloke! What the fuck is going on here?"

"Ask Frag and Sheila! They're the ones ye assigned to do the snatch, remember? I'm just doing what Sheila told me to do," protests Niall.

"Fuck!" curses Patrick as he leaves the room. "Sheila, what the fuck? I thought I told ye to snatch Sarah, not Michael."

Sheila stands up and hugs her *daidí*, tears in her eyes. "I'm sorry, *Daidí*. The bitch wasn't home and he was the only one in the apartment."

Sheila tells him everything from the start, from her relationship with

Michael to the part when they snatched him. Patrick can't stay angry with his daughter, even though she made a fatal mistake that could probably cost him his whole organization. His guilt for abandoning her when she was a baby always catches up with him.

When he was the RSM of the Royal Irish Regiment and Sheila joined, Patrick instantly recognized her as his daughter. He took Sheila under his wing and introduced her to Muireann. He finally felt he had a family when he saw that Muireann and Sheila clicked instantly and loved each other very much. Patrick and Muireann taught Sheila everything, and both were immensely proud of her when she passed Selection and became a special forces operative.

"Go home and I'll take care of this," says Patrick softy. "I'll catch up with ye and we shall all go to Jakarta tomorrow morning, all right?"

"Aye, *Daidí*," says Sheila. She starts walking unevenly towards the lift.

"Be careful driving home," says her *daidí*, "and put some fucking clothes on!"

Sheila doesn't answer him. Patrick returns to Niall, still grumbling for not being the one to finish off his victim.

"Go clean yerself up while I take care of yer fucking mess," orders Patrick.

Niall does what he's told. Patrick sees Carraig and waves him over. He has to teach him a lesson for failing.

"Cut him up so we can feed him to the fucking pigs," orders Patrick.

"I'm no fucking butcher, Paddy!" protests Carraig, his pale face turning even paler.

"I don't give a shite! Take the saw and cut off his fucking head, arms, and legs before we send him to the pigs," orders Patrick. He then sees Gwilliam coming out of the toilet. "Gwilliam, help him out cutting up Michael."

"Hey! I'm not the one who fucked up," protests Gwilliam.

Patrick gives him a deadly look, instantly shutting him up. "I'll have the other fellas decommission this place. Once ye're finished, ye can come with us to Jakarta tomorrow morning."

Patrick knows that the SAS will eventually find this location so he orders his men to pack everything for smuggling to Jakarta. After spending two and a half hours there, Patrick and Niall start their return journey to Sandalwood Farm... not knowing that the only person still breathing there is an MI5 officer.

00:59 GMT
Sunday September 27, 2026
Sandalwood Farm
Nether Alderley, Cheshire, England

On Congleton Rd, Patrick sees dozens of police cars, ambulances, and even a police helicopter heading towards his house. Rory has managed to conceal their HQ for years and Patrick wonders how the coppers finally found it. He doesn't know whether Sheila or Steve have been apprehended or not and this worries him.

Patrick calls Carraig and Gwilliam at Liverpool, but they don't answer. Assuming the worst has happened, there's nothing more he can do except vanish and head to Jakarta. He destroys his smartphone in case they try to track him.

00:59 GMT
Sunday September 27, 2026
Kempston Warehouse
Islington, Liverpool, England

"Boss, could you please unload and make safe your weapons?" asks Al carefully.

Sarah gets angry with herself for neglecting the most basic of firearms safety and immediately unloads all her weapons. She doesn't feel anything at the moment. She knows this is because there are a lot of things she must do first and adrenaline is still surging through her system. But she also realizes that the emotions will hit in a few minutes so she starts concentrating on the work at hand.

Sarah observes that all the windows are mined with IEDs. If the assault force had made entry from the roof and abseiled through the windows, the blasts would've claimed many casualties. As EOD experts, Sarah and her men have the skills and experience to dispose them, but they didn't bring an ABS with them. Sarah faces her team, who already look devastated, knowing they've failed to save Michael's life.

Sarah finds her command voice again. "Right! Go on stag to cover all entrances on the ground floor. Use the lift because there is still a UXO on the stairs leading to the second floor. Al, please call and update your CO once everyone is on stag and tell him to have one of the EODs handle the IEDs and the UXO. Carry on!"

The four men freeze and look confused. Instead of jumping to action, they just stand there, looking back at Sarah with glassy eyes and open mouths like complete dickheads. Sarah finally loses it and fully reverts back to her role as an Indonesian special forces commander.

"Carry on, *jullie klootzakken!*" yells Sarah, absolutely furious.

Sarah cuffs Dave and George roughly on their heads, cursing all the while at them in Dutch. She doesn't get the chance to hit the others, who finally snap out of it and hurriedly execute her orders. While pushing them on towards the lift, she briefly checks the dead bodies to see if she recognizes anybody from James's files. This proves impossible as almost all have had their heads blown off. Her men can only watch her work as the door of the lift starts closing.

A minute later, Al's voice is heard on her headset. "Charlie, this is Alpha. All call signs in position."

"Charlie roger," answers Sarah. Her command voice is so strong that the men under her command have to fight the urge to stand to attention.

Through her headset, Sarah can hear Al brief Cormac by phone, but she ignores him and concentrates on her work. After checking the bodies, she finally goes back to Michael. For a few minutes, Sarah can do nothing but look. Michael's skull is clearly visible and his body is a complete mess. Right in the middle of his forehead, Sarah sees two small gunshot wounds, probably from a .22 calibre pistol. Sarah checks the back of his head and sees no exit wound, meaning the bullets mushroomed perfectly inside his brain. Sarah looks around and sees a wooden board with nails hammered through, still covered in blood and flesh. Sarah can't even imagine the pain and suffering her fiancé felt before they finally ended his misery.

In the corner of the room, there's a sound system and TV that shows images from their CCTV. They're extremely lucky that no one was watching when they made entry. The floor and walls are covered in plastic sheets, decorated with blood, skin, and flesh. There are plastic bags on the floor and a couple of them have Michael's legs wrapped up inside. There's little blood from the stump, meaning that at least his legs were cut off post-mortem. Seeing the wood-saw still embedded in his shoulder, Sarah concludes that they were in the middle of cutting Michael up before feeding him to the pigs. Sarah checks the *rigor mortis* and guesses his temperature compared to the room temperature. Michael's body is already cold, but not overly stiff, meaning he was probably killed in the last three hours, about the same time Sarah started her recce. If Niall began his work immediately after getting him here, this means Michael was tortured for at least eight hours before someone finally finished him off.

Sarah knows that there was nothing she could've done to save him, but she still regrets not getting to her flat quicker, even though if she had've, she would probably be disembowelled right now next to Michael. The words 'what if' might haunt her for the rest of her life. Sarah feels the adrenaline leaving her system and she's getting more emotional by the second, but there's one more job she must do. She takes out her smartphone and calls Broussard, who has been trying unsuccessfully to reach her.

01:17 GMT
Sunday September 27, 2026
Sandalwood Farm
Nether Alderley, Cheshire, England

"You called, Chief?"

"Sarah, you're on speaker. I'm still at Sandalwood Farm with the rest of the team. James said that you and the SAS have deployed to Liverpool to assault their warehouse. Could you please send the latest sitrep?" orders Broussard in Steve's room.

The other team members are helping with the SSE. They stop what they're doing to listen in.

"Another drug factory and distribution centre for England is here," reports Sarah. "The SAS and I have secured it, but there are no signs of any senior members. They must've buggered off before we began the assault. The rest of the SAS are on their way here."

"Right, we'll be on our way in a few minutes. I'll have Paul coordinate with the Merseyside Police. Did you find Michael there?" asks Broussard expectantly.

"Affirmative... he's here."

"Thank God!" says Broussard, relieved. "How's he doing?"

"He's dead, Chief... tortured," answers Sarah, her voice starting to break up.

Broussard is silent for a few seconds. "Oh, fuck no! Fuck no! Fuck! Fuck..."

The call disconnects when Broussard throws his smartphone into a wall and then sits down crying. The others do the same.

The Interpol Incident Response Team has once again lost one of its finest members.

01:19 GMT
Sunday September 27, 2026
Kempston Warehouse
Islington, Liverpool, England

Sarah's legs feel weak and she falls on her knees in front of Michael's body. She stays like that for a few moments, looking at what's left of her fiancé. She quickly prays 'Padre Nuestro' and 'Ave Maria' before she's too emotional to do so. She forces herself to leave the room and can only sit down on the floor, hugging her rifle.

The grief starts coming in waves. She tries hard to cry silently so her men don't hear her crying through her headset. She doesn't know that her men are doing the same thing. From afar, she finally hears the distinct sounds of a Chinook helicopter. Cormac and the rest of B Squadron have finally arrived.

"Charlie, this is Zero. Radio check," says Cormac.

"Charlie roger," answers Sarah.

"Charlie, this is Zero. Send your sitrep," orders Cormac. He already received a situation report from Al, but he wants to hear it directly from Sarah.

Sarah sobs as she reports to Cormac. "Zero, this is Charlie... the stronghold is secured... Yankee is on the second floor... IEDs are on the second floor windows... A UXO is on the stairs leading to the second floor... The roof has not been cleared yet... *Do not* abseil or land on the roof! I say again, *do not* abseil or land on the roof! Elements of B Squadron are on stag on the ground floor... the Interpol team with the Merseyside Police are mobile to the stronghold... heads up for blue-on-blue... over."

Cormac is silent for a few moments. "Zero roger, we are ETA two mikes."

"Charlie roger," answers Sarah.

Sarah stands and tries to wipe the tears from her eyes. She is too sad to stop crying so she gives it up and uses the lift to go downstairs. Sarah's embarrassed to deliver a report to Cormac while sobbing, but she can't help it.

"Charlie descending to the ground floor via lift," she reports through her headset.

"Roger that," answers her team.

On the ground floor, Sarah observes that her men can't look at her and avert their eyes when she looks at them with tears streaming down her cheeks. Sarah knows they must be embarrassed to see their commander unable to control her emotions.

The heli is hovering next to the building. It can't land on the narrow street so the men fast-ropes down. A few seconds later, Cormac enters the stronghold with St John directly behind him carrying an ABS and EOD kit. St John has brought the same kit he'd taken with him when he'd secured Swan's Mill with Al the month before.

"Zero complete and I have control. Sinjin, your call sign is Sierra. Charlie, could you please lead Sierra to the IEDs and UXO?" orders Cormac.

Sarah nods and helps St John into his ABS. Without her realizing it, she has stopped crying. She has her orders and there's work to be done. Cormac heads towards the men. Sarah sees her men turn off their headsets and meet with Cormac to debrief him, while the rest of B Squadron cordon the area. Sarah knows that her men will criticize her leadership while they were under her command. She regrets treating them like they were her men in Indonesia, especially as they didn't deserve it. Sarah keeps looking at them, but they try hard not to meet her eyes. They're extremely emotional as they debrief Cormac and keep looking away when they see Sarah looking towards them. This adds to Sarah's sorrow, though she can understand their behaviour. She too would be disappointed if her commander failed to lead her properly.

Sarah and St John take the lift to the second floor and she directs him to the IEDs on the window in the office area. St John asks Sarah to wait by the lift while he disposes of the IEDs. Sarah sits on the floor accompanied by the X-Rays she'd killed a few minutes earlier. The pungent reek of urine, faeces, burnt flesh and hair makes her gag.

As he enters the office room and sees what's left of Michael, St John curses out loud and starts crying. His cry is contagious and Sarah starts crying again. St John keeps cursing and sobbing as he finishes his job. "All call signs… this is Sierra… IEDs secured… White-7-2… White-6-2…"

"Charlie roger," says Sarah. She stands up and walks towards the White side.

"Zero roger," says Cormac.

Sarah directs St John to the UXO's location on the stairs and sits down on the floor in front of the office area. She hugs her rifle as if it could comfort her. After their battle at Carluccio's, Michael calmed and comforted her. He can't do that now because she failed to rescue him.

Sarah will be held responsible for this failure because she was in command. Tears start streaming from her eyes again, not just for losing someone she loves very much, but also because she failed the mission. She failed despite having the best special forces operatives in the world under her command. She has never failed a mission before, making this failure doubly painful.

BOOOM!

The grenade blast sends Sarah jumping to help St John. She sees the wooden stairway collapse to the ground floor and St John's hanging for dear life on what's left of the rails. Just before the rails collapse, Sarah manages to grab his ABS. She struggles to drag him to safety. This proves extremely difficult for Sarah, because the ABS St John is wearing is almost as heavy as he is. The lift opens and Cormac and her men sprint towards them, just as she manages to secure St John. Sarah takes off his helmet. He's still conscious, but pink blood is starting to flow from his mouth and nose, meaning that St John's suffering from 'blast lung'. She must open his ABS and have him lie face-down so he won't drown in his own blood.

Sarah's still trying to open the ABS when the others reach them. Sarah backs away so St John can receive medical attention. Once she sees that he's in good hands, she returns to her original place and hugs her rifle again. She can't cry because of the sudden surge of adrenaline. The lift opens once more and several troopers run over, carrying a stretcher and medical kits.

A few minutes later, Cormac goes into the room where Michael is. After only a few seconds, he exits the room and sits beside Sarah. She can see that Cormac is as sad as she is, but he's holding back his tears. They sit in silence watching St John being taken care of. They hear another heli approaching from afar and police sirens heading towards their location. Sarah feels the adrenaline leaving her and the grief is starting to overwhelm her.

"I'm sorry, Mac," says Sarah.

"For what?" asks Cormac.

"I couldn't save him... this time..."

Cormac is silent for a few seconds before he responds. "You can't save everyone, but I saw you save Sinjin's life. If I hadn't known anything else about your actions today... that would've been enough."

"But I failed..." says Sarah, starting to cry again.

"Your mission was to lead the team and do whatever it took to save Michael. You did what you were ordered to do to the best of your ability," says Cormac.

Sarah closes her eyes, but the tears keep on streaming. When they deployed to Liverpool, Sarah was confident in her ability to lead her team. It turns out her leadership ability was nowhere near Michael's. She was in command of this mission and she failed. "I apologize for disobeying your order, Mac. I'll take full responsibility for the failure of the mission... so please don't court-martial or RTU the men.... Please, Mac... I was in command... and they were just following my orders..."

Cormac is silent once again. What Sarah and her team did was intolerable. In wartime, those kinds of insubordination could get them hanged. Cormac nods slowly and his eyes finally gloss over. "You did the right thing... If you had followed my orders, they probably would've cut him up, removed him, and sent him to the pig farm by now... and we would never have found him..."

Sarah feels some relief knowing that Cormac won't punish her teammates. She doesn't want the careers of her teammates to suffer because she made such an amateurish commander. She's amazed with herself. She was trained by the SAS for only a day and a half. How could she possibly think she'd be able to lead a team of the finest special forces unit in the world in a real operation? Did she really think she was in the same league as Michael? She suddenly realizes she's still just a policewoman from Indonesia. Sarah's disappointed with herself for letting her teammates down. She also deeply regrets treating them so badly.

"I guess the men are disappointed with me now…" says Sarah, head bowing down.

Cormac frowns and looks at her quizzically.

"I failed the mission and I haven't led the men properly, have I?" asks Sarah.

The CO of the SAS is lost for words and can only give Sarah an incredulous look. Before he can respond, the lift opens and the Interpol team finally arrive along with the Merseyside Police. Sarah hurriedly gives Cormac her rifle and her kit and then runs towards Liz, who's already running towards her. They hug and cry hysterically in the middle of the floor while the others secure the crime scene.

Cormac escorts his men carrying St John on a stretcher towards the lift. He takes out his smartphone to call someone and can only watch the two women cry hysterically. The B Squadron men with him can only stare as they pass by. Sarah thinks that the SAS men must be disappointed and disgusted with her behaviour. As an officer, she's required to be fully in control of her emotions at all times. Besides being overwhelmed with grief, she's also embarrassed for not being able to control her emotions. As tough as she is, Sarah is only human.

A few minutes later, a police car takes Sarah and Liz to Liz's flat at the Dreamhouse Apartments. Liz will take Sarah in while her flat's still considered a crime scene.

10:15 WIB (GMT+7)
Sunday September 27, 2026
Terminal 3, Soekarno-Hatta International Airport
Kota Tangerang, Tangerang, Banten

At the airport, Santoso picks up Rory Hanrahan.

"*Apa kabar*, Santoso?" greets Rory. *How are you, Santoso?*

"*Baik-baik saja, pak* Rory," replies Santoso in his usual friendly manner. *Fine,* pak *Rory.*

"*Bagaimana keluarga?*" *How's the family?*

"*Istri saya sedang demam, pak,*" replies Santoso without changing his expression. *My wife has a fever, pak.*

"*Oh, semoga cepat sembuh ya. Bisa tolong bawa bagasi saya? Saya harus ke kamar kecil terlebih dahulu,*" says Rory without missing a beat. *Oh, I hope she gets well soon. Could you please take my luggage? I have to go to the loo.*

"*Baik, pak* Rory," says Santoso.

Rory leaves him with his luggage and heads back towards the terminal. As he turns around, he observes several people in mufti eyeing them. Predictably, some of them start following Santoso to his car and only one stays back to follow Rory. After exiting the loo and terminal, Rory unexpectedly hails a taxi. He smirks when he sees his tail frantically calling someone on his smartphone. Rory asks the taxi driver to go around town, which the driver happily obliges because it will rack up his fare. The taxi driver doesn't know and doesn't care that Rory is conducting counter-surveillance drills.

A few hours later, and after Rory has changed taxis half a dozen times, he finally receives a text from Santoso. Rory breathes a sigh of relief when he reads it. The text reads '*istri saya sudah sehat*', which translate into 'my wife is now healthy'. This means that he managed to lose the people following him. If Santoso had texted '*saya berhasil lolos dari mereka*', which translates into 'I've managed to lose them', this would've meant that he had been caught and sent the text under duress. Santoso is good at his job and Rory makes a mental note to give him a big raise.

Rory goes to the Central Park Mall where Santoso is waiting near the entrance. To be extra safe, Santoso conducts another counter-surveillance drill before finally reaching the house. On arriving, Rory immediately calls a meeting with Frank, Richard, and a senior Cartel member named Brian Turner. Brian was once a captain in the Royal Logistics Corps, but took the Army 2020 package. He's groomed to be part of the organization's top echelon and will be responsible for exporting their goods to Australia and distributing them to the local market. Unlike most Cartel members, Brian is English. Rory can see all three of them are badly shaken.

"What's the whole fucking story?" asks Rory.

"Sheila fucked up and snatched the SAS bloke, she did," says Frank, his Welsh accent sounding more pronounced than usual. "The SAS somehow found out about her and they raided our HQ and also Kempston. Paddy and Niall are on the way here, everyone else is fucking dead."

"Everyone?" asks Rory, incredulously. "Steve? Sheila? Gwilliam? Frag?"

"They're fucking dead, Rory!" says Frank.

"Jesus fucking Christ!" curses Rory. "When will Paddy arrive?"

Richard looks at a calendar. "They should get here Friday afternoon."

Rory's the most senior in the organization until Patrick gets here. He has to make lots of decisions before the INP and that policewoman finally find them.

"Leftenant!"

Lieutenant Richard Callaghan stands to attention. "Sir!"

"We'll have to relocate because it's only a matter of time before the INP find this place. Could ye please find us another location for our HQ and factory somewhere in Central Java? Make sure it's a highly defendable stronghold."

"Aye, sir!" says Richard. He stands at ease.

"Leftenant-Colonel!"

Lieutenant-Colonel Frank Llywelyn stands to attention. "Sir!"

"Ye should halt the construction of the escape tunnel. Ye are now 3 i/c and besides handling the supply chain, ye're also in charge of logistics and administration. For now, could ye please coordinate with the suppliers regarding our relocation plans?"

"Yes, sir!" says Frank. He grins as he stands at ease, happy being appointed Steve's successor.

"Captain!"

Captain Brian Turner stands to attention. "Sir!"

"I'm promoting you. Since we've lost our export to Ireland, could ye please expedite the distribution of our product to the local market?"

"Yes, sir!" says Brian. He stands at ease, grinning broadly. This promotion means he's now a part of The Cartel's top echelon.

"We should also beef up security and put one of the longs in the guardhouse so Santoso can fire some bursts for early warning if the coppers raid us. This is just in case he doesn't have the chance to call us first. Leftenant!"

Richard stands to attention again. "Sir!"

"Could ye please brief Santoso on this?" orders Rory.

"Aye, sir!" says Richard. He stands at ease.

"Back to work, lads. Falling out, to-the-riiight… Fall out!" orders Rory.

They fall out to the right without saluting because they have no headdress on. Rory must execute Phase Five, which means gathering intel on the INP's top men and women. If they can't be bribed, Niall will take care of them and their families. The main priority is to snatch the most dangerous of them - the head of Badan Narkotika National (National Narcotics Agency) and Police Brigadier General Prasetyo, the head of Densus-88. To be on the safe side, they'll take their families too.

But first, Rory must concentrate on gathering intel on Sarah Dharmawan and her family. That policewoman helped kill six of his closest friends and hundreds of their men. Rory wants to make sure Sarah and her whole family get what they deserve.

10:54 GMT
Sunday September 27, 2026
Dreamhouse Apartments
Deansgate, Manchester, England

Sarah wakes up alone in Liz's flat. She just lies there on Liz's bed, contemplating her fate. After a few minutes, she looks around. She sees an Old Bushmills Irish whiskey on the nightstand with a note from Liz saying it's for her. Sarah has to suppress the urge to drain it in one sitting. She checks her smartphone and finds out that Broussard has ordered her to take a warm-down period. Although it's a Sunday, Sarah wants to work so she can ignore her sorrow. She grabs her tablet to fill out the AAR form. It takes almost the whole day for her to do it, as remembering what happened to Michael makes her cry. Only when she's finished with her job does she start drinking the whiskey.

Broussard and his team are in a meeting with officers from the NCA, Cheshire Constabulary, and Merseyside Police. The amount of dead bodies at the crime scene is stretching the capacity for both constabularies. Sarah's AAR arrives by e-mail to all members of the Interpol team. Broussard and the others read it in disbelief. Sarah led four soldiers of the SAS killing up to eighty members of the Irish Drug Cartel. It's a phenomenal achievement!

When Liz returns to her flat, her teammate's already asleep, an empty whiskey bottle on the nightstand.

06:13 GMT
Monday September 28, 2026
Dreamhouse Apartments
Deansgate, Manchester, England

"Good morning, Sarah," says Liz, smiling. "Fancy some breakfast?"

Sarah wakes up and sees that Liz has cooked a full English breakfast for both. Her stomach rumbles as she hasn't eaten in two days and she has a severe hangover from the whiskey. She struggles to return Liz's smile. "Good morning, Liz. Thank you very much for this… and for the whiskey."

"Ye're welcome. Do ye need something for yer head?" asks Liz.

"No, thank you," replies Sarah. The events of these past few days have made her hate drugs even more.

While having breakfast, they talk about everything except work. Sarah's grateful that Liz doesn't ask her how she feels or other stupid questions that would remind her about these past couple of days. Even so, Liz looks just as sad as she does.

A few hours later, they go to GMP HQ. In the Interpol area, her teammates shake her hand and hug her. She then enters Broussard's office. Her commander has visibly aged since she last saw him a couple of days ago. This is the second time he's lost a team member and he must be feeling incredibly stressed out. Sarah knows on top of that he's worked all night and all through the weekend.

"First, my condolences to you. I know you and Michael had become very close so this must be a terrible blow for you," says Broussard.

"Thank you, Chief," says Sarah softly.

"Michael's body…" Broussard has to stop a few moments to compose himself. "Michael's body is currently being held by the Liverpool Coroner's Office for autopsy. They will release his body within three working days."

"Funeral arrangements?"

"Michael's parents has been notified and they have requested Michael be buried at the SAS Cemetery across the road from their barracks at Credenhill. The burial is planned for this Friday and the SAS will arrange everything. There will be a church service in the morning inside their barracks and a military funeral at the cemetery afterwards. The whole team will attend, of course. My secretary has arranged for us to go there by train on Thursday evening and we will stay at The Green Dragon Hotel."

Sarah can only nod.

"Second, because MACP is still in effect and you were officially seconded to the SAS, all of your kills were considered 'lawful killing' by the authorities. You won't have to worry about the killings of Steve Dunbar and Sheila Neeson, nor the kills at the warehouse in Liverpool," says Broussard. He looks uncomfortable, because what Sarah and the SAS did was close to murder, especially as most of the people killed were shot while sleeping.

"Third, I recommended you for a George Cross. The Home Secretary won't be awarding you that exactly, but he has upgraded your KGM to a George Medal. You will be entitled to use the post-nominal letters GM."

Sarah doesn't feel any joy whatsoever in being invested with the GM, even though it's the second highest award for a civilian. She failed her mission and failed to save her fiancé, and she feels she doesn't deserve anything.

"Fourth, as of this morning, your apartment's status as a crime scene has been lifted. I had a company licensed in trauma and crime-scene cleaning take care of cleaning your apartment. It should be done by now so you can return there this afternoon. The Cartel knows where you live now so the GMP will heavily patrol your area as a precaution. You might want to consider moving."

Sarah only nods again.

"And finally, Cormac has informed me that as of today, your secondment to the SAS has concluded and you have been returned to the Interpol IRT. We still have a lot of work to do, but I'd prefer you take a few days' leave of absence."

"Please don't make me stay at home, Chief," says Sarah, almost inaudibly.

Broussard looks at her for a while and finally nods. He then receives a text on his smartphone.

"James and Paul have prepared the results of the raid on Sandalwood Farm and the warehouse at Liverpool. Let's go and meet them," invites Broussard, standing up.

Sarah follows him into the meeting room. After everyone takes their seats, the two empty seats reserved for their slain teammates stand out starkly. Paul stares at the empty seat beside Liz for several moments before starting his presentation.

Paul tells them that the price of MDMA has skyrocketed throughout the UK and Republic of Ireland. The price is getting higher each day as the stock in the hands of the distributors and dealers slowly decreases. It appears The Cartel is no longer active in the UK and Republic of Ireland. The NCA and the territorial police forces are monitoring the price. If the price ever comes down again, this means The Cartel has returned or another criminal organization has taken over the MDMA market.

James presents the results of the SSEs on both sites. Sarah and the SAS killed fifty-two narcoterrorists at Sandalwood Farm, including Sheila Iona Neeson and Steve Dunbar. Sheila is considered a member of The Cartel's top echelon because of her family relationship with Patrick and Steve Dunbar. At Liverpool, Sarah and the SAS managed to kill twenty-six narcoterrorists, including Carraig 'Frag' O'Lenihan and Gwilliam O'Donnel. At the time, Sarah couldn't recognize them because their heads were blown off, but DNA testing shows that they've killed two more senior members.

This means that Sarah and four SAS men eliminated seventy-eight narcoterrorists in a single night, including four of the Irish Drug Cartel's senior members. Unlike after Operation Crankshaft, none of the team members are happy with the news, because this extraordinary achievement was achieved at the cost of one of their own.

The analysis of phones recovered from the two sites failed to reveal the location of the other senior members. Just like the Interpol team's own SOP, The Cartel probably changes smartphones and numbers when one of them is killed. At Sandalwood Farm, James found evidence that Patrick Dunbar, Niall Schroeder, and other senior members had stayed there. They've most likely escaped from the UK and will now be on their way to Indonesia. MI5 is trying to find out how they managed to escape the UK.

Grenades, Claymore mines, and other explosives were found at Sandalwood Farm and the Kempston warehouse. An EOD team from the SAS found the roof of Sandalwood Farm and the Kempston warehouse filled with IEDs. This means that if they had assaulted from the roof, there would've been heavy casualties among the SAS. They found numerous AK-47 and M16A2 assault rifles. James is sure The Cartel has hundreds of M4 Carbines, but none of them were recovered. The worst-case scenario is that they've already been smuggled to Indonesia.

The results of the SSE cannot determine the location of their drug factories in Indonesia, but they now have the names and addresses of all The Cartel's distributors and dealers across the UK and Republic of Ireland. Today, James will give the list to all concerned territorial police so the distributors and dealers can be apprehended. James also sends the list to Cormac, currently at Credenhill. Paul will coordinate with the territorial police forces to apprehend all of The Cartel's associates at exactly the same time. This is to prevent any one of them getting tipped off. They will start the massive arrests early on Wednesday morning.

Once the distributors and dealers have been apprehended, the Interpol Incident Response Team will have completed the bulk of their mission, leaving it only up to Sarah to find The Cartel's drug factory in Indonesia. Although Sarah has played a huge part in eliminating The Cartel in the UK and Republic of Ireland, she's disappointed being the only one not to have achieved her primary mission, locating their drug factory in Indonesia. Because the supply chain to Ireland has been broken, their factory in Indonesia will probably continue to operate distributing goods to the local market. The INP must find it as soon as possible, before The Cartel start their narcoterrorism in Indonesia.

Sarah spends the rest of the day making a report for NCB Indonesia while her teammates return to their units to lead the arrests of the distributors and dealers. Sarah is left alone in the office. Unconsciously, her eyes keep glancing towards the desk beside her, as if hoping Michael will suddenly sit there. Cormac suddenly texts her and asks what time they'll arrive in Hereford and where they'll stay. Sarah lets him know that the Interpol team will arrive on Thursday afternoon and stay at The Green Dragon Hotel. Cormac doesn't respond to her text, which makes Sarah briefly wonder.

Then she receives an e-mail from NCB Indonesia. They've sent her a list of all the foreign companies located along the Mayor Oking Jayaatmaja road. NCB Indonesia also tells her the Bogor Police Precinct is checking the companies one by one. They are also trying to locate the lorry driver from PT. Horizon Turbines and Propulsions, who has suddenly disappeared.

The next couple of days, Sarah receives regular reports from her teammates. The distributors and dealers were arrested without a hitch. On Wednesday afternoon, Sarah receives the final report that, from the list of 1,431 people, 1,299 have been successfully apprehended.

The West Mercia Police and Dorset Police are on the lookout for the remaining 132 distributors and dealers. Both of those territorial police forces are disappointed to be the only ones failing to arrest the distributors and dealers on their list. They don't know, and will never know, that the 132 they're looking for were all simultaneously snatched by groups of four men.

The fate of the distributors and dealers is never known... except to the men who snatched them.

11:21 WIB (GMT+7)
Wednesday September 30, 2026
PT. Westershire Chemicals Manufacture Indonesia
Citeureup, Bogor, West Java

An Indonesian policeman ranked Brigadir Satu (Briptu) from the Bogor Police Precinct enters the main gate. An employee greets him at the security post.

"*Selamat siang*," greets the policeman, giving the man a salute. *Good afternoon.*

"*Selamat siang, pak*," returns Santoso, unconsciously returning his salute.

"I'm Briptu Nano Suwarno from the Bogor Police Precinct. May I meet with the head of this factory? I tried calling for an appointment, but there was no answer."

"For what purpose, *pak*?"

# THE POLICEWOMAN

"I'm assigned to check all factories in this area," answers Briptu Nano. "Here's my assignment letter from the Bogor Police Precinct."

"Our factory is a mess, *pak*. Does it have to be today?"

"*Iya, pak*, I have to check every company on my list," says Briptu Nano, showing him the list.

"Wow, that's quite a lot! There's nothing in our factory, *pak*. Why don't you just tell your superiors that you've already checked it? Give him my number and if he calls, I'll tell him you've done your job. How about it, *pak*? How about we just 86 it?" 86 (*delapan-enam*) is a code word Indonesians use when they're trying to bribe a policeman.

"I'm sorry, *pak*, I have to check this factory."

Santoso keeps trying to bribe the policeman, but he's having none of it. Briptu Nano needs the money, but his commander gave him a direct order to check each one of those factories on his list.

"I'm sorry, *pak*, I still have to check this factory," says Briptu Nano firmly.

"Let me call my boss first. Okay, *pak*?"

"Sure, go ahead," answers Briptu Nano.

Santoso goes inside the security post and closes the door. He calls Rory with his smartphone.

"*Ya*, Santoso?" answers Rory in Bahasa Indonesia.

"There's a policeman out front, *pak* Rory. He wants to see you and he wants to check the factory," reports Santoso.

"How many are there?" asks Rory.

"Just one, *pak* Rory. I already tried to bribe him many times, but he wouldn't accept it."

Rory is silent for a few seconds. Having a copper show up means the INP suspects their factory is in this area. As he expected, it's now only a matter of time before the INP finds them. Rory calls Richard and Brian to handle the copper. He also orders Frank to call the distributors and dealers in the UK, especially those that have military experience, and make them core members of The Cartel. Rory plans to send them to Jakarta to reinforce his team because he doesn't want to be too dependent on the local workers.

"Okay then, we'll just have to execute the SOP for this situation. *Lanjutkan!*" orders Rory. *Carry on!*

"*Siap, Komandan!*" answers Santoso. *Yes, sir!*

Santoso exits the security post. "*Pak* Nano, can you wait here for five minutes?"

"Why?"

"Our office is a mess, *pak*, let us clean it up a bit before you meet with my boss."

"Oh, okay," answers Briptu Nano.

Santoso and Britpu Nano sit and chit chat at the bench outside the security post. Five minutes later, Santoso receives a text to tell their guest he may enter the office. The policeman rides his worn-down motorcycle towards the office. The road there has only one lane, with a forest block to either side. The road forks and circles around the whole factory area, surrounded by high walls. The two-storey factory looks huge and formidable. Briptu Nano enters the lobby and sees a foreigner across the room, giving him a friendly smile. The policeman returns his smile and walks towards him.

The last thing Briptu Nano sees is the foreigner's smile turn nasty. A bullet from an S&W Model M&P22 pistol with a sound suppressor enters the back of his head. Brian shot him from behind while Richard diverted his attention from the front. Brian moves forward and empties his pistol into the convulsing policeman. After he's dead, Richard frisks him and Brian calls seven of their core members, Jason, Errol, Vinnie, Bert, Chris, Tommy, and Liam, to clean the office and bury the dead body in the forest.

Briptu Nano Suwarno's body will be found a couple of weeks from now. He died on duty, leaving behind a son and a pregnant wife.

08:58 GMT
Thursday October 1, 2026
Interpol Manchester
Central Park, Manchester, England

A day before Michael's funeral, the team is invited to a meeting by Broussard.

"I have some good news and some bad news. Contrary to custom, I will deliver the good news first. Since all drug manufacturing plants and distribution centres of The Cartel have been decommissioned and the remaining members have buggered off, most likely to Indonesia, as of today His Majesty's Government has decided to lift MACP. Besides successfully assisting the MoD in locating The Cartel members and decommissioning their drug factories and distribution centres, we have also successfully supported the constabularies in apprehending almost all distributors and dealers of MDMA throughout the UK and the Republic of Ireland. That is a grand total of 1,299 arrests. We have accomplished the mission the Home Office and ICPO-Interpol gave us and all of this is because I have an extraordinary team under my command. This is, by far, the best Incident Response Team I have ever commanded and I thank you very much for your work on this mission. You will each receive a Letter of Recommendation from ICPO-Interpol HQ for your support."

Everyone claps their hands, but it doesn't sound that cheerful. Everyone can clearly see the sorrow on Broussard's face, even before he delivers the bad news.

"And because we have succeeded in our mission, ICPO-Interpol HQ has decided that this Incident Response Team will be disbanded by the end of this week. By Monday next week, you will all be required to report to your previous units and I've been recalled back to Lyon to handle another team for another mission."

Everyone is stunned. They knew that they would be disbanded someday, but not so abruptly.

"But I still haven't accomplished my primary mission, Chief, and I still need intel support from the UK to find their factory in Indonesia," protests Sarah.

"I have made the exact same argument to my superiors at Interpol and to the Home Office. However, as you know, there is evidence that the rest of The Cartel has relocated to Indonesia. The Home Secretary's position on this, not to put too fine a point on it, is that The Cartel is now Indonesia's problem. This is now INP's mission and Interpol, MI5, and the NCA will still provide intel support for the INP through NCB Indonesia whenever anything comes up."

Sarah can now empathize with the men of the Royal Irish Regiment, who were 'rewarded' with the disbanding of three of their battalions after their success in Operation Banner. Sarah is sad and disappointed, but understands why it has to be done. Her teammates look as if they are still too stunned to react.

"Because tomorrow we will head for Hereford, and unless you want to work throughout the weekend, all of you will have until the end of today to get your affairs in order before you return to your units. Sarah, this is your airline ticket to Jakarta for tomorrow evening via Manchester International Airport. If I may suggest, you should pack all your things and then send them to a deposit at the airport so you can depart for Indonesia immediately after Michael's funeral," says Broussard, giving her a British Airways e-ticket.

Interpol has sent Sarah to England, and Interpol will also send her back to Indonesia, giving her no say in this matter. There's nothing more to do than pack her things. Sarah doesn't have much to sort out at the office so she returns to her flat and starts packing. After sending most of her luggage to a deposit at the airport, she takes the train with her teammates to Hereford.

19:13 GMT
Thursday October 1, 2026
The Green Dragon Hotel
Hereford, Herefordshire, England

Sarah has checked in to the hotel and is now in her room. She's sorting out her luggage when the doorbell rings. As is her custom, Sarah looks through the peephole, but she literally can't believe her eyes when she sees who's standing there! She quickly opens the door and hugs her visitor.

"*Kak!*" exclaims Sarah, giving her brother a ferocious hug.

"*Halo, Dik!*" greets Tony, returning her hug.

"How on earth did you get here?" asks Sarah incredulously as she drags him into her room.

"Last Sunday, Cormac suddenly called me and he told me Michael was killed in action. I was shocked, but he didn't tell me anything else. He only told me that it'd be better if I go to England to keep you company because you were close to Michael. So I took some leave and the next flight to London. From Heathrow I took the train and Cormac told me to come to this hotel. So, what's this all about, *Dik*? How did you get to know Michael and the CO of the SAS?"

As is their family custom, Sarah never told her family about her work. This time, though, Sarah tells Tony everything, about her job at Interpol, how she met Michael, their activities in Ireland, their battle at Carluccio's, and the time she was trained by the SAS.

Tony looks at his sister in awe, listening to her incredible experience. Sarah starts to look sad when she tells him about her engagement to Michael and then his snatching and murder by The Cartel. Tony looks pale when she tells him about the unexploded grenade. He then hugs his sister when she tells him about the failed mission to rescue Michael. Tony is also sad, because Michael was the one who trained him and his unit.

Once Sarah has calmed down, Tony takes her to the hotel's restaurant, the John Spice's Restaurant & Bar. The buffet is excellent and now it's Tony's turn to ask questions.

"What did they teach you at PATA?" he asks.

"The most useful thing for Densus is the SAS Colour Clock Code for Immediate Actions. Have you implemented it for Bravo yet?"

"Of course I have," answers Tony. "By the way, you're not military. How the devil could you get into PATA?"

"The Director said it was the least he could do for saving Michael's life at Carluccio's," says Sarah. "He also invested me with an MC. Next year, King William will also invest me with a GM."

Sarah can see that her brother is fiercely proud of her. However, there's a glint in Tony's eyes that reminds Sarah of her mum when she announced to the family that she was hand-selected into Densus-88. Sarah remembers her whole family looking at her proudly. She then noticed her mum, who was looking at her with fierce pride in her eyes. But behind that pride, Sarah could also feel her deep worries. Sarah notices that Tony is looking at her the same way as their mum did that time.

"When will you go back to Jakarta?" asks Sarah, changing the subject.

"Tomorrow afternoon, with you through Manchester."

"How did you know when I will go back?"

"Cormac told me. He said that he got it from your commander at Interpol," answers Tony.

Sarah is touched because Cormac had thought of her, even though he must surely be busy arranging for Michael's funeral. After dinner, they keep talking in the hotel room. After the lights are out and just before they go to sleep, Tony is still curious about a few things.

"How did you do at the Fan Dance?" he asks.

"Three hours and thirty-eight minutes," answers Sarah, a bit curtly.

"What happened? Did you get lost or something?" asks Tony, smirking.

Sarah doesn't take his bait.

Tony's happy because she didn't defeat his time, but he's actually impressed because he knows her timing is good, even for the SAS. "Have you ever been inside their base in Credenhill?"

"Of course I have," answers Sarah, even more curtly. "In fact, I've been into B Squadron's Interest Room."

Tony doesn't respond and now he's turning pale. It's fortunate the room is already dark so Sarah can't see his expression.

"Watch it, *Kak*, I'm going to get you for that!" says Sarah as she turns over to sleep.

'Now I'm dead...' thinks Tony worriedly.

10:18 WIB (GMT+7)
Friday October 2, 2026
PT. Westershire Chemicals Manufacture Indonesia
Citeureup, Bogor, West Java

These past few days, Rory has been looking for Sarah's sister on Facebook. He finally found someone who's a dead ringer for her sister. Since she also has the same surname, Rory is sure that the girl named Cindy Monica Dharmawan is the one he's looking for. Fortunately, Cindy has a public account so everyone can see her wall. Rory is in the middle of studying it when Frank enters his office.

"What now?" asks Rory on seeing Frank's expression.

"Almost all our dealers and distributors in the UK and Ireland have been arrested," answers Frank.

"Almost *all of them*?" asks Rory incredulously.

"Except for the blokes at Shropshire, Herefordshire, Worcestershire, and Dorset, who've disappeared. Either they've all managed to escape the coppers or…" says Frank, shrugging.

Frank doesn't have to continue. Rory knows those distributors and dealers will never be found because they live not far away from the SAS and SBS bases. The Cartel is more vulnerable now than they've ever been, because they can't recruit new men to replace the ones they've lost.

06:54 GMT
Friday October 2, 2026
Regimental Church, Memorial Garden, SAS Barracks
Credenhill, Herefordshire, England

The Regimental Church is inside the Memorial Garden of the SAS Barracks. In front of the church, there's a Regimental Clock Tower with the names of SAS members who 'failed to beat the clock', which is their way of saying men who were killed in action before they could retire. Sarah sees hundreds of names and notices Michael's name is already etched among them. A large wreath is in front of it, sent by His Royal Highness Prince Henry of Wales as Colonel-in-Chief of the 22$^{nd}$ Regiment. Sarah is disappointed she couldn't meet Prince Harry, but the prince is still abroad and sent a representative from The Blues and Royals.

There's a plaque on the tower with a verse from James Elroy Flecker's 'Hassan: The Story of Hassan of Baghdad and How He Came to Make the Golden Journey to Samarkand'.

'We are the pilgrims, Master, we shall go,
Always a little further; it may be,
Beyond that last blue mountain barred with snow,
Across that angry or that glimmering sea.'

Sarah doesn't understand the quote and doesn't know why it's there. She enters the church and sits beside her fiancé's coffin with Tony accompanying her. She's wearing a black dress with a black hat she bought before going to Hereford and Tony's wearing his dark blue Indonesian Air Force uniform, holding the orange beret of the Korps Pasukan Khas in his hand.

The coffin is draped with the Union Flag. In front of the coffin is displayed Michael's old photo. He looks dashing in his blue temperate ceremonial uniform with the rank of Second-Lieutenant and the maroon beret of the Parachute Regiment. He looks young, and the picture was taken before he had scars on his face. It's been a while since Sarah saw Michael with his cheeky grin and she can't stop looking at his picture. Beside the picture is a board displaying two of Michael's medals, the George Medal (GM) and An Bonn Míleata Calmachta Le Tuillteanas (BMC) from the Republic of Ireland. Sarah briefly wonders why there are only two medals for a highly decorated British Army officer.

'His other medals are classified then,' thinks Sarah.

All members of B Squadron are already inside the church, wearing the temperate parade uniform from their previous units. Among them, Robert seems to be the most shaken. He sits sadly in the front pew, head down and with a thousand-yard stare. Sarah sees Al, George, and Dave pass by several times, but they don't even glance at her and seem to be trying hard to avoid her, adding to her sorrow. Sarah knows that they're disappointed with her for failing the mission and for her poor leadership. She can understand them, though, as she would probably do the same if her commander had failed her. Sarah is sad, not just for losing Michael, but also her teammates, although Cormac and the other B Squadron members are treating her nicely. Before she takes the train to Manchester, Sarah has to apologize to them for her poor leadership and for treating them badly during the operation. Sarah hopes they will forgive her and accept her as their friend again.

Michael's parents and little brother arrive and Cormac introduces them to Sarah and Tony. Michael's brother looks a lot like Michael, but Sarah has to admit that he's much better looking, especially wearing the Irish Guards' temperate parade uniform.

"Second-*Lef*tenant Scott Adrian, Irish Guards," says Michael's brother, blinking while he shakes her hand.

Looking at him blinking like that, Sarah suddenly remembers the first time she met Michael.

"Inspector Sarah Dharmawan, INP," she says, trying hard to smile at him.

"Goodness, ye're so beautiful, Sarah," says Lady Patricia Adrian.

"Thank you, Lady Adrian."

"Aye, ye look even lovelier in person than ye do in yer picture," says Sir Geoffrey Adrian, KCB.

Scott clears his throat and Sarah gives Tony a nasty look.

"Picture? What picture?" asks Lady Adrian to her husband, who starts going red-faced.

Fortunately, the Director comes to greet them. It turns out Sir Charles and Sir Geoffrey know each other already.

"Excuse us, please," says Sarah, taking Tony's hand to sit with the other B Squadron troopers while they wait for the service to start.

15:15 WIB (GMT+7)
Friday October 2, 2026
PT. Westershire Chemicals Manufacture Indonesia
Citeureup, Bogor, West Java

Rory finally finds something useful on Cindy's wall. Near the beginning of her account, Cindy invited her friends to her house to swim and there's a Google Map showing the way. Rory receives information from the GMP that the Interpol IRT has been disbanded and Sarah is no longer seen at GMP HQ. Rory also receives info from his other contact in the UKSF Group that Sarah is attending Michael's funeral and will return to Jakarta from Manchester International Airport the same day.

Rory takes a car to pick up Patrick and Niall at the city's other airport.

09:54 GMT
Friday October 2, 2026
New SAS Cemetery
Credenhill, Herefordshire, England

Michael will be buried at the SAS Cemetery, across the street from the main gate of the SAS Barracks. They follow the coffin, carried by six members of Air Troop from all squadrons including George. Sarah sees that George is a Staff Sergeant. The six Air Troop men are wearing the uniform of the 2$^{nd}$ Battalion, Parachute Regiment with their maroon berets. The bearer party is led by Robert, wearing the Coldstream Guards uniform.

When they arrive at the cemetery, Sarah stands between Tony and Liz. Across from the coffin stands Michael's family, with everyone else behind them, wearing the temperate parade uniforms from their previous units. It feels as if every regiment in His Majesty's Armed Forces sent a representative to attend Michael's funeral. All of B Squadron can attend because they are still 'On The Team'. Sarah sees St John among them, looking pale and feeble, wearing a Corporal's uniform of the Royal Welsh. He ran away from the hospital just so he could give his last respects to his commander. Derek, with his AGC uniform, is recording everything on his video camera.

Sarah sees several people from the Training Wing. Some are missing an arm, a leg, an eye, or a combination of all three, but they look proud in their uniform. Among them, Sarah sees the DS from the checkpoint on top of Pen y Fan where she did the Fan Dance. He's wearing the uniform of the 3$^{rd}$ Battalion, Yorkshire Regiment (Duke of Wellington's) with the rank of Warrant Officer Class 2. He looks the saddest among them and Sarah notices him crying all throughout the church service.

On her right, the Band of the Royal Scots Dragoon Guards stands to attention, flanked by the Hereford Cathedral Choir. In front of the band stand twelve men holding SA80A3 rifles in the 'Reverse Arms' position, meaning their rifles are held upside down to honour their fallen comrade. The firing party is led by Dave, wearing the uniform of the King's Royal Hussars. The temperate parade uniform of that regiment looks the oddest, with a crimson-coloured hat and pants. Like George, Dave is also a Staff Sergeant.

The Director comes forward to deliver his eulogy and he is the only one wearing the SAS uniform. "Michael Adrian, born in Belfast, County Antrim, Northern Ireland, twenty-eight years ago, spent five years in The Regiment. He was one of the youngest officer ever to become an Officer Commanding of a sabre squadron. This came as no surprise to those who knew him, as he always excelled in everything he did. After graduating from secondary school at St. Patrick's College, he immediately enrolled into the Royal Military Academy Sandhurst where he graduated as the best British Army Officer Cadet of the Course, and was awarded the Sword of Honour from the Commandant…"

Sarah listens carefully as Sir Charles tells them about Michael's career. She still doesn't know how he rose up the career ladder so fast.

After telling them about Michael's career, the Director starts telling them his impressions of Michael. "Major-General Adrian, Lady Adrian, and Second-Leftenant Adrian, we all know that Michael was a true Irishman, fiercely loyal to his land and heritage. During one of my many discussions with Michael about poetry, however, he once told me that his favourite poem came from The War Sonnets, by Rupert Brooke - who happens to be an Englishman. And I quote:

'If I should die, think only this of me;
That there's some corner of a foreign field
That is forever England. There shall be
In that rich earth a richer dust concealed;

'A dust whom England bore, shaped, made aware,
Gave, once, her flowers to love, her ways to roam,
A body of England's, breathing English air,
Washed by the rivers, blest by suns of home.

'And think, this heart, all evil shed away,
A pulse in the eternal mind, no less
Gives somewhere back the thoughts by England given;
Her sights and sounds; dreams happy as her day;
And laughter, learnt of friends; and gentleness,
In hearts at peace, under an English heaven.'"

Sir Charles pauses to let the words resonate through the crowd before continuing his eulogy. "Major-General Adrian, Lady Adrian, and Second-Leftenant Adrian, let me assure you of this, that there is a corner of a field here in Credenhill… that will be forever Ireland."

Sarah is touched and almost cries hearing Sir Charles's words. But his next words shock almost everyone.

"God bless you, Michael, and God bless your family. Leftenant-Colonel Sir Michael Adrian, VC, KCB, GM, BMC… may you Rest in Peace."

Sarah's jaw drops. She looks at her Interpol teammates and they're equally stunned. It turns out Michael had been invested with a Victoria Cross, the UK's highest military decoration. The VC is equivalent to the US's Medal of Honor or Indonesia's Bintang Sakti and the KCB is the

Knight Commander of the Most Honourable Order of the Bath, the same honour bestowed on Michael's father.

The KCB makes Michael a knight, entitled to a 'Sir' as a prefix to his first name. If he were married, his wife would be entitled to a 'Lady' as a prefix to her surname. As far as Sarah knows, the KCB can only be bestowed to officers with a minimum rank of Colonel, making her even more intrigued why Michael was given an exception. With those kinds of honours, it's no wonder Michael's career soared so fast. Because they weren't displayed awards, this means Michael won them in classified operations. The Director shouldn't have mentioned them, but he doesn't seem to care today, because he wants everyone to know that Michael is a hero and a knight.

Sarah looks towards Michael's family and sees they're equally surprised. The Director salutes the coffin and returns to his original place. The next eulogy is from Al, wearing the brown uniform and black hat of The Rifles infantry regiment, rank Warrant Officer Class 2. He's also wearing black gloves and a black armband on his left arm, worn only during funerals.

"Sir Michael Adrian, the late OC of B Squadron, 22$^{nd}$ Regiment, Special Air Service, is no more. I guess we're all thinking how sad it is that a man of such talent, of such capability, of such unusual intelligence, should now so suddenly be spirited away at the age of only twenty-eight, before he had achieved many of the things of which he was capable, and before he had enough fun."

"The first time I met the wanker was during his Selection…"

Sarah can't help but laugh. Even Michael's family is laughing out loud. Only Sir Charles, Broussard, and Cormac are maintaining straight faces, though Sir Charles is maybe stifling a laugh. Al tells the gathered about the silly antics Michael got up to with everyone and people are openly enjoying themselves. But Sarah can clearly see that behind all the funny stories, Al is feeling deep sorrow for losing his close friend.

After the laughter ceases, Al ends his eulogy. "Well, Michael, it has been really fun and a true honour to serve under your command." His voice starts to break up so he stops for a few seconds. "We will miss you… old buddy."

Al salutes the coffin, tears streaming from his eyes as he returns to his original place. The bearer party then starts 'undressing the coffin' and folds the Union Flag. Cormac, wearing the uniform of the Royal Scots Dragoon Guards (Carabiniers and Greys), gives the flag to Michael's father. Cormac shares a few kind words of comfort with the Major-General. Cormac then returns to his original place while the firing party prepare.

Dave's command voice echoes throughout the cemetery. "Party, present – arms!"

"Shoulder – arms!"

"Volleys with blank cartridges!"

"Load!"

"Present!"

"Fire!"

"Reload!"

"Fire!"

"Reload!"

"Fire!"

"Unload!"

"Shoulder – arms!"

"Present – arms!"

Dave's last two orders make everyone stand to attention and then salute the coffin. A trumpet from the Band of the Royal Scots Dragoon Guards starts playing 'Last Post'. The song accompanies the bearer party lowering the coffin into the grave. There is a Two-Minute Silence after 'Last Post'. After the two minutes, 'Reveille' suddenly bursts out, making most people jump.

"Shoulder – arms!" orders Dave. He then gives the order for the firing party to leave.

Four women from the Band of the Royal Scots Dragoon Guards prepare to sing, unaccompanied.

'Oh Danny boy, the pipes, the pipes are calling,

From glen to glen, and down the mountain side…'

Sarah knows that she will cry anyway so she lets go of any control of her emotions. The singers from the Band of the Royal Scots Dragoon Guards have sung perfectly, touching everyone. Sarah glances at Tony and sees him wiping his eyes with a tissue.

After a round of applause, a bagpipe starts playing the notes of 'Amazing Grace'. After the solo bagpipe, the rest of the bagpipes join in.

The four women start singing the words, backed by the Hereford Cathedral Choir and music from the Band of the Royal Scots Dragoon Guards.

'Amazing grace, how sweet the sound,
That saved a wretch like me..."

The women's voices, backed by the choir, mesmerize everyone. When they finish, they receive a long round of applause. Unlike 'Danny Boy', 'Amazing Grace' gave Sarah spirit and helped her finally accept Michael's death. The song signals the end of Michael's military funeral.

The band starts playing 'Going Home' as everyone departs. Sarah goes over to Michael's grave with Tony behind her. Just like in the song, 'Danny Boy', she bends over to touch his grave marker.

"*Vaya con Dios*, Michael. Sleep in peace until I come to you... *sayang*," she whispers.

Sarah prays 'Ave Maria' and takes a moment of silence. She then sees Michael's family approach and quickly wipes the tears from her eyes.

"Sarah, we would like ye to have this," says Lady Adrian, giving her Michael's beret.

Sarah is touched and almost cries again upon receiving the beret. "Thank you, ma'am, I don't know what else to say," she says, hugging Michael's mother.

"There's no need for ye to say anything. We know ye love him very much so at least ye will have something to remember him by," says Sir Geoffrey.

"I will always remember him, sir," says Sarah, hugging him too.

Cormac approaches. It turns out the Director has invited them all to the RHQ. The sound of 'Scotland The Brave' accompanies them as they walk towards the RHQ.


11:19 GMT
Friday October 2, 2026
Main Briefing Room, Regimental Headquarters, SAS Barracks
Credenhill, Herefordshire, England

Sarah takes off her hat as she enters the Blue Room, already filled with SAS personnel in parade formation. The Director and her Interpol team are also there, standing in the middle of the room. Cormac guides them towards the Director and then takes a position on the back-left of the Director. Derek keeps recording with his video camera.

Sir Charles greets Michael's father warmly. "I do hope the funeral service was in accordance with your usual high standards, Major-General."

"It was beautiful, Director, and an honour to have the legendary Band of the Royal Scots Dragoon Guards and the Hereford Cathedral Choir perform for us," says Sir Geoffrey.

"Well, Major-General, before you return to Belfast, there is one more thing we would like you and your family to bear witness to," says Sir Charles.

Major-General Sir Charles Mountbatten, GCB, DSO receives a parchment from Cormac and reads it out loud. "Inspector Sarah Michelle Dharmawan, MC, GM, of the Indonesian National Police,

"On Saturday, September 26, 2026, Inspector Sarah Michelle Dharmawan, on secondment from Interpol Manchester, led an officer, a warrant officer, and two senior non-commissioned officers on a mission to locate and rescue a highly decorated British Army officer from the hands of the Irish Drug Cartel. She conducted a one-up Close Target Reconnaissance on a stronghold in Cheshire, England and then infiltrated the stronghold, which was later confirmed as the headquarters and drug manufacturing plant of the Irish Drug Cartel. She defeated two members of The Cartel in unarmed combat before the rest of her unit arrived and successfully secured the stronghold."

"After performing a careful and thorough Sensitive Site Exploitation with a teammate from Interpol Manchester, she located the whereabouts of the British Army officer and immediately led the team in planning and executing a rescue operation at a warehouse in Liverpool, England, where they faced unknown odds. The assault on the first two floors of the warehouse was a textbook Direct Action assault on a stronghold. However, while ascending the stairs leading to the second floor, a member of The Cartel rolled a fragmentation grenade down towards the team. Without any hesitation and with complete disregard for her own life…"

Sir Charles's voice starts to break up and he has to stop for few seconds. He then continues with a stronger voice. "Without any hesitation and complete disregard for her own life, Sarah fearlessly threw herself on top of the grenade. She willingly sacrificed her own life in the hopes her teammates would live and continue the mission. Fortunately, the grenade failed to detonate. But most incredibly, Sarah then rose and fearlessly resumed command of the operation. Due to her superior tactics against overwhelming odds, she and another teammate eliminated the remaining narcoterrorists. In the process, Sarah again saved the life of her teammate from enemy fire.

"Although the rescue of the British Army officer was unsuccessful, Sarah led the four British Army men in a mission that eliminated an astonishing seventy-eight narcoterrorists, eliminating the threat of narcoterrorism in the United Kingdom of Great Britain and Northern Ireland. Quite astonishingly, her gallantry and heroism did not end there. After the rescue operation had ended, she further saved the life of an Explosives Ordnance Disposal specialist, who was disarming an unexploded device which unexpectedly detonated.

"During the debriefing attended by the entire group, the four men from the British Army under her command could not stop praising how incredibly brave she was and how excellent and courageous her leadership was throughout the entire operation. She is definitely a shining example of outstanding and exemplary leadership for every officer in the British Army.

"Inspector Sarah Michelle Dharmawan, MC, GM of the Indonesian National Police, for most-conspicuous bravery and preeminent acts of valour and self-sacrifice in the presence of the enemy, and for fearlessly and successfully leading a British Army unit during active operations, His Majesty King William the Fifth is graciously pleased to approve the award of… the Distinguished Service Order," says Sir Charles.

Sarah didn't expect to be invested with another medal! Her jaw drops as she accepts the citation and medal, to the applause of everyone in the Blue Room.

Sir Charles shakes her hand. "Congratulations, Sarah."

"Thank you for this, Director… but the citation is incorrect. I was terrified when I landed on top of that grenade and I was an emotional wreck after the operation. I am still quite ashamed of my behaviour that day," says Sarah, trying to smile.

Sir Charles Mountbatten shakes his head. "Your emotional state *after* the operation was understandable… and irrelevant. What matters, however, was the extraordinary leadership you displayed *during* the operation," he says, giving his men a hard look. "Regarding the fear you felt, well, let me quote something that I once heard, that 'courage is not the absence of fear, but rather the judgement that something else is more important than fear.' The lads knew you were afraid at that time, but your ability to act and successfully lead your team in the presence of fear is what makes you quite special.

"You are truly an exceptional combat leader and commander, Sarah. Each one of the lads has stated that it was a true honour for them to fight under your command and that they would not hesitate to follow you into battle anywhere. You deserve to wear Michael's beret, Sarah, and you are welcome here at the SAS Barracks anytime," says Sir Charles Mountbatten, giving her a Green Pass.

Tears stream from Sarah's eyes upon receiving the Green Pass, which means she is now free to enter the SAS Barracks unaccompanied. Sarah makes a decision and hands over everything she's holding to Tony. Although Sir Charles told her that she deserves to wear Michael's beret, she still feels unworthy of it because she hasn't passed their Selection. Once her hands are free, she replaces her black hat so she can give the Director a proper salute. She then stands to attention in the INP manner.

But Sir Charles suddenly touches Sarah's right arm, preventing her from giving him a salute.

"I beg your pardon, Sarah, but I will not accept your salute," says Sir Charles, softly but firmly.

Sarah's surprised Sir Charles doesn't want to accept her salute. Probably because she's just a civilian or something. She can now only look down, tears streaming from her eyes, feeling dejected and disappointed.

Sir Charles releases her arm and takes a few steps back. "Inspector Sarah Michelle Dharmawan, DSO, MC, GM, of the Indonesian National Police… it would be an honour if you accept ours."

"Parade, paraaade 'shun!" orders Cormac in his strongest command voice.

The sound of hundreds of boots slamming the floor sounds like a cannon! It echoes throughout the Blue Room, making Sarah, Tony, Major-General Sir Geoffrey Adrian, and Second-Lieutenant Scott Adrian stand to attention too.

With damp eyes, the Commanding Officer of the 22$^{nd}$ Regiment, Special Air Service gives another order. "Saluting, to-the-frooont... Salute!"

Sir Charles, Cormac, and every member of the SAS give Sarah a crisp salute. Sarah's so shocked that she doesn't immediately return it. She looks towards the SAS men and sees Robert, Al, George, and Dave at the front, crisply saluting her with tears in their eyes. It turns out all this time they've considered Sarah a hero, not someone who failed to lead them. This means so much to her. She looks towards Michael's family and they seem impressed, especially Sir Geoffrey and Scott, who are also saluting her. Sarah looks toward Broussard and her teammates, who are giving her a look of immense pride with tears streaming down their cheeks. Tony is also saluting her, fierce pride in his teary eyes.

There is nothing else Sarah can do except return their salute with a salute of her own... and her own tears streaming down her cheek.

# CHAPTER 15
# TIGER KIDNAP

17:21 WIB (GMT + 7)
Friday October 2, 2026
Halim Perdanakusuma Airport
Halim Perdanakusuma, East Jakarta, Jakarta

Patrick and Niall finally arrive at Jakarta's smaller, less conspicuous airport, where they're picked up by Rory. Patrick can see from Rory's face that he's bringing bad news. Inside the car, Niall immediately goes to sleep in the back.

"Let me have it," orders Patrick, taking the heavy disguise off his face.

"The SAS raided our HQ and our factory in Liverpool. Frag, Gwilliam, Steve, and Sheila are dead and so is everyone else," says Rory.

Tears stream from Patrick's eyes. He'd feared the worst had happened when he'd seen the coppers headed towards his HQ. "How did they die?"

"My intel says that Gwilliam and Frag got their fucking heads blown off, but Frag managed to chuck his grenade before he died. I don't think he managed to slot anyone, because Michael was the only fella they buried. Steve died with a fucking knife in his heart."

"How the fuck did they manage that?"

Rory can only shake his head.

"What about Sheila? Was it quick?" asks Patrick.

Rory glances at the rear-view mirror and sees that Niall is asleep. "They gutted her and then blew her face off. They buried her without a face, Paddy."

"Jesus fucking Christ!" curses Patrick, crying.

Niall is only pretending to be asleep and he finds himself getting hard imagining Sheila with her guts out. He wants to return to England just so he can see her dead body.

"Did ye find out which of the bastards slotted them?" asks Patrick.

"It was the same bitch from Densus that slotted Steve and Sheila," says Rory. "She somehow led the SAS fellas assaulting both places. Our other contact in the UKSF Group said she will even get a bloody medal from their fucking DSF for doing it!"

"Find out when that bitch is returning to Jakarta!" orders Patrick.

"My intel says she'll arrive here Saturday evening," says Rory.

"Powerful! We'll just let Niall have fun with her," says Patrick, grim-faced. "In the meantime, have Brian conduct a recce on her house."

"Right," answers Rory.

Niall doesn't want to return to England anymore. Sarah is much sexier than Sheila and he wants to see what her guts look like. He imagines her screaming as he opens her up. Her intestines must surely look better than other women he's dissected. Niall can't wait to see what's inside Sarah's stomach and can't wait to open up other Indonesian women.

11:40 GMT
Friday October 2, 2026
Regimental Headquarters, SAS Barracks
Credenhill, Herefordshire, England

Sarah is congratulated by everyone present. The last person to congratulate her is St John. Sarah heard that even though St John was badly wounded in the hospital, his mates still gave him a severe slagging for failing to dispose the UXO. One of his mates even gave him a Kashmir goat doll with a toy grenade strapped to its neck.

"Congratulations, Sarah," says St John, shaking her hand.

"Thank you, Sinjin. How are you feeling today?" asks Sarah, smiling at him.

"Still under the doctor and a tidy bit wanged-out, I am," says St John in his Welsh way of saying things. "I'm glad I have this chance to personally thank you for saving my life," he continues, eyes starting to tear up.

"I'm sure you would've done the same thing for me, Sinjin," says Sarah. She then kisses him on his cheek and gives him a warm hug. The other troopers get jealous they didn't receive the same treatment.

"Of course I would, wouldn't I?" says Corporal St John Williams, BSD happily. He no longer looks pale.

## THE POLICEWOMAN

Sarah goes to see Michael's brother, who's eyeing the SAS men with awe.

"I'm sorry I couldn't save your brother, Scott," says Sarah.

"Oh, I know you did your best," says Scott, shrugging, "and if you and the SAS couldn't save him, then no one else could've."

Sarah smiles. Scott shares his brother's talent for cheering her up.

"After listening to your citation back there, I only hope that one day I can be half as good an officer as you," continues Scott. "Michael would've been proud of you, you know."

Sarah's smile grows even wider. She likes Scott and he reminds her of Michael. She's sure that Scott will be as good an officer as his brother.

"Did you know that he was invested with a VC and KCB?" asks Scott.

"No," answers Sarah, shaking her head.

"Did he ever tell you how he got all those scars?"

"No and I never asked him. Why? Did he ever tell you?" asks Sarah.

"Yeah," answers Scott. "He told me he got kicked by a donkey."

Scott's pout reminds her of Michael, but it only makes Sarah laugh. Scott acknowledges her laughter with a wry grin, then returns to staring at the SAS men in front of them.

"Are you planning to join The Regiment?" asks Sarah.

"Of course! I'm going to do Selection after I receive my Captaincy."

"No ye're not, Scott!" yells Lady Adrian, overhearing their conversation.

Scott doesn't respond to his mother, but winks at Sarah, making her laugh again. They exchange numbers and e-mail addresses. Broussard and Sarah's teammates approach them to say their goodbyes. Sarah shakes hands and hugs them.

"Sorry we have to leave, Sarah, we have to catch the 12:30 train to Manchester," says Broussard.

"No problem, Chief," says Sarah.

"And thank you dearly for your support on this mission. My superiors at Lyon have sent the Secretariat of NCB Indonesia one hell of a Letter of Recommendation for you."

"Thank you, Chief."

"Please convey my best wishes to Prasetyo and don't forget to show him all your medals," says Christopher Broussard, smiling broadly.

351

"I'll do that, Chief," says Sarah, laughing, "and thanks again for everything!"

"Please remember ye still have yer mission to find their factory in Indonesia," says James Hicks. "We'll keep in touch, all right?"

"Of course, James."

"We'll send *yee* intel support from the NCA whenever anything comes up, *pet*," says Paul Elliot.

"Thank you, Paul."

"Make sure you come see me when you go to Buckingham Palace next year, all right?" says Detective Chief Inspector Arthur Grimes.

"I'll look you up at The Met, Arthur."

"I hope ye can visit me in Belfast after ye receive yer medal," says Detective Chief Inspector Matthew Gallagher.

"Of course I will, Matt."

"Be sure to visit me in Dublin also and please keep in touch, my good friend," says Cigire Elizabeth O'Connell, her eyes moist.

"I will, Liz, and have a safe trip," says Sarah.

Cormac approaches her with Tony behind him. "How about we all have a piss-up before you go home?"

"That would be lovely, Mac, as long as you let me pay for it," says Sarah, wiping her eyes with a tissue.

Sarah, Tony, and Cormac say goodbye to Michael's family and the SAS men still in the Blue Room. The last person they see is Major-General Sir Charles Mountbatten, GCB, DSO.

"Do you have any more missions for me, Director?" asks Sarah, smiling at him.

"Indeed, Sarah. Be sure to find the rest of The Cartel in Indonesia and avenge Michael for us," says Sir Charles.

"Yes, sir! But please take care of my team for me, Director," says Sarah, reminding him that they also played a huge part in destroying The Cartel.

"Of course, Sarah," says Sir Charles, giving her a warm smile, "and after you receive your medal next year, I do hope you and Tony can visit us at the barracks for a couple of days. I'm sure Al and the others could teach both of you a few more tricks during your visit."

"That would be lovely, Director!" says Sarah, genuinely delighted.

"Thank you for the invitation, Director!" says Tony, shaking his hand.

Robert, Al, George, and Dave are already waiting for them next to the Q car they will take. George is driving, Cormac riding shotgun, Sarah and Tony in the middle, and everyone else in the back. They head towards The Barrels at St Owens Street, not far from Castle Green. Everyone is sombre and in no mood for bantering.

"You know, Sarah, when we heard that the Director had only recommended you for a DSO, we were all upset. We think you deserve a VC," says George.

Everyone in the back agrees with him.

Cormac explains. "I asked the Director about that and he said, and I quote, 'if that bloody grenade had detonated while she was on top of it, then yes, she would have definitely received the VC.' Which would you prefer she receive, George?" he asks, giving George a wry look.

George only snorts. He still thinks Sarah should receive UK's highest military decoration.

"The DSO is more than enough, George!" says Tony, shuddering to think of the grenade exploding, ripping his sister apart. "And I hope that none of us is ever involved in a combat situation that merits the VC," he continues while giving Sarah a frightening look.

Sarah is genuinely scared by the look Tony's giving her. She remembers the day before when she told him about throwing herself on top a grenade to save her teammates, Tony looked pale enough to pass out. He then looked as if he were torn between hugging her tightly and slapping her hard across her face. He eventually chose the hug.

"And if I ever see you do any of that shit in front of me, I'll fucking shoot you myself!" continues Tony, still giving her a frightening look.

Sarah almost believes him.

"Spoken like a true, professional rupert of the special forces, Tony," says Cormac, smiling at him.

"In any case, I apologize if I disappointed you," says Sarah to her friends. "I failed you and I hope you forgive me for mistreating you while you were under my command."

The men are having none of it, including Cormac. "Your leadership was bloody perfect, Sarah! You led the chaps slotting almost eighty players without sustaining a single fucking casualty. I, on the other hand, almost lost Sinjin after the operation was already over! I was given a slagging from B Squadron for that, you know."

"You treated us no better nor worse than what we deserved. We should be the ones saying sorry to you," says Robert.

"And there's no way we could be disappointed with you. We're disappointed with ourselves… ashamed more like it," says Dave. "After the debriefing, the Director gave us a severe bollocking for our behaviour under your command, you know."

"But I was in command of the mission!" protests Sarah.

George explains. "The mission was a failure from the beginning and there was no way anyone could have saved him. Michael was a dead man the moment he was snatched and I think even *he* knew that. We did everything we could to try and save him, including disobeying a direct order… but we failed *you*."

"Oh? How is that?" asks Sarah.

"You told the Director that you became an emotional wreck *after* the operation, r*oi*ght?" asks Al.

"I think so," says Sarah, trying to remember her own words.

Al has to stop for a moment from getting emotional. "Well… as you saw yourself, we became emotional wrecks also. However, like a bunch of dickheads, we let ourselves get completely overwhelmed by it *before* the job was done. That's why the Director gave us a severe bollocking after the debriefing. That's why he gave us the evil eye after reading your citation. We exhibited unprofessional, unacceptable behaviour *before* the operation was over."

"We apologize for avoiding you all this time, but frankly, we were just too embarrassed to meet you," says Robert. "I mean, how the fuck could we look you in the eyes after you saw us perform like that?"

Sarah remembers them looking shaken after finding Michael's body. She remembers them literally freezing when she gave them the order to pepper-pott. Then, after all X-Rays were taken care of and there was still a lot of work to do, they just stood there like complete dickheads even after Sarah gave them a direct order. That incident made them embarrassed; not because Sarah had slapped them around, but because they'd messed up. In other words, they'd let themselves get overwhelmed by emotions *before* the job was finished. Everyone was impressed by Sarah's leadership because even though she was almost killed and lost someone she loved very much, she could still focus on finishing the job before she let her emotions overwhelm her. Her men are the most senior in their squadron and they should've been an example for Sarah, not the other way around.

"On behalf of myself and the blokes, I apologize for our behaviour and performance while we were under your command, Sarah," says Al.

"Don't worry about it, my brothers," says Sarah, relieved knowing they still consider her their friend.

"That's settled then. Now let's just get on the piss and try to forget the whole thing, shall we?" says Cormac.

They are quiet for a few moments. George seems to be taking his time driving to Hereford.

Sarah suddenly asks, "Mac, may I ask how Michael won the VC and KCB?"

Tony nudges Sarah with his elbow. He's frowning and shaking his head because Sarah asked something that Cormac can't answer.

The CO of the SAS doesn't respond for a few seconds. "That information is strictly confidential and I would be RTU'd, and maybe even court-martialed if I told you about it."

"I understand, Mac," says Sarah hurriedly.

"Well, now that you know what I have at stake, let me tell you about it," says Cormac.

Sarah, Tony, and Robert are surprised. They hadn't expected Cormac to risk his career by telling them classified information. They listen intently. The others seem to already know the story.

"I was OC of B Squadron at that time and Michael was in Air Troop. Three or so years ago, elements of B Squadron including myself, Al, George, and Dave here were deployed to... a certain middle-eastern country. We were tasked with training the government troops at a remote garrison, when hundreds of insurgents attacked it. Whether by coincidence or not, they attacked when Prince Harry was there to inspect the garrison. They staged a frontal assault on the garrison with mortars in support. They managed to destroy the Prince's helicopter with their first few rounds and killed the pilots and crew. They were Prince Harry's close friends, whom he'd known for years. Michael saw that one of the OPs with a Gimpy was being targeted by the insurgents so he immediately ran there to support it, dodging heavy enemy fire along the way. It was a miracle he didn't get hit. The OP was a vital defence position and we all knew that the loss of it would collapse the garrison's defence. It was manned by B Squadron's SSM and a couple of local troops he was training at that time. The insurgents knew about the OP position and started concentrating their attack on it. They also fired mortars at it. Before Dave managed to slot the mortar crews with his sniper rifle, the OP took an almost-direct hit. Both of the locals were killed instantly."

Cormac has to stop for a moment before continuing. "The SSM was severely wounded, losing an arm and his left eye. Despite his own wounds, Michael gave the SSM whatever first aid he could, whilst also operating the Gimpy. He knew that his position was vital and the loss of it would be the end of the garrison and Prince Harry. The insurgents came to within metres of his position when, incredibly, Michael gave the order for our mortars to fire directly on to his own position. We all knew the importance of keeping the machine gun out of the possession of the insurgents and that it had to be destroyed before it could fall into their hands. Michael's order meant that he was in imminent danger of being overrun. However, Prince Harry countermanded Michael's order and ordered Al, who was in charge of our mortar crew at that time, to fire immediately ahead of Michael's position, which was almost as dangerous, since a stray round could've killed them instantly. Thanks to Al's skill with the mortars and Michael's Gimpy fire, they kept the insurgents from overrunning the position.

"I finally managed to contact a flight of F-35B Lightning from the 809 Naval Air Squadron aboard the HMS Queen Elizabeth for close air support and another Chinook helicopter and a couple of Apache escorts to get the Prince to safety. The combination of close air support and Al's mortar fire finally managed to repel the attack, so the rest of B Squadron went forward to check on Michael's position. The SSM was still alive and Michael took shrapnel all over his face and body, bleeding all over the place. Michael was so angry with the insurgent attack that he refused treatment and insisted he lead a counterattack after he'd made sure the SSM was casevac'd in the Chinook. Michael and the lads slotted all 113 insurgents, with the help from elements of G Squadron and the support of Prince Harry in one of the Apache helicopters."

"Prince Harry supported Michael in the counterattack?" asks Tony. "I thought you'd sent a helicopter to take him to safety?"

"Prince Harry refused evacuation and became angry at his bodyguards for insisting, even punching one of them out and threatening the others with his sidearm when they tried to throw him into the Chinook. He ordered the Chinook to casevac the SSM to one of our military hospitals and then ordered one of the Apaches to land, and then literally threw the pilot out of the cockpit. The poor sod almost cried when the Prince took away his helmet and took off with his helicopter. Anyway, Prince Harry piloted the Apache and helped give close air support during Michael's counterattack. I managed to coordinate with elements of G Squadron at another garrison to set up defensive positions behind the insurgents while B Squadron and the Apaches directed the insurgents into the ambush. All the insurgents were caught in the hammer and anvil tactic, and every single last one of them was slotted. It was only at that point that Michael collapsed from loss of blood and exhaustion."

"Did the SSM make it?" asks Sarah.

Cormac smiles. "He's still in the Training Wing. You've already met him, Sarah. He was the DS you met at the top of Pen y Fan. Michael and Prince Harry saved his life. Fred is currently the proud owner of The Nag's Head restaurant, which he bought soon after he recovered from his wounds. He has a wife and three kids now."

Sarah remembers the friendly DS from the top of Pen y Fan, who kept spurring her to keep up with the rest of B Squadron. That's why he looked so sad at the funeral, because Michael once saved his life. Sarah can't even imagine how terrible it would feel if she owed someone her life and the person died before she could return the favour.

"Michael was covered with bandages from head to toe like a mummy and the Prince was in the hospital room with us when he regained consciousness. Michael panicked at first, thinking that he was blind, but we calmed him down and assured him it was because his whole head was covered in bandages. The first thing Michael asked was whether Fred was all right. After we told him he'd made it, the second thing he asked was whether Prince Harry was all right. Michael didn't know that Prince Harry was in the room at the time and Michael seemed so genuinely concerned for the Prince's well-being that the Prince was touched. Michael was surprised when Prince Harry himself answered his question and thanked him for saving his life."

"After the Prince left, we all took the piss out of Michael for brown-nosing the prince. But then he said, and I quote, 'I wasn't brown-nosing him, you muppets. If Prince Harry had gotten killed or wounded, our careers would've been over!'"

Everyone laughs.

"The Prince personally recommended Michael for both awards; the Victoria Cross for his actions defending the garrison, saving Fred's life, and successfully leading the counterattack, and the KCB for saving the life of his sovereign and the Colonel-in-Chief of the 22$^{nd}$ Regiment. Just so you know, he also invested me with a DSO, Al and Fred with CGCs, and everyone involved, including Dave and George here, an MC for their roles in the action. We're not allowed to tell anyone about it or wear the medals on our uniforms because the mission is still classified. Just remember that my career is at stake here, so please do not repeat any of this to anyone."

"Repeat what, Mac?" asks Tony, winking at him.

Cormac smiles. George parks the Q car at Bath Street and they walk towards The Barrels. Even though it's only just opened, it's already mostly full. In their varied uniforms, Cormac's group makes quite a sight, and the pub patrons keep looking their way as they seat themselves in the corner. They order lunch and Cormac orders several pitchers of beer. After their drinks arrive, everyone except Cormac stands up for the Loyal Toast. Cormac must stay seated during the Loyal Toast because of a Royal Scots Dragoon Guards tradition.

"My lady and gentlemen! The King!" says Al.

"The King!" says everyone, including Sarah and Tony.

They sip their beers, but they're already starting to get emotional before the next toast.

"To Michael!" says Cormac.

"To Michael!"

They sip their beers again.

"And to Sarah!" says Robert, eyes already moist. "Our leader... our hero... and most of all... our friend."

"Hear, hear!" say the others, also with tears in their eyes.

Sarah raises her glass, tears streaming down her cheeks. Her lips say 'thank you', but no words come out. They all sit and enjoy their beer in silence. Sarah cries silently on Tony's shoulder while everyone else is coping in their own personal way. Their lunch arrives and Cormac keeps ordering pitchers of beer. They eat and drink in silence. As before, Robert

# THE POLICEWOMAN

is designated driver and Sarah feels sorry for him because it looks as if he could really use a drink. After spending a couple of hours there, it's time for them to go to Hereford Railway Station. Cormac asks the waiter for the bill.

"Mac, let me pay for this!" protests Sarah.

"Don't worry, I got it," says Cormac, taking out his wallet.

"Sir, your bill has already been taken care of," says the waiter.

"Oh? By whom?" asks Cormac.

"All the patrons here, the owner, and all of the employees have chipped in and taken care of it, sir."

"That's very generous and we thank all of you, sir… but may I ask why?"

"We heard about what happened to one of your squadron commanders, sir, and this is the least we could do for you. God bless you, sirs, and we thank you for your service," says the waiter, giving them a bow.

Everyone in the pub gives them a standing ovation. Cormac and the others are touched as they shake hands with the waiter and everyone at the pub. They exit to the continued applause of everyone inside.

14:23 GMT
Friday October 2, 2026
Hereford Railway Station
Hereford, Herefordshire, England

Everyone is silent on the journey to the railway station, deep in their own thoughts and emotions. Once they reach the station, they help Sarah and Tony with their luggage. The SAS men look sad because their comrade-in-arms, who they already consider a sister, is returning to Indonesia. Tony shakes hands with them and Sarah hugs them and kisses their cheeks.

"The Director was serious about that invitation you know," says Cormac. "Be sure to bring your Green Pass when you visit us next year, all right?"

"Of course, Mac. Thank you for telling my brother to come here and pick me up. That was thoughtful of you."

"It was the least I could do for you, Sarah," says Lieutenant-Colonel Cormac McLaughlin, DSO, BMC, smiling warmly at her.

"I don't think I've thanked you yet for saving my life," says Robert. "I owe you one, Sarah."

"Oh, I bet you would have done the same for me, Robert."

"Yes, I definitely would have," says Captain Robert Covington, BSD seriously.

"You are the only person I know besides Michael to earn three medals for gallantry," says Staff Sergeant David Bancroft, MC, BSD. "It's an honour to have you as my friend."

"It's an honour for me also, Dave. Michael once told me you shot three insurgents with only four rounds from 1,900 metres away. I don't know anyone else able to do that," says Sarah, making Dave smile happily.

"Yeah... but he's still a dickhead for wasting that one round," says Staff Sergeant George Hastings, MC, BSD.

"He's a better shot than you, George," quips Sarah, reminding him about his missed targets.

They all laugh.

"Is there anything else I can do for you?" asks Al.

"There is indeed, Al," says Sarah.

"Anything, old buddy," says Warrant Officer Class 2 Al Spencer, CGC, BSD.

"If I ever die before you, please don't deliver my eulogy," says Sarah. She's joking, but her eyes are starting to tear up.

Everyone laughs out loud and they wave goodbye. Sarah and Tony sit and Sarah is crying once again because she will miss her brothers. She suddenly understands why she considers them her brothers and a quote from Shakespeare's Henry V comes to mind. Just before the Battle of Agincourt, King Henry V said these words to his men, 'we few, we happy few, we band of brothers; for he to-day that sheds his blood with me, shall be my brother.' Sarah and her friends have spilled the blood of their enemies together. The camaraderie that developed between them makes them feel like they're part of her family.

"*Kak?*"

"*Ya, Dik?*"

"If Michael was still alive, would you've been okay with me marrying him?" asks Sarah.

# THE POLICEWOMAN

Tony smiles. Sarah trusts his judgement, so she always introduced him to her partners. Tony didn't like any of them and Sarah eventually broke up with them.

"Well, there are some things about him that I don't like," says Tony.

"Really? What sort of things?"

"First, he was probably the only boyfriend you had that could kick my arse."

"Agreed," says Sarah, smirking.

"Second, he was younger than I am, but had the same rank as I do. He'd most likely outrank me someday," says Tony. "And I can't have that."

"Yeah, right. *I'll* probably outrank you someday," quips Sarah.

Tony visibly deflates before her eyes and Sarah almost laughs out loud. Tony knows that his sister has a lot of combat experience. Officially, Tony has never experienced any combat. Unofficially, Tony and his team have several times conducted highly-classified military operations. Like Michael and their friends at B Squadron, Tony's medals are classified and he may not wear them on his uniform.

Tony has risen fast for someone who's not a fighter pilot in the Indonesian Air Force. Sarah has the rank of Ajun Komisaris Polisi, which is more or less the same level as a Captain in the TNI, which is extraordinary for somebody only twenty-four years old. After her assignment in the UK, Tony knows that her career will skyrocket.

"And if I had married him," teases Sarah, "not only would you have to salute me first, you'd also have to call me Lady Adrian."

Tony is even more deflated imagining just that. He looks like he's thinking of other things he'd rather call her. They're silent for a few moments.

"I guess that will never happen…" says Sarah, almost inaudibly.

Tony sees that she's starting to get emotional again. He hugs her and they don't talk much the rest of the way home.

18:04 WIB (GMT+7)
Friday October 2, 2026
Jaya Ancol Seafront
Pademangan, North Jakarta, Jakarta

Brian enters the main gate and reports to the two on-duty security guards. He can see a CCTV camera directed towards his disguised face.

"*Selamat malam,*" greets Brian.

"*Selamat malam, pak. Bisa saya bantu?*" asks the security guard. *Good evening, pak. May I help you?*

"Yes, I would like to go to Sarah Dharmawan's house," says Brian in English. He can speak fluent Bahasa Indonesia, but intentionally used English to put the guards on the back foot. "Could you please show me the way?"

"It would be my pleasure, sir," answers the security guard without missing a beat, "but could you please deposit your passport before you enter our complex?"

Unexpectedly, the security guard can speak posh English! This really surprises Brian, who was born in the London East End. Brian doesn't know that Sarah is appointed as their commander and taught them English. She also gave them a standing order to be extra careful if anyone asked about her or her family.

"I-I-I'm sorry, but I didn't bring my passport," stammers Brian.

"I beg your pardon, sir, but we can't let you enter our complex unless you deposit your passport or at least a copy of it with us," answers the security guard.

Brian tries to bluff his way in, but the security guards are having none of it. Although they still sound friendly, Brian can tell they're suspicious of him. As he turns his car around, he sees in the rear-view mirror that one of the security guards is taking down his plates.

"Fuck!" curses Brian, slamming his hand on the steering wheel.

He immediately debriefs the others when he arrives at their factory.

"I don't think we can snatch her from her fucking house. The bloody security guards there are ridiculously thorough," says Brian, taking the disguise off his face.

"How about if we infiltrate from the seaside?" suggests Richard.

"We'd need Muireann and the other fucking divers for that and they're all fucking dead!" snaps Patrick.

Everyone falls silent, but Rory offers them a solution. "We don't have to snatch her from her house. Her sister Cindy's Facebook page says she's meeting her friends at the Grand Indonesia Mall this Sunday morning. We'll just snatch the little girl on the way there and then force Sarah to come to us."

This operation is known as tiger kidnap and was developed by the Irish Republican Army (IRA) during The Troubles. They would snatch someone and then force their significant other to do something they wouldn't do under normal circumstances. In this instance, they'll snatch Cindy and force Sarah to come to them.

"When will I gut her wee sister?" asks Niall excitedly.

"She hasn't come of age yet, Niall!" protests Brian.

"So?"

"We don't slot children," says Brian firmly.

"But it's okay for ye to give them drugs?" challenges Niall, smirking.

Brian snorts. "That's different."

Their conversation makes everyone uncomfortable. They don't mind Niall torturing and killing Sarah, but her sister is under-aged. Niall, the psychopath, doesn't care about that.

"That's enough!" snaps Patrick. "Once Sarah is dead, then we'll decide what to do with the weean. Liam, Bert, and Chris will do the snatch and Frank and I will plan the decommissioning and the relocation of the plant to Central Java. Richard, have the local fellas produce overtime on Saturday so they can start packing on Sunday."

"Aye," answers Richard.

Liam, Bert, and Chris aren't looking forward to their assignment, but they see that Patrick isn't in the mood for argument. Patrick knows that most of his members will object to this. No matter how vicious they are, they won't kill an under-aged girl. But Patrick must make sure the INP daren't harass them. He has to show that he won't hesitate to kill Indonesian policemen and their families if they harass them. Patrick decides to himself that he'll hand Cindy over to Niall once he's finished with Sarah.

With the plans for snatching, torturing, and killing the Indonesian policewoman and her family underway, narcoterrorism activities by a foreign drug syndicate will soon commence.

21:44 WIB (GMT+7)
Saturday October 3, 2026
Jaya Ancol Seafront
Pademangan, North Jakarta, Jakarta

Sarah and Tony finally arrive by taxi at the family's housing complex. They observe the security guards thoroughly perform all their procedures. Sarah realizes that all this time, her security guards have been scared of her. First, because they suspect she's a member of Densus-88 and second, because she could easily defeat any of them during hand-to-hand combat training. She has no qualms about slapping them around when they repeat mistakes. However, that was in the past. Sarah is determined to change her leadership style, starting with them.

The two security guards salute them crisply, knowing their commander is in the taxi's backseat. The taxi stops at her house and the driver helps them with their luggage. Cindy and the family dog welcome them home. The German Shepherd is extremely excited to see Sarah again.

"*Moin*, Jürgen," greets Sarah in German. She kneels and hugs the large dog. "*Ich vermisse dich so sehr. Vermisst du mich?*"

Jürgen answers with a loud bark. They play with each other for a while before finally entering the house.

"Where's Mum and Dad, *Dik*?" asks Sarah.

"They have to go to a wedding reception in Bandung. They'll be home tomorrow evening," answers Cindy, dropping two of Sarah's suitcases in her room.

Tony brings the rest. Sarah opens one and gives her siblings some souvenirs from England.

"Thanks, *Dik*," says Tony. "I have to go right away, I'm on duty tomorrow."

"Thanks a lot, *Kak*," says Sarah. "By the way, that package you're holding is from B Squadron."

"Really?" asks Tony, looking like Christmas came early.

Tony kisses his sisters on their foreheads and goes downstairs, opening his package on the way.

"Do you have any plans for tomorrow, *Kak*?" asks Cindy.

"I already have an appointment with the commander of Densus. Why do you ask?"

# THE POLICEWOMAN

"My friends and I are going to see a movie at the Grand Indonesia Mall. Isn't tomorrow a Sunday?" asks Cindy, her cute lips pouting.

"Sunday doesn't mean anything for a Densus operative, *Dik*," says Sarah, smiling. She's missed her sister.

"So when can I hang out with you? I haven't hung out with you in a long time, you know," says Cindy, her pout growing bigger.

"Next year I'm invited to Buckingham Palace. King William is going to invest me with a medal. Do you want to go to England with me?" asks Sarah.

"Yeah!" answers Cindy excitedly.

While helping her sister sort out her luggage, Cindy starts telling Sarah what she'll do if she meets Prince George, which makes Sarah laugh. Sarah's finally home and everything is back to normal again. The only thing *not* normal is Tony's loud laugh from downstairs. Sarah and Cindy briefly share a look before running downstairs. Their brother's rolling on the sofa, laughing his arse off while holding a framed photograph.

"What's up, *Kak*?" asks Sarah quizzically.

Tony still can't say anything and gives her the framed photograph, face-down. Sarah reads what's on the back. 'A copy of this photo has replaced the one in the Interest Room.' She flips it over. Sarah is instantly red-faced when she sees the picture, which is her surprised, furious face from when she first saw her picture in B Squadron's Interest Room. Compared to her bikini picture, this photo is her ugliest and in fact, she looks as if she's constipated. There's a caption at the bottom that reads 'Inspector Incontinentia Buttocks, MC'. Sarah sighs and gives the picture to Cindy, who immediately starts rolling on the sofa beside Tony.

"Hey! That picture's not up-to-date, you know. The caption should read 'Inspector Incontinentia Buttocks, DSO, MC, GM'," says Sarah, pouting exactly like her picture and making her siblings laugh even louder.

Sarah can only shake her head as she returns to her room. She must now figure out a way to stitch-up her friends at B Squadron, now on the other side of the world. Once everything is sorted out, Jürgen accompanies Sarah to the main security post inside the town hall of the housing complex. When they see their commander approach, the guards exit the post and give her a crisp salute before inviting her inside.

Sarah asks them to debrief her on what happened during her absence.

Unlike other security guards, they're required to debrief her in English. Before she was deployed overseas, Sarah used to chew them out when their grammar was wrong or if they mispronounced a word. But not anymore. She now patiently teaches them the correct way. The security guards are pleasantly surprised when she praises their English. After the debrief, she asks a couple of them to accompany her inspecting the other security posts around the housing complex.

Before they go, they tell her that a foreigner asked about her house, but they had to turn him back because he wouldn't deposit his passport. As per procedure, they noted down the number of his car and they show her the CCTV recording. Sarah doesn't recognize the man so she calls POLDA Metro Jaya to check the numbers. The on-duty policeman tells her to check back tomorrow because he doesn't have access to the database.

Sarah smiles and praises her security guards once again for following procedures. The security guards can sense that their commander's leadership style has changed. She's far more patient with them than she was before she deployed. They like being praised by their commander, not just because she's beautiful, but also because they know she's extremely skilled at her day job.

They used to fear her. But now they have nothing but the utmost respect for her and would follow her anywhere.

04:56 WIB (GMT+7)
Sunday October 4, 2026
Jaya Ancol Seafront
Pademangan, North Jakarta, Jakarta

Sarah starts the day with her crunches in her room, accompanied by Jürgen. She really misses Michael, who always caressed her stomach during her morning workout. It feels hard doing her crunches now, with no one there to admire her abs. She's even thought about quitting.

But Sarah's self-discipline pushes her to the end. She then feels disappointed with herself for just *thinking* about quitting, so she punishes herself with extra crunches. She finally stops at 1,500, making her abs as hard as a rock. She wants to continue to 2,000, but she has to start preparing for work.

Today, she takes her Lamborghini Huracán. She's in mufti, wearing a simple white shirt, light-blue jeans, and running shoes. The only unusual thing about her appearance is a black, skull-themed balaclava covering her face like a ninja, showing nothing but her clear blue eyes. Masked individuals like her are often seen near the Densus-88 Building and the other policemen are used to it. Sarah's height, body shape, and eye colour make other policemen think she's one of the foreign female instructors for Densus policewomen. A traffic policeman once tried to hit on her in his broken English, but was completely confounded when she answered him in French. Sarah enters the Densus-88 Building, takes off her balaclava, and goes into her commander's office.

"*Selamat pagi, Komandan*," greets Sarah, saluting him crisply. *Good morning, Commander.*

"*Selamat pagi*," greets Police Brigadier General Prasetyo, returning her salute. "Have a seat, AKP."

"*Terimakasih, Komandan*," says Sarah, taking a seat in front of his desk.

"How's your arm?"

"Optimum, *Komandan*," answers Sarah. The medic was so good he didn't even leave a scar.

"How did it happen, AKP?" asks her commander. Broussard has already briefed him and he's read her report, but he wants to hear the story first-hand.

Sarah tells him everything. The commander of Densus-88 is impressed and this confirms his opinion that Sarah is his best police officer, maybe the best police officer in the INP. Sarah's competitive and this makes her want to excel in everything. Because Sarah comes from an affluent family, she doesn't care about her salary so she can concentrate on her passion, which is crime-fighting. Her career rise has been the fastest ever in the INP, making other police officers jealous of her. But they all have to admit that she's highly capable, intellectually and physically, and she's proficient in many foreign languages. Sarah works harder than most police officers and always goes home late at night. She almost never takes a day off, to the point where her commander often has to order her to take a break.

According to Prasetyo, Sarah's only weakness is that she's too easily disappointed with herself when an operation doesn't go exactly as planned, although she's able to adapt herself quickly when things go wrong and she's accomplished every mission assigned to her. Sarah will eventually overcome this weakness through operational experience, as every field commander knows that every plan, no matter how meticulously planned, will always go to shit as soon as the bullets start flying.

But Prasetyo fully realizes that there will be political factors inhibiting her career in Densus-88. She already has what it takes to be the commander someday. Her charisma and command presence is powerful. Her men follow her lead without question, although some of the men complain she's too tough on them and too much of a perfectionist. A few police generals have cynically suggested that Sarah rose so fast just because of her looks, but they all changed their minds when Prasetyo introduced them to her and they talked to her for a few minutes.

Sarah then starts telling her commander about her experience being trained by the SAS. Prasetyo is surprised and calls one of his subordinates to join them. Komisaris Besar Polisi (Kombes) Hanafi, the Commander of Densus-88 for POLDA Metro Jaya, enters the room and listens to Sarah as she tells them about her CQB training at PATA. Both men look enthusiastic as they learn the SAS CQB methods, which are quite different to what they're taught by their US instructors. They ask Sarah to teach them the SAS Colour Clock Code on the spot. Both commanders agree that the colour clock code is perfect for Immediate Actions.

Over the next few hours, Sarah tells them about the UKSF Selection process, their organization structure, the planning stages and assault on Swan's Mill, and, finally, the progress of the investigation into The Cartel's factory in Indonesia. They already know from the Secretariat of Interpol NCB Indonesia that next year Sarah will be invited to Buckingham Palace to be invested with a George Medal, but this is the first time they've heard she received two more medals from the British Army.

They're empathetic when Sarah tells them about the raid in Cheshire and Liverpool when she tried to save one of her teammates. Sarah reports the mission professionally, but they can still feel the sorrow behind her mask.

"You were close to that SAS squadron commander, weren't you?" asks Hanafi.

"*Siap, Komandan!*" says Sarah. She can't help it, but her eyes are starting to dampen.

Prasetyo gives her a couple of letters. "Before you go home to rest, here's a couple of letters for you. I think they will cheer you up."

The first letter is a transfer order as per Monday for her return to Densus-88, which indeed cheers her up a bit. Although her assignment at Interpol turned out to be quite interesting, she prefers a more direct approach to crime-fighting than being a liaison officer.

The second letter tells her as per Monday she will be promoted to Komisaris Polisi, making her instantly happy. This is unexpected, as she was promoted to Ajun Komisaris Polisi just earlier this year. Sarah can't wait to see Tony's expression when she tells him they'll be the same level.

Both commanders smile wryly at her reaction. They've had to quickly promote her to counteract a 'threat' from Interpol, who intended to keep Sarah in Interpol unless Densus-88 could absolutely guarantee her career in Densus-88 would be better than in Interpol. ICPO-Interpol HQ has recommended NCB Indonesia keep Sarah in Interpol. They believe she already has what it takes to be promoted and sent to Interpol HQ to handle an Incident Response Team.

After Prasetyo negotiated with the Secretariat of Interpol NCB Indonesia, it was decided that Sarah could be transferred back to Densus-88, on the condition they were able to promote her once she returned to Indonesia. In the future, once Sarah has gone as far as she can go at Densus-88, they will have to let her move to ICPO-Interpol HQ.

The Secretariat of Interpol NCB Indonesia and Prasetyo both know that if Sarah is transferred to ICPO-Interpol HQ, her career could know no limits. Between 2012 and 2016, the President of ICPO-Interpol was a French-Italian policewoman named Mirelle Ballestrazzi, and there's no reason Sarah couldn't equal that. Sarah has already mastered the four official languages of Interpol, which are English, French, Spanish, and Arabic, so she'd be ready to skyrocket through the ranks. Fortunately for Densus, the Chief of the INP instantly approved her promotion because her achievements have been extraordinary.

"With your promotion, your responsibilities will be even greater, AKP," reminds Prasetyo. "I want you to become the commander of the Special Actions Sub-detachment."

"*Siap, Komandan!*" answers Sarah. She looks even more cheerful because she has been eyeing that position.

"Besides that, I order you to help us adopt what you learned from the SAS for implementation at Densus-88, especially the SAS Colour Clock Code. Please present your concept next week on Friday. I also order you to revamp our selection methods for Densus operatives according to the UKSF Selection. I'm hoping the trials can be started next month," orders Prasetyo.

With her promotion, Sarah's workload is now three times heavier, though it's nothing she can't handle. Her commander asked her to present the SAS methods Friday next week, but Sarah should be able to finish everything assigned to her within a couple of days. Sarah almost says '*Siap, Komandan!*' like she usually does, but then she remembers something she learned from Michael.

"Is there a problem, AKP?" asks her commander when he sees her hesitate.

"I... ehm... still have a mission from Interpol to find The Cartel's factory in Indonesia, *Komandan*. I think it will be almost impossible to accomplish everything according to your timetable," answers Sarah with a straight face.

Both men are taken aback by Sarah's answer. They are so confounded that they don't know how to respond.

"But I will do my best to finish everything on time, *Komandan*," continues Sarah.

She's then dismissed. After Sarah leaves them, both men look at each other and laugh out loud. Besides learning a lot about the SAS CQB methods, it turns out their best police officer has also picked up some of their bad working habits as well...

09:42 WIB (GMT+7)
Sunday October 4, 2026
Jaya Ancol Seafront
Pademangan, North Jakarta, Jakarta

Several hours earlier...

Cindy's parents taught her to be independent and this means she must go everywhere using the Transjakarta busway system. From the front gate of her housing complex, she walks toward the deserted R.E. Martadinata road. Both her siblings and parents always tell her to be extra careful in this high crime area. Cindy has never experienced or witnessed any crime, but she's fully alert. She can sense a car stop behind her and a couple of people getting out. She quickens her walk and can sense that two people are trying to catch up with her. When one of them grabs her from behind, Cindy is ready. She pulls his hand, bows down, and slams him to the ground. She executed the move perfectly because she's been drilled by her dad and siblings in unarmed combat.

"Fuck!" curses Chris as he slams head first into the pavement.

Because of her lack of experience, Cindy takes too long to admire her work and doesn't immediately run or scream for help. Having successfully floored one of her attackers, she becomes overconfident. When she turns around to face his friend, a telescoping baton hits the top of her head. Cindy's dazed for a moment before she passes out, head gushing out blood. Chris and Bert hurriedly pick her up and put her in their car before anyone sees them. Liam steps on the gas once everyone is inside.

Bert hit Cindy's head a bit too hard, so it's several hours before she regains consciousness. Even though she has a tremendous headache and is feeling nauseous from the blow, Cindy immediately realizes that she's been abducted. Inside the hot and humid room, she feels her body already drenched in sweat. She's tied to a chair wearing some sort of heavy vest. There's an old handphone wrapped in wiring sticking out of one of the pockets. To her right, Cindy sees a foreigner tinkering with her smartphone in front of an open laptop. Another foreigner enters the room.

"Well?" asks Patrick.

"Her smartphone is active and she's currently mobile. She's on her way home and will probably arrive in a few minutes," says Rory.

"I'll wait a couple of hours before I call her. Has Brian deployed yet?"

"Aye, he'll take a position right across the street from POLDA Metro Jaya and he should be able to see whether there are any extraordinary activities across the street," answers Rory. "He'll immediately distribute the Mandy to the local dealers once we're finished here."

"Have the fellas started packing yet?"

"Aye! We're on schedule, Paddy!" answers Rory, starting to get impatient.

The Cartel has found a perfect location for their factory and HQ in Central Java. It's in a remote area and highly defendable in an assault, even from above. Patrick heads over to Cindy, who doesn't look even remotely scared of him. Cindy's attitude reminds him of Sheila, making him suddenly feel sad for the loss of his only child.

"How's your head? Does it hurt much?" asks Patrick in Bahasa Indonesia.

Cindy doesn't give him a reaction, even though she's surprised the foreigner can speak her language fluently. Patrick softly cleans the cut on Cindy's head. He then helps her drink from a bottled water. He doesn't want her to get dehydrated and needs her to be conscious for a few more hours.

"Are you hungry? Do you want something to eat?" asks Patrick.

Cindy shakes her head. Niall enters the room and sees Cindy tied to a chair. She's adorable, like a super-cute version of her older sister, with more of an Asian look. Cindy's skin has a deeper shade of tan than her sister's, and Niall likes her exotic look. He actually prefers Cindy to Sarah. He keeps looking at Cindy with his leery smile. Cindy's afraid of him, but she still won't give him a reaction.

Patrick says to Niall. "When she gets here, ye only have one hour."

"That's not even remotely enough time!" protests Niall.

"Once we're finished packing, we'll take the weean with us. After we reach our new stronghold in Central Java, ye can take all the time ye want with the weean."

Niall looks at Cindy for a few seconds before nodding. Cindy looks confused so Patrick gives her an explanation. "Your sister has killed my wife, my brother, and my daughter. Today, I will get my revenge. I will call your sister here so my friend can disembowel her. If Sarah won't come here, my friend will disembowel *you!*"

Cindy's eyes finally go wide in panic, especially when she sees the other man's sadistic smile.

12:14 WIB (GMT+7)
Sunday October 4, 2026
Jaya Ancol Seafront
Pademangan, North Jakarta, Jakarta

Sarah parks her Huracán and enters her house. No one is home except Bibi and Jürgen.

"Bibi, has Cindy gone yet?" asks Sarah.

"Since morning," answers Bibi. "Have you had lunch?"

"Maybe later. It's scorching outside so I'll have a swim first," says Sarah. "If my phone rings, just send it to the pool, all right?"

"*Baik.*"

Sarah places her smartphone on the dinner table and goes to her room. She undresses and puts on a plain white bikini. She then dives into their Olympic-sized swimming pool. The water is warm, but refreshing. She starts swimming laps to release the stress of these past few days.

Whenever Sarah's swimming or sunbathing during the weekends, her twelve-year-old back-door neighbour always opens his bedroom window, takes out a pair of binoculars, and watches her. This adorable kid is named Bona and he likes to come over to play with Cindy. They've been friends since they were babies. This time, only Bona is watching her every move. One time, there were up to six boys jostling each other on the window with their binoculars, watching her sunbathe. Sarah ignored them, but finally felt uncomfortable when Bona's dad joined them with his own binoculars. After a couple of hours swimming, Bibi brings over her smartphone with Jürgen in tow.

"Someone's calling," says Bibi, placing the ringing smartphone on the table by the pool. She immediately heads inside. "Jürgen! *Komm herein!*"

The German Shepherd meekly follows Bibi inside. Their Javanese housekeeper has had to learn some German too, just so that she is able to give commands to the family dog. Sarah exits the pool and dries her hands before answering the phone, which turns out to be from Cindy.

"*Ya, Dik?*"

"*Kak!* Don't come here!" shouts her sister's voice.

"Cindy!"

"Sarah, this is Patrick Dunbar."

Sarah is stunned and can't answer for a few seconds, dreading what she will hear. "What do you want?"

"We have yer sister. If ye want to see her in one piece, go to the PT. Westershire Chemicals Manufacture Indonesia in Bogor before 15:00 local time. I will send ye the GPS coordinates to find it. We have a couple of fellas watching yer training centre at Bogor and at POLDA Metro Jaya and they are in constant contact with us. If they see just one fucking heli arrive or deploy, the weean will die. Understand?" threatens Patrick.

"What do you want with me?"

"Oh, just revenge. That's all. I just want ye to experience the same agony ye dished out to Muireann, Sheila, and Steve," says Patrick. "Be here by 15:00 or the weean's dead."

The call is disconnected and Sarah runs to her room without bothering to dry herself. She puts on her jeans and running shoes. She grabs her shirt on the way out of her room and slips into it as she heads towards her Huracán. She doesn't waste time to button the shirt and just ties the ends together. Sarah races out of the complex, ignoring the salutes of the security guards on duty, and heads towards Bogor.

She calls Tony.

# CHAPTER 16
# SATUAN BRAVO – 90

13:58 WIB (GMT+7)
Sunday October 4, 2026
Detasemen 902, Satuan Bravo – 90, Korps Pasukan Khas, TNI – Angkatan Udara
Rumpin Airfield, Bogor, West Java

Tony is doing administrative work for his detachment. He absolutely hates paperwork so he concentrates fully to finish everything in one sitting. He's on-duty with five other men this Sunday. They're all in mufti and they're even *prohibited* from wearing their air force uniforms. They have to appear and act like civilians, and this goes for all CT units under Komando Operasi Khusus (KOOPSUS), Indonesia's equivalent to the UKSF Group.

During their morning briefing, Tony told his men about his sister's adventures in the UK and his men were impressed. They could see that their commander is immensely proud of his sister's achievements. They too were sad to hear the fate of Michael Adrian, the SAS squadron commander who trained them a couple of years ago.

Tony is pouring some mineral water from a dispenser when his smartphone rings. It's his sister. "*Ya, Dik?*"

"*Kak*, Cindy's been abducted!"

"What? Who snatched her?" asks Tony, eyes wide as saucers.

A couple of Bravo men inside the room with him look towards their commander and frown. Tony goes into his office and closes the door.

"The Cartel snatched her and took her to some factory in Bogor, called the PT. Westershire Chemicals Manufacture Indonesia. I'll send you the GPS coordinates."

"Where are you now?" asks Tony.

"I'm on the way there. If I don't get there before three o'clock, they're going to kill her!"

"But if you go there, they'll kill *you*!" shouts Tony.

His booming voice is heard by his men outside his office.

"They won't immediately kill me. They're going to torture me first," says Sarah.

Tony almost drops his smartphone. "Torture you?"

"One of their members is a psychopath. His name is Niall Schroeder. He's the one who tortured Michael. If he's the one who's going to torture me, I'll still have a chance."

Tony feels weak in the knees imagining his sister being tortured like Michael. "How the fuck could you take being hit by a board full of nails like that?"

Tony notices his men hurriedly leaving the office.

"He doesn't do that to his female victims."

"What will he do to you?" asks Tony.

His sister doesn't answer.

"*Dik*, I'm asking you a fucking question! How will he torture you?"

Tony hears Sarah give a long sigh before answering him. "He's going to disembowel me."

"What? You stand down! Right the fuck now!" orders Tony, taking his Glock 19 pistol and holstering it into his tactical holster on his thigh.

"No way! They're going to kill Cindy if I don't get there before three o'clock. I can't ask Densus for help. They said they have lookouts watching POLDA Metro Jaya and the training facility at Megamendung. If they see anyone deploy, they'll kill her, *Kak*! Just get here as fast as you can before that psycho opens me up. Remember to bring extra kit for me. If I don't make it... save Cindy! All right, *Kak*?" says Sarah.

Tony can hear his sister let out a sob before she disconnects the call. Tony is stunned for a moment before running outside to his Toyota Fortuner. He sees five of his men standing next to it, carrying weapons and various kit. They're all in mufti, but carrying HK MP5SD3 submachine guns and wearing load bearing harnesses and tactical holsters with the same type of pistol Tony is carrying. Sersan Satu (Sertu) Nyoman is carrying a MOLLE pack and a combat medical kit and Sersan Kepala (Serka) Pranoto is bringing sets of tactical holsters for pistols, load bearing harnesses for submachine guns, HK MP5SD3 submachine guns, Aitor Jungle King II combat knives, and CQB Headsets. Besides Sertu Nyoman and Serka Pranoto, there's Sersan Mayor (Serma) Suprayitno, Sertu Dedi Suhendri, and Sersan Dua (Serda) Zulkarnaen, every Bravo member on-duty today.

"What are you doing here?" asks Tony, frowning at them.

"We're coming with you, *Komandan*," answers Suprayitno.

"Negative!" says Tony firmly. "If I survive this, I will definitely be court-martialed. You men return to your duties. If you go with me, you'll be considered AWOL and get court-martialed too."

"*Siap, Komandan!*" say the five Bravo members without hesitation.

"That's not all. There's an unknown number of armed criminals. You could get wounded or even killed!"

"*Siap, Komandan!*" say the five Bravo members, once again without any hesitation. They're more afraid of being court-martialed than of getting wounded or killed.

"Your sisters are part of our family too, *Komandan*," says Pranoto. "Let us help you save them."

Tony feels a lump in his throat and can't say anything else. He can clearly see that they won't budge. Even though they're armed, they most likely still don't have enough manpower or firepower to take on the entire Cartel. Tony can't delay anymore because his sisters' lives are in danger. He can't even imagine how he would react if he saw Sarah with her guts hanging out.

"Get in," orders Tony.

Everyone enters and Tony races his car towards the GPS coordinates Sarah sent him. His men are just as horrified as he is when Tony briefs them on what'll happen to his sister if they don't get there in time. They're committed to helping their commander no matter what consequences they'll face.

14:01 WIB (GMT+7)
Sunday October 4, 2026
Jagorawi Toll Road
Citeureup, Bogor, West Java

Several minutes earlier…

Sarah disconnects the call before she starts crying. She realizes that this might be the last day of her life. The almost-empty toll road lets her make full use of her Huracán's speed and she only slows down when she exits the toll road, almost an hour later. After a couple of minutes, her GPS shows her that their drug factory is only a hundred metres away. Sarah glances at her watch and it turns out she still has plenty of time.

Sarah parks her car on the side of the road, covers her face with both hands, and starts crying. Of all the battles she's experienced, the only time she was wounded was at Carluccio's. Right before an operation commenced, it always crossed her mind that within the next few minutes she could get wounded, disabled, disfigured, or even killed. With all her training, she's confident that she can avoid all the above, but the danger's there. Sarah remembers the motto of the Training Wing of the SAS 'Train hard, fight easy. Train easy, fight hard – and die.'

But this time is different to her previous combat experience. This time Sarah *knows* that within the next few minutes, she's going to feel the most excruciating pain ever! No training in the world could prepare her for such horrendous torture. Sarah has never felt so much fear in her life, not just for own fate, but also for the life of her little sister. Sarah must endure the torture for as long as possible so Tony can at least save Cindy.

As she worries about her sister, Sarah recalls the quote from Sir Charles Mountbatten when he invested her with the DSO. He said that 'courage is not the absence of fear, but rather the judgment that something else is more important than fear'. Thinking about those words, Sarah realizes she cares more about Cindy's life than her own. She doesn't care anymore about her own life and is willing to give it up for her sister. She decides to give everything she has today. If she dies, at least she'll meet Michael again.

In a much calmer state of mind, Sarah drives her car to The Cartel's factory. She's ready for any kind of pain awaiting her inside.

14:50 WIB (GMT+7)
Sunday October 4, 2026
POLDA Metro Jaya
Kebayoran Baru, South Jakarta, Jakarta

In the middle of the city of Jakarta, Police Brigadier General Prasetyo and Komisaris Besar Polisi Hanafi are still at POLDA Metro Jaya, discussing the SAS Colour Clock Code and other methods of the SAS. They're excited to implement much of what Sarah told them about for Densus.

A female Densus operative knocks on the door and enters. She reports that there's a suspicious foreigner out the front of the Crowne Plaza Hotel, across the street from the exit of POLDA Metro Jaya. His car seems to have broken down, but he's refusing all offers of assistance. He's standing outside, even though it's scorching hot outside.

The two men take their binoculars and look out the window. The foreigner looks like he's playing with his smartphone. He doesn't look dangerous, but they make preparations in case it turns out he's up to some mischief.


14:57 WIB (GMT+7)
Sunday October 4, 2026
PT. Westershire Chemicals Manufacture Indonesia
Citeureup, Bogor, West Java


Sarah enters through the main entrance. Someone at the security post directs her to the office. Sarah catches a glimpse of an M4 Carbine inside the security post. It's eighty metres to the office, with a forest block on either side of the single lane road. Sarah parks her Huracán in the parking lot, filled with dozens of Toyota Innovas. She enters the lobby, but it seems to be empty. There's a door at the back that she heads towards. She's not gone a foot when the silencer of a pistol is suddenly pushed inside her ear. This is to prevent the victim from being able to swat the pistol away before the attacker can squeeze the trigger.

"Turn left, put yer hands against that wall, and spread yer legs," orders Niall.

Sarah does what she is told.

"Any sudden moves and I'll blow up yer wee sister, all right?" threatens Niall.

Sarah only nods. Niall frisks her thoroughly and professionally with one hand. The other keeps the gun pressed against her.

"Now go towards the door on yer right. Slowly!" orders Niall.

Again, Sarah does what she's told. She opens the door to the spacious room. It's several degrees hotter than the scorching heat outside, so she's instantly sweaty. Across the room, there's a doorway that presumably leads to the factory area. Sarah hears plenty of noise from behind the door. To the right of the door, there's a table with an old laptop on it and a video camera on a tripod. To the right of the tripod and in the corner sits Cindy tied to a chair. Her eyes and mouth are covered with cloth and she's wearing what looks like a suicide vest filled with explosives. The explosives are shaped in such a way that if they explode, they'll blow inwards, killing only Cindy and no one else. An old handphone, wrapped in wires, is in one of the pockets. Sarah boils up in anger when she sees dried blood on Cindy's shirt and pants. Niall pushes Sarah towards the laptop and Patrick's image suddenly appears.

"We finally meet, Sarah," says Patrick through the webcam.

"Let my sister go, then you can do anything you want with me," says Sarah.

Cindy reacts when she hears her sister's voice, but she's unable to say anything.

Patrick laughs. "We don't slot weeans. We'll let her go, of course, but only after Niall is done with ye. And that's going to take a while, right Niall?"

As a police officer, Sarah knows that Patrick's lying. She can feel Niall smirk behind her, but she doesn't give him a reaction. Cindy can only squirm in her seat.

"Sarah doesn't seem afraid of what ye'll do to her, Niall. Go ahead and do what ye do best, make her death as excruciating as possible."

"Aye, Paddy!" says Niall excitedly.

Cindy squirms even harder, but she can't make a sound. She's starting to cry.

"We leave in an hour," says Patrick. "Make sure she's dead by then."

The webcam disconnects. Niall turns on the video camera and points it at Sarah. He's already holstered his pistol, but his left hand is holding something as big as an old handphone with some sort of small antennae sticking out of it.

"I have the detonator in my hand in a dead man's switch. If ye try anything bone, I'll make a mess out of yer sister. Understand?" says Niall, showing her the detonator.

Niall's thumb keeps pressing on a button. A 'dead man's switch' means that the IED will explode if Niall releases the button. Sarah only nods. She won't take any risks. She'll just wait for her brother to arrive.

"One more thing. Patrick and Brian can also detonate this. If I'm not back within the hour, Patrick will blow her up. If Brian sees any unusual activities at POLDA Metro Jaya, he'll blow her up. All they have to do is call the number on that phone. Understand?"

Sarah doesn't know who Brian is, but she can figure out that he's the lookout watching POLDA Metro Jaya. This means that Patrick lied to her when he said that one of his men was watching Megamendung. Sarah nods once again.

"Now take off yer shirt," orders Niall.

Sarah removes her sweat-soaked shirt and throws it on the floor. She's now in her white bikini-top, light blue jeans, and running shoes. Her light-tanned skin is gleaming with sweat, making all her muscles stand out beautifully, especially her perfectly-shaped six-pack abs. Niall can only stare at Sarah's magnificent body as he takes out his knife. Sarah sees that it's the same tanto-tip Gerber Guardian he used to disembowel Karen.

"Ye will certainly be the most beautiful of all my victims," says Niall.

"Thank you," says Sarah, looking at him with her sharp blue eyes.

Niall laughs. "Ye're courageous and I love yer eyes. Maybe I should stick my knife into them?"

Niall suddenly lunges forward and stabs his knife at Sarah's left eye! He diverts the knife at the last second, missing her eye by millimetres. Sarah only blinks and resumes looking at Niall without changing her expression.

"Naah... yer eyes are too pretty. I want to see them when ye scream for mercy."

Niall traces the knife down to Sarah's neck.

"How about if I slit yer throat?" asks Niall, placing the knife against her throat as if he's about to slit it.

Sarah doesn't react.

"Naah... too much of a mess."

He traces his knife down again and points it towards the middle of Sarah's chest.

"How about if I stab ye through the heart?"

"I thought you wanted me to die slowly," says Sarah.

Niall smirks at Sarah's defiance. Niall slowly traces the knife downwards, from her sternum, down between the ridges of her abs, then down again towards her navel. Sarah knows that in a few moments she will feel the most excruciating pain she has ever experienced in her life, which makes her heart beat faster. But Sarah is determined to face it as calmly and as courageously as possible. Cindy can hear everything happening in front of her and Sarah doesn't want her to be traumatized by hearing her sister being tortured.

The tanto-tipped knife finally passes the upper lip of Sarah's navel and Niall starts pressing it in. Sarah holds her breath and clenches her abdominal muscles, as if trying to prevent the knife from entering her belly. Niall is struggling, but the sharp tip finally punctures through the outer skin. The knife starts going in smoothly, but Sarah manages not to react. It turns out it isn't as painful as she thought it would be.

Sarah suddenly flinches and gasps when the tip of the knife pierces her innards. The pain she feels when the knife punctures her intestines almost takes her breath away! But Niall stops pushing the blade in and releases his grip on the knife. Sarah breathes a sigh of relief and looks down. The knife is halfway embedded in her navel, but no blood is coming out. She looks sharply at Niall again, but with watery eyes from the pain.

"Now what?" asks Sarah.

"Honey, I'm just getting started," says Niall as he punches her in the stomach.

Sarah manages to clench her abs before his fist hits her, but she still feels as if her stomach has exploded. She doesn't make a sound, but her face hardens from the pain. She can still look at Niall with her deadly sharp eyes, but her lips are clenched shut.

"My knife looks good on ye," says Niall, smirking.

He flicks the knife with his finger and Sarah flinches in pain. Niall quickly punches her again in the same place. This time, Sarah doesn't have time to clench her abs and it feels like her stomach's been shot with a shotgun! Sarah staggers back and clutches her stomach. She almost falls, but manages to control herself at the last second. Her left knee and left hand hit the floor, her right hand still clutching her stomach. Sarah hasn't recovered from the blow when Niall kicks her right shoulder, flooring her on her back. She clenches her mouth shut and makes no sound, but her beautiful face is contorted in immense pain.

Niall's aroused watching Sarah writhing around sensually on the floor, her athletic body gleaming with sweat. He stares at her for a while and then kneels beside her. He starts caressing her body and squeezing her firm breasts. Sarah ignores him and takes the chance to control her breathing. Niall starts caressing her stomach.

"Such perfect abs…" he mumbles.

His words and touch make Sarah think of Michael. Sarah briefly forgets her pain and recalls her time together with him. But Niall suddenly grabs the handle and plunges it down! Sarah gasps in pain and before she can recover, Niall starts wiggling the knife. Sarah can feel the blade ripping her intestines apart. She has never felt this much pain in her life! Her face is showing extreme agony, but Sarah suffers in silence. Niall continues wiggling the knife and Sarah starts to cough up blood.

"Scream," orders Niall.

He keeps looking at Sarah's face as he wiggles the knife. For him, she looks even more beautiful with her face in agony like this. However, he's frustrated she isn't screaming. He's only satisfied when his victims cry for mercy and he doesn't have much time. Sarah knows this so she tries hard not to make a sound. If she screams, Niall will start disembowelling her.

"Scream," orders Niall again.

Sarah tries hard to put her thoughts elsewhere. Her memory of Michael helps her ignore some of the pain. She once again thinks about their lovely time together. When they walked around town, had dinner, and worked out together. When she thinks about running with Michael at the Brecon Beacons, Sarah suddenly realizes that the Fan Dance was more painful than what she's currently experiencing. The pain she's feeling right now is like the time she ran out of steam during her ascent on Corn Du.

"Scream!" orders Niall, sounding frustrated.

Sarah doesn't make a sound and now she's able to give Niall her sharp look. She then clenches her abs, squeezing her muscles around the blade in her belly. Niall tries hard to wiggle the knife, but fails, and this makes him even more frustrated. He starts punching Sarah in the stomach as hard as he can, as if forcing her to unclench her muscles. Each blow feels like being hit by a ballistic hammer, but Sarah stays silent. From where she's lying on her back, she can see Cindy crying, and it makes her determined to deal with this torture as quietly as she possibly can.

After hitting her stomach for the umpteenth time, Niall gets tired. Sarah enjoys a moment of relief and tries to control her breathing. She steals a look at her belly and sees that only a little blood has come out. The worst of her risks right now is that Niall will nick her aorta, which will lead to profuse blood loss and a fast death. As long as he doesn't do that, the next biggest risk is peritonitis from perforating abdominal trauma. But if she's treated quickly with strong antibiotics, she could survive hours and even days like this.

Sarah once read about a young Viet Cong during the Vietnam war, who got shot in his abdomen during a battle with the Americans. He retreated with his guts hanging out of him, then went into a farmhouse and borrowed an enamel cooking bowl. He put his intestines in the bowl and strapped it to his waist. He then continued fighting for three days until the GIs finally captured him. Despite being enemies, the Viet Cong earned the GIs' respect and admiration for his dedication and bravery. That incident inspired a memorable scene in the famous war movie called Apocalypse Now.

If that Viet Cong could keep on fighting for three days with his guts hanging out of him, Sarah thinks she can handle another thirty minutes with Niall. She can only hope that Tony will arrive before Niall opens her up. But no matter what condition Sarah's in when he saves her, she's determined to wipe out the people who killed her fiancé and hurt her little sister. Every time Sarah sees the blood on Cindy's shirt, the more determined she becomes to make them pay.

"Scream... and I will end yer agony," says Niall, panting.

Sarah looks at Niall and considers her words carefully. She knows that what's she's about to say will only make her suffer more, but she has to try to stall until her brother arrives.

"Honey, this doesn't hurt that much," says Sarah, smiling at him. She even puts her hands behind her head as if she's lying on the beach. "I'm actually starting to enjoy it."

Niall's jaw drops.

"You're not very good at this, are you?" quips Sarah.

Niall's jaw drops even further.

"Just wondering, Niall, what were Michael's last words?"

Niall is speechless and it takes a while before he can answer her. "He said 'the knife appears somewhat blunt' after I stuck him in the eye with this knife."

Sarah smiles even wider and looks towards Niall's groin. "Hmm... it seems your knife isn't the only thing that appears 'blunt' today, Niall."

Niall looks offended and furious. He grabs the knife and starts wiggling it again.

"How does this feel, ye bitch!"

Sarah feels the knife shredding her guts. She's in more pain than before and almost chokes as more blood gushes out of her mouth. She remembers Michael was tortured for hours before they finally ended his misery. Even though Michael experienced much, much worse than what she's enduring, he still wouldn't tell them where she was or give them her phone number. This thought keeps her going and even lets her ignore the extreme pain she's experiencing. Her hatred towards the people who tortured and killed her fiancé, then snatched and hurt her little sister, enables her to dismiss her pain.

"Scream, damn it!" shouts Niall.

Sarah clenches her abs and he has trouble wiggling the knife again. Niall starts hitting her stomach, forcing her to unclench. Sarah only looks at him and even smiles again. Niall looks both amazed and extremely frustrated at the same time. No woman has ever withstood this much torture without screaming.

The door to the factory suddenly opens. Someone sticks his head in and just as quickly pulls it back out, and the sound of machinery fills the room. Niall stops what he's doing and glances towards the door. Sarah tries to control her breathing. She can do this quickly because she's in top shape. She then notices that the door to the factory is unlocked, opens outward, and the handle is on the right side.

"Ye have thirty minutes left, Niall," says someone's voice.

"Right!" shouts Niall. After the door closes, he focuses again on Sarah. "I guess it's time to see whether the inside of yer belly is as lovely as the outside."

Niall likes to disembowel a woman when she's screaming for mercy and he's disappointed that Sarah hasn't made a sound. He unbuttons her jeans and opens the zipper, while Sarah just calmly looks at him, hands still behind her head. He grabs the handle of the knife and is gearing to open her up. He looks at her face so he can watch her expression as he disembowels her, but is amazed to find that Sarah's smiling at him. Niall's so frustrated, he fails to notice a shadow cross underneath the door to the lobby.

"Hmm... my intestines are lovely, Niall," says Sarah, winking at him. "It's such a shame you'll never see them."

Niall can only give her a quizzical look. Several things suddenly happen at the same time! Sarah's right hand shoots out towards Niall's left hand, pressing on the dead man's switch, at the same time the door flies open. A third of a second later, a couple of bullets slam into Niall's head. With her left hand, Sarah throws Niall's body to the side, while her right hand keeps his left hand clutched tight. Sarah sees Serka Pranoto approach Niall's convulsing body and empties his suppressed sub-machine gun into his head, shattering it to pieces.

"Clear!" says Pranoto.

"Room clear!" says Tony.

Pranoto heads towards the laptop to gather intel while Serma Suprayitno, an EOD specialist, heads towards Cindy to disarm the IED. Sertu Dedi Suhendri heads towards the door to the factory to cover it while two more men drag someone's body inside the room. The body has two gunshot wounds in the middle of his forehead and a look of surprise on his dead face. One of the men dragging it in is Tony. The other is Sertu Nyoman Sukarya, putting down an M4 Carbine and a couple of mags taken from the security post. Serda Zulkarnaen is the last to enter. He closes the door and covers it.

"The detonator's here... it's a dead man's switch," says Sarah.

Tony takes out his Aitor knife from the holster on his left waist and starts cutting Niall's hand off. Tony takes over his hand so Sarah can release her grip. Nyoman helps his commander wrap Niall's dead fingers to the detonator with duct tape.

Tony helps Sarah to her feet and then frisks Niall's dead body. Sarah takes her shirt off the floor and wipes the blood from her mouth and belly. Suprayitno has just disarmed the IED and is now untying Cindy's hands. Sarah throws her bloody shirt away and helps untie Cindy's legs. Both bonds are untied at the same time and Cindy takes off the cloth covering her eyes and mouth.

"*Kak!*" exclaims Cindy, hugging her sister.

Sarah flinches in pain when Cindy's leg accidentally snags on the knife still embedded in her. Cindy feels something on her leg and releases her hug. She looks down and her eyes go wide.

"*Kak...* your belly!" exclaims Cindy, reaching for the knife.

Sarah catches Cindy's hand before she pulls the knife out. "Leave it there, *Dik.*"

Cindy turns pale and can only look at her sister with wide eyes.

Sarah smiles to calm her down. "If you pull it out, everything inside will come out with it."

"But... but..." says Cindy. She suddenly faints into Sarah's arms.

Suprayitno helps Cindy while Sarah stands up again, buttoning her jeans closed. She faces Tony.

"Get her out of here," she orders. "Give me your smartphone and lend me a weapon. Densus and I will take care of this."

Tony has finished frisking Niall's body. He stands up and faces his sister. "I think I outrank you, *Dik.*"

Sarah gives her brother a sharp look. "*Tu n'as pas la juridiction, eikel. T'es militaire, pas policier. Tu es probablement en difficulté déjà assez.*" Sarah hates seeing officers arguing in front of their men so she reverts to French so Tony's men won't understand what they're arguing about. *You don't have the jurisdiction, stupid. You're military, not a law enforcement officer. You're in enough trouble already.*

"*Tu peux pas faire ça tout seul, Dik,*" says Tony, trying to reason with her. *You can't do this alone, Dik.*

"*C'est pas ta lutte!*" says Sarah firmly. *This isn't your fight!*

Nyoman breaks out his medical kit. He gives Sarah a pill from of his pill pack and a canteen of water.

"What's this?" asks Sarah.

"*Moxifloxacin*, AKP, to prevent sepsis," replies Nyoman, pointing at her belly.

Sarah swallows the antibiotic with just a sip of water. Nyoman makes sure she doesn't drink too much. Sarah returns to Tony while Nyoman goes back to his medical kit.

"*C'est pas ta lutte, Kak,*" repeats Sarah.

"*Il ya une force étrangère ici qui menace notre société. Il est grand temps que le militaire s'implique dans les opérations de manutention de la drogue,*" says Tony firmly. *There's a foreign force here that threatens our society. It's high time the military's involved in handling drug operations.*

"*C'est pas ta decision,*" says Sarah. *This isn't your decision.*

"*Alors, tu devrais appeler quelqu'un qui peut prendre cette decision,*" suggests Tony, giving her his smartphone. *So you should call someone that can make that decision.*

Meanwhile, Nyoman returns to Sarah, bringing an auto-injector.

"What's that?" asks Sarah, curtly.

"Morphine, AKP."

"I don't need it," says Sarah, waving him off.

Nyoman looks towards Tony, who only shakes his head. Tony knows that his sister absolutely hates drugs and it's a waste of time trying to persuade her. Nyoman goes over to treat Cindy. Meanwhile, Pranoto has finished checking the laptop and puts it inside Nyoman's MOLLE pack. Without saying anything, he goes to a corner and starts vomiting. Sarah ignores him and calls Prasetyo with Tony's smartphone. She puts the call on speaker.

"*Selamat sore,* Major Dharmawan," answers the commander of Densus-88 warmly.

"This is AKP Sarah Dharmawan, *Komandan,*" answers Sarah.

Prasetyo is taken aback and doesn't answer for a few seconds. "What is it, AKP?"

"I'm at the office of PT. Westershire Chemicals Manufacture Indonesia in Bogor. This place is The Cartel's drug factory. They snatched my little sister and took her here. They have someone staking out POLDA Metro Jaya and possibly Megamendung. If they'd seen anyone deploying, they would've killed my sister, *Komandan*. I had to ask Major Dharmawan to help me free her. Major Dharmawan and five of his men killed two Tangos and rescued my sister. There are still approximately a hundred members of The Cartel in the factory… and…"

Sarah suddenly covers her mouth and coughs a few times. She pauses for a moment to wipe the blood dripping from the corner of her mouth. She then continues her briefing despite the intense pain in her belly. "There are indications… they're going to leave the area… and distribute their MDMA… in about twenty minutes… *Komandan*."

Prasetyo doesn't answer for a few seconds. "Are you all right, AKP?"

"I... ehm... just have a stomach ache, *Komandan*."

Tony snorts and curses out loud in Dutch and the other Bravo men wince. Prasetyo again doesn't answer for a few seconds. He can sense that his subordinate is concealing her true condition.

"A few minutes ago, I received a report of a suspicious foreigner in front of the Crowne Plaza Hotel. He's been there for over an hour and he could be one of their lookouts. I'll send a team from the Special Actions Sub-detachment to take care of him. There are no reports from Megamendung, but I'll give them a call," says Prasetyo. "AKP Dharmawan!"

Sarah stands to attention. "*Siap, Komandan!*"

"We have to prevent the suspects and their goods from leaving the area. To prevent collateral damage, you should assault them while they're all in one place. Your mission is to assault them and prevent them from escaping. I say again, your mission is to assault them and prevent them from escaping. Your call sign is Bravo-Niner. Are you ready to lead this operation, AKP?"

"*Siap, Komandan!*" says Sarah. She stands at ease.

"Major Dharmawan!"

Tony stands to attention. "*Siap, Komandan!*"

"Right after this, I will coordinate with the Chief of the INP, the commander-in-chief of the TNI, and the Minister of Defence. I order you and your men to be seconded to Densus-88. This is an anti-narcotics operation, not a military operation, so it *must* be led by AKP Sarah Dharmawan from Densus-88. Do you agree to this, Major?"

Tony glances at his sister's belly. He's anxious to kill the people who hurt his sisters, but right now he'd rather take them both to the nearest hospital. Sarah can guess what Tony is thinking so she punches him hard in the chest and gives him a sharp look.

Tony relents. "*Siap, Komandan!*"

"Thank you for your support on this operation, Major. We will deploy as soon as we take care of their lookout. It's an honour to have you and your men with us on this, Major Dharmawan."

"It's an honour for Satuan Bravo, *Komandan*," says Tony. He hangs up.

With Tony and his men under Sarah's command, the commander of Densus-88 has initiated *darurat sipil*, or civil emergency, somewhat equivalent to MACP. Indonesia is now the third country in the world after the UK and Republic of Ireland to involve their military in the War on Narcoterrorism.

"Now what, *Komandan*?" asks Tony, facing his new commander.

Sarah glances at her MTM watch. "We have only ten minutes of preparation before they leave this place. If we don't do this now, they might escape forever." She then looks at Pranoto, who has finished throwing up and is looking quite pale. "What's wrong with him?"

"Hmph, he always does that after killing someone," answers Tony without thinking.

Sarah frowns and gives Tony a quizzical look. As far as she knows, her brother and his men have never been in combat before. Tony suddenly realizes that his mouth has run away from him and tries to change the subject.

"Are *you* alright?" he asks, giving his sister a sharp look.

Sarah takes a deep breath and looks down at her own belly. The small knife is embedded up to its hilt and she's in incredible pain. Michael once suggested that whenever she's enduring hardship, she should remember herself running the Fan Dance. She does that now. She's just reached the top of Pen y Fan and now she's descending the Jacob's Ladder. She can take it easy for now, but she'll have to suffer for a few more hours before the run is finished.

Sarah looks at her brother. "Can you guess what Michael's last words were after Niall stabbed him in the eye with this knife?"

Tony can only wince and shake his head.

"He quoted Lord Uxbridge, from when a surgeon amputated his leg."

"You mean the line about the knife being blunt?" asks Tony. "So?"

"This is nothing compared to what Michael had to endure before they finally killed him, *Kak*."

Tony stays silent.

Sarah knows her brother is worried about her so she smiles and winks at him. "Anyhow, I could do the Fan Dance with this thing in me."

"Yeah, right," Tony snorts.

Although Tony is worried about Sarah, he greatly admires her dedication and fighting spirit. Tony also doesn't mind being under her command. Her combat experience far exceeds his own. She's been trained by the SAS and even led an SAS team in a special operation. Tony orders Nyoman to help Sarah put on her kit.

Sarah finds her command voice. "Gentlemen! I'm Ajun Komisaris Polisi Sarah Dharmawan from the Indonesian National Police and I'm in command."

Everyone looks towards their new commander and listens intently.

"For the Preliminaries: Serda Zulkarnaen, you will take Cindy and escort her out of the premises and to safety. Take her to the nearest police precinct, identify yourself, and have one of them take care of her. Please coordinate with the local police and Densus-88 before they arrive and then, as soon as possible, get as many policemen to take an overwatch position from the front entrance. After securing Cindy, your Mission is to ensure that no X-Rays escape the stronghold from the front entrance. I say again, your Mission is to ensure that no X-Rays escape the stronghold from the front entrance. Is that clear?" Although he's the youngest sergeant in Tony's team, Sarah knows that Zulkarnaen is extremely reliable.

"*Siap, Komandan*," answers Zulkarnaen.

Zulkarnaen carries the unconscious Cindy in a one-shoulder fireman's carry on his left shoulder, carrying his submachine gun in the other hand. Tony gives him the keys to his car and he exits the building. Pranoto covers Zulkarnaen and Cindy until they've entered Tony's car and then takes position to cover the front door.

Sarah continues her briefing. "Here's the Situation: There are, at the very least, a hundred X-Rays in the factory next door. We do not have intel on the exact number of X-Rays, but around fifty of them are from the UK and the rest are local criminals. We have no intel on their weapons, so we must assume all of them are armed with M4 Carbines. All suspects are to be considered armed and extremely dangerous. We do not have either the manpower or firepower to contain them so we will have to initiate the assault. We do not have to worry about Yankees besides Cindy. We also don't have intel on the building layout and can only assume from the exterior that it has two storeys. The only thing we *do* know for sure is that they plan to leave the premises within the next fifteen mikes."

"Our Mission is to 'shoot-to-kill' all suspects before they disperse to distribute the narcotics. I say again, our Mission is to 'shoot-to-kill' all suspects before they disperse to distribute the narcotics."

"For the Execution: We will go silent unless compromised and all weapons should be in semi-automatic fire. Assume all X-Rays are wearing body armour so you should aim for headshots and shoot with controlled pairs. Use full-auto if, and only if, we go noisy. We will be using the SAS Colour Clock Code. You should always call out your targets and their positions after you eliminate them.

"The Command structure and call signs will be as follows: Our team's call sign is designated as Bravo-Niner. I will be Bravo-Niner-Six and Strike Force commander, Major Dharmawan will be Bravo-Niner-Five and 2 i/c. Serma Suprayitno is Charlie-One, Sertu Dedi is Charlie-Two, Serka Pranoto is Charlie-Three, and Sertu Nyoman is Charlie-Four."

"The stack will be as follows: The pointman is Charlie-One, number two is Charlie-Two, number three is Bravo-Niner-Six, number four is Bravo-Niner-Five, and the MOE specialist is Charlie-Three. After the entry, Charlie-Three will stand firm and provide overwatch from the entrance to the factory."

Sarah gives a direct order to Pranoto. "Charlie-Three, use the MP5, but hold fire unless there is an immediate threat or imminent danger of being compromised. You may use the M4 Carbine if we go noisy."

"Roger that, Bravo-Niner-Six," says Pranoto (Charlie-Three).

Charlie-Three field-strips and checks the M4 Carbine taken from the security post. All special forces operatives know that the use of weapons and/or ammo from the opposition is highly *not* recommended, except in the most extreme conditions, such as they are currently facing. Meanwhile, Nyoman finishes helping Sarah with her kit and replaces Pranoto covering the front door. Sarah takes a moment to give Nyoman a nod and a smile for his initiative.

Sarah then gives a direct order to Suprayitno. "Charlie-One, since we don't have any explosives, please rig the IED into an improvised satchel charge. Bravo-Niner-Five will be in charge of explosives."

"Roger that, Bravo-Niner-Six," says Suprayitno (Charlie-One).

Charlie-One starts turning the IED into a satchel charge. If detonated in the right place, it can bring down half of the factory. Tony regrets not having enough time to bring more firepower and explosives, but then quickly dismisses the thought. If they had been just two seconds late, he would've seen his sister with her guts hanging out of her. Tony shudders to think how close they came to that.

## THE POLICEWOMAN

Sarah continues her briefing. "As you know, this is at least a fifteen-to-one odds situation. We are nowhere near the manpower or firepower needed to do this properly. Charlie-Four will serve as rear guard and combat medic. You will stand firm behind Charlie-Three and cover the White-6 front office entrance. You will deploy forward if, and only if, anyone needs combat first aid."

"Roger that, Bravo-Niner-Six," answers Sertu Nyoman (Charlie-Four). He's disappointed being made rear guard, but he doesn't show it.

"We will receive Support from Densus-88, but it is unclear when they will arrive. In the meantime, we have to assume that we are on our own."

All the Bravo members nod and Tony gives Sarah a smile. Despite being in much pain, his sister gave them a professional briefing. Tony agrees to all her tactics and feels immensely proud of her.

Sarah ends her briefing. "Gentlemen! A foreign force has invaded our country and they have disrupted our society with narcotics. In a few minutes, we will battle against local criminals and highly trained ex-soldiers of the British Army armed with automatic weapons. We will be facing overwhelming odds, but this is what we've been trained for! This is why we joined the special forces! My brothers of Bravo, you are one of the finest counterterrorist units in the world… and it's an honour to share this field of battle with you."

Sarah's fighting spirit is infectious! Tony can feel himself and his men getting pumped up.

"Bravo-Niners, are you ready?" asks Sarah.

Sarah looks fearsome wearing all the black combat kit. On her right thigh is a tactical holster for the Glock 19 pistol, a load bearing holster is on her torso with mags for the HK MP5SD3 and pistol, an Aitor Jungle King II knife is in a holster on her left waist, and a CQB Headset on her head. The small knife embedded deep in her belly only serves to make her even more frightening! The members of Detasemen 902, Satuan Bravo-90, Korps Pasukan Khas, TNI-AU can clearly see that their new commander is as smart and tough as her brother. They are confident in the abilities of their new commander and would follow her anywhere.

"Ready!" answer the Bravo men without any hesitation whatsoever.

"Make ready and stack up!" orders Sarah.

# CHAPTER 17
## DETASEMEN KHUSUS – 88

15:34 WIB (GMT+7)
Sunday October 4, 2026
Gatot Subroto Road
Setiabudi, South Jakarta, Jakarta

A few minutes earlier…
Brian is near the entrance to the Crowne Plaza Hotel on the Gatot Subroto road. He's leaning on his car and watching the exit of POLDA Metro Jaya. He has his back to the target, but can see it clearly in selfie mode on his smartphone. The bonnet of his car is open, as if his car has broken down. Not much is happening at POLDA Metro Jaya this Sunday. Brian's bored with this task and has spent most of the time playing games on his smartphone.

From Plaza Semanggi, a mall next to the hotel, Brian sees two Chinese women walking and talking on the pavement, heading his way carrying shopping bags. They're both attractive, in tight tank tops and short jeans-shorts, showing off their perfect white legs. As they approach, Brian hears them speaking Mandarin.

An old, beaten-down pick-up truck passes the two women and parks behind Brian's car. The driver gets out of the truck and helps two men, his passengers, take down a large roll of carpet. The driver and the two men, who are as worn-down and dirty as the truck, are having trouble lowering down the heavy roll of carpet. They pay no attention to Brian and Brian pays little attention to them. He briefly wonders why they don't just enter the hotel, but realises, looking at the way they're dressed, the hotel security probably wouldn't let them in.

'Poor buggers,' he thinks. Not much fun being stuck outside working on this baking hot day. He should know.

The two Chinese women finally pass the three struggling men on Brian's left. One of the women's talking Mandarin on her phone, and the other, who has hair down to her waist, looks at Brian and smiles at him sweetly. He returns her smile and keeps his eyes on her for as long as it takes them to walk past him.

'Nice aris and bacons,' he thinks, admiring the woman's perfectly round arse and shapely legs. He likes her perfect white skin, but her body is too athletic for his taste.

Just after they pass Brian, the long-haired woman's phone rings. She stops to take it from her handbag.

BRAAAK!

Brian turns his head left towards the men struggling with the carpet. The lead man has tripped on the pavement and fallen. The heavy carpet has fallen too and unrolled.

"Ah, geblek loe!" curses the driver, looking severely pissed-off. *You dickhead!*

Distracted by the sight, Brian doesn't see the long-haired woman take a telescoping baton from her handbag. The first he knows of it is when she hits him on the back of his head. At the same time, the man who was holding the middle part of the carpet turns around and catches Brian's limp body before he hits the dirt. The man slams Brian into the open roll of carpet. The three men quickly roll the carpet up with Brian inside and, without any trouble at all, pick it up and put it in the back of their pick-up truck. One of the men goes to secure Brian's car and the driver races the pick-up away from the scene. The long-haired woman has secured her baton and walks away calmly with her friend, who says "HVT secured, mission accomplished" in Mandarin into her phone.

From the first man falling to 'mission accomplished', it only took thirteen seconds.

There were twenty people around them, but not one of them realised that five members of Densus-88 had just conducted a perfect snatch of a foreign drug syndicate member. Only a professional can fully appreciate how difficult it is to conduct this sort of operation in broad daylight with next to no time to prepare.

Less than five seconds later, two traffic police cars escort four black Toyota Innovas as they exit POLDA Metro Jaya at high speed. The four Innovas contain every member of Densus-88, Gegana, and Brimob on duty at POLDA Metro Jaya that Sunday. At the same time, an Enstrom 480B helicopter takes off. The small, aging heli, at POLDA Metro Jaya since the morning, races towards Bogor.

The events of today mean Brian meets the same fate as his mates from Shropshire, Herefordshire, Worcestershire, and Dorset. What happened to Brian Turner, one of the senior members of the Irish Drug Cartel, is never known... except to the people that snatched him.


15:34 WIB (GMT+7)
Sunday October 4, 2026
PT. Westershire Chemicals Manufacture Indonesia
Citeureup, Bogor, West Java

Sarah, Tony, and her team stack on the left side of the door. The pointman is Suprayitno (Charlie-One) and number two is Dedi (Charlie-Two). The number two position should've gone to the second most experienced member of the team, Pranoto, but Sarah needs him as a sniper instead to cover their entry from the rear. Too bad he didn't bring his sniper rifle. The M4 Carbine taken from the guard post will have to do. Numbers three and four are Sarah (Bravo-Niner-Six) and Tony (Bravo-Niner-Five). Pranoto (Charlie-Three) is at the back of the stack as MOE specialist and sniper. After letting the others in, he'll cover them from the door. Nyoman (Charlie-Four) will be the rear guard, covering the door to the lobby until Zulkarnaen arrives with reinforcements.

At the back of the stack, Pranoto is ready. He squeezes Tony's left shoulder with his left hand. Tony's ready, so he squeezes Sarah's left shoulder. Sarah does the same to Dedi and he does the same to Suprayitno. Suprayitno gives an exaggerated nod and Dedi copies him. Sarah sees Dedi's nod. Everyone in the stack is now ready.

"Execute the entry in five," says Sarah. All weapons are in the low ready position with the safety off and switched to semi-automatic fire.

"Four."

"Three." Pranoto moves forward and stands on the right side of the door.

"Two."

"One." Pranoto starts turning the handle.

"Execute!" says Sarah.

Pranoto opens the door and steps back to let the team into the factory. Suprayitno makes his entry and starts securing the right side of the factory. Not even a second has passed before he fires his first controlled pair.

"X-Ray down, White-5," he whispers. He shot an X-Ray on the right-front side of the factory and, in accordance with SAS CQB doctrine, now crisscrosses so he can dominate the extreme right of the building.

Dedi is right behind Suprayitno. He sees Suprayitno crisscrossing to the right, but then sees an X-Ray straight ahead. He fires a controlled pair, buttonhooks to the left, and fires another controlled pair.

"Two X-Rays down, White-6 and White-7."

Two more suppressed shots are heard. "X-Ray down, Red-4," whispers Suprayitno.

Sarah hasn't even entered the factory yet and the two men in front of her have already killed four X-Rays. Sarah finally enters and takes the centre-right position. For the first time, she sees the interior of the factory.

The first thing Sarah sees is one of the X-Rays, a white man, two metres in front of her, dropping down with a pair of gunshot wounds in the middle of his forehead. She recognises the face of the man who stuck his head into the room while Niall was torturing her. He falls with his right hand on his pistol, still in its holster. His left hand is clutching his phone. It looks as if he was heading for the front office to check on Niall again. If they had delayed their entry, their assault would've been compromised before it even started. There are exits at the right-middle and left-middle of the factory, and dozens of chemical reactors, chemical drums, and pill-making machines all the way to the back. Sarah also sees sixteen pillars holding up the roof. There are maybe 130 people working inside, dismantling all the machinery. By the looks of it, there's not much more for them to do.

At the rear of the factory, in the middle, there's a large exit. The back of a container lorry is parked there and the X-Rays are storing their kit and goods inside the container. To the left and right of the back exit are rows of offices. In the far right is a steel stairway to the first floor. Fortunately, the first floor is only at the back of the factory and only consists of offices, which span the length of the factory from left to right. All the offices have darkened windows, so Sarah doesn't know how many X-Rays are inside.

Next to the stairway, on the ground floor and first floor, there are toilets. Sarah doesn't know how many X-Rays are in the toilets either. As in Swan's Mill, Sandalwood Farm, and the Kempston warehouse, The Cartel's drug factory has CCTV cameras everywhere. Sarah can only hope no one's watching them.

The situation is much, much worse than Sarah imagined! The six of them will have to face some 130 X-Rays, who all seem to be armed with pistols. Fortunately, the noise of machinery being dismantled will mask their assault.

Sarah's highly-trained observation skills and situation awareness let her notice all of this within seconds of entering the factory. Sarah senses Tony taking her left and he's also firing controlled pairs. There are repeated whispers of 'X-Ray down' and positions. Suprayitno and Tony's TAOR overlaps Sarah's, so she can concentrate on being a team leader rather than just another assaulter.

"Charlie-Three, cover first floor, Black side," whispers Sarah.

"Roger that," answers Pranoto.

"Charlie-Four, stand firm. Other call signs, stay silent, carry on forward, and engage," whispers Sarah.

"Roger that," answer her men.

Sarah moves forward as one with the others. Her body is bent forward and her MP5 in the low ready position. Her posture pushes the blade deeper into her belly, but she ignores the pain. She's more concerned with the mission and her men's safety than her own suffering. Sarah feels like she's running the five kilometres of the Roman Road with a fifty-pound bergen on her back.

"Reload," whispers Suprayitno.

Sarah starts assaulting to cover Suprayitno's Tactical Area of Responsibility (TAOR). SCAN. She sees three X-Rays twenty metres to her front-right. Two of them are facing her right and the other has just looked towards her. His eyes are widening and he looks ready to shout. He's the immediate threat. ACQUIRE. Sarah aims her MP5. SHOOT. She fires towards his head. ACQUIRE. She recovers from the slight recoil and reacquires her target. SHOOT. She shoots his head again as he falls. ACQUIRE. She makes sure both her shots have hit the target. SCAN. She sees the two X-Rays reacting to their friend's fall in front of them. SHOOT.

ACQUIRE. SHOOT. ACQUIRE. SCAN. ACQUIRE. SHOOT. ACQUIRE. SHOOT. ACQUIRE. SCAN. Throughout, she's moving forward.

"Ready," whispers Suprayitno, already firing his weapon.

It took Suprayitno only two seconds to reload and fire again, but Sarah has managed to kill three X-Rays within that short timeframe.

"Three X-Rays down, Red-2," whispers Sarah.

"Bravo-Niner-Six, this is Charlie-Three. Two X-Rays sighted, Black-11-1, foxtrot towards Black-1-1," whispers Pranoto.

Sarah sees two white men exiting one of the offices on the left side of the first floor, laughing their arses off. They're carrying M4 Carbines, but they don't seem to know the ground floor's being assaulted. Pranoto holds his fire.

"Copy, engage when necessary," whispers Sarah.

"Roger that," says Pranoto, sounding extremely tense.

Everyone can understand Pranoto's anxiety, because hitting a target from eighty metres away with an HK MP5SD3 is almost impossible to do accurately and silently. The HK MP5SD3 submachine gun uses the same rounds as a pistol. They are subsonic when leaving the muzzle and their accuracy starts to fall after thirty metres.

Sarah has given Pranoto a lot of responsibility and his aim is now essential for the success of the mission. If Pranoto fails, the team will have to 'go noisy', which would be unspeakably dangerous. Just like the 4-man team assault on Sandalwood Farm, Sarah's confident they can accomplish the mission safely, even though they're outnumbered and outgunned, so long as they can maintain speed, aggression, and surprise.

"Reload," whispers Dedi.

Tony must cover Dedi's TAOR so Sarah helps cover Tony's. SCAN. She sees two X-Rays. One is facing left, working and listening to music on earphones. The other is facing right, yawning. ACQUIRE. SHOOT. ACQUIRE. SHOOT. ACQUIRE. SCAN. ACQUIRE. SHOOT. ACQUIRE. SHOOT. ACQUIRE. SCAN.

"Two X-Rays down..." Sarah doesn't get the chance to finish.

PYAAAR, PYAAAR, BRAAAAAKKK!

There are sounds of breaking glass and someone crashing down from the first floor. A moment later, the sound of assault rifles blasts from the office on the first floor towards the front of the factory. The eyes of all the

X-Rays inside the factory follow the sights of the assault rifles and they finally see the people assaulting them.

"Contact front!" shouts Pranoto.

"Go noisy!" shouts Sarah, switching her MP5 to full-auto.

They don't have to go for headshots as none of the X-Rays are wearing body armour. They now shoot until the X-Rays don't move anymore. They've lost the element of surprise and Sarah is extremely worried for her men.

"*Dios nos ayude*," she prays to herself.


15:36 WIB (GMT+7)
Sunday October 4, 2026
Back Office Area, PT. Westershire Chemicals Manufacture Indonesia
Citeureup, Bogor, West Java

Several minutes earlier…

"Where the fuck is Vinnie?" Patrick asks the people around him. "He was supposed to call back after he made sure Niall had slotted that bitch."

Jason, Errol, Tommy, and Richard are in the office with Patrick. No one answers him. Instead, they continue eating chips and drinking Bintang beer, watching football on the 50" TV under a cold AC. Guinness is available in Indonesia, but these men have fallen in love with the local Bintang beer. There's a smaller TV in the corner showing CCTV images from the factory, but no one's watching it because Chelsea is playing The Toon on the big screen TV. Jason stands up.

"Jason, go check on Niall and Vinnie," orders Patrick.

"Sorry… gotta take a shite," says Jason, smirking.

Errol stands up also.

"Errol, ye fucking go then," orders Patrick.

"Gotta go to the bloody loo too, Paddy," says Errol, also smirking.

The two Cartel members don't want to see Niall's victim. They exit the office carrying their carbines, laughing their arses off as they head towards the toilet. Patrick looks like he's about to explode.

"I'll fucking go then," says Tommy, taking his carbine. He doesn't fancy being in the same room as Patrick when he looks like that.

"And tell them to haul their fucking arses in five minutes!" shouts Patrick as Tommy opens the door.

Tommy nods and then exits. As he faces forward, he's stunned when he sees what's happening at the front of the factory.

"Jesus fucking Christ!" he shouts, readying his carbine. "Contact fr…"

Tommy doesn't get the chance to finish before his head snaps back twice; a bullet enters his left eye and another enters his mouth. He's dead before he hits the floor.

"Bloody hell!" curses Richard.

Errol and Jason hear Tommy cursing behind them and when they turn around, they see what he saw. A 4-man team's assaulting them, and no one on the ground floor even seems to realize it. Before they can react, a couple of bullets are already heading towards Jason. Errol hears sounds like a couple of raw eggs cracking when those two rounds enter Jason's head. Errol freezes when he sees Jason fall like a rag doll, but then snaps out of it and starts running towards cover. A bullet passes through his throat, swirling him to the right. He drops his carbine and clutches his throat with both hands. He staggers forward and then backwards towards the rails. Seven 9mm jacketed hollow point bullets slam into his back, as if to prevent him from falling backwards. They fail. Rounds that missed their target shatter the windows of the office. Errol finally hits the rail and he falls arse over teakettle to the ground floor, smashing into some pill-making machines.

At the same time, Patrick and Richard take cover as bullets shatter the windows of their office. They ready their carbines and fire blindly towards the front of the factory.

15:37 WIB (GMT+7)
Sunday October 4, 2026
Factory Area, PT. Westershire Chemicals Manufacture Indonesia
Citeureup, Bogor, West Java

After Sarah says 'go noisy', Pranoto switches to the M4 Carbine. He fires three-round bursts towards the offices on the first floor, the occupants of which are firing blindly in his general direction.

"Reload!" shouts Tony, taking cover behind one of the pillars.

Sarah gives him covering fire until she empties her mag and then takes cover behind a pillar to her front.

"Ready!" shouts Tony at the same time Sarah shouts. "Reload!"

Sarah changes mags in record speed while Tony covers her. "Ready!" she shouts.

Sarah starts firing again. Most of the X-Rays return fire with their revolvers, but the others retreat to the rear exit. All those retreating are The Cartel's core members from the UK. Unbeknownst to Sarah and her team, there's an armoury at the rear of the factory containing all their carbines and ammo. Many of the X-Rays have been killed, but her team has barely reached the halfway point of the factory.

Sarah has to make a decision to maintain their advantage. "Bravo-Niner-Five, ready explosives!"

Three seconds later, Tony shouts. "Explosives ready!"

"Bravo-Niner-Five go! All Bravo-Niners, suppressing fire!" shouts Sarah.

Everyone except Nyoman starts spraying in full-auto towards the X-Rays, panicking them into taking cover. Tony moves forward, carrying an IED in his left hand and firing his Glock with his right.

"Stoppage!" shouts Pranoto.

Tony decides to keep moving forward despite the lack of covering fire from Pranoto. He plans to throw the IED, set to explode in fifteen seconds, into the container lorry. Twelve metres from the target, Tony throws the IED. In the middle of his throw, a round grazes his left cheek and takes off most of his left ear. His throw falls short of the lorry.

"Fire in the hole! Fire in the hole! Fire in the hole!" shouts Tony, emptying his pistol as he falls back.

"Ready!" shouts Pranoto, already firing his M4.

"All call signs, move back and take cover! Charlie-Three, cover Black side!" shouts Sarah.

"Roger that!" answer her men.

Everyone moves back and takes cover behind a pillar, while Pranoto keeps firing.

BOOOOOM!

They can hear screams amid the blast of the IED. They catch a glimpse of the first floor collapsing before black smoke covers the carnage. Of all the armed people inside the factory, only Pranoto is still firing his weapon, finishing off the X-Rays he can still see.

Sarah scans her surroundings. They're a little more than halfway through the factory. She can't see through the black smoke covering the rear of the factory, but she can hear people dying and crying. She knows lots of X-Rays managed to escape the blast.

"All Bravo-Niners, anticipate X-Ray flanking manoeuvre... Charlie-One, cover Red-3 exit... Charlie-Two, cover Green-9 exit... Charlie-Three, anticipate counterattack... and continue covering Black side," orders Sarah, panting.

"Roger that," they answer, also panting.

"Charlie-Four, continue covering White-6 front office."

"Roger that," answers Nyoman, restless at not being able to join the fight.

"All Bravo-Niners, send your sitrep," orders Sarah.

"This is Charlie-One. Four primary mags down, secondary full, over," says Suprayitno.

"This is Charlie-Two. Three and a half primary mags down, secondary full, over," says Dedi.

"This is Bravo-Niner-Five. Three primary mags down, one secondary mag down, lightly wounded, over," says Tony.

Sarah sees that Tony's left cheek looks as if it's been sliced open and most of his left ear is gone, blood dripping from both wounds. Sarah's order has disfigured her handsome brother. This is the first time someone under her command has gotten hurt, making her feel doubly guilty. She tries to ignore that feeling and returns her focus to her mission.

"This is Charlie-Three. M4 dry, switching to MP5, one primary mag down, secondary full, over," says Pranoto.

"This is Charlie-Four. No action yet, over," says Nyoman, sounding irritated and making the others smile briefly.

"What's *your* sitrep, Bravo-Niner-Six?" asks Tony, looking worriedly at his sister.

Sarah takes a deep breath. The pain in her belly is excruciating. She now feels as if she's reached the checkpoint at Torpantau. She still has a long way to go, but at least she can take a short break.

"This is Bravo-Niner-Six. Two primary mags down, secondary full, mild stomach-ache, over," she says, smiling and winking at her brother to calm him down.

She fails.

"Don't joke about that again, *Dik!*" Tony snaps, furious at her.

Sarah ignores him and throws one of her mags to Suprayitno. Her brother is sometimes overprotective of his sisters. If they were anywhere else but here, she'd tell him off, but right now she needs him completely focused on the mission. She then gives some orders to her team. "Charlie-Four, distribute reserve ammo and then return to previous position, over."

"Roger that, moving to Charlie-One at Red-3," says Nyoman.

Sarah glances towards the back of the factory. The black smoke has stopped moving towards them, but she still can't see beyond it. They've lost speed, aggression, and surprise, and Sarah has run out of ideas. She's also extremely worried that the opposition will counterattack.

"Suggestions, *Kak?*" she asks.

Tony's also hesitant. There are too many fields of fire to cover and they are severely lacking in manpower and firepower. "Let's just wait for reinforcements," he suggests.

Sarah nods. "Call Zul for me, would you?"

Tony calls Zulkarnaen and throws his smartphone to Sarah.

"*Siap, Komandan!*" answers Zulkarnaen.

"Zul, this is Bravo-Niner-Six and I'm in command of this special operation. Send your sitrep, over," orders Sarah.

"Roger that. I am mobile with five policemen from POLSEK Citeureup armed with SS-1 rifles and FN pistols, ETA in six mikes and more reinforcements to follow. Yankee is secured at the police precinct with one policewoman taking care of her. I've coordinated with Delta-Eight-Eight-Actual. They've just taken care of the lookout and deployed all hands with one heli and four Innovas full of policemen. ETA of heli is seven mikes, Innovas are twelve mikes. Be advised that the heli is only carrying a sniper team. Acknowledge!" says Zulkarnaen.

"Affirmative, wait one," says Sarah, relieved. She gives a thumbs-up to Tony who also looks relieved.

Meanwhile, Nyoman has finished distributing the reserve ammo and has returned to his original position.

Sarah closes her eyes to think hard for a few seconds before giving Zulkarnaen further orders. "Zul, this is Bravo-Niner-Six. When you arrive, split your forces into two fireteams and cover Delta Mike Papa exits Green-9 from White-7 front entrance and Red-3 from White-5 front entrance. Engage all X-Rays who appear from outside Black-11 or Black-1. Relay to Delta-Eight-Eight-Actual that X-Rays are still in control of Black side and have the heli cover Black-12 exit. Half of the Innovas should immediately double envelop to Black-11 and Black-1 and cover Black-12 exit, but *do not* enter Delta Mike Papa. I say again, *do not* enter Delta Mike Papa. The rest will provide reinforcement through White-6 front office. Report using headset when you are in range, over."

"Affirmative, Bravo-Niner-Six," answers Zulkarnaen.

"Bravo-Niner-Six out," says Sarah, glancing at Tony, who gives her a thumbs-up.

Tony looks at his sister with fierce pride in his eyes. He can clearly picture her tactics and his respect for his commander has gone through the roof!


15:46 WIB (GMT+7)
Sunday October 4, 2026
PT. Westershire Chemicals Manufacture Indonesia
Citeureup, Bogor, West Java

A few minutes earlier…

The blast knocks Patrick and Richard down, but they're mostly unhurt.

"We can't stay here!" whispers Patrick.

Richard nods and finds his carbine amid the rubble. He's shaking from seeing Tommy die in front of him and his own near-death experience. The whole first floor has collapsed, killing the men on the ground floor offices. Only the toilets on the first and ground floor remain standing. They crawl towards the rear exit. It looks like most of the men from the UK have made it out alive and Patrick does a quick headcount. They've only lost Niall, Vinnie, Tommy, Jason, and Errol in the first wave of the assault and Chris and Bert in the blast. The ground floor offices are mostly occupied by locals. Clearly none of the locals survived the collapse of the first floor on top of them.

"How many are left?" asks Patrick when he sees Rory.

"Forty or so went with me to the back," says Rory. "We can't stay here!"

"I know, for God's sake!" snaps Patrick. He watches as his men take the M4 and ammo from the armoury. "Who the fuck are those fellas? They can't be Densus unless Brian has fucked up, but they still shouldn't get here this fast. Are there any fucking special forces stationed in this area?"

"Kopassus of the Indonesian Army and a Brimob HQ are near this area. KOOPSUS HQ is nearby. Satuan Bravo-90 of the Indonesian Air Force is also headquartered in Bogor," says Rory, starting to go pale. "Sheila said Bravo trained with the SAS a couple of years ago."

"Fuck! Isn't Sarah's brother in Bravo?" asks Patrick.

Rory can only nod and Patrick sees some of his men go pale. They all know that Satuan Bravo-90 is one of Indonesia's counterterrorist units.

"Let's just surrender!" suggests Liam, voice shaking.

Patrick takes out his suppressed pistol and shoots Liam in his temple.

"Does anyone else have any more fucking bone ideas?" asks Patrick, giving his men a deadly look.

His men shake their heads, no.

Patrick continues. "I think I saw only four or five of them, so here's what we're going to do…"

He lays out his plan.


15:46 WIB (GMT+7)
Sunday October 4, 2026
Mayor Oking Jayaatmaja Road
Citeureup, Bogor, West Java

Zulkarnaen and five policemen from the Citeureup Police Precinct are racing towards the factory in Tony's Fortuner. Other policemen will follow shortly. Before they deployed, the head of the police precinct (called Kapolsek) coordinated with the commander of the Brimob base at Kedung Halang, not too far from their location. They'll deploy all on-duty Brimob personnel.

After Zulkarnaen coordinates with Prasetyo, Komisaris Polisi Hendro Kistono, the Kapolsek, asks him a question. "Can you repeat our orders? I don't understand any of the code words."

## THE POLICEWOMAN

"We were ordered to split into two teams. One will cover the left side of the factory and the other the right side. If anyone shows up from the back of the factory, we're free to engage," explains Zulkarnaen patiently.

The policemen can only look blankly at the air force sergeant. They've never been involved in this sort of operation before.

Zulkarnaen continues his briefing. "Briptu Heru will come with me to the left. *Pak* Hendro, please take three of your men to the right. If anyone shows up, just keep shooting at them, but cease fire when Densus arrive. Please have one of your men guard the entrance to prevent civilians from entering the area and to direct Densus-88 on arrival."

"*Siap!*" answers Hendro. The head of the police precinct defers to the air force sergeant's lead because this operation is beyond his own experience and capabilities.

From 300 metres away, they can see black smoke from the location. Zulkarnael turns on his headset. "Bravo-Niner-Six, this is Zulkarnaen. Comm check, over."

"This is Bravo-Niner-Six and I read you five-by-five. Your call sign is designated as Zulu-Six, over," says Sarah.

"Affirmative, Bravo-Niner-Six. Zulu-Six and Zulu-One will provide overwatch from White-7 front entrance, Zulu-Two will provide overwatch from White-5 front entrance. Zulu team will be in overwatch position within two mikes, over."

"Copy, out."

A couple of minutes later, they park the car ten metres from the front entrance. They debus and split up according to their orders. Curious onlookers from the surrounding neighbourhood try to gather around, but one of the policemen prevents them from entering the compound. Zulkarnaen then hears his commander through his headset giving orders to somebody else.

The sharp cracks of assault rifles are heard from inside the factory. Amid the noise, Zulkarnaen can hear a diesel engine roaring to life from the rear of the factory.

Half a minute later, Zulkarnaen reports. "Bravo-Niner-Six, this is Zulu-Six. Zulu team is in overwatch position, over."

There's no answer. Only the sounds of M4 Carbines fill his ears.

"Bravo-Niner-Six, this is Zulu-Six. Zulu team is in overwatch position. Do you copy?"

"Copy, Zulu-Six... Engage when necessary," orders Sarah.

His commander sounds like she's under a lot of pressure. Briptu Heru looks toward Zulkarnaen and sees that the air force NCO is looking extremely worried. This makes *him* absolutely terrified!

15:50 WIB (GMT+7)
Sunday October 4, 2026
PT. Westershire Chemicals Manufacture Indonesia
Citeureup, Bogor, West Java

Several seconds earlier...

Sarah glances at her military watch. Zulkarnaen should be in position soon so she gives orders to her men. "Charlie-Four, assist Charlie-Three in covering Black-12 to Red-3."

"Roger that, moving to Charlie-Three at White-6," answers Nyoman.

"Charlie-Three, cover..." Sarah doesn't get the chance to finish her orders when a group of X-Rays suddenly come out of the black smoke behind her, blindly firing their M4 Carbines in Pranoto's direction and screaming at the top of their lungs.

At the same time, someone starts the engine of the lorry and drives it away. Pranoto and Nyoman return fire, but then they have to take cover from the heavy enemy fire. Sarah releases the sling from her HK MP5SD3 and prepares herself for hand-to-hand combat. She sees her men have already done the same. They wait behind the pillars for the opposition to change mags.

Once the X-Rays stop firing, Sarah gives an order. "All Bravo-Niners, return fire!"

Sarah and her men return fire on the X-Rays counterattacking them. Three metres to her front-right, Frank Llywelyn tries to change mags. Sarah is about to shoot him when his head snaps back, shot by Nyoman from Sarah's rear. Seven other X-Rays are quickly dispatched by the others. With the lorry gone, the black smoke starts to dissipate. There are six X-Rays still firing at them from the ruins on the Black side. They took cover there when they saw their counterattack had failed. Zulkarnaen reports for the second time that he's in position and Sarah finally answers him.

15:50 WIB (GMT+7)
Sunday October 4, 2026
PT. Westershire Chemicals Manufacture Indonesia
Citeureup, Bogor, West Java

Zulkarnaen sees the lorry driving towards him.

"Open fire!" he orders Briptu Heru.

Both men empty their first mag at the lorry's cabin, shattering the windshield. They don't know whether they've hit the driver or not, but the lorry keeps heading towards them. X-Rays are taking cover behind the lorry, like infantrymen advancing behind a tank.

"Shoot the engines!" orders Zulkarnaen.

Heru fires at the engine with his assault rifle and Zulkarnaen fires his MP5 at the front tyres. The lorry finally stops and both men start firing at the X-Rays, who are themselves already firing their M4s at them. At the same time, Zulkarnaen hears the loud cracks of assault rifles to his right. Zulkarnaen can see the Kapolsek looking extremely pale giving orders to his men, who are equally pale.

Zulkarnaen panics when he suddenly realises what the X-Rays are up to and shouts into his headset. "Bravo-Niner-Six, this is Zulu-Six! Imminent enemy double envelopment manoeuver to Green-9 and Red-6 from outdoors! I say again, imminent enemy double envelopment manoeuver to Green-9 and Red-6 from outdoors, over!"

"Copy, Zulu-Six. You are free to engage from your position," orders Sarah in her calm, assertive voice.

Sarah's command voice calms Zulkarnaen down... and makes him ashamed of himself for panicking. "Roger that."

Meanwhile, reinforcement from POLSEK Citeureup finally arrive. Six policemen join Zulkarnaen carrying SS-1 assault rifles. Zulkarnaen orders four of them to stay where they are and keep firing their weapons at the X-Rays, and tells the rest to follow him towards the Kapolsek's position. He sees that the Kapolsek and his men are pinned down by enemy fire. Fortunately, the trees can absorb the high-velocity rounds of the M4. When he finally reaches the Kapolsek, Zulkarnaen sees that, unlike the Green side of the factory, the Red side is strewn with building materials, which the X-Rays are using as cover. He sees only one X-Ray down, still writhing on the ground. He takes careful aim and puts the X-Ray out of his misery with a couple of shots to the head.

Zulkarnaen realizes that his MP5 is not fit for this kind of battle so he trades his weapon and ammo with one of the policemen. Normally he wouldn't swap his weapon with somebody else on the battlefield, but here he has no choice. The SS-1 with FMJ ammo is much more powerful than his MP5. Zulkarnaen starts shooting his new weapon. After a few shots, he feels a tap on his arm.

"*P-p-pak*, h-h-how d-d-do you change m-m-mags?" asks the policeman Zulkarnaen had traded weapons with.

The policeman looks so scared that his whole body is shaking. Zulkarnaen quickly but patiently teaches him, before returning fire.


15:52 WIB (GMT+7)
Sunday October 4, 2026
PT. Westershire Chemicals Manufacture Indonesia
Citeureup, Bogor, West Java

Several minutes earlier...

Sarah hears from Zulkarnaen that the X-Rays are double-enveloping them from outside. She thinks hard for a few seconds. The sound of gunfire and the excruciating pain in her belly is making it hard for her to concentrate. Sarah feels like she's climbing the Jacob's Ladder towards the top of Pen y Fan. She's struggling to reach the top.

"Charlie-Three, move forward and reinforce Charlie-Two covering Green-9," orders Sarah.

"Roger that, moving to reinforce Charlie-Two."

"Charlie-Four, do the same covering Red-3," orders Sarah.

"Roger that, moving to reinforce Charlie-One."

"Bravo-Niner-Five, standby to fire and manoeuvre to Black-12," orders Sarah.

Tony hurriedly shuts off his headset. "Are you out of your fucking mind?"

Sarah also turns off her headset. At the same time, the loud cracks of M4 Carbines are heard from both sides of the factory.

# THE POLICEWOMAN

"Do we have a choice?" asks Sarah, eyes wide open in panic. She suddenly doubts her own orders.

Tony forces himself to take a deep breath and thinks hard for a moment. The fire and manoeuvre tactic, known as pepper-potting in the British Army, is bold to the point of reckless. The risk is extremely high with just two people, especially for whoever's doing the final assault. Ideally, the assault force should outnumber the defenders three-to-one. What they're facing now is the exact opposite. On top of that, the HK MP5SD3 submachine gun is hardly the right weapon for this tactic. Although there are M4 Carbines strewn around, they don't dare use them.

But if they don't do anything, they'll be annihilated by an attack from both flanks. The only reason why the enemy counterattack failed was thanks to Zulu-One and Zulu-Two, covering both flanks. Another option available is to fall back to the front office. However, they're extremely low on ammo. If the opposition throws everything they have at them, the team will most likely not survive their attack.

'It's better to attack instead of retreating in a situation like this,' thinks Tony. 'It looks like attacking is our only option.'

His sister was right all along. Tony now feels guilty for doubting his commander. He reactivates his headset.

"I will follow you anywhere, Bravo-Niner-Six," he says firmly.

Tony has just given his sister the highest praise a soldier can offer his commander. Sarah only smiles at her brother and reactivates her own headset.

The voice of Police Brigadier General Prasetyo suddenly comes through. "This is Delta-Eight-Eight-Actual onboard heli. Comm check, over."

"Delta-Eight-Eight-Actual, this is Bravo-Niner-Six. We read you five-by-five, over."

"Airborne sniper team hovering in position half a click above and behind Black-12. Send your sitrep, over."

Sarah is grateful she had the chance to pass her knowledge on to her commander this morning. "Delta-Eight-Eight-Actual, this is Bravo-Niner-Six. X-Rays are still in control of Black side and most are double-enveloping to Red-3 and Green-9 from outdoors. Be advised that friendlies are in White-5 and White-7 front entrance area. Please provide sniper cover for Black side, over."

"Affirmative, Bravo-Niner-Six. Ground forces are commanded by Kombes Hanafi, call sign is Golf-Two-Three, ETA is four mikes. Acknowledge!"

"Affirmative, Delta-Eight-Eight-Actual. Golf-Two-Tree ETA four mikes, over," answers Sarah.

"Charlie-Mike, Bravo-Niner-Six. Good luck and good hunting, out."

"Bravo-Niner-Six, this is Charlie-One. Last primary mag," says Suprayitno.

"Copy," answers Sarah.

Sarah throws one of her mags to Suprayitno and Tony does the same to Dedi. Sarah and Tony then exchange looks. They'll be out of ammo soon and they don't have four minutes. They have no choice but to attack. They can't wait until Densus gets here.

15:53 WIB (GMT+7)
Sunday October 4, 2026
PT. Westershire Chemicals Manufacture Indonesia
Citeureup, Bogor, West Java

Sarah had asked Densus to double envelop the factory from both flanks, but Zulkarnaen sees that that tactic no longer fits with the battlefield. The Green side is blocked by the lorry and the Red side is filled with building materials. The Densus policemen deployed to those flanks won't be able to do much good, and might even endanger them.

Zulkarnaen takes the initiative. "Delta-Eight-Eight-Actual, this is Zulu-Six at White-5 front entrance, over."

"Go ahead, Zulu-Six."

"Be advised that both the Red side and Green side of the factory are blocked. Please deploy all reinforcements from White-6 front office, over."

"Copy, Zulu-Six," says Prasetyo, who immediately forwards the order to Hanafi in one of the Innovas.

An air force sergeant has just ordered a Police Brigadier General to change combat tactics, but Prasetyo followed his command without any hesitation whatsoever. The commander of Densus-88 knows that soldiers on the ground know more about the situation than he does. He also knows that the members of Bravo under Major Dharmawan are the finest men in the Indonesian military.

15:53 WIB (GMT+7)
Sunday October 4, 2026
PT. Westershire Chemicals Manufacture Indonesia
Citeureup, Bogor, West Java

Tony glances towards the Black side. He looks like he's counting something. Incoming fire from the six remaining X-Rays at the Black side is still intense.

"All right, *Komandan*, this is our last dance. You go first, okay?" says Tony.

Sarah nods and gives him an order. "Bravo-Niner-Five, suppress fire in three, two, one, go!"

Tony gives suppressing fire towards the X-Rays and Sarah runs as fast as she can to the next pillar. Once she's gone firm, she gives a signal to Tony, who runs towards the next two pillars while Sarah gives suppressing fire. Once Tony's there, he signals Sarah, and lays down suppressing fire as she runs to the next two pillars. Sarah's last movement takes her only a few metres away from the X-Rays, still firing at them from cover. As she runs toward the pillar, she finally realizes why Tony wanted her to go first. Tony's next move means that he's the one who'll do the final assault on the X-Rays' position. The risk for her brother is huge! To minimize casualties, Sarah should be the one doing the final assault. She looks extremely worried when she gives the final signal to Tony.

Tony rushes towards the X-Rays' position, screaming at the top of his lungs. Sarah provides suppressing fire with her last mag. Sarah's shots are both accurate and effective, forcing the X-Rays to take cover. Five X-Rays are still alive and one is writhing on the floor, both hands covering his bloody face. When he reaches them, Tony manages to shoot two X-Rays before they can react. Another stands up to try to shoot Tony, but Sarah shoots him in the neck from behind Tony. The remaining two X-Rays throw themselves towards Tony, who has just run out of ammo. Sarah rushes forward to help her brother and throws away her empty MP5.

As she throws away her submachine gun, Sarah sees Patrick suddenly emerge from another position, pointing his pistol straight at her…

15:55 WIB (GMT+7)
Sunday October 4, 2026
PT. Westershire Chemicals Manufacture Indonesia
Citeureup, Bogor, West Java

Patrick meets Sarah, face-to-face for the first time. He's taken aback seeing Sarah in her white bikini top and blue jeans, reminding him of Sheila the last time he saw her. For a second, Patrick's not in Indonesia anymore… he's back in Liverpool… back with his daughter. Remembering his only child, he hesitates squeezing the trigger of his .22 calibre pistol…

15:55 WIB (GMT+7)
Sunday October 4, 2026
PT. Westershire Chemicals Manufacture Indonesia
Citeureup, Bogor, West Java

Sarah draws her sidearm from her thigh holster and fires at Patrick without pausing to aim. The Glock 19 is deafening compared to the HK MP5SD3.

Patrick staggers when a couple of bullets hit his hip and leg. He limps towards the back exit before Sarah can change mags and shoot him again. He plans on hiding in the escape tunnel at the rear of the factory. As it's not yet finished, he won't be able to escape. Like his wife, Patrick plans on killing as many people as possible from inside the tunnel before they can finally kill him.

"How the fuck do ye slot that bitch?" Patrick mumbles to himself.

He was sure that the one and only shot he'd fired had hit Sarah in the centre mass, but why is she still fighting? His round must've been a dud or something. In the middle of his thoughts, a .338 Lapua Magnum bullet fired from a Remington Model 700P sniper rifle hits him in the centre mass and blows out his spine. He drops face first like a sack of potatoes.

"Tango down, Black-12 outdoors," says Prasetyo, in his usual calm manner.

## THE POLICEWOMAN

Before the leader of the Irish Drug Cartel bleeds to death on the floor of his own drug manufacturing plant, Sarah empties her pistol into the back of his head. Sarah then focuses on helping Tony. He's managed to take down Richard Callaghan, who's still writhing and moaning with an Aitor knife stuck in his chest. The other X-Ray, Rory Hanrahan, is on top of Tony and trying to stab her brother in the neck with a piece of rebar.

Sarah calmly changes mags, aims her pistol, and shoots Rory in the head with a controlled pair. Rory drops dead on top of Tony. Tony throws him to one side and gets up, quickly wiping Rory's blood and brains off his face. Sarah sees a deep cut on her brother's face, near his left eye down to his jaw. His waist has been grazed by a bullet and his left ear is still dripping blood.

Sarah doesn't give her brother time to catch his breath before ordering him into action. "Clear the toilets, I'll cover you from here."

Tony nods, changes mags, and moves to secure the two toilets that survived the IED blast. They both know that those toilets are most likely empty, but they're trained not to assume anything. Sarah finishes off the last of the X-Rays around her by shooting them twice in the head. As an Indonesian police officer, she's violating the incredibly stupid directive from KOMNAS HAM, but she doesn't care anymore. They can punish her if she survives this mission.

After changing mags, Sarah covers Tony with her Glock in her right hand and clutches her stomach with her left. She feels as if she has reached the top of Corn Du and is now running towards Storey Arms. Only adrenaline is mitigating the pain in her abdomen, allowing her to still fully function. After the adrenaline leaves her system, Sarah knows she'll experience the most excruciating pain in her life.

"Black-1-0 toilet cleared," says Tony. He then goes upstairs to clear the first floor toilet.

"Two Tangos down, Black-11 outdoors," says Delta-Eight-Eight-Actual. As usual, Prasetyo's voice sounds calm and assertive, no matter how dire the situation or crisis is.

Sarah slowly turns towards the front of the factory. She can see the fierce battle raging on the Green and Red side. If either side carried any explosives, the battle would've ended by now, not still be in a stalemate like this. On her left, Serma Suprayitno is firing his pistol with his left hand, his right arm shattered up to his elbow. Sertu Nyoman Sukarya is helping him cover the Red side exit with the last mag of his MP5.

On her right, Sertu Dedi Suhendri is also hit. The lower-left side of his face is missing and what's left of his jaw and tongue hangs grotesquely from his face. Dedi's on top of an X-Ray, bashing his head open with the butt of his Glock. Sarah sees two dead X-Rays near him, one with an obvious broken neck and the other with an Aitor knife stuck in his left eye. Serka Pranoto is covering Dedi with his pistol. Sarah is deeply saddened seeing her men gravely wounded like that. She's their commander and they're her responsibility.

Several pistol shots suddenly go off from the toilet on the first floor!

"Two X-Rays down, Black-1-1 toilet, Black side clear," says Tony. There were X-Rays hiding inside the first floor toilet after all.

"All call signs, this is Golf Two-Three-Actual. All Golf-Two-Three are foxtrot, entering from White-6 front entrance, over," says Hanafi. The ground force has debussed and is now running towards them.

Sarah takes a deep breath. These will be her last sets of orders. "Golf-Two-Three-Actual, this is Bravo-Niner-Six. Split into two fireteams after entering Delta Mike Papa from White-6 front office and immediately deploy to Red-3 and Green-9 exits. Bypass friendlies in the area and unleash hell with frags and willie-peters. Black side is clear, friendlies also in the area. Acknowledge!"

"Affirmative, Bravo-Niner-Six. Golf-Two-Three will deploy to Red-3 and Green-9 exits from inside Delta Mike Papa. Friendlies in all areas, over," says Hanafi as he runs.

"All Bravo-Niners, this is Bravo-Niner-Six… Black side is clear… reinforcement coming in from White-6 front office, over."

"Roger that," answers everyone under her command except Sertu Dedi.

"All call signs… this is Bravo-Niner-Six… Bravo-Niner-Five is now in control…" says Sarah, her command voice starting to fade. "Bravo-Niner-Six… signing off…"

Sarah says those words with the last of her remaining energy. Only her excellent physical condition keeps her on her feet. Sarah knows that she'll fall if she tries to move, so she decides to just stand there and watch the battle unfold in front of her. Sarah now imagines herself running behind D

Squadron. After running up and down the Brecon Beacons for almost twenty-four kilometres with a fifty-pound bergen on her back, she finally sees the finish line at Storey Arms. The members of G Squadron are already there, cheering for her, spurring her to finish the run. Their cheers echo in her head.

"Go, Sarah, go!"

"Come on, Sarah!"

"You can do it, Sarah!"

And now she's determined more than ever to accomplish her mission. As she thinks about this, Sarah suddenly understands the quote from James Elroy Flecker, written on the Regimental Clock Tower in the SAS Barracks.

"... *we shall go,*

*Always a little further; it may be...*"

As a special forces operative, Sarah's physical and mental toughness have been drilled so hard that she will never quit until she's accomplished her mission. She will force her body to go 'Always a little further; it may be...' like she always does.

"Golf-Two-Three is complete," says Hanafi.

A couple of seconds later, Sarah sees Densus personnel in black kit armed with HK 416s enter the front door to the factory. They've deployed according to her last order. The sounds of HK 416s intermingle with the sounds of M4s. Shouts of 'Tango down' are heard repeatedly. Sarah sees a Densus member stagger and fall from a shot to his chest. A female Densus member starts dragging him to safety, but is shot in her lower left leg, blowing it off completely. Sarah's tears start streaming down her cheek. Her orders have left her teammates wounded.

She has failed them.

Meanwhile, Tony has been worried since Sarah suddenly turned over her command to him. From the first floor, he sees Sarah standing below, tears streaming from her eyes and blood dripping from the corner of her mouth. Her right hand is holding her Glock and her left is clutching her stomach. Tony hurriedly limps down to the ground floor. One of the X-Rays in the toilet shot Tony in the leg before Tony had a chance to shoot him with his Glock.

BOOOM! BOOOM! BOOOM! BOOOM!

Several grenades go off at almost the same time on both sides, making the whole factory shake. They can hear the screams of agony from the X-Rays amid the blasts. Blasts continue to explode for the next minute, finally blowing up the lorry outside. Fire rages from both sides of the factory.

Tony finally arrives. He gives a worried look to his sister. "*Dik...* are you all right?"

Sarah doesn't answer and only releases her left hand from her stomach. Tony's eyes go wide seeing blackish blood flow like a river from the small gunshot wound in his sister's stomach.

Tony is barely in control of himself when he shouts into his headset. "*Godverdomme!* All call signs, this is Bravo-Niner-Five! Bravo-Niner-Six is hit! Charlie-Four, get to Black-12! Delta-Eight-Eight-Actual, take control of the operation! Bravo-Niner-Five out!"

"Roger that, moving to Black-12," says Nyoman, limping towards their position. His left thigh has been shot.

"Copy, Bravo-Niner-Five. Delta-Eight-Eight-Actual is in control," says Prasetyo. He starts giving orders to set up a triage system. In stark contrast to his usual demeanour, the commander of Densus-88 now sounds extremely emotional.

Sarah finally loses energy in her legs and starts falling. Tony manages to catch his sister before she hits the floor. He holds her with her head in his arms. He then releases and throws away Sarah's headset. He doesn't want her to think about the mission anymore.

Meanwhile, Tony hears Hanafi's voice in his headset. "Delta-Eight-Eight-Actual, this is Golf-Two-Three-Actual. Red-3 and Green-9 exits clear!"

"All call signs, this is Delta-Eight-Eight-Actual. All clear and mission accomplished!" says Prasetyo. No one is cheering because they all know that some of their comrades are severely wounded.

"*Kak...* the mission..." says Sarah, starting to lose her breath.

"All clear and mission accomplished, *Komandan*. We did it!"

"Stronghold... secured?" asks Sarah, trying to smile at her brother.

"*Siap, Komandan*. Stronghold secured!"

Sarah breathes a sigh of relief. Her thoughts wander to her teammates in the UK, who counted on her to locate and destroy The Cartel's drug factory in Indonesia. She has accomplished the mission assigned to her by

Christopher Broussard, Sir Charles Mountbatten, and by the commander of Densus-88 this afternoon. She misses Broussard, Liz, Arthur, Matt, James, and Paul; her team in England who she came to love. Sarah suddenly remembers when they looked at her with tears of pride in their eyes when Sir Charles invested her with a DSO.

Nyoman finally arrives and, according to SOP, he first takes Sarah's pistol and clears it. He checks the small gunshot wound in the middle of Sarah's abdomen, right between her sternum and the small knife still embedded deeply in her navel. The size of the gunshot wound means that she was shot with a .22. The blackish blood coming out of her stomach means that the small but deadly round has shredded Sarah's liver. Nyoman checks her back and can't find an exit wound. The round must be a hollow point, mushroomed inside her liver. The hollow point round is deadlier because all the kinetic energy of the round after it's fired is transferred to the target.

Sarah looks towards Nyoman, who is checking other parts of her body to see if there are wounds more severe than the obvious ones in front of him. She sees that Nyoman's left thigh is shredded. Sarah feels sad for all the wounded men under her command.

"*Kak*... the men..." she asks, more blood dripping from the corner of her mouth.

"Don't worry, all of them will make it. You've led us so well, *Komandan*," says Tony, starting to choke. "I love you and I'm proud of you. You're a hero!"

Tony checks Sarah's pulse. It's weak and irregular. Nyoman glances at Tony, but looks down again without saying anything. He doesn't want to see his commander cry. He also doesn't want his commander to see him crying himself.

"Help the others," orders Tony, almost inaudibly. Densus has set up a triage system, and Nyoman's skills and medical kit are needed elsewhere.

"*Siap!*" answers Nyoman. He takes the time to wipe Sarah's mouth of blood before leaving the brother and sister behind him. "Charlie-Four to Green-9," he says, starting to cry openly.

Amid all the noise, Tony hears Pranoto start retching again. This indicates to Tony that the operation is completely over and there's nothing else he can do.

"*Kak...*" says Sarah, her beautiful face contorted in pain.

"*Iya, Dik...* the pain is temporary... don't fight it..." says Tony, gripping hard onto her left hand.

"I'm... scared..." says Sarah, tears streaming from her blue eyes.

Sarah's grip is as hard as Tony's, as if she doesn't want to let go... as if she doesn't want to give up. Tony wants to cry, but he must be brave for his sister as she faces the Ángel de la Muerte.

"I'm here, *Dik*," says Tony, kissing her forehead softly. "Just close your eyes... and go to sleep... I'm here for you... I'm here for you... *Vaya con Dios, Dik*... shhh... shhh...*"

Sarah closes her eyes. Her thoughts start wandering again and now she's reached the finish line at Storey Arms. All she has to do now is rest. Her body is hurting all over, but she's happy because the SAS men are congratulating her for finishing the Fan Dance. Among the SAS men, she sees Cormac, Al, Robert, George, and Dave, her friends in the SAS whom she loves and considers as her own brothers. The last one she sees is Michael, whom she loved very much. Michael is hugging her and trying to calm her down, just like he did at the 888 Restaurant & Bar in Manchester.

'*Je t'aime tellement*, Michael!' shouts Sarah in her mind as she cries from the unbearable pain in her stomach.

'*Aku cinta padamu juga, mo ghile mear,*' says Michael, smiling at her, the morning before The Cartel snatched and tortured him to death.

Sarah keeps crying from the pain and Tony can't bear watching his sister in agony like this. He remembers their childhood together at Poole. Sarah likes to sleep in his arms like this while he sings her an Indonesian nursery rhyme.

"*Kupu-kupu yang lucu,
Kemana engkau terbang...*"

Sarah's breathing starts to get ragged. She coughs out blood and her body tenses up, but she's still gripping hard onto Tony's hand, still unwilling to give up. Only Sarah's excellent physical condition is what's keeping her alive.

Sarah's last thoughts are about her family. Her loving parents who raised her so well... her gallant brother... and her adorable sister. Sarah is calmer knowing she saved Cindy's life. Before she loses consciousness, she remembers her whole family looking at her with immense pride when she told them she was hand-selected to join Densus-88. Sarah remembers noticing her mum, who looked at her with fierce pride in her eyes... but behind that pride, Sarah can also sense her deep worries...

"*Maafkan* Sarah... mummy..." says Sarah, tears streaming down her cheek. *I'm sorry... mummy...*

After hearing those words, Tony senses that Sarah has lost consciousness. He carries on singing to his sister for the very last time.

"*Kupu-kupu yang elok,*
*Bolehkah saya serta,*
*Mencium bunga-bunga,*
*Yang semerbak baunya...*"

Tony can feel the exact moment when his sister leaves him. Sarah's body tenses up and a gush of blood flows from her mouth. Sarah exhales her last breath and her body finally goes limp. Her beautiful face, that a few moments ago was contorted in extreme pain, now looks at peace, as if she's sleeping in his arms. Crying, Tony carries on singing until the song is finished.

"*Bolehkah kuturut,*
*Bersama pergi...*"

In the War on Narcoterrorism in Indonesia that lasted less than an hour, ICPO-Interpol and Densus-88 have lost their finest police officer.

And in less than a week since Michael's death, the United Kingdom of Great Britain and Northern Ireland has once again lost one of their heroes...

# EPILOGUE

08:48 WIB (GMT+7)
Wednesday October 7, 2026
Jaya Ancol Seafront
Pademangan, North Jakarta, Jakarta

The ceremony is about to begin. An Interpol and a Security Service officer, accompanied by three UK policemen and a policewoman from the Republic of Ireland, give her parents a medal and a citation from His Majesty's Government for her role in eliminating a vicious drug syndicate from the UK. The medal is an upgrade from the GM and it's the highest gallantry award the UK government can invest to a civilian.

A Major-General from the British Army arrives to invest her brother with a CGC and the five men under her command with MCs. The six members of Satuan Bravo-90 can all attend, though some are severely wounded. Those who are wounded have forced their way here so they can attend the funeral of their commander, who had led them so well.

The Major-General, in a sand-coloured beret, is escorted by five soldiers wearing the temperate parade uniform of various regiments in the British Army, from the Royal Scots Dragoon Guards, Coldstream Guards, The Rifles, King's Royal Hussars, and the Parachute Regiment with their famous maroon beret. The six soldiers cannot hide their sorrow over losing their close friend, who they considered a sister. They are extremely emotional when they salute the body of their fallen comrade.

After the ceremony, an ambulance leaves the house, escorted by eight police motorcycles called *vooriders*. The *vooriders* lead the ambulance out of the front gate towards a crematorium in the northeast side of the city.

At the front gate, sixty-three security guards and some 150 men and women in mufti are standing in parade formation. The men and women in mufti are all extremely athletic. They stand to attention and salute when the ambulance passes by. Everyone has tears in their eyes when the ambulance containing the body of Komisaris Besar Polisi Anumerta Sarah Michelle Dharmawan, GC, DSO, MC passes in front of them.

Their commander has left them...

# ABOUT THE AUTHOR

Justin W. M. Roberts was born in London, England. He has travelled widely in Europe, Africa, and Asia and has lived in Indonesia for the last twenty-five years. He has a degree in PPP (Psychology, Philosophy, and Physiology) from Hull University, England. He lives with his wife and two children in Jakarta.

Printed in Great Britain
by Amazon